In the Land of the Postscript

In the Land of the Postscript

The Complete Short Stories of Chava Rosenfarb

TRANSLATED FROM THE YIDDISH
BY GOLDIE MORGENTALER

EDITED BY GOLDIE MORGENTALER

In the Land of the Postscript: The Complete Short Stories of Chava Rosenfarb
Translated and edited by Goldie Morgentaler

White Goat Press, the Yiddish Book Center's imprint
Yiddish Book Center
Amherst, MA 01002
whitegoatpress.org

Printed in the United States of America at The Studley Press, Dalton, MA
10 9 8 7 6 5 4 3 2 1

Hardcover ISBN 979-8-9877078-4-5
Paperback ISBN 979-8-9877078-3-8
Ebook ISBN 979-8-9877078-5-2

Library of Congress Control Number: 2023903970

Book and cover design by Michael Grinley

Grey Day, Prince Arthur Street (Montreal, 1937) by Jack Beder.
Reproduced with the generous permission of MNABQ.

For Jonathan

Made possible with the generous support of
Larry and Muriel Gillick.

Contents

Introduction

IN THE LAND OF THE POSTSCRIPT

Much has been written about the Holocaust, but comparatively little about its aftermath and the lives of the survivors. How did the horrific experiences they lived through affect those who migrated from Europe to find safe haven in North America? How did they deal with their memories of the traumatic past once they had established new lives in a new country?

Between 1974 and 1995 the Yiddish-language novelist Chava Rosenfarb wrote a series of short stories in Yiddish that explored the afterlife of Holocaust survivors. Most, but not all, of these stories were published in the prestigious Yiddish literary journal *Di goldene keyt*. With one exception—"Serengeti," which is set in Africa and features an American protagonist—all of Rosenfarb's stories deal with Holocaust survivors who have settled in Canada after the war. This volume collects all of the short stories that Rosenfarb, herself a Holocaust survivor, published after the war when she had settled in Canada and begun her literary career.

The roots of Yiddish literature in Canada go back to the turn of the twentieth century, when Eastern European Jews, seeking refuge from persecution and poverty, began arriving in large numbers, settling primarily in the cities of Montreal, Toronto, and Winnipeg. Montreal, where most of the immigrants settled, provided particularly advantageous conditions for the establishment of a literature written in Yiddish. From 1900 to the outbreak of World War II, Jews made up Montreal's largest immigrant community, and Yiddish was, after French and English, the city's most widely spoken language. The result was a Yiddish-speaking culture of remarkable self-sufficiency and vitality, which earned Montreal a reputation among Jews as "the Jerusalem of North America." After World War II, Canadian Yiddish literature was given another boost by the arrival of survivors of the European conflagration—among them Chava Rosenfarb, who settled in Montreal in 1950.

In general, Yiddish literature written in Canada focused on Europe and on European concerns, despite the fact that many Canadian Yiddish writers lived the greater part of their lives in North America. Even J. I. Segal, arguably the most Canadian of the major Yiddish writers who settled in the country, was essentially European in outlook, filtering his vision of Montreal through the sieve of an Old World sensibility.

In her novels, Chava Rosenfarb—the youngest of the major Yiddish writers to settle in Canada—conforms to this pattern of Canadian creation and European subject matter. But her short fiction does not. Rosenfarb's novels tend to be conceived in epic terms, dealing as they do with the impact of the Holocaust on the Jews of her hometown, Lodz, Poland. Her three novels, *The Tree of Life*, *Bociany*, and *Letters to Abrasha*, are European works by an essentially European writer who just happened to be living in North America.

It was only in her short fiction that Rosenfarb permitted Canada, her adopted home, to play a role in her work. She did this by effecting a synthesis between her primary theme of the Holocaust and the Canadian milieu in which she found herself, so that Canada becomes in these stories the land of the postscript, the country in which the survivors of the Holocaust play out the tragedy's last act.

Rosenfarb's short fiction is thus a different take on a theme that has been explored by Saul Bellow in *Mr. Sammler's Planet* and by Isaac Bashevis Singer in several of his short stories—namely, the afterlife of the survivor. But Chava Rosenfarb was one of the few writers on this theme who was a survivor herself and thus intimately acquainted with the subtle undercurrents of pain, confusion, anger, and despair in the lives she wrote about. Her characters may be strangers in a strange land, but they are neither ennobled by their suffering nor necessarily embittered by it. Instead they represent a gallery of all conceivable human types and all conceivable human reactions to devastation.

Chava Rosenfarb was born in Lodz, Poland, on February 9, 1923. She attended a Yiddish secular school and a Polish-language Jewish high school from which she graduated in 1941. By that time she and her family had been incarcerated in the Lodz Ghetto, and it was in the ghetto that she received her diploma. The Lodz Ghetto was liquidated in August 1944; Rosenfarb and her family were deported to Auschwitz. From Auschwitz she, her mother, and sister were sent to a forced-labor camp at Sasel, where they built houses for the bombed-out citizens of Hamburg. Rosenfarb and her family were then sent to Bergen Belsen concentration camp from which they were liberated by the British army in 1945. After the war she crossed the border illegally into Belgium, where she lived as a stateless person until her immigration to Canada in February 1950.

Rosenfarb was profoundly affected by her experiences during the Holocaust, and her prodigious output of poetry, novels, short stories, plays, and essays all deal with this topic in one way or another. She began as a poet, publishing her first collection of poetry, *Di balade fun nekhtikn vald (The Ballad of Yesterday's Forest)*, in London in 1947. This was followed by three other poetry collections and a play, *Der foigl fun geto (The Bird of the Ghetto)*, which was translated into Hebrew and performed by Israel's National Theatre, the Habimah, in 1966. It has since been performed in English in Toronto and in the original Yiddish in a Zoom production by the New York–based Folksbiene.

Finding that neither poetry nor drama could begin to express the depths of her feelings about the Holocaust, Rosenfarb turned to fiction. In 1972 she published her masterpiece, *Der boim fun lebn (The Tree of Life)*. This three-volume epic chronicles the destruction of the Jewish community of Lodz during the Second World War. It was followed by *Bociany* (published in the author's own English translation by Syracuse University Press as *Bociany* and *Of Lodz and Love*) and *Briv tsu abrashn*

(*Letters to Abrasha*), which is, as yet, unavailable in English.

Rosenfarb was a frequent contributor of essays to the Yiddish literary journal *Di goldene keyt*, where, beginning in the early 1980s, she also began to publish a series of short stories about the lives of Holocaust survivors living in Canada and the United States. These are the stories that make up this collection.

At first glance, the stories contained in this volume belong to the general category of immigrant literature, because they attempt a synthesis of the Old World and the New. But this is immigrant literature with a difference, because the Old World in this case incorporates the stain of the Holocaust, which the New World is incapable of washing away. The stories therefore exist within a symbolic framework that addresses the relationship between Europe and North America. For instance, in the story "Last Love," an elderly Jewish woman's dying wish is to make love to a handsome young Frenchman. All the characters in this story are European. Amalia, the heroine, is the representative of all those survivors who found refuge in Canada after the ravages of the war. But when Amalia learns that she has only a short time left to live, she begs her husband to take her back to Paris, the city where the couple had first met after the war. Once there, she announces that her dying wish is to make love to a young man. It is as if she hopes to incorporate within herself a more innocent Europe, cleansed of atrocities and pain. Amalia herself represents the dying order of an Old World corrupted as much by the presence of its victims as by that of its aggressors.

Canada in these stories does not wipe out Europe—not even symbolically. It cannot nullify the European past. Canada here plays the role of Spam in a sandwich; it is bland, neutral territory that is nevertheless deadly, because its unflavored ahistorical terrain, like a tabula rasa, permits the intrusion of a corroding European reality. In these stories Canada is the neutral land of refuge that, like blank paper, patiently permits the survivors to impose their past on its present.

I use the blank paper analogy advisedly, because the dominant season in Rosenfarb's depiction of Canada is winter. This is not really surprising given the harshness and duration of the Canadian winter.

Furthermore, the winter season can have many meanings. In "The Greenhorn," the earliest of the stories, originally published in Yiddish in the 1950s, the newly arrived immigrant Barukh refuses to stop wearing his winter coat even when it is long past the season for it. "He cannot seem to get warm in this country," writes the narrator, "and he does not find the coat too heavy for spring."

But the chill that Barukh feels is not the chill of the Canadian climate but of the memories frozen within him. In this story Montreal is portrayed as a hot place—hot with the steam of a *shmateh* factory and with the warmth of sexual allure. Barukh, a Holocaust survivor, is working his first day at a garment factory in Montreal. The factory foreman is also a transplanted Jew, as are several of the other workers. The Jewish workers in fact are a mix of newly arrived greenhorns, mostly Holocaust survivors like Barukh, and of Jews from earlier migrations. But the Jews are not the only inhabitants of this factory world. There are also French Canadians. One of these, a flirtatious young woman, tries to befriend Barukh.

The dialogue between the two reveals the chasm that separates them. The young French Canadian is envious of Barukh's European past, which to her suggests romantic, far-off places that she can never visit. When Barukh tells her that he has lived in Paris, she immediately imagines the Paris of the tourist brochures: nightclubs, opera, theater . . . the Paris of elegance and the high life. But Barukh has known none of these enchantments. In Paris he lived the life of a penniless displaced person. She, for her part, has no idea what a DP is. The cataclysmic events that Barukh has lived through have barely penetrated her consciousness. Barukh and the young French Canadian flirt their way through a conversation in which they talk past each other, her side of the exchange made up of unrealized dreams and fantasies, his side made up of the searing memories of a barbarous past in which he lost his wife and children. There is no way these two versions of Europe can be reconciled, so it is not surprising that the underlying sexual play of the encounter misfires, disintegrating in the grubby present reality of steaming factory presses and the need to earn a living.

Barukh carries his past with him wherever he goes. When the young French Canadian eagerly quizzes him about living in Warsaw, he replies, "I no longer have any feeling for Warsaw." She suggests that this is because he has been away from the city for too long. To which Barukh replies, "No, I am still there."

This theme of the persistence of Europe and European memories within the context of what should be a new beginning in North America recurs in several of the stories. In "Edgia's Revenge," a tangled relationship of gratitude and resentment that began during the Holocaust plays itself out against the backdrop of Montreal. The story is narrated by Rella, a former kapo. Kapos were concentration camp guards, often Jewish themselves, whom the Nazis put in charge of their fellow inmates. Rella, who had become a kapo through bestowing sexual favors on a guard, lorded it over the other women in her barracks, beating them and indulging in the petty cruelties her position permitted. Her one good deed was to save the life of Edgia, another camp inmate, by hiding Edgia under a bunk during roll call. After the war, the two women, Rella and Edgia, meet again in Montreal, where each has settled unbeknownst to the other. "Edgia's Revenge" chronicles their desperate attempts to come to terms with their past and with each other.

Rella tries to cope by blotting the past out and throwing herself wholeheartedly into the cultural life of Montreal. She becomes a self-confessed "culture vulture," desperately running after every new fad and diversion. She also runs after Edgia's husband, Lolek, another Holocaust survivor who seeks to bury the past in the distractions of the present. Edgia, however, cannot shake the past, and she continues living the life of the victim, even on Canadian soil, although now the oppressor has become her husband, who belittles, betrays, and torments her for her inability to put the past behind her.

"Edgia's Revenge" is one of the most complex of Rosenfarb's stories, containing many levels of meaning. Among the most interesting of these are the varying emotional reactions of the survivors to their new North American reality. For instance, Rella, in her determination to remake herself, masters English and judges her acquaintances by how well they speak the language. She is thrown into despair, however, by the thought that she will never lose her accent. "The accent prevented me from becoming a new person," she laments. Despite this, Rella is not above exploiting the advantages of that accent. She opens a ladies' dress shop she calls "La Boutique européenne," and she admits, "My European accent contributed to the Continental ambience of the shop, which in turn appealed to the predilections of my customers. This made me realize how attractive Europeanness could be in a non-European setting."

This ambivalence about their European roots haunts all the characters in "Edgia's Revenge," who, as a group, live dual lives. Outwardly they adapt very well to their Canadian reality, learning English, making a success of their various business enterprises, and participating in the cultural life of their city—but inwardly, as the author makes clear, they have never left the Europe that tortured and rejected them. Like Barukh in "The Greenhorn," they are still there. "The truth was," writes Rella, "that we felt alien in this new world, that we were so caught up with modernity because we found it so frightening."

"Edgia's Revenge" is about dealing with the unfinished business of the European past. Toward this end it exploits its Montreal setting for symbolic and contrapuntal resonances. For instance, Rosenfarb puts to good use the winding wooden staircases that are so distinctive a feature of Montreal architecture. These external staircases, which curl up to the second and third floors of the city's older triplexes, are certainly picturesque, but they are steep and slippery hazards in both summer and winter. Edgia and her husband live in one such triplex with a winding staircase, and Rella's deep fear that Edgia intends to do her harm centers on this staircase, which must be negotiated in order to get to the floor where Edgia lives with her husband, who is also Rella's lover. In the end, it is Edgia's husband, not Rella, who slips on one such ice-covered staircase—this one outside a brothel—and breaks his neck. This is death by architecture, an ironic and pathetic Canadian demise for a man who had managed to survive the much greater dangers of the European Holocaust.

Another feature of Montreal that finds its way into this story concerns the cross atop Mount Royal, the mountain in the center of the city. This cross can be seen from wherever in the city Edgia chooses to live. Even when she marries her second husband and moves to a wealthier part of town, the cross is visible from her window. This is, in fact, an accurate reflection of the geography of Montreal. Because the cross is the highest point in the city, it can be seen from poorer neighborhoods as well as from richer ones. The fact that the cross follows Edgia through her various permutations of personality, fortune, and changes of address hints at the symbolic underpinning of Rosenfarb's story. As Edgia notes, the cross is missing something. "Every cross should have its Jesus and every Jesus should have his cross . . . The cross is the question and Jesus is the answer."

The cross on the top of Mount Royal—first planted, according to tradition, by Paul de Chomedey, Sieur de Maisonneuve, to thank God for sparing the nascent colony from flooding—attests to the strong Catholic presence in Montreal and to the city's beginnings as a colonial outpost. It thereby alludes obliquely to the place of the Jews in Western history as well as to their victimization, a victimization that culminated in the Holocaust. But while Edgia's remark underlines the victimization of the survivors, it is also a statement of incompletion, of a lack of closure. The cross follows Edgia everywhere in much the same way as the past haunts the future of all the survivors, bleeding into their present with intimations of incompleteness, of something missing that can never again be found.

Many of the stories recount bad marriages. "The Masterpiece" describes an apparently harmonious marriage between two survivors that masks the seeds of its own destruction. In "A Friday in the Life of Sarah Zonaband" and "Edgia's Revenge," postwar marriages contracted out of the desperate need to reestablish normal family bonds persist in misery despite the incompatibility of the survivor couples. One form this incompatibility takes is a divergent attitude toward dealing with the trauma that the Holocaust inflicted on survivors. The husbands in these stories want to forget what happened, to bury it in the past and pretend that all is well, because remembering is too painful. The wives, on the other hand, cling to the past and seem incapable of moving beyond it.

"François" is an account of one such crumbling marriage. Leah and Leon are survivors who met and married after the war. As their echoing names suggest, their union should have been a harmonious one based on their shared experiences of pain and loss. Both have, in fact, responded to the emotional emptiness inside them with a similar obsessive restlessness, an incessant searching for something that they cannot find.

Leon has silenced the "howling void" inside him by denying it. He has made a fortune in real estate, buying and selling Canadian land. The land of Canada has been good to Leon in more ways than one. But his wealth has transformed him into a crass vulgarian, a man who exorcises his demons by denigrating his wife. His wife, for her part, tries at first to silence her own inner demons by drowning them in activities. She takes courses at universities, volunteers at hospitals, and participates in community work and good causes; she tries painting, attending lectures, and keeping a diary, moving frantically and aimlessly from one thing to another. Finally, after many years, she takes a lover. He is an imaginary lover, formed to her own specifications out of her own needs, a French French Canadian. He is Frenchness squared, and not surprisingly his name is François. François tells Leah what she wants to hear, comforts her in her misery, compliments her, caresses her, and converses with her on matters of the human heart.

Acting on impulse, but probably with an arrière-pensée of trying to save his marriage, Leon suddenly decides to take Leah to South America. There they do touristy things like journeying to the famous Angel Falls, swimming in the Amazon River, and flying out to visit Machu Picchu. But wherever they go, Leon and Leah encounter people who remind them of their European past—a tour guide who may or may not also be a Holocaust survivor; a German couple who own a lodge on the Amazon River and who may or may not be former Nazis.

The presence of François in this story suggests the complicating element in Rosenfarb's depiction of Europe. Europe in these stories is not just the ravaged and desecrated Eastern Europe, ancient homeland of Ashkenazic Jews. Rosenfarb's Europe also contains France, the country of elegance, style, civilization, and romance—the country that dreams are made on. Not only does this French element provide Rosenfarb with a dual image of Europe as both barbarous and ideal, it also permits her to meld Europe to America through the presence of French Canadians in her stories.

For instance, the chimeric François in the story of the same name is described as a Parisian Frenchman living in Montreal, a professor of French literature at Montreal's French university, hence an amalgam of Europe and America. The fact that François is a creature of Leah's imagination suggests how, when it comes to creating an ideal lover, Leah's mind attempts to synthesize Europe and America. Yet the story exploits the ambiguity inherent in such doubleness, for instance in the like-sounding names of the mismatched couple Leah and Leon.

"François" also exploits the duality inherent in the couple's experience of the two continents, North and South America. The North America of Leah's Canadian experience is snowy, dreary, and devoid of Old World associations. The South America of her trip, by contrast, is overgrown with European allusions. In the ruins of Machu Picchu lies America's claim to harboring a civilization older than that of Europe. Thus, the two continents of America bracket Europe. In Blakean terms, South America is the land of experience, North America that of innocence. In between lies the ambiguity of Europe—its horrific past and its romanticism.

The geographical juxtapositions add symbolic weight to the stories for which they serve as backdrop. Rosenfarb's survivors cannot be still; their afterlives are marked by relentless voyaging. Many of the stories in the collection contain a trip beyond the initial transplant of European Holocaust survivors to North America. For instance, "Little Red Bird" is about the abduction of a child to Mexico, while "Serengeti" describes a safari in Africa. These trips constitute a nod in the direction of the legendary wandering Jew. Yet they are wanderings in which the traveler does not get very far, because, all the while, behind these per-egrinations there hovers the pursuing shadow of the inescapable European past ruthlessly dictating the terms of a North American present.

"Serengeti" is in fact an anomaly among the stories, since it features a Jewish protagonist who is neither a Holocaust survivor nor a Canadian. Dr. Simon Brown—his surname is a shortened form of "Brownstein"—is a third-generation Jewish American psychiatrist who is leading a group of other psychiatrists on a safari in Africa. Among this group of psychiatrists is a Holocaust survivor, Marisha Vishnievska, who was formerly one of Dr. Brown's patients. Dr. Brown has always felt an antipathy toward this woman, although he could not have said why. The narrator suggests, however, that this antipathy has to do with Simon Brown's projected hatred of his own Jewishness, a Jewishness he has been trying to deny and evade all his life. However, during the course of the group's visit to the Serengeti, Simon's antipathy toward Marisha resolves itself into an attraction.

But Simon is already married, and his wife, Mildred, has accompanied him on this trip. Mildred is not Jewish, and this, it seems, is why Simon loves her: "He loved Mildred, and through her, he loved America. Thanks to her he not only felt himself more of an American but also more of a citizen of the world . . . Every time that he held her in his arms he had the feeling of coming home from a long voyage. The history of America that he had mechanically absorbed in his childhood and youth became, after his marriage, as familiar and near to him as Mildred's heartbeat."

At first glance, Rosenfarb seems to be preparing us for the classic triangular plot, albeit with a Jewish twist, in which a self-hating Jewish male awakens to the self-delusional quality underlying his attraction to Gentile women and comes to accept himself for the Jew he really is, an acceptance usually signaled by a romantic passion for a Jewish woman. (The non-Jewish Victorian novelist George Eliot pioneered the prototype for this Jewish twist on the traditional triangle in her 1876 novel *Daniel Deronda*.)

But Rosenfarb's story is more complex than this. To begin with, the

Jewish side of the triangle, Marisha Vishnievska, is as full of self-hatred as Simon Brown. Thrown from an Auschwitz-bound train at the age of two by a Jewish mother trying desperately to save her child from certain death, Marisha is found and raised by a Polish peasant woman. But Rosenfarb consistently confounds expectations. Marisha's mother does not die in the gas chamber at Auschwitz; she survives the war and returns to reclaim her daughter, setting up in the girl a tension between the Polish mother who raised her and the Jewish one who took her back. To further complicate the child's feelings, Marisha's mother, having escaped the Nazis, is murdered by anti-Semitic Polish thugs in a post-Holocaust attack on Jews. Marisha is then raised as a Pole by an assimilated Polish-Jewish couple. Thus Marisha's feelings about her own sense of identity are no less complex, no less filled with self-disgust and self-hatred, than Simon Brown's. Simon is the offspring of American-born Jewish parents whose highest ideal was to melt into the melting pot. "Simon Brown ascribed everything he disliked about himself to the disheveled little Jew who dwelled within his well-groomed, sportive, modern American body." The attraction between Simon Brown and Marisha Vishnievska is thus based as much on a recognition of their shared ambivalence about their own Jewishness as it is on their shared Jewishness itself.

But Simon's attraction to Marisha does not obviate his love for Mildred. Interestingly, he expresses this love in terms of the concept "home," declaring to Marisha, "I love Mildred. She is my home." To this Marisha replies: "I am your home. Your real home." To complicate matters still further, this tug-of-war over the allegiance and love of a man, this semantic tussle over what is an appropriate home for the Jew, is played out against the backdrop of the Serengeti, a perfect showcase for the demonstration of the survival of the fittest, where nature is red in tooth and claw and life is at its most elemental: eat or be eaten. At the same time the natural cruelty of life on the Serengeti is constantly compared to the unnatural cruelty of human beings, especially during the Holocaust. When Simon Brown sees a lioness stalking her prey, he remarks to Marisha that the scene reminds him of a photograph he saw of a concentration camp where Dr. Mengele was making a selection. "Don't insult the lioness, Professor," is Marisha's only reply. Thus, it is not only Rosenfarb's Holocaust survivors who cannot escape the long shadow of the event, no matter where they travel; it is also third-generation American Jews, like Simon Brown, with a more peripheral connection to the great disaster, who cannot evade its impact.

"Serengeti" straddles three continents and yokes all three together through a focus on recent Jewish history and Jewish dilemmas. But even more interesting is that the story achieves its effects by taking on a series of Jewish stereotypes and clichés and presenting them in a new light. Thus, underlying the character of Dr. Simon Brown we can find the combined stock figures of the Jewish American psychiatrist and of the generic Jewish male who marries a Gentile wife with a pedigree going all the way back to the *Mayflower*. In Marisha we have another common Jewish literary type—the sweaty, unkempt, vulgar, loud-mouthed Jewish woman who has no sense of grace or decorum, elegance or self-restraint. And, of course, we have a theme that has become the sine qua non of post-Holocaust Jewish fiction, namely the allusion to the Holocaust as the fountainhead of Jewish angst. Yet the stereotypical elements evoked here seem to be evoked precisely in order that they may be reexamined, and that reexamination takes place against the backdrop of a safari in Africa, an activity and a location not usually associated with Jews; indeed, an activity and a location that tend to consign problems of Jewish identity to the margins of concern.

It is because of this need to reexamine some of the stereotypes of Jewish life that Rosenfarb defines her main character as American rather than Canadian. Canadian Jews—much like Canadians themselves—have few identifiable tags that can immediately stamp and label them in the popular imagination. For Rosenfarb, Canada is a country empty of history and—ironically—empty of Canadians, unless they be French Canadians. For this reason, Canada serves her well when she wants to describe the afterlife of the Holocaust survivor who imprints the reality of his or her horror-filled past on the blank, patient page of a Canadian present. It is only when she seeks to portray Jews who are second and third generation, who have a history outside of Europe, that Rosenfarb automatically shifts her focus to the United States. The reason for this is not that there are no second-, third-, and even fourth-generation Jews in Canada, nor that there is a lack of Jewish psychiatrists in Canada. The reason for Rosenfarb's southward reach is that the fight between dual allegiances, between where to belong and which national reality represents home, seems so much more urgent in a Jewish American context than in a Jewish Canadian one.

Yet whether she locates her survivors in Canada or the United States, whether vacationing in South America, wandering across the plains of the Serengeti, in a cottage in the Laurentians, or attending a ghetto memorial in the Miles End section of Montreal, Rosenfarb's depiction of the Holocaust survivor remains the same. As in the story "Letters to God," her survivors are those for whom the present, not the past, is a foreign country. They are haunted by their Holocaust experiences, but haunted in all the diverse and individual ways that make one human being different from another. Rosenfarb's survivors are too complex to be labeled as the walking wounded, yet they are people who can never again live happily ever after—not in America, not in Canada, not in Europe, not even in Africa.

ACKNOWLEDGMENT

Heartfelt thanks to my friend, Lilian Nattel, for insisting that the first seven stories in this collection needed to be republished after their Canadian publisher put them out of print. And sincerest thanks to White Goat Press for agreeing with her.

—*Goldie Morgentaler*

The Greenhorn

"Why do you stand there like a wooden pole and don't say a word? You want the job, okay; if not, get lost. There's plenty of others to take your place."

This is how the foreman speaks to Barukh, all the while dialing a telephone number.

Barukh, a slender young man with a bent back who wears a pair of glasses with cheap frames, blinks at the foreman as if straining to see him better. Finally he answers: "Yes, I will take it."

The foreman does not hear. He is busy speaking into the phone. His English sounds like Polish Yiddish, but the words are incomprehensible. Finally he finishes the conversation, hurriedly replaces the receiver, and turns his eyes again on Barukh. "*Nu? Ni?* Well?"

"Yes," Barukh answers again. He stares at the ring the foreman wears on the little finger of his right hand. Mechanically, Barukh slides his hand into his left pocket and rubs his bare ring finger with his thumb, a habitual gesture whenever he feels lost. It was she who had once given him a ring. Their friends had mocked the gift as hopelessly bourgeois, but he had worn the ring with pride. Until that day . . .

"All right," the foreman exclaims. Barukh jumps as if jarred from sleep. "You punch in at ten o'clock." The foreman steps quickly behind a counter made of raw plywood, pulls a pencil from behind his ear, and prepares to write. "How do you spell your name?"

Barukh spells his name.

"How old are you?" "Forty-one."

"Wife? Children?"

"Gone."

"All right. Go and punch in. There under the clock. You mean you never punched a card before?"

"Never."

The foreman accompanies him to the clock and punches the white card for Barukh. "Your number is sixty-one. Your card must always lie right here. You punch in four times a day. What did you do before?"

"I've only been here for three weeks."

"I mean there, over there."

"In Warsaw I was a typesetter for a Polish newspaper."

"Go hang yourself up over there," the foreman chuckles, motioning toward Barukh's coat. "I'll put you to work at the press. Do you know how the press works?"

"No."

"All right. François!" The foreman's voice booms over the noise of the machines. From somewhere deep within the shop there is a flash of a striped red shirt. A scrawny, blond young man appears from between the racks hung with finished coats. He looks about sixteen years old. Two knots of curly hair cling moistly to his forehead. With both hands, he wipes the sweat from his boyish face.

Barukh hangs his coat on an empty coat rack. The solitary coat looks forlorn and even more bedraggled than it actually is. It is no longer the season for wearing heavy winter coats, but Barukh cannot help himself. He cannot seem to get warm in this country, and he does not find the coat too heavy for spring. He notices that the foreman and François wink at one another in amusement as they glance mockingly at the heavy coat.

"*Montrez garçon* pressing," the foreman says to François, indicating Barukh.

Barukh smiles shamefacedly at François and follows him through the shop, negotiating his way first among the racks of coats and then between the rows of roaring machines. Here and there workers look up as he passes. Some glance at him indifferently, then drop their eyes back to their work. Others stare at him with curiosity. The indifferent eyes belong to men, the curious ones to women. The men working at the machines are all middle-aged, and almost all are bald. The women are almost all young and pretty. They are French. That little one over there, for instance, the one sewing buttons—what big, warm eyes she has. And the ringlets around her head are thin and so light that the glow from the lamp shines through them.

François and Barukh come to a place in the shop where eight presses are arranged in a large rectangle. Next to each press stands a half-naked young man with unkempt hair. Steam rises from the ironing boards.

The heat hits Barukh in the face. "Speak English?" François asks him with a smile.

"No. French a little."

"Vous êtes français?"

"No. I just lived in Paris for a while."

"Ah, Paris!" Barukh can feel his stock rising in the young man's eyes.

The work, it seems, is not too difficult. One must lay out the pockets, the belts, and other small items on a board and then lower the press by hand. The first few pieces Barukh tries do not come out well, but François assures him that he will learn. Of course he will learn. If only it weren't so hot here. He is covered in sweat even though the window fans are constantly whirring. There should be some air, even a little breeze. Why is it so hard to breathe? He had better take off his tie, unbutton his collar, and roll up his shirt sleeves. It's airier that way. But in another minute he again feels the sweat running down the back of his ears and onto his neck. The shirt sticks to his back and rivulets of moisture tickle his spine. He will just have to get used to it. It's merely a question of becoming acclimatized, he tells himself. But his head aches as if a thousand hammers were pounding inside, and his legs buckle beneath him—just as they did on that hot, dark day that has not yet come to an end.

A bell. What is that ringing suddenly? As if by magic all the machines stop. The shop catches its breath in the momentary silence. Of course: it is noon—lunchtime. At a loss, Barukh stands by his press and stares at the others rushing past him. No one looks at him.

Suddenly he finds himself confronted by a pair of warm eyes. The girl who sews the buttons is standing next to him. *"Comment-ça va?"* she asks. For the first time it strikes Barukh that French-Canadian French is full of charm. He attempts to smile but immediately senses that his smile is foolish and without cheer. *"Vous êtes Parisien, n'est-ce pas?"* she asks.

How could she know this so quickly? Barukh wonders. "Yes . . . no," he stammers, and explains that he only lived in Paris for a year.

"Oh, as a visitor."

"No, as a DP."

"Oh." She nods knowingly, but from the expression on her face he realizes that she has no idea what this means. "Have you punched your card?" she asks. He shakes his head. "So come."

He lets her lead him to the clock and slides his card in upside down. "No, not that way," she exclaims, taking the card out of his hand and sliding it in the proper way. She has a small hand. The pallor of her skin is even more evident against the bright red of her polished nails. She smiles at him in a friendly way. "Aren't you going home for lunch?"

"I have no home."

Her smile displays two rows of tiny, perfect white teeth. "So where do you sleep? On the street?"

"I have a room that I rent, but I have no home."

She finds this amusing and bursts into laughter, giving him a friendly slap on the back. "Let's go eat. You can get some Coke outside at the counter. Bon appétit."

He looks after her as she walks back down the length of the shop to her table. Her high-heeled shoes click against the floor with a light wooden tap. The white nylon blouse she is wearing trembles against her skin, and the large flowers on her colorful skirt wrap themselves around her legs like a dancing bouquet. The girl possesses a carefree lightheartedness that makes Barukh feel more acutely the weight of the despair that he carries within himself.

He glances around the shop. Here and there workers sit by their machines absorbed in eating. Next to the window stands a group of Jews, chatting. The smoke from their cigarettes hangs in a cloud over their heads. Across the way, in the darker side of the hall, are groups of young men and women, some of whom lie stretched out across mounds of raw fabric. Barukh can hear their whistles and their laughter. They are French Canadian. Why didn't a Jewish girl come over to me? he wonders. He looks about him. Where are all the young Jewish women? Better they should be anywhere rather than here in this damp, sweaty shop. Better they should work in offices, or study, or be the mothers of small Jewish children.

Suddenly his thoughts focus on his own two children, who perished during the war. They are dressed in their holiday clothes and are seated on a high sofa. They peer into the camera and wait for the birdie to appear.

Barukh walks slowly over to the window. On the large table nearby lies an open *Forward*. A young man with an uneven bald spot, which he has attempted to cover with a thick strand of hair, lifts his dark, unshaven face as Barukh approaches. Barukh asks if that is today's *Forward*. The young man shakes his head and once more lowers his bald head over the paper. Barukh's eyes skim the headlines. Nearby stands a group of Jews, discussing politics. A heavy-set Jew waves his index finger threateningly in the face of his listeners. He is wearing a green Bermuda shirt with a flowery design in loud colors, and his collar is open.

"You have to be an American to appreciate who MacArthur was. Small thing, MacArthur! A folk hero!" he thunders. "What do you know about MacArthur? Listen . . ." He grabs the sleeve of one of his listeners, but the other, a flabby, middle-aged Jew with a pointy nose and small, merry eyes, laughs and interrupts him.

"Listen, shmisten." The flabby Jew pulls up his baggy pants. "Better ask us greenhorns who the folk heroes are. Believe me, mister, the biggest folk hero would be a lot bigger if you made him a head shorter. And you better cut out that song and dance about being an American."

"Did I knock the crown off your head when I said that you have to be an American?" asks the Jew in the Bermuda shirt, nervously winding the large gold watch on his wrist.

"Heaven forbid, my friend! You're too short to reach my crown! Do you really think that we greenhorns know nothing and understand nothing? Believe me, there are many things you could learn from us."

"Like what, for instance?"

"A little bit of humanity, a little bit of friendliness."

"*Oh va!* No more, no less!"

"You should know that," intercedes another greenhorn. "If you had come to us, after the kinds of troubles we've lived through, we would have welcomed you with open arms."

"Oh, when will there ever be peace between the old-timers and the newcomers?" one of the listeners sighs.

"When the Messiah comes," smiles the Jew with the merry eyes.

"Do you think that they will welcome the Messiah better than they did us? He will be a greenhorn, after all."

"Their Messiah has already come. They don't need anything more, those old-timers."

"Why are you talking nonsense?" explodes the Jew in the Bermuda shirt. "Do you think that my Messiah has come already? Of course he has. I've blackened my life with forty years' work at the sewing machine. Forty years, I tell you. And I'm still at the same level as you. What do you want from me, anyway? What have I taken from you? What do I owe you? I like this country. What are you going to do about it? You don't approve, so go back where you came from."

An uncomfortable silence falls on the group, which disperses slowly and with seeming regret. For the first time someone takes note of Barukh. "Are you new?"

Barukh nods.

"Where do you come from?"

"From Paris."

"A Parisian?"

"No. From Warsaw."

6

"Were you in Russia?"

"No. In the camps."

"Did you run into anyone from Ozorkov?"

"Only after the war."

"Did you ever hear of the family Zlotnik?"

"No."

A new circle has formed around Barukh and his questioner. Someone else eagerly addresses a question to Barukh: "Did you say you are from Warsaw? Where in the city did you live?"

"On Krochmalna Street."

"I'm from Otvotsk. My father had a cigarette stand next to the highway. You probably know . . ."

Otvotsk. Barukh sees himself with her on one of their first excursions together. He breathes in the air of Otvotsk, inhaling deeply. Cigarettes! He is suddenly overcome by a powerful urge to smoke. He deserts his companions and hurries away to the stand where his coat is hanging solitary and forsaken. He puts his hand into his pocket, extracts the pack of cigarettes, and lights one. He inhales deeply. The air of Otvotsk burns and grates against his throat.

Suddenly the little French Canadian with the warm eyes is at his side again. The unease inside him grows. "Give me a cigarette," her red lips smile at him. He extends the pack of cigarettes toward her. She pulls one out and puts it in her mouth, waiting for a light. Her mouth is close to him, and there is a pleasant coolness emanating from her fingers. He feels drawn to this carefree girl, just as earlier he had been drawn to his cigarettes. "Did you enjoy it?" she asks, seating herself on a nearby table.

He watches her. "What?"

"What do you mean *what*? The lunch."

He smiles crookedly and shakes his head. She plays with the folds of her colorful skirt and stares at him steadily with her laughing eyes. "Tell me something about Paris," she implores in an oddly childlike voice. "To have lived for a whole year in Paris! *Mon Dieu!* Some people have all the luck."

He looks at her legs dangling from the table. Small blonde hairs peek through her nylon stockings. "Paris?"

"Yes, Paris."

Suddenly the girl vanishes, and Barukh sees himself in a dirty Paris hotel room. He remembers how he had to be constantly registering with the police and how he had to stand in line for days on end in front of the JOINT distribution offices. He remembers all the worries about having proper papers, about getting the proper tickets for the boat. "Yes, certainly, a beautiful city," he mutters.

"*N'est-ce pas?*" she exclaims. "Paris is my dream. What sorts of things did you see there? Tell me."

"Oh, the Eiffel Tower . . ." He remembers a walk he took on a brilliant Saturday. The Trocadero was bathed in light. The fountains spat streams of crystalline water into the air. He did not have enough francs to buy a ticket to ride up the Eiffel Tower.

"And I'm sure you went walking on the Champs Élysées," she remarks with enthusiasm.

"Of course." He sees the Champs Élysées as it was in the blue summer twilight. He spent many hours wandering about there until, one day, he was accosted by a vision that froze his heart. He saw a woman standing by the exit to the metro. It was she! His wife. She had a suitcase in her hand and was looking uncertainly about her. He knew that this could not be his wife because he had seen his wife in the Umshlagplatz, the gathering place for those about to be deported to their deaths. Even so, with bated breath, he started to run toward the woman only to be confronted by a pair of strange, frightened eyes as he drew near her.

"And how are the Parisian women dressed? Very stylish and elegant, *n'est-ce pas?*" The girl looks into his face as if she could find there the entire splendor of Paris. "Why are you silent? Tell me." Suddenly she giggles. "I guess you're not an expert on women's clothing. You certainly don't look like one. But you surely went to the opera and the theater every night, didn't you?"

He remembers the few open-air concerts that he attended in Paris, and the gnawing despair that accompanied his return home after each one. His wife had played the violin. On their way to the ghetto the violin had fallen from her hand, and an oncoming wagon filled with furniture had run over it.

"They have some wonderful nightclubs there, don't they?" The girl's eyes are no longer laughing. They are large and eager. There is such a thirst in them! "They drink champagne there as if it were water, the music plays, and people dance in the half darkness while the voice of Edith Piaf comes over the loudspeaker, '*Je vous aime . . .*'" She bends closer to him and flutters her lashes seductively. But his desire for her has dissipated. "And tell me"—she is not yet tired of questioning him—"have you seen other countries as well?"

"I've seen them."

"And I've never been anywhere except Montreal and Trois-Rivières. That's where I was born. If you only knew how much I like to hear stories about other countries!" Once again her face takes on a childish, dreamy quality. He would gladly stroke her head as if she were a little girl. "Where else have you been? Tell me," she implores.

"In Poland," he answers. "That's where I was born, in a city called Warsaw."

"Oh, Warsaw is really far! Did you like the city?"

"In the past I did."

"And today?"

"Today the city seems alien to me."

"Why? Well, of course, it's been a long time since you've been there."

"I am still there."

"What do you mean?"

"My childhood is there, and my youth is there, and my dearest possessions are all there. Everything that mattered to me is there, and it is all gone."

"I don't understand what you're saying."

"How can you understand? You were born in Trois-Rivières."

"Never mind that stuff. Tell me where else you've been. Go on. Tell me."

"I was in Czechoslovakia, in Austria, in Germany, in Italy . . ."

"Jésu Marie! You've seen the entire world! Were you so rich? You must have been one of the richest people in the world."

"No, one of the poorest."

"You were a businessman, weren't you?"

"No. A DP."

"I don't understand."

"In English it's called a 'displaced person.'"

"Oh, you mean a displeased person. That's what I am too." She breaks into a full-throated laugh. Her voice is lusty and youthful. How long it has been since Barukh heard such laughter! But he cannot join in her mirth. He does not even smile. He feels suddenly claustrophobic and ill at ease. He leaves the girl sitting where she is and strides toward the door.

At the exit, behind the plywood counter, sits the foreman, holding a bottle of Coke to his mouth. "Hey, you! Come over here," he calls to Barukh.

Barukh's heart skips a beat. Someone else once called to him in just that tone of voice. The foreman takes Barukh's measure with a pair of cold eyes. Someone else once took his measure in just that way. Barukh has a feeling that this coming encounter is a replay of an encounter that happened some time in the past. Yes. He is in the concentration camp. There is about to be a selection. He hides behind the barrack. If he shows up at the selection he is lost. He is too bloated. Suddenly he hears a voice. "Hey, you, come over here!" Before him he sees the Jewish kapo. A raised fist lands on his back. Barukh falls into the mud. "Come. You are going to clean the latrines!" the kapo barks. At that moment Barukh feels the stirrings of love for the fist that knocked him down. He is ready to kiss it in gratitude because it has granted him his life.

"So how do you like the job?" The foreman's voice sounds mocking.

All of Barukh's senses are awake. This is not the camp. This is freedom; this is the God-blessed country of Canada. The foreman's voice grates on him. "I told you already, I like it," he snaps.

The foreman rises and bangs the bottle of Coke against the plywood table. "So you told me already, eh? So now the question is, do I like you? He's told me already, the big shot with the manicured fingernails! That's some way to talk!" From under the counter, he abruptly pulls out the work Barukh has done in the previous few hours and lays it out with jerky fingers on the countertop. Curious workers gather around, holding sandwiches in their hands and guzzling drinks. The foreman stares at them and shouts self-righteously. "Good work, eh? Ruined a few dozen pockets and belts."

"I told you that I'm not a presser," Barukh coldly replies.

"So you told me again! You never stop telling me. Maybe you will tell me now how to run my business."

"I don't know what you want from me."

"He doesn't know what I want from him! You hear that? The guy ruins a few dozen pockets and belts and hasn't got a clue what the matter is. I ask you again, do you want this job?" Barukh carefully nods yes. The foreman wags a finger at him. "So once and for all you should know that I am the boss here and not you, greenhorn! You do as I say and as I please. And if you don't like it, you can go to hell." Having said his piece, the foreman reseats himself on the stool.

Barukh can feel his hands knotting into fists. One stride and he is standing in front of the plywood counter, his hot face breathing into the face of the foreman. "You can't talk to me like that!" he shouts.

But the foreman's eyes have lost their metallic edge. Unconcerned, he pushes Barukh out of the way, unpacks his smoked-meat sandwich, and bites into it with large, eager teeth.

Barukh is transported by his own rage. "Don't you talk to me like that! This is a free country. Understand?"

The foreman chews, shrugs, puts a finger to his temple, and smiles at the others, motioning toward Barukh. "Crazy."

The others smile back meaningfully.

Barukh is beside himself: "You are not the boss of my life, do you hear? I am a human being, just like you. Just like you!" he shouts, his voice growing increasingly louder the smaller he feels inside. "You will not curse me! No! I've heard enough curses in my life."

"So why don't you get lost!" the foreman laughs. "Did you ever hear such a thing?" He turns to the others. "I'm supposed to talk to him through a silken handkerchief. Who do you think you are, greenhorn? And *where* do you think you are? In Bronfman's living room, maybe? This is a shop."

"Yes, a shop," Barukh retorts hotly. "But a modern shop, not from a hundred years ago. Those curses were fine then."

"Really? You would prefer some modern curses, then? Well, I'm an old-fashioned foreman. Go, do me something!"

"But we are modern workers. We won't stand to be insulted by such nothings like you. We have unions."

The workers, who have been listening to this exchange in silence, suddenly break into laughter. One of them slaps Barukh on the back in a comradely way. "Here is not like back home, my friend."

Someone else waves his hand derisively. "This one is a real greenhorn from greenhorn land."

Barukh gives up the argument. He feels lost. He is alone, utterly alone, in this strange place. All around him the workers are conversing in heated tones, discussing unions and wages. The foreman stares at Barukh with mock-innocent eyes. He unpacks another smoked-meat sandwich and bites into it with obvious enjoyment. Barukh feels silly. He wipes the sweat from his forehead with a dirty piece of Kleenex and does not know what to do with himself. The bell rings. Still conversing, the workers go to the clock and, one after another, punch in their cards.

The little French Canadian appears next to Barukh. "Here. Have a Chiclet." Her white hand pushes a piece of chewing gum between his lips. The tips of her fingers are wonderfully cool against his mouth.

Suddenly the foreman stands up and calls, "François!" The thin boy with the large mop of hair appears by his side. "*Montrez garçon* pressing! Good pressing. Remember! And if you don't, may the holy plague take you, you goyish blockhead."

"Okay, boss," François nods smilingly, revealing two protruding front teeth. He pulls Barukh by the sleeve. "Come on."

Barukh would like to run away, but the foreman is smiling at him. "Why are you standing there like a wooden pole with your eyes popping out? Go punch your card." The foreman's voice sounds paternal, forgiving.

Barukh punches his card. This time he does it correctly. Then he returns to the press machine. The heat beats against his face. Once again the sweat runs in streams down his back. The fans whir, the machines roar rhythmically. The little French Canadian is sewing buttons somewhere between the racks of finished clothing. Barukh chews on his gum. A drop of sweetness melts in his mouth and soothes his temper.

Last Love

For the first two weeks of her stay in Paris, Amalia felt quite well. For hours on end, day after day, she would sit between the tall, shuttered casements of the open hotel room window with her knees resting against the black wrought-iron railing that was molded as fine as a piece of filigree. From there she would gaze down into the Tuileries Gardens across the street. The pills she was taking had completely dulled her pain, and if she happened to feel an ache in her chest, Gabriel would double the dose of her medicine.

Ever since the Second World War she had suffered from tuberculosis. She had spent time in a number of sanatoria and had thought herself cured—especially during the years she lived with her former husband—when suddenly, for some mysterious reason, she suffered a relapse. Now she was in the last stage of her illness, from which, the doctors said, there was no hope that she would recover.

Gabriel had brought her to Paris to grant her what she—partly in jest, partly in earnest—had called her "final request." She wanted to die in Paris, she had told him in a coquettish tone of voice. She wished to embark on her journey into Eternal Darkness from the City of Light, the city where she had gone directly after the war, the city where she had been young, where her beauty had come into bloom, and where she had fallen in love for the first time.

There, many years later, she had also met Gabriel. At that time he had been an unsuccessful sculptor with a family to support, while she was an elegant matron who had run away from her wealthy husband in

Montreal. Alone in Paris, she had sought out her favorite spots, which included the Tuileries Gardens, where she wandered about the Jeu de Paume Museum and the Musée de Flore. Having refreshed herself by gazing on the works of her beloved Impressionists, she stepped outside to stroll at a leisurely pace among the Henry Moore sculptures in the garden. There Gabriel too had been strolling.

It was his first visit to Paris since he had emigrated from Europe. He too lived in Montreal, where he had left his wife and children in order to make the trip to Paris alone, a trip he considered of great importance to his survival as an artist. His creative output had begun to decline; his imagination had lost its wings. Like a wanderer in the desert he was frantically searching for an oasis, for a revitalizing spring. And so he had launched himself into the world again in quest of the stimulation he hoped would save his soul.

In Montreal Gabriel and Amalia had never met. They might have heard each other's names mentioned, or noticed one another from a distance at a vernissage or a prize-giving ceremony or some similar function where money and art met, but that was all. And here too, in the Tuileries Gardens, they almost escaped each other's notice. Amalia, having distracted herself at the art exhibit, walked among Henry Moore's rocklike masterpieces absent-mindedly, lost in the labyrinth of her own inner world, her thoughts stumbling along the stony paths of her own life.

She was, of course, aware of the stranger who, like herself, had been strolling among the bronzes. On such a rainy, pre-spring day, when there were not yet many tourists in Paris, the gardens were deserted. Gabriel's tall, slightly stooped figure had immediately caught her eye. He was clad in a not overly clean raincoat, while the unkempt strands of his graying hair extended in all directions like exclamation marks. A number of times she had even been obliged to step aside and let him pass, so absorbed was he in scrutinizing the sculptures. Yet she did not notice him—not really.

As for him, he definitely did not notice her. He was preoccupied with comparing Henry Moore's artistic idiom to that of Picasso. At the same time Moore's massive creations transported him, through the shortcut of association, back to the majestic Canadian Rockies, which he loved.

He suddenly realized how late it was and automatically turned to the strange, trim lady who wore a white suit that did not yet match the season but was a refreshing contrast to the gray of their surroundings. Her blonde hair, loosely gathered in a bun, fell with charming negligence against the white ermine collar hugging her neck. He walked up to her and asked if she knew where he might take the metro to the Bastille.

"To the Bastille?" She raised an eyebrow as if in surprise, and before his eyes this mysteriously alluring woman acquired the look of a young girl whose facial expression suggested that she was being robbed of something that belonged exclusively to her.

"Yes, to the Bastille," he nodded.

They recognized the racial kinship in each other's accent and eyes—a Jewish gaze from Jewish eyes. In the same instant they both exclaimed, she a question, he the answer.

"First time in Paris?"

"First time in Paris since the end of the war."

A stream of more typically Jewish questions and answers followed in rapid succession. They both, it seemed, hailed from Montreal. Each vaguely recalled having heard the other's name mentioned; perhaps they had even met. Surely they had met, the day before, or years earlier, or eternities ago. From the depths of their eyes a magnetic force drew them together. They continued questioning each other but had ceased listening to the answers. No, he was in no particular hurry to get to the Bastille, nor did she have any pressing business to attend to.

That day Gabriel did not go to the Bastille. He and Amalia spent the day in the Tuileries, with no food or drink. They sat on the ironwork garden chairs, which grated unpleasantly against the gravel. The seats were painted orange and looked like rectangular slices of sunshine against the gray. They reminded Amalia of the color of the bougainvillea that grew in the small Japanese town where she had been stranded when the war broke out. When they grew tired of sitting, Amalia and Gabriel walked about the garden, then returned to the Moore sculptures, sat down again, and continued their conversation, increasingly fascinated by and absorbed in each other's world.

On the whole they exchanged banalities, laying out the patterns of their respective lives for their mutual perusal. Gabriel confessed that he was a deplorable breadwinner, that when he had been forced to put away his chisel and carving knife in order to concentrate on earning a living he had cursed his life; that he had worked at a regular job until his children were grown and that during all those years, he had barely done any sculpting. Now he was feeling the effect of having neglected his skills. Apart from the fact that his creative vigor had vanished, his technique, too, was faulty and inadequate for his needs. He also told her that his wife resented him.

"She . . ." he began.

"She doesn't understand you." Amalia finished the sentence for him with a discreet chuckle, aware that such a statement could be both a cliché and a painful truth.

"She's about to divorce me," he said, and in turn asked her the customary question that one asks a woman alone—namely, why is she alone?

Her reply was candid and direct: "My husband had an affair with another woman. So I've come here to sort out my feelings." She also told him that she suffered from tuberculosis but that at present she was almost completely cured.

It was good, gratifying, to be frank and not feel obliged to embellish one's story or hide behind a mask of half-truths. No doubt this foreign city contributed to that ease, to that open-heartedness. So did the fact that they were strangers and that, although receptive, friendly, and curious about each other, they would probably never meet again. It was like getting undressed in front of a doctor and finding a partial remedy for one's ills in the mere expectation of a cure.

Actually, it was not a matter of what they said to one another but of what they did not say yet allowed each other to sense. There was something in the air between them, a radiance of spirit that enveloped them both and set them apart in a distinct and harmonious sphere.

With the gray of dusk, they left the Tuileries, crossed the street to the Arcades, and had a baguette sandwich and a cup of coffee in a tiny bistro. They both laughed at the fact that Paris was a cure for the torments of the heart.

Afterward Amalia, in the most simple and direct manner, invited Gabriel to her hotel room. She was staying nearby, at the distinguished Hotel Meurice, once part of the building complex that had housed the Gestapo headquarters during the German occupation. There, in the room with the tall, shuttered windows that faced the Tuileries Gardens, they spent the night.

The following morning she said goodbye to him. She had no intention of seeing him again. It was true that life with her husband had lost its meaning, but she was not yet ready to become involved with another man, let alone to fall in love with one.

It was then that Gabriel said to her: "I shall never leave you. Nor will I ever be unfaithful to you."

He did not visit the Bastille that day either, but waited for Amalia in front of her hotel. At length he saw her appear, wearing the same white suit she had worn the day before. She entered a nearby travel agency, and he followed her inside. Before she had time to sit down at the agent's desk he strode over and seized her arm.

"You are my destiny. I feel it in my bones," he said to her. "Wherever you go, I will follow. Wherever you are, I will be there too, now and forever."

She was startled. There was an edge of rawness and heat in his voice, as well as a forceful sincerity that made her head swim. To see such a face, to meet such a gaze and hear such words from a man of this type, could only happen once in a lifetime. She knew that. This was not the first time in her life that she had listened to a declaration of love from a man. But the declaration she heard at that moment, as they stood facing each other in the travel bureau, had nothing in common with other love declarations. What she herself felt for Gabriel was of no importance. Just as she had not managed to sort out the feelings that she had brought with her from Canada, so she could not disentangle the chaos of emotions that had overtaken her during the last twenty-four hours.

So he made the decision for her, and she allowed him to do so. She, who had lived through her own series of trials and tribulations, was reckless for perhaps the first time in her life. She trusted him, although she hardly knew who he was. But in the forcefulness of his words she heard the command of Fate, for better or worse, the confirmation that they were meant for each other.

She postponed her departure from one day to the next, and he did the same. They spent the days and nights together, never leaving one another for longer than was absolutely necessary. Often when they made love, tears would flow down Amalia's cheeks.

* * *

Gabriel kept his promise. He never deceived Amalia. Nor did she deceive him. She felt good with him. She never discovered whether her feelings for him were as powerful as his for her, but that did not seem to matter. His love for her, their lovemaking, and his readiness to serve her filled her heart with such gratitude and enriched her days so abundantly that being with him, talking to him, or keeping silent with him became as necessary to her as the air she breathed. She grew more sensitive, more sensuous than she had ever been before, as if Gabriel had removed the dust from some delicate chords that had lain untouched for a long time in the deepest recesses of her heart. She felt a kind of ecstatic tenderness for him and could find no other name to call it but love. Like a plant starved for nourishment and receiving finally what it had lacked, she came back to life. She unfolded like a flower in bloom, infusing the air about her with a kind of soul perfume that permeated her surroundings.

As soon as she and Gabriel were divorced from their respective spouses, they rented a studio apartment at the foot of the mountain in the center of Montreal. There Gabriel could devote himself to his work. They lived modestly, frugally, on Gabriel's earnings from the infrequent sale of his sculptures and on Amalia's salary. In Japan she had taken lessons in flower arrangement, which stood her now in good stead, and thanks to her attractive appearance and her fluent French she found work as a saleslady in a high-class flower shop.

She liked flowers of a warm, rich hue, and the wide window ledge in Gabriel's studio was crowded with pots of blooming azaleas the color of deep coral sunsets—although her favorite color, the one she herself liked to wear, was white. She cared a great deal for her flowers and talked about them so often that Gabriel would sometimes call her "my white azalea."

In his heart he also bestowed on her two other names that were connected in meaning. He called her "my white Dame aux Camélias" or "my white geisha." Both names suited her, not only because La Dame aux Camélias had worn a white camellia in her hair or because she too had suffered from tuberculosis, and not only because "geisha" evoked Amalia's Japanese interlude, while the porcelain pallor of Amalia's face reminded Gabriel of the artificial whiteness of a geisha's complexion, but also because the reawakening of her illness—of which they had both been unaware at first—stimulated her sexual appetite. Thus he lovingly compared her to a refined courtesan who maintained a knowing balance between decency and vulgarity, and in this way she made him want her even more. As Amalia's illness progressed, a delicate flush caused by fever colored her cheeks, and she became even more beautiful.

The years wore on, one month followed another, weeks came and went, not always in perfect harmony. Periods of boredom occasionally punctuated their time together; discord and misunderstandings occurred more than once. But these usually gave way to moments of clarity, of consciously rising above the workaday tedium, and once again the light of devotion would illuminate the gray, monotonous plateau of routine with a warm glow.

It was usually Gabriel who saw to it that their hours of estrangement after a quarrel should end quickly. Whatever elements of mediocrity may have existed in him as a sculptor, he proved himself a true artist in his love for Amalia. His life with her became his masterpiece. And it was precisely this feat of creativity in his daily life that began to stir his potential as a sculptor. The inventive power of his love stimulated his artistic imagination. Gabriel and Amalia, both touched by war and personal tragedy, treated each one of their days together as if it were a symphonic poem or a chapter in a romance.

Gabriel's sculptures began to sell. As soon as their financial situation improved he bought a car, a Jaguar. Amalia covered the seats with warm-colored fabrics, and they traveled a great deal all over Canada. Once he drove her all the way west to the Rocky Mountains to view the turquoise blue of crystalline Lake Louise, a lake whose magic-mirror surface reflects the surrounding mountains, which recline like queens with snowy veils on their heads, each peak demanding to know who is the fairest of them all.

But Amalia's health began to deteriorate rapidly. She gave up her job, although, thanks to the excellent medical care she received, there were still times when she led a perfectly normal life. She remained active at home, caring for the household, tending to her flowers, and reading. She spent long hours sitting with Gabriel in his studio watching him work while the phonograph played their favorite music, most often Gustav Mahler's *Kindertotenlieder.*

Amalia's beauty acquired a new delicacy and fragility. She grew ethereal in appearance; from the grayish green of her eyes there emanated an intense inner light. She released a kind of soul heat into the atmosphere around her. Sometimes, when Gabriel watched her moving about the room, wrapped in her long, white dressing gown, her eyes glowing with the high fever devouring her body, she appeared to him like a statue chiseled out of burning coal and wrapped in a cloak of white ice, or like a marble lamp covered by a marble lampshade; but most often she seemed like a white ghost who had gathered the whole of the sunset to her bosom.

Gabriel was possessed by the impulse to carry her around in his arms, to touch the flame that burned within her. While she, for her part, yearned for his touch, for his caress, and could never get enough of their lovemaking.

His grief at her illness was overwhelming, and the only means by which he could forget his sorrow was to immerse himself in his work. From dawn until late at night he stood at his workbench, hammer, chisel, or carving knife in hand. His only inspiration, his only subject, was Amalia. He began to shape her likeness in countless variations of delicately formed, ethereal figures. He made the transparency of her soul sing from the clay, from the metal or stone with which he worked. He wanted to fix her forever in these forms, to prevent her from slipping away from him. He wanted to imbue his sculptures with his love song, with his boundless devotion.

His studio became full of her. A room full of Amalias. And still it was not enough. He was like a man possessed, in a continuous trance, in a state of uninterrupted intoxication. He found himself at the very bottom of despair, like a beggar, while at the same time he was as elated and proud as a king, as if he had only just discovered the artist within him.

Never before had it been as difficult for him to part with his works as it was now, when he had to sell one of his Amalia figures. Each piece he packed in a crate gave him the impression that he was placing both Amalia and himself in a coffin, as if their joined selves were about to leave the house forever. It was only Amalia's encouraging smile that gave him the heart to deliver the package to its buyer. And he was compelled to make this effort with increasing frequency when Amalia was finally forced to enter a sanatorium in the Laurentians.

To live without her in their apartment was like living in hell. It gave him a foretaste of what her actual absence from his life would be like. Occasionally he had the impression that he could hear her rustling steps behind him, that at any moment she might emerge from some shadowy corner. In the studio where he spent his days, he drank in her radiance from the figures he had made of her, and they gave him support. With tenderness, deeply moved, he took care of her flowers, the coral-colored azaleas on the window ledge of his studio, which he now addressed as "my beautiful Amalias." He could hardly wait for the weekends, when he set out to visit her in the mountains.

Nurtured by his longing for her, by his sorrow and his fear of losing her, his muse flourished. Overnight he became famous. His Amalia figures cast a magical spell over their viewers, as if each piece of bronze or stone exhaled the warm breath of love. Women looking at the figures recognized their own souls revealed in their fullest beauty, while men saw the features of the women who haunted their dreams.

The harder it became for Gabriel to part with his statues, the greater the demand for them grew; and the more he raised his prices in order to discourage buyers, the more eager did the buyers become to possess his work. Thus after each exhibition of his sculptures, in Canada or abroad, when his studio was left depleted and empty, Gabriel felt himself orphaned, ill, without support. And he immediately set out to create new Amalias, formed in humility, carved out of his fantastic visions of her. The sicker Amalia became, the deeper grew Gabriel's grief and the greater grew his fame as an artist, as if his creative genius were feasting on her illness. And so his victory went hand in hand with his defeat; his creative health and prowess went hand in hand with the greatest pain of his life.

When it became clear to Amalia that there was no hope for her and that her life was drawing to a close, she asked Gabriel to take her to Paris. Her physicians had no objections, since there was nothing more to be done but to satisfy her last wishes. They recommended a competent nurse to accompany the couple on their journey, and Gabriel made the necessary arrangements. Since Amalia wished it, they installed themselves in the same Hotel Meurice, across from the Tuileries Gardens, where they had spent their first night together.

* * *

After their first two weeks in Paris Amalia began to feel that the last springs of her life were draining away. She sat at the open window of the hotel room. It was the beginning of autumn. The trees in the gardens across the street stood dipped in the red-gold and yellow-brown of sunset, colors she so admired.

It was the best time of year to be in Paris. The weather was not hot but pleasantly warm. Amalia could guess the temperature by observing the people in the street, noting what clothes they wore and the expressions of leisurely contentment on their faces. She herself felt the usual heat in her body and the fever bugs crawling over her skin. Young couples strolled in the Tuileries Gardens, while excited children raced after the falling leaves. Seen through the haze of suffering and the thin veil in front of her eyes—the effect of the pills she was taking to soothe her pain—the sky above the treetops resembled a painting by an Impressionist master.

Amalia's mind, dreamily awake, was worried by a vague craving as it wandered about its inner autumnal world, where scraps of memory were scattered by the winds of time, like golden leaves with burnt, dark edges. Only one leaf, still fresh and green, not yet fully unfurled, as if it were waiting for a summer that would never come, remained firmly rooted to the stem of her memory. Now, as all the other leaves of recollection fell away, this single leaf became the focus of her attention, like a scream within a void.

A question, both tragic and amusing, picked at her mind. "Who was the idiot," she asked herself, "who said that the unexamined life is not worth living? What a fool! Life is like wine. All you need is to feel its taste on your tongue. Let the wine producers or the scientists analyze it if they like; for me it is enough to feel the intoxicating stream flowing through my veins. And yet . . . and yet I wouldn't mind knowing . . . I would like to discover what was the strongest force propelling me through life. What was my most powerful passion?"

* * *

Another bright, sunny morning. Paris was flooded with sunshine, made colorful by crowds of well-dressed strollers. Gabriel was still in his pajamas. Amalia, clad in her white dressing gown, sat in a cushioned armchair. The room service waiter had just rolled in a table on tiny wheels with breakfast for the couple. There was, as usual, a bowl of strawberries. Amalia never ate the strawberries; she just liked to look at them.

Amalia's long hair, which had once been blonde, was now knotted in a loose gray braid that lay limply against her bosom. Gabriel served her. It was usually he who attended to her needs, who served her and took care of her. They had brought along the nurse whom the doctors had recommended, but they availed themselves of her services only in medical matters. Until recently the nurse had also assisted with Amalia's morning toilette and with her bath. But then Gabriel decided that he alone would be responsible for that. They both felt good about this, although Gabriel's heart contracted with grief at the sight of his wife during these daily ablutions.

Whenever he touched her body, it seemed to him that he was engaged in an unsuccessful attempt to mold a sculpture by adding handfuls of clay that refused to adhere to the frame and kept falling away. He felt that his reason was leaving him. There were moments when he wished her dead—because he loved her so, because he was incapable of watching her die—and wished to have it all behind him. Yet these moments of tactile intimacy with her were precious to him.

They would talk frankly about her leaving him and about what would happen after her death. She had even sent him out to buy himself an entire wardrobe of coats, suits, shirts, shoes, and ties that he was to wear after she was gone so that she might have an idea of how he would look. The more life dimmed within her, the more she loved him. And she realized that she knew the answer to the question she had asked herself the other day.

That morning she said to him, "Do you know, Gabriel, what the most powerful forces were that shaped my life? They were love and the fear of death. And they both expressed themselves in erotic passion, in my sexual excitement. It is true that the climax of pleasure and death are related." Then she added quickly, brutally, "And do you know what my last wish is, Gabriel? My very last wish is to make love to a young man."

A spasm intended as a smile twisted his face. "Amalia . . ." he stammered.

"Don't laugh at me, dearest. Why are you so red in the face? You're not a prude. And you can't tell me that I mustn't give way to such lustful cravings at this point in my life, or that my body is simply too repulsive, since just this very morning, when you washed me, you remarked how youthful, white, and soft my skin is. As delicate and smooth as silk, you said. And I know it is so. I saw myself in the mirror when you wiped me dry with the towel. Even on her deathbed a woman wants to look beautiful. I would not have dared to entertain such a wish had I not been sure that I was still pleasing to the eye. Yes, beautiful . . . because you think that I am beautiful, because you have sculpted me so. You shaped me, with the chisel of your gaze, with the caresses of your hands, and with your telling me year after year how much you loved me, my face, my body, my limbs; how you loved to look at me, to touch me. This was how you kept your plant flourishing. And you still do. Because the thing that is so hopelessly ill within me, my darling Gabriel, is nothing but a sick sunset, which is, at the same time, a sunrise somewhere else. It must be so, Gabriel, my dearest. Because the sun never stops shining, does it?"

"Amalia . . ." he groaned. He had started to eat before she began speaking. Now his hand was unable to lift the food to his mouth.

Amalia continued talking, oblivious to his discomfort. "Perhaps my face betrays me a little bit, after all. What do you think?" She smiled faintly, and a small, playful spark lit up the grayish green of her eyes. "Yes, my face is like an azalea that has stood in the sun too long and become burnt around the edges. On the other hand, it is possible that only you would notice this, because you know . . . Anyway, I will try to fix it somehow, to adorn myself. You will help me, won't you? You will make me up with the hands of an artist; you'll add some color, a tiny bit of rouge on the cheeks to cover the pallor. You'll enhance me ever so slightly, only enough to render homage to the aesthetic sense of man. I don't want to play-act by masking myself. Because the curtain is almost touching the stage. And, dearest, why have you put down the croissant? Why don't you drink your coffee? Are you weeping? But, Gabriel, why?"

He did not answer. When she began to insist he jumped to his feet, walked over to the window, and through blurry eyes searched for an escape. But she would not give up so easily, and although his back was turned, she continued whispering tenderly, insistently, nagging him for an answer.

He turned to her abruptly, but all that could pass through his constricted throat was a hoarse whimper. "Please, Amalia!"

"Of course, I understand . . ." She placed her hot hand on top of his as he stood holding on to the railing, yet she did not stop talking. "And you must understand me too. I know you will. That is why I want to ask you . . . And please forgive me, my only one, for putting you through all this. But I know that your love for me ennobles everything I do and allows you to tolerate and forgive my wildest whims and caprices. Gabriel, I wish to ask you . . . no, not because I am capricious. But do find me a brown-haired . . . Someone of your height, perhaps a little taller . . . an attractive young man. Do it. Of course, I know how unbearably difficult this must be for you. And it may not be so easy to find him. But if someone like me exists, someone capable of having such a need, then someone like him must exist too, someone willing to respond to that need, prompted by a need of his own, by a secret wish. Forgive me, my sweet Gabriel, for my arrogance and for daring to hurt you so, but the need is stronger than I am, more powerful than life itself, more powerful than . . ."

He could not bear to listen any longer. Every one of her words cut into his heart. "Amalia . . ." he implored.

Still she continued: "And you must not pay him. Do you understand, dearest?" She feverishly stroked his hand. "Because if you do, the whole thing would lose its meaning; it would cheapen it. And you must tell him about me, about the state of my health. He must be aware of it. So I suppose it will take you some time, and you know how much time I have left . . ." She surprised him with a mischievous giggle. "This will also give you the perfect excuse to leave me for a while. I know that you need a rest. And from the artistic point of view, this might turn into quite an interesting experience for you. The nurse will stay with me, so you have no need to worry."

It was the first time that he burst into tears in her presence. His shoulders began to shake violently. "Why do you talk so cruelly, Amalia?"

"No . . . no," she stammered, moved by his sorrow. "I am not cruel. Fate is cruel. Understand—I never loved you as much as I do now. Perhaps it is merely that the manner in which I express my feelings has changed."

* * *

Gabriel could not make peace with Amalia's strange demand. It seemed to him that it was madness on her part, and that to comply with her wish would be madness on his. His despair acquired a new dimension. He was convinced that the high fever brought on by her illness had begun to confuse Amalia's mind and that she was dragging him down with her into the macabre entanglements of a reality in which everything was twisted and distorted as if reflected in a crooked mirror.

For the next two days he never left the hotel room. During that time they both refrained from mentioning the "mission" she had entrusted to him. On the third day he decided to venture out into the street and leave the nurse to stay with Amalia. When Amalia saw him take up his coat she did not stir, but a Mona Lisa smile played on her lips, which were tinted dark red by the fever. She said goodbye to him with a slight motion of her finger, from a distance, since he had not drawn near to give her a kiss nor a caress, nor had she called him over to receive one.

He wandered about the arcades in front of the hotel eyeing the luxurious window displays in the elegant shops at the same time as he scanned the faces of passersby. But he saw neither one nor the other. Instead he saw Amalia's chalk-white face and her long gray braid. The air was mild, yet he felt chilly. He wrapped himself in his raincoat, tightened the belt around his waist, and thrust his hands into the pockets as if he were trying to hold himself together.

Absently he crossed the street and entered the Tuileries Gardens, as though the subconscious recollection of his first encounter with Amalia propelled his feet in that direction.

Kicking a pebble along the gravel path he approached the Henry Moore sculptures and wandered about among the bronzes—reclining women who were cut up into raw, compartmentalized masses, heads askew, arms and legs asunder, bosoms like huge open gates, wombs like hoops made of granite, full of air, full of emptiness. Theirs was the majesty of the Rocky Mountains with only the icy glaciers of eternity missing from their backs. A cold wind breathed through the massive forms and through his own heavy thoughts. He felt hollow, drained, without a drop of energy left inside him—an unbearable existence, with a knife piercing the very core of his being, the blade lingering in the wound, the heart in one ceaseless spasm. He was overcome by a yearning to be transformed into a mass of stone.

He approached one of the iron chairs and slumped down so heavily into its orange-painted seat that the chair slid across the gravel. Before long his chin fell against his chest, and he drifted into a restless sleep. The sun warmed his back, beads of sweat formed pearls on his forehead, yet in his sleep he shuddered.

He woke to find himself the object of a stranger's gaze. Across from him sat a young man wearing threadbare jeans and a creased windbreaker. A scarf with long fringes was loosely draped around his neck; his arms encircled a knapsack on his knees, and a rolled-up copy of *Time* magazine protruded from one of his fists. The young man smiled broadly at Gabriel and offered him the magazine.

"It fell out of your pocket, Monsieur," he said in thickly accented English. "I did not dare to slip it back into your pocket in case I woke you. You look catastrophically tired, Monsieur."

His use of the word "catastrophically" caused Gabriel to look more closely at the young man. He saw before him an unusually bright, part-manly, part-boyish face from which there emanated a kind of radiant serenity. But when Gabriel peered more attentively into the stranger's brown eyes, which seemed to have the size and shape of a pair of plums, he noticed that there lurked a restless little flame in their depths; the young man's gaze was jumpy, like that of a startled rabbit. His brown, disheveled hair trembled with every breeze that brushed past his forehead.

"Thank you," Gabriel said, taking the magazine from the young man's hand.

When Gabriel stood up, the young man did the same. "You're an American, aren't you?" he asked.

"A Canadian," Gabriel replied.

"Really? You don't say!" the young man exclaimed enthusiastically. "I've always dreamed of visiting Canada, the Canadian Rockies. I'm a mountain climber. I've just come back from the Alps."

"Is that so," Gabriel said indifferently. Out of politeness, he asked, "What attracts you to mountain climbing?"

"I like to flirt with death," the young man retorted nonchalantly. Observing that he had not aroused any interest in his listener, he added guiltily, "I am a Parisian. My English is not very good, *n'est-ce pas*?"

"Passable," Gabriel grinned.

"I'm learning English from my fiancée. She is an American, studying French at the Sorbonne." He said this with obvious pride. "As a matter of fact, I'm waiting for her here. We are going on a picnic. She was with me in the Alps too. You understand, Monsieur, mountain climbing is a kind of erotic drive. Every mountain is like a woman you want to win, to conquer, and in the process you are liable to break your neck and lose your soul. But we had to return to Paris because her classes are soon to begin."

Gabriel was barely listening and did not react to his words. But the stranger continued to tramp along beside him, although at a distance. Finally Gabriel turned to face him.

"What is it that you want of me, Monsieur?" The young man drew nearer and asked, "Monsieur, are you in favor of peace in the world?"

The word "peace" pronounced with a French accent sounded comical. Gabriel had to smile. "Of course I'm in favor of peace."

"I don't mean you personally, *mon ami*. I mean you Canadians, in regard to your foreign policy."

"No one wants war except those who don't have to take part in it or those who profit from it," Gabriel replied curtly.

The young man was delighted with this response. He began to talk very quickly, grabbing hold of Gabriel's hand and pumping it vigorously up and down, then patting him cordially on the back. "My name is Jean-Pierre. I'm an activist in the Peace Movement. Perhaps you wish to make a small contribution?"

With a feeling of contempt for such undisguised begging, Gabriel thrust his hand into his pocket in the hope of retrieving a couple of francs but instead pulled out an American twenty-dollar bill. In order to rid himself of the nuisance as quickly as possible, he handed the money to the young man. "Bonjour!" he said sharply, turning away. He listened to his own heavy steps on the gravel, trying to determine whether or not the stranger was following him.

The next moment the young man was standing before him, the twenty-dollar bill in his outstretched hand. "Just a minute, Monsieur," he panted. "I have to give you a receipt, and my fiancée has the receipt book. Will you wait with me for her? Please do, *cher ami*. It won't be long."

Their eyes met. The anxiety in the young man's face was more evident now, his expression more frantic. Gabriel scrutinized him again. He slowly and carefully let his eyes travel over the figure of the young man in the creased windbreaker and the worn jeans.

Jean-Pierre was taller than Gabriel. He had a high, unshaven neck with a large Adam's apple, which was visible above the loose scarf that was wrapped around his neck. His mouth was broad and strong and his nose prominent; his jaws joined the chin in a sharp, decisive line. He had a pair of large, finely shaped ears; a few curly strands of his disheveled hair, cut in the Parisian style, were tucked behind his earlobes. However, these hard, masculine features were softened by the warm glow of the large, brown, plum-shaped eyes that illuminated his entire face. There was an air of nobility about the face, although its former radiant serenity now seemed faded. As for the young man's hands—Gabriel was capable of reading a great deal into the appearance and shape of a hand—he had just now felt their suppressed strength in Jean-Pierre's handshake.

Nevertheless Gabriel was suspicious. Perhaps this was some kind of scam? True, no one knew him in Paris, but he could be kidnapped just the same, or he could be robbed. Automatically he thrust his hands into his pockets and glanced stealthily about him, checking the gardens for passersby.

"Really, Monsieur," Jean-Pierre continued in his strongly accented English. "I would like very much to have your twenty dollars for the Peace Movement. I am appealing to you to wait here with me. My fiancée will be here any minute. She was supposed to be here already. She was supposed to be here an hour ago. *Vous comprenez?* I sense in you . . . I can see the catalog of the Louvre sticking out from your pocket . . . Monsieur, I beg of you."

Gabriel looked directly into his eyes. "What do you really want of me?"

"Really, Monsieur, I want you to wait with me for my fiancée."

"Why can't you wait for her by yourself?"

"I can, but I want to give you a receipt, and . . . I'm afraid she will not come. I need simply someone to talk to."

"Why shouldn't she come?"

"Because she was supposed to be here between eleven and twelve. Usually she is here about eleven. We meet beside the Moore sculptures. And today was supposed to be a most important day for us. We are supposed to fix the date when we register as man and wife. *Comprenez-vous*, Monsieur? We are so much in love and everything goes so well. And her parents in Philadelphia agree, and my parents also agree. But, Monsieur, we study the facts of reality. Contemporary life and the contemporary world, they stink, forgive the expression, Monsieur. So I am afraid that something may happen to our love. Because it is so holy, so sacred, and so unreal. This is my problem, Monsieur. I am trembling over my happiness. I have the feeling that I ought to pray, to make some sacrifice. To become husband and wife is no small thing, *n'est pas*, Monsieur?"

Something stirred within Gabriel. The young man's disarming, almost boyish candor was clearly genuine. He put his hand on Jean-Pierre's shoulder and patted him amicably. "It will all work out just fine, I assure you."

"What makes you so sure?" Jean-Pierre glanced at him searchingly.

"Your love and your imaginary problem."

"I know, I am crazy."

"Right. So am I."

Jean-Pierre smiled at him compassionately. "You are in love with a young woman?"

"No, I am in love with an old woman, an old woman who is dying. And you see, it is I who have the real problem. You want me to wait with you for your fiancée? Let's sit down, and I will tell you about my problem while we wait."

* * *

It was not easy for Gabriel to start talking to the strange young man, and at first he could only stammer out broken sentences between long gaps of silence. Both he and Jean-Pierre were preoccupied, each with his own anxiety, his own insecurity. Gradually, however, Gabriel's reluctance to talk gave way to an increasingly compelling need to liberate himself through words, to purify his soul with confession and burst open the boil that had festered in his heart for so long. He saw a pair of human ears before him intent on hearing what he had to say. There were the large, plum-shaped eyes concentrating on him, their restlessness muted. It seemed as if the stranger had moved his own soul in with Gabriel's and was a stranger no more.

Gabriel told Jean-Pierre about Amalia and himself and also about the mission on which she had sent him. Just at that moment, a young beauty with long, wispy blonde hair came running breathlessly up the garden path in the direction of the two men sitting on the iron chairs.

Both men jumped to their feet. The young couple fell eagerly into each other's arms as if they had not been together for an eternity. A long time seemed to pass before Jean-Pierre recovered himself and introduced his fiancée to Gabriel.

"This is Rose . . . Rosa."

She did indeed look like a newly opened rosebud. Her large blue eyes, moist from the wind, were smiling. Her flushed cheeks were the color of coral, and they reminded Gabriel of sunrise. As she brushed the long strands of hair away from her face, she tried to explain to Jean-Pierre why she was late. They were standing very close to one another, hand clasped in hand, yet they pressed together still more firmly in order to be even closer.

Jean-Pierre gave Rosa the twenty dollars for the Peace Movement. She wrote out a receipt and handed it to Gabriel. He wished them both much happiness and walked away, his mind calmer than it had been before. He prepared himself inwardly to refuse Amalia's request. He did not have the strength to fulfill her impossible wish, especially now that he had had this encounter with health and beauty.

As he entered the hotel room, Amalia, who had been lying in bed, opened her eyes. She smiled faintly at him and, without a word, again lowered her eyelids. For the rest of the afternoon and evening he could not bring himself to speak to her.

The following morning Gabriel went down into the street for a walk, something that had suddenly become a necessity for him. As he took his first undecided steps along the colonnade, Jean-Pierre suddenly emerged from behind a column and walked up to him.

"Monsieur," Jean-Pierre said, a note of suicidal resolve sounding in his voice. "I will help you. In the name of love, I will help you. I will offer myself as a sacrifice to earn absolution and blessing. When should I come?"

Gabriel replied without hesitation, "Tonight! Eight-thirty! Hotel Meurice, room number 639!" He ran into a kiosk, bought himself a pack of cigarettes, and hurried back to the hotel.

Once inside he slowed his pace and strolled slowly through the carpeted lobby, which was filled with photographers and journalists. Elegantly dressed men and women of various nationalities were standing around in loose groups. Waiters carrying champagne glasses and hors d'oeuvres on large silver trays navigated from one cluster of people to the next. The door to the Grand Salon stood open, and inside everything sparkled with the reflected light of mirrors and chandeliers.

Gabriel moved toward the Grand Salon. He glanced inside the room, then inquired of a man nearby what was going on.

"A luncheon for the delegates to the Peace Conference, sir. A dinner and ball to follow tonight," a tall, unhappy-looking Englishman informed him politely. Gabriel thanked him with a slight bow and entered the lift with peace in his heart. He got off at the sixth floor, unlocked the door to his room, and once inside was immediately met by Amalia's hazy, gray-green stare. He smiled at her broadly and sank to his knees beside her bed. He took her hot hand in his.

"I found him, dearest," he said softly. "As handsome as Adonis, with a warm heart, full of passion. Our kind of man." He kissed her white arm and her delicate, dark red lips.

From that moment on, Gabriel and Amalia were particularly careful with one another, particularly affectionate, but few words passed between them. Gabriel hardly noticed that Amalia did not finish her sentences, that she mumbled rather than spoke, and that she barely moved, as if she were paralyzed. He was too busy with his own state of mind, with his victory over himself, and with absorbing the tragic beauty, both real and unreal, of this particular day in his life. He did not finish his sentences either, although his head was buzzing with talk, with prayer, and with the motifs of Mahler's *Kindertotenlieder*. It seemed to him that he should walk about on tiptoe so as not to waken anyone.

In the afternoon they slowly began to prepare for what was to follow, and they stopped talking altogether. At dusk Gabriel gave Amalia a bath and saw to it that the linen on her bed was changed and the bed itself made up. He dressed her in her most beautiful nightgown—at least the two of them thought it the most beautiful, although it was very old. She had worn it the first night they had spent together in Paris. It looked like a white satin evening gown, and she had more than once whispered in his ear that she wanted to be buried in it.

He ordered a dozen royal roses up to the room and put them in a vase. Unaware of what he was saying, he murmured, "Rose, Rosa . . ." as he nestled each flower between the delicate green ferns in the vase. He placed the vase on the marble top of a small Louis Quinze table that stood near the window. The flowers filled the room with their intoxicating perfume, and Amalia asked him to open the window a little. Outside the sun was about to set, and Gabriel opened the window much wider than she had asked. He drew aside the heavy brocade drapes and let the light of the entire Parisian sky with its symphony of pastel colors pour into the room. Far in the distance, in the faint blue of the horizon, Gabriel caught sight of a glimmering star.

Amalia asked him to turn on the light on the night table, even though it was still quite bright in the room. He dabbed her wrists and earlobes with the drops of a French perfume whose fragrance he liked. He looked at her as she lay in her white nightgown against the white pillow under the white blanket. The long, gray braid of frayed, stringy hair lay against her bosom, rising and falling with each breath like a snake in agony. Her face—to which, at her request, he had applied a little makeup—seemed to glow. She was unbelievably beautiful, and he wanted to sink to his knees beside her and beg her forgiveness—for her fading life, for the extinguished desire that he felt for her, for the peace in his heart.

A few minutes past eight-thirty, Jean-Pierre knocked at the door. He was wearing tight black pants and a neat white sport shirt with an open collar from which protruded his dark-skinned neck with its large Adam's apple.

As if she had been saving her last smile just for him, Amalia smiled at Jean-Pierre so generously, so radiantly, that the young man blushed. He stammered something in response, then burst into loud laughter and, assuming an air of self-assurance, firmly shook Gabriel's hand, as if he wanted him to leave.

"I'm on my way," Gabriel muttered.

In the manner of an experienced babysitter, Jean-Pierre patted him reassuringly on the shoulder and accompanied him to the door.

"I will be waiting in the lobby," Gabriel whispered to him.

The young man closed the door behind him and turned the lock.

Gabriel sat in the downstairs lobby. The figures of men and women, blacks and whites, glided past him, the men in dark frock coats, the white women in long black dresses, the black women in long white dresses. An orchestra played in the Grand Salon with its glittering mirrors and crystal chandeliers. Couples danced round and round, while Gabriel's head whirled along with them, between suns and moons, nights and days, in and out of constellations of stars, round and round between now and eternity, in dull indifference, with no pain or sorrow, with neither love nor hate but in a frozen, never-before-experienced loneliness.

He had no idea how much time had passed since he sat down when suddenly he saw Jean-Pierre run out of the elevator with his hair disheveled, his clothes in disarray, his eyes wild, and his face aflame. He rushed toward Gabriel, who had jumped to his feet, and almost toppled him.

"She's dead!" he cried. "She died in my arms! Is your name Sebastian?"

"No!"

"She called me 'Sebastian.' That was the last word she said. Do you want to call the police?"

"No. What for?"

Gabriel took the key from Jean-Pierre's hand. Jean-Pierre turned abruptly and ran out of the lobby.

Gabriel hurried to the elevator. On his way up he remembered that Sebastian was the name of the young man who had charmed Amalia after her return from Japan, when she had come to Paris for the first time. She had met Sebastian on Bastille Day, she once confided to Gabriel. She and Sebastian had danced together, and she had fallen in love for the first time in her life. She had arranged to meet him again the next day at the Bastille metro, but he never appeared. She never saw him again. It was foolish to be jealous of such a love. Amalia had never been alone with Sebastian, not even for a second, and besides, it had all happened so many years ago. So Gabriel had thought when she told him about it.

* * *

That night Jean-Pierre did not visit Rosa but wandered instead through the streets of Paris. He had the impression that during that one evening he had aged a decade. It was strange that he thought so little about Amalia's death and so much about her living, delicate, submissive body, which he had held in his arms. He thought about the awesome and eternal force—for which he could not find the proper name, since he was ignorant of its nature, and knew only that it was godly—Amalia had poured into him, an unencompassable force he would never be able to describe in words, although he could feel it so clearly coursing within him, in the marrow of his bones. It was something magical; it filled him with piety and elation; it devoured him with its heat. Shudders crept up and down his spine. It filled him with horror.

Over and over again his mind replayed the scene with Amalia. Her body was still beautiful, her skin smooth and white, without the faintest blemish. A virginal purity, a chaste innocence, permeated it. He traced the vague outlines of her loose breasts in his memory. Even the aureoles around the nipples had been white, bloodless. She was all whiteness, as if she had been molded from a white bedsheet or a kind of hot snow, because she had burned in his arms. And he had wanted her; he had wanted to absorb her desperate passion for life, a life whose last drops had dripped through his fingers. She reminded him of the thirteen-year-old girl with whom he had once been paired, a long time ago, in a brothel. That time he had run away; this time he had not. He had not turned his back on a dying old woman.

Now he was in love with Rosa, who was somewhere high up at the peak of Mount Blanc while he was climbing up toward her, clinging to the chain of love, rising toward her from the very bottom of the abyss.

How strong this chain was! How powerful was his love! He had never felt it more intensely than in that deep pit, on the threshold of Amalia's eternity. There he had found himself in a state of ecstatic delirium compounded of pain and pleasure, which no other sensation could equal. When he had awoken and touched his own cheek he found his fingers wet with his own tears. Only then had he realized that the body entangled with his own was limp and lifeless.

For the next few days he prepared himself to tell Rosa what he had done and why. But he did not dare. She was too beautiful, too healthy, and too much in love with him to understand his reasoning. Besides, talking was liable to complicate the matter even further. So he postponed making his confession from one day to the next. And in order to clarify the whole experience to himself, and because he felt "unclean"—not on account of what he had done but because he had not told Rosa about it, which was a form of cheating on her—he punished himself by keeping away from her, using any excuse that came to mind.

Before long he and Rosa became man and wife. It was a memorable day for both of them. Exhausted yet exhilarated after the modest celebration at his parents' house, they left for their new apartment and fell on the bed in each other's arms. Jean-Pierre immediately fell asleep. Rosa did not wake him. They had a long life before them with many nights to stay awake together. And she too fell asleep with a smile on her lips.

It was not until some months later that Jean-Pierre began to realize that something had gone wrong in his relationship with Rosa. Being with her no longer gave him the same feeling of joyous exaltation as it had in the past. Every time that he took Rosa's supple young body into his arms he would see the dead Amalia beckoning him from somewhere nearby, calling out to him with overwhelming urgency. After a while, Amalia began to haunt him even when he was not holding Rosa in his arms but merely sitting next to her. Rosa, beautiful and blossoming, seemed faded somehow, drained of her vitality as if it were she who were withered and old, while Amalia lured him with promises of an eternal life that was beyond age and time. He yearned for that powerful "something," for the magnificent hymn of love and ecstasy, for the marriage of life and death.

So it happened that he, who had once been so talkative and so adept at letting Rosa know with both words and caresses what he felt for her, now turned into a mute, wooden, and awkward man.

Rosa could not understand what had happened to him. She was tormented by the fear of losing him. Anxiously she dressed in her most alluring clothes and tried to make herself as beautiful and enticing as she could. She tried to seduce him with her gaiety, or she tried to be serious and romantic. She ceased being herself altogether and no longer knew how to talk to him or how to behave. Finally she could bear it no longer; she was exhausted from trying to jump out of her own skin. And clinging to what she called the last straw, she attempted to regain the honesty and frankness that had once been the rule between them.

"Don't you love me anymore, Jean-Pierre?" she asked him one day.

"Of course I do," he replied, fearing to add any more enthusiastic confirmation of his love as he had often done in the past when she had playfully inquired about the state of his feelings for her. He too wanted to be honest with her. Honesty had become the only path left to take. Nevertheless, he could not bring himself to tell her about Amalia.

She sensed caution in his reply, but her woman's intuition misled her. In a trembling voice she said, "You've been seeing another woman."

"No. Heaven forbid!" he protested, but without conviction in his voice. He realized that he could dissemble no longer, and was on the verge of making his confession, when Rosa burst into tears.

His eyes too filled with tears. In that instant he knew beyond any doubt that he pitied her but loved her no more.

Not long after this he left Rosa for good. He grew a beard, and his long vagabondage began. He became a professional mountain climber and joined all possible expeditions. He never again loved a woman as he had loved Rosa. However, between one expedition and the next, he compulsively pursued women, in search of the one who would bewitch him, but he could not find her. For a time he even sought the company of older women in the hope that one of them would again awaken that powerful feeling he sensed was waiting for him somewhere. But the older women were too greedy for him; they devoured him with their passion and spoiled him. They possessed too much last-chance vitality and lacked the otherworldly enchantment he craved.

At length his travels brought him to North America. He flew into Montreal with the intention of buying a secondhand car and driving across Canada to the Rocky Mountains. He scanned the newspaper ads to see what was available. Responding to one of the ads, he found himself on a street at the foot of Mount Royal, in the center of the city. He entered the studio apartment of an old, gray-haired sculptor. One look at the sculptor immediately brought back to Jean-Pierre's mind the macabre sexual incident in his past, an incident he had tried to banish from his memory.

The sculptor bore no resemblance to Gabriel. He was too old, too skinny, too stooped, and he wore thickly rimmed glasses. Nor was Jean-Pierre inclined to inquire after Gabriel. What for? He refused to spoil the pleasure of his trip. And for this reason too he wished to leave town as quickly as possible. He had, in any case, little opportunity to engage the old man in conversation or to look at him more closely, since there was something else in the apartment that caught his attention.

The sculptor had led Jean-Pierre into his atelier, which was filled with sculptures of breathtaking beauty. The sculptures had a strange effect on Jean-Pierre. He had never been particularly interested in sculpture; certainly, he was no more interested in it than he was in any other art. But he possessed an innate sensitivity, a modest aesthetic appreciation, which was not unusual in a man of average education who had grown up in a city like Paris and been exposed to its treasures. Now, however, he could not take his eyes off the statues he saw in the studio.

At length the old man grew impatient. "You've come about the car, haven't you?" he asked severely.

Jean-Pierre, his eyes on the sculptures, replied with a question: "Why do you want to sell it?"

"I have no use for it," the old man answered. "I am not well. Whatever I need, I can get here in the neighborhood."

They went out into the garage. The car was not at all to Jean-Pierre's liking: an old-fashioned, quaint-looking Jaguar with orange-colored seats. However, the motor seemed to be in excellent condition, and there was relatively little mileage on the odometer. He got in and drove the car around the block a few times, noting that despite his initial reservations he felt comfortable and relaxed at the wheel. He decided to buy the car.

During their sparse exchange of words, Jean-Pierre and the old man had hardly looked at one another, each being immersed in his own mood, in his own world. The old man seemed sentimental about the car, while Jean-Pierre suddenly began to feel festive and could not understand why. When they had completed the sale of the car, Jean-Pierre said, "I would like to buy one of your sculptures, Monsieur."

The old man shook his head sharply. "They're not for sale!" he replied.

Jean-Pierre left Montreal in the Jaguar. The longer he rode in it, the better he felt. He began to develop a tender feeling for it, a kind of affection. It performed superbly, as if it were driving itself. When, after much traveling, he crossed the prairies and saw the Rocky Mountains looming ahead, he was already so taken with his vehicle that instead of renting a room in a motel he slept in the car at night. He felt strong and stimulated and excitedly planned his climb to the snow-covered mountain peaks. His thinking was amazingly clear and easy in this car, and dreaming was easier still. Never in his life had he felt so free and happy. Perhaps this was due to the vastness of the enormous country through which he had just traveled or to his feeling of wonder and awe in the shadow of the majestic mountain range here in the north, where in the middle of August one could read a paper or a book outdoors at midnight. The mystery of life seemed so near and tangible that one could practically touch it with one's hand.

Once when he was driving high up in the mountains he decided to continue on his way through one such night that seemed like day. A mood of dreaminess overcame him; everything he saw was real and unreal at the same time. He began to appreciate the warmth of the orange material covering the empty seat beside him. It seemed to infuse the air with a glow as though the seat were not empty at all but occupied by a strange, luminous presence. The road before him was white and empty; on both sides lay the majestic, snow-covered peaks, like gigantic, reclining women covered with white bedsheets. What a glorious feeling of both infinity and cozy intimacy!

From a distance he noticed a human form, a woman waiting by the roadside. She looked like a piece of granite sculpted by the winds of time, set apart and yet of a piece with the outlines of the massive clusters of stone and earth that hovered all about her. For a moment he remembered the Henry Moore sculptures in the Tuileries Gardens back in Paris, sculptures he knew intimately because he had so often waited for Rosa beside them. The woman had her arm outstretched as if she wanted to stop the car and ask for a ride. As he drew nearer he saw her more clearly. She was dressed in white, with a long, white, flowing veil wrapped around her shoulders. She seemed transparent, hollow. He smiled at his own strange equation of a work of art with the form of a living woman. He chuckled to himself. No doubt the sculptures he had recently seen in the old sculptor's atelier had inclined his mind in that direction. He stepped firmly on the accelerator and raced toward the woman.

—He caught up with her on the opposite side of the precipice over which he had taken flight.

A Friday in the Life of Sarah Zonabend

Before she went to the hospital for her operation, Sarah had thrown all the pages of her latest diary into the incinerator. This was not the first time that she had destroyed her personal notes, which she had been keeping on and off throughout most of her literate life. Somehow she had always felt like jotting down a few more-or-less sincere accounts of happenings and feelings yet had always been careful not to leave such intimate documents behind.

She hardly knew why she was writing these pages. She justified the habit to herself using her bad memory as an excuse: she was having difficulties recalling what had happened a year or two ago. Only her concentration camp memories stood out in her mind like an island of sharp, blistering clarity amid a sea of forgetfulness. But as far as the rest of her life was concerned, the past had turned into a terrifying blank that slipped through her fingers as if all the living she had ever done had occurred in her childhood and youth and in that surrogate "life" she had endured in the concentration camp. She told herself that by making notes she would feel more alive; she would supply herself with the tangible proof that something—no matter how meaningless and insignificant that something was—had actually happened to her.

Although in her diary entries she mostly gave an account of her suffering as a lonely wife, or of the illnesses and problems of her children, or of the loss of loved ones, she always hoped—while writing—that in the future she would be able to detect between the lines a reflection of that other form of life, that elusive inner life of the soul, whose exact nature she found impossible to describe. As a matter of fact, she seldom reread her journal entries, and when she did it was with a sort of dread.

Occasionally she told herself that she was writing these diaries with a dedication in mind—a dedication to her children, who might read them one day and learn of her experiences and so come to know her better as the person she really was, although in her heart of hearts she knew perfectly well that nobody learns from someone else's experiences, that her children would never be able to see her in the same light as she saw herself, that there was no other way for children to know their mother than by watching her with their own eyes, by being exposed to her through daily contact. She also knew that her concentration camp experiences could never serve as an excuse for the messy chaotic quality of her present-day existence.

And so she continued to write her diaries, not really knowing why, until one day she was overcome by an attack of devil-take-it desperation and destroyed them—only to start a new diary in a moment of renewed hope.

She had now gone without a diary for the whole stretch of that short, sunless summer, which had vanished more rapidly than the summer before and the one before that. Blotted from her memory, the past had turned into what she called a "black hole."

* * *

Today was Friday. Sarah had a dread of Fridays. She had a superstitious anxiety about this day, an apprehensive fear of approaching danger she could not shake in spite of all attempts to reason with herself. She had always gotten the worst marks at school on a Friday. The war had broken out on a Friday. Her mother had died in the camp on a Friday. President Kennedy had been shot on a Friday. She had discovered, on a Friday, that her husband was unfaithful to her. On a Friday she had gone to see the doctor, and on a Friday she was operated on. In addition, she retained the memory of one late Friday afternoon, after a selection in the camp. Those women whose lives had been spared returned to their barrack and climbed up onto their bunks in the dark.

It was then that Crazy Bluma had exclaimed: "Children, have you forgotten? Today is Friday, Sabbath eve! Quick! Let's light the candles and bless them!" And in the dark Bluma went through the motions of lighting the Sabbath candles, while all the other half-mad women in the barrack—those whose lives had so recently been spared—covered their faces with their hands and mumbled the blessing of the lights, whether they knew the words or not.

So every Friday morning Sarah's superstitious self was apprehensive even though her reasonable, enlightened self looked forward to the oncoming day with a heart full of hope.

Her morning went as usual. She sent the children off to school, tidied the kitchen, and served breakfast to Moniek, her husband, who discussed the news in the morning paper with her. He spoke to her of the racial problems in South Africa and discussed Poland's stand with regard to the Common Market. She did not wish that he would speak of something more personal, more intimate, that he would murmur a few affectionate words, because this had not happened for a very long time; perhaps it had never happened.

Sarah had always clung to the unrealistic belief that two people who loved each other before the war and had found each other after the war were touched by divine grace, so to speak—that they were bound to one another by an exceptionally powerful bond of devotion and that such a man and woman were different from other couples by virtue of their love's miraculous salvation. In her mind such a marriage, even when not cemented by religious vows, was sacred. Such a woman and such a man had been appointed by fate to alleviate and comfort each other's pain and distress.

As a matter of fact, Sarah had once worked up the courage to raise this topic with Moniek, albeit in a vague form, presenting her thoughts in a less romantic wrapping. But Moniek's response was to burst out laughing, and he laughed so heartily that she was forced to laugh along with him. Such a fool she had made of herself.

She had no idea how long ago this scene had taken place. Her memory was terrible. All she could remember was that, in the past, her heart had often filled with longing for an intimate moment during breakfast that would supply her with energy and good cheer for the rest of the day. But the need for such a moment had faded, and she now considered this fading to be a charitable gift from fate. Nevertheless, it was unfortunate that the older a woman grew the less affection she received, although she needed affection more than ever. But perhaps this was nature's refined way of preparing her for death, numbing her before she tasted the real thing.

As she sat at the breakfast table opposite Moniek, Sarah kept her eyes fixed on the door. It was too early for the mailman, yet sometimes a nice bundle of letters did slip through the slot in the door just at breakfast time. She did not recall that anything exciting ever arrived in that bundle of letters, which usually consisted of bills, city hall circulars, bulletins, and business letters for Moniek. Yet the sudden leap of her heart at the sight of the envelopes falling onto the floor gave her pleasure. She could still feel the taste of excitement as she tore her lips from the cup of coffee and rushed to the door to pick up the mail.

She hoped that this pleasurable experience would happen again during today's breakfast. When it did not she went about her housework, hoping that perhaps something pleasurable would happen later on. It was a new day, a new morning, carrying the secret of unknown hours to come, each one liable to reveal the seed of a new beginning. Her superstitious self remembered that it was Friday, but during the morning hours her optimistic, life-loving self got the upper hand over her dread.

And so she continued to expect the arrival of the mail, without fully admitting to herself that she had not yet given up on it. The slot in the front door was a window of promise. Perhaps it would bring a solution to her loneliness, a solution to her troubles with Moniek and the children; perhaps it would bring her recognition as a valuable human being, perhaps a message of love or praise, something to heighten her sense of dignity, to make her feel like somebody special, like a person to whom people wrote letters and with whom they needed to communicate; perhaps it would make her feel like a person who was fully alive and whose days did not fall into black holes of nothingness.

Sarah's Saturdays and Sundays were the dullest, drabbest days of her week because there was no mail on Saturday or Sunday. She scolded herself for making a deus ex machina out of the mail. But her superstitious belief in the power of the mail was stronger even than her superstitious fear of Fridays. She doubted whether she would ever be rid of these weaknesses.

The mailman had probably passed while she was busy at the sewing machine, stitching felt flowers onto the decorative pillow slips on the living room sofa. With Moniek gone and the children at school, Sarah had the day to herself, and the best part of it was the morning, when she sat at the sewing machine deciding on the designs for the pillow decorations, when all her ideas about color and fabric texture were just right and everything she did had an air of beauty and excitement about it. Yes, in the morning, when she could still feel the imprint of Moniek's cold peck on her cheek, she gave herself the treat of doing something of value for herself alone. She did not mind the untidy house. There was time enough to be wasted on house cleaning.

Then, when she rose from her seat at the sewing machine to take another cigarette, she glanced at the floor beneath the slot in the door to make sure that there really had not been any mail today. She lit her cigarette and went back to the sewing machine. She worked for a while, executing her original designs, but the work went more slowly. Her head ached; she was sleepy. What a sham art was after all! Once she had thought art to be the ultimate expression of truth, coming just after love in importance in her life. But nowadays she was confused about love and no longer knew what art was all about. She abhorred the canvases displayed at the art galleries, the so-called masterpieces of contemporary art. They irritated her. They seemed to mock her with their displays of childish doodles in crazy colors. The same was true for modern music, which drove her out of her mind with its deafening noise, producing visions and sounds aimed at dulling the senses. The musical instruments boomed, the singers shouted, their bodies and faces distorted by passion. Was this ugliness art? Had all the beauty seeped out of life after the war?

The flowers she had stitched onto the pillow case began to hurt her eyes with their clashing colors. They too were lies. They were ugly, nauseatingly so—or was it the cigarette that was ugly? She hardly derived any pleasure from that lazy puffing. However, she continued working and puffing until she grew tired. Then she stood up and turned her attention to the disorderly house. Her nausea increased. She felt like weeping and sleeping.

She started to make the beds. As she straightened her son's bed, so disorderly from his playing on it, her eyes filled with tears. She threw herself on the untidy blanket and spread her arms across the bed as if she were embracing his body. She loved that boy of hers. She imagined him next to her and caressed his slim figure. He was so busy discovering the world, he had little time for her. She missed him badly. "What does he really feel for me?" she asked herself, thinking of the boy who was about to leave his childhood behind. Could need be described as love? And what would be left of it when he needed her no more?

She reproached herself for wasting her time, squandering her life, for sleeping so much during the day, for her frequent attacks of weeping. It was her indulgence in self-pity that nauseated her, she thought. She got up from the bed and cleaned the boy's room, collecting the piles of comic books from the floor, putting away his clothes, replacing his guitar and accordion in their usual places.

She moved on to her daughter's room. There was little to do here, thank heaven. The bed was made, and the things lying around were probably meant to be lying around. Of late Sarah had been feeling a little like a stranger in her daughter's room. Here lived a beautiful somebody who had once been part of her—so long ago, she hardly even remembered when. Sarah swept the floor while in her imagination she saw the girl's graceful body, her budding breasts and the flow of her long blonde hair, which reflected the sun's luster. She saw her smiling, saw the dreamy sparkle of her blue eyes, which could change into panther green when she was in a rebellious rage, calling her mother a liar. And perhaps Sarah was a liar after all but in a different sense of the word. She just no longer knew what was true. She no longer knew who she was herself—or whether she was at all.

She stepped out of her daughter's room and entered her own bedroom. First she dusted off the night tables and arranged the stacks of books that stood on them. Lately she could read no more than a page or two before falling asleep. Somehow the books, even the best works of fiction, had lost their magic. They had betrayed their promise. Was there something wrong with literature, with art in general? Or was the problem life itself? Perhaps the books no longer served as a substitute for some other needs within her. Had she lost the ability of entering another reality besides her own, of being capable of imagining herself into someone else's life because she was so absorbed with her own?

All she felt was that if everything was a lie, literature was the greatest lie of all. She had been raised on literature. It had fed her dreams and provided her with an education. But now she could not forgive its shortcomings, could not forgive the fact that it had so poorly prepared her for life, although she still loved books, piling them up on her bedside table, collecting them on her library shelves. She was constantly adding new volumes since she could not pass a bookstore without going in, returning home with a neat package under her arm. Would she ever read all the books she now owned? Of course not. But if she did read them, what difference would it make?

She turned to face the double bed. How vast that bed sometimes seemed! A white-sheeted desert between body and body. If a bed could listen, or feel, or tell a story—would the story it told be the truth?

* * *

Sarah had two scrambled eggs for lunch. While eating she remembered that she had to run across to the grocery store; there was no milk left in the refrigerator. As she wrapped herself in her old, worn-out coat, the thought of her fur coat flashed through her mind. She seldom wore it anymore. There was hardly any occasion for it. She did not mind this.

She felt more at home in her familiar shabby, old coat. It better suited her disposition. In fact, she felt guilty for possessing a fur coat. Even though she was not an ardent animal lover, she nevertheless felt an affinity for animals.

She glanced quickly at herself in the mirror and tidied her hair. She should start going to the beauty parlor again, she thought, as she ran out into the street. She hated spending long hours at the beauty parlor, and she hated the stiff, fluffed, teased hair that resulted from her sessions there. She even hated the smell of the hairspray. But taking care of her hair might give her a lift. She might acquire a more youthful look by covering the gray. All women dyed their hair nowadays. There seemed to be no older woman around with natural hair color and a natural hairdo and a natural face to go with it, a face that bore witness to the passing of time. So what? The main thing was that women were more beautiful today than they had been in the past, although their beauty was of a superficial kind.

But shouldn't she at least start taking care of her figure? What a shame to be walking around wearing those flat Hush Puppies! They looked like slippers. She should get used to wearing shoes on raised heels, which made a woman look and feel uplifted and less flat-footed. And why not wear the fur coat after all? The animal whose fur it had been was dead anyway. Wrapped in the fur she might perhaps better demonstrate her affinity with the living creature whose pelt she now wore.

The fresh breeze and the mild sunshine of an early fall afternoon caressed Sarah's face. The unbuttoned sides of her old coat flapped like wings around her. She felt dirty and sloppy. It was not an apt comparison, yet a trace of that same self-disgust she had sometimes felt in the concentration camp because of the rags she wore returned to haunt her.

But what did she care? Where was she going, and who was going to see her? Except for an occasional "excursion" to the grocery store, she was alone in the house all day long, and when Moniek was home, he rarely noticed what she was wearing. On those rare occasions when she dressed for the theater or for an acquaintance's family celebration she could only get compliments from Moniek by begging.

"How do I look?" she would ask.

And he would answer, obligingly, "Nice," or more generously, "Very nice," looking through her rather than at her.

Perhaps she should buy herself a dress in spite of everything. In the past buying a new dress, or any other item of clothing—something bought exclusively for herself—would have helped to lift her spirits. But she no longer felt like shopping for clothes; she was unable to work herself into the proper frame of mind to undertake the excursion.

She grinned at herself as she imagined her picture in a quiz magazine and underneath it the caption: "What is wrong with this woman survivor? Why can't she enjoy the life fate has bestowed on her?"

Then she noticed the mailman standing on the corner of the street, his mailbag utterly, painfully empty. There he stood next to her, his work done, waiting to cross the street on his way home. She nodded at him, but he did not respond. Perhaps he did not recognize her. After all, hers was only one door in a street full of doors.

She ran ahead of him, paying no attention to the lights. Suddenly she heard a harsh squeak, a raw screech of tires against asphalt. She did not turn her head, yet she knew. There had been an accident. The mailman. Her heart began to pound. She ran into the grocery store without turning her head. She asked for a bottle of milk, and while she waited she thought she saw the dead mailman lying sprawled on the street. Serves him right—for his empty mailbag, for not responding to her greeting. That took care, also, of another unlucky Friday.

Sarah took the bottle of milk in her hand. What a pleasant, cool whiteness it had; how good it was to hold it in her hand. She would have loved to cool her hot face against the bottle that very minute or open it and take a few sips. But no, she would not do that in public.

She left the store. At the bus stop on the corner the mailman was still standing, waiting for the bus to take him home. She was relieved. There had been no accident. She smiled at him. He glanced at her and this time he lifted two fingers to the rim of his mailman's hat in a kind of military salute. How lovely that was! She fell in love with him on the spot! Yes, she fell in love, and perhaps that was really the only solution, the only answer to all the questions: that rare moment when one person's loneliness saluted the loneliness of another, that moment was happiness. That was all there was to it.

With her entire being she felt the beauty of this sunny, fall afternoon. Yes, she was madly in love with life and therefore terrified of her particular brand of loneliness, which heralded the approach of death. She was not the suicidal type at all. It would have never occurred to her to willingly stop her own heartbeat. Quite the contrary. She could never get her fill of living. Hadn't she once written a story for her children about a fly born in fall and how it was better to be alive in that season than not to be alive at all?

She knew what she would do. She would go home, prepare dinner for her husband and children, and then pack—take a valise, throw in a few items of clothing, take the few hundred dollars that she had saved, write a note to the children telling them not to worry about her, and leave. She would go somewhere in search of the mail that never came, in search of the exciting news that never reached her, in search of friendship, that honest, serious friendship that she had known in the camp. She would take action to make things happen. Take a step toward your goal and it will take a step toward you. She, Sarah Zonabend, would do it! She would be free again.

The breeze playing with the sides of her coat gave her a delicious feeling of abandonment; it seemed to be lifting her up on wings. Her steps were light, her body ready to soar. She swung the bottle of milk in her hand just as she had her schoolbag long ago, when she had run home full of the joy of life and freedom: "No homework today! Hurray! Today is Friday! No school tomorrow!"

* * *

She entered the house and looked around. Scattered around the sewing machine lay the colorful pillow slips she had worked on that morning. Slowly she approached them. The work looked definitely unprofessional and shabbily executed. She was a dilettante in everything she did.

Everything came out half baked from under her hands, devoid of any masterful finishing touch. Yet the sight of her work stirred something within her and brought tears to her eyes. Perhaps all that was needed was to remove the brown patch in the center of the design and replace it with some blue . . .

She set down the milk on a nearby table and, still wearing her coat, sat down by the machine. Her eyes filled. She knew that these were not the tears she sometimes shed when admiring a work of beauty. It was rather that so many of her tears seemed to have filled the clumsy flower cups sewn onto the pillow cases; so much of her own self was embodied in that disjointed, amateurish piece of work. Her eyes were so full that she could hardly see the flowers she wanted to fix. Anyway, it was time to prepare dinner.

She stood up, took off her coat, and picked up the milk. On her way to the kitchen she noticed the telephone. It had not rung even once that day. Nor had it rung yesterday. Perhaps it was out of order? She smiled a bitter smile and picked up the receiver to check for a dial tone. The buzzing sound mocked her. The telephone was functioning, all right. There was something else that did not function. Perhaps she should get rid of that obnoxious buzzing by telephoning somebody herself? But whom should she call? Perhaps one of her former camp sisters, who after liberation had turned into ersatz friends, full of meaningless chatter and phoniness. What would she and the woman on the other end of the line talk about? They could not bring up the subject of the camps this Friday afternoon. And how much entertainment would they derive from cheerfully discussing the insignificant details of their daily lives? And even if Sarah launched into a topic close to her heart—how sincere could she be on this Friday afternoon, when the person on the other end of the line was as confused as she was and just as preoccupied with her own loneliness and her own dinner preparations?

Sarah entered the kitchen and started to peel some potatoes. She washed the lettuce. Suddenly she dried her hands and reached into the table drawer for a pencil. The next moment she was sitting at the kitchen table, bent over her old notebook from which half of the pages—those filled with the notes from her former diary—were missing. Next to her lay the shavings of the peeled potatoes, and next to the bowl of freshly washed salad stood the white milk bottle, which she had forgotten to put in the refrigerator.

"Dear diary," she wrote, laughing softly to herself like a little girl enthralled by the act of confiding a secret to her diary. "You are the only trip I am capable of taking, the only phone call that I am capable of making, the only letter I am both writing and receiving. Today is Friday, and thank heaven, nothing has happened."

EDGIA'S REVENGE

Ever since Edgia disappeared beyond the horizon of my life, the desire to put an end to myself has grown stronger within me. This is Edgia's victory over me, her definitive act of vengeance. I am ready to submit, ready to surrender to the perverse law that still seems to rule over the psyches of those survivors whose souls remain trapped in the concentration camps and who will never break free. I refer to the law that says that for every life saved, another must be sacrificed. The account must tally. For having saved Edgia's life I must put an end to my own, if not today then tomorrow, if not tomorrow then twenty or thirty years from now.

At the same time I feel a need to resolve for myself the conundrum that Edgia represents in my life. I mean my life after the war, because in the camps there were no conundrums, and all complications of the soul resolved themselves by themselves or were thrown overboard like so much extra ballast. In the camps only one question mattered—how to survive another hour, another day.

But how can I indulge in ruminations about my life in the camps when even today my hand is incapable of writing the words "concentration camp" without trembling? It is incomprehensible to me, it is silly and ludicrous, that even now, just as I am about to unlock the gate to eternity and free myself from all entrapments, I should still fall prey to the fear of my memories from there. For this reason I must limit myself in this account to touching on only the most necessary points.

Just now, as I wrote the words "the gate to eternity," my hand did not shake. That's not surprising. How many times have I peered through that gate? I do so even now, and will continue to do so until I myself pass through. But my indifference in the face of eternity is not a consequence of habit. One may grow accustomed to gazing at the gates of nonexistence in order to watch how others pass through—or are driven through. Don't modern intellectuals, who were never there, speak about the banality of evil? The annihilation of others may be banal, but when it's a question of one's own personal one-time-only demise, then banality vanishes and so does indifference. I am no exception. On the contrary. My own salvaged life is precious to me. I have paid a higher price for it than other survivors did for theirs. I have paid for it with my conscience. From this stems the sangfroid with which I approach this particular subject.

My voluntary passage through the eternal gate has become for me a categorical imperative, a final summing up. In order for a sum to tally there can be only one correct answer; no ifs or maybes. Edgia's disappearance from my life has once and for all brought this fact home to me. The revulsion I feel for my precious life has finally conquered the revulsion I feel for death.

* * *

I first got the idea of supplying myself with sleeping pills in the first weeks after my liberation from the camp. As soon as the German guards disappeared from behind the barbed wire fence I fled the camp. I then drifted from one end to the other of that devastated German countryside, trying to escape from myself and from others, regardless of whether they were the conquerors or the conquered. The sight of a human face disgusted me. But with the passing of time, loneliness set up such a howling inside me that I could no longer endure it, and I attached myself to a group of former concentration camp inmates who were wandering from one camp to another in search of relatives. They had come from the English Zone, and not one of them was a native of my hometown. I myself had no relatives to find, but I trailed along with them because I was overcome by panic at the thought of being alone, and because I hoped that with them or through them I would discover the quickest way out of Germany.

It was a bright spring day. Along with my group of wanderers I was sitting on the edge of an unplowed field near the highway. The normal means of transportation had not yet been restored, so we waited for a military truck to come along and give us a lift. After a while such a truck drove up. The American driver jumped out of his seat, dropped the back flap of his vehicle, and we climbed up. And here unexpectedly we came upon another former camp inmate sleeping on the floorboards of the truck. The noise of our clattering aboard woke him. He jumped to his feet, took our measure with a quick glance, and retreated to the farthest corner of the truck. As soon as we started to move, he turned his back and caught hold of the truck's vibrating sides. We moved closer, anxious to question him about which camp he was from, where he was heading, and what information he had.

Just at that moment one of my group cried out: "I know him! He was a kapo in my camp! We called him Romek the Executioner!" He pointed a bony index finger at the stranger's face as if he were aiming to poke out his eyes.

A moment later the stranger lay stretched across the swaying floorboards of the truck as my companions unloaded the burden of their pain-filled hearts on his prostrate body with kicks and jabs, cursing and yelling all the while. The stranger made no attempt to defend or shield himself. He endured the blows with muffled groans from between compressed lips. Perhaps he desired these blows, craving the ritual purification that such a beating would confer in the hope that having paid the price he too would have the right to enjoy his freedom?

I was so disturbed by the beating that I felt each blow as if it were landing on me. But I had been even more shaken by that first cry of "I know him! He's a kapo." The cry reverberated in my ears and would not die away. That must be the worst—the shock of being recognized, the inner trembling at the sight of a pointing finger. The mere thought of this took my breath away.

What happened afterward to Romek the Executioner I do not

know. As soon as we came to the next town some of the group dragged him to a military police station. I took advantage of the confusion to steal away from my companions.

Somehow I managed to make it to Munich, where I sought the advice of a compassionate, terribly naïve, and ignorant UNRRA doctor. I went to see him because I was suffering from insomnia, and I begged him for sleeping pills. "It's no wonder, my child, that you can't sleep," he said, affectionately patting my shoulder. "After all that you've lived through, you must be having nightmares even in the daytime, when you are wide awake." How could I explain that I wanted the pills not only to squelch the nightmares evoked by my past but also to squelch the nightmares inspired by my present-day, wonderful, dearly bought life?

* * *

And so I escaped from Germany in my one and only civilian dress, which I had managed to "organize" for myself out of a German house. But in my knapsack I carried the twenty-five sleeping pills that the good doctor had given me. These pills were the only possessions that I brought with me to Canada from the European continent. They took the place of my parents, my grandparents, my sixteen-year-old brother, and my ten-year-old sister, my darling Maniusha. They took the place of all my aunts, uncles, and cousins, of my hometown, my childhood, my early adolescence, and my first and only love. Sleeping pills became my life—and my death. And now they have become my only road back to innocence.

Throughout all the years that I carried the pills around with me, I found strength in the promise I had made to myself that should the day ever come when someone recognized me and pointed a finger at me, I would turn to my brightly colored, beadlike saviors. I told myself that it was my prerogative to set the limits of my post-liberation hell and that I had no intention of letting others decide the boundaries for me. If I was to be devoured by guilt then let me be the one to measure its immensity and the extent to which I had earned it. Because I am not the true culprit. What happened would have happened even without my assistance. I did not add a single drop to the cup of poison. I just kept order among the imbibers.

If there was such a thing as a good kapo, then that is what I was. The only reason that the inmates of the women's camp called me Black Rella was because I have black hair, dark eyes, and dark skin. I am not a murderer; I do not even have a violent nature, although I did beat people, and I suppose you could say that I had a hand in murder. I grew up in a cultured, middle-class home. I had good manners. I liked people. I enjoyed life. And I loved my little sister Maniusha, to whom I was a second mother, since our own mother was sickly. I took pleasure in the long, sun-drenched days of our summer vacations and delighted in the mild, caressing evenings at our country house, when we all sat on the veranda and Maniusha recited children's poems. I loved poetry with a passion.

In the camps I saw my entire family float heavenward with the smoke from the crematorium chimneys. I wanted to save myself. I was nineteen years old. I wanted to survive. I didn't choose the means by which to do it. There were no choices to be made. Everything depended on luck. The means chose me. Perhaps, in my dazed state, I was helped by blind instinct. But instinct is itself the slave of luck. It doesn't always function as it should.

* * *

It was the second week of my incarceration in the camp. I hardly knew what was happening to me. A sandy, smoky phantasmagoria whirled ceaselessly before my eyes: whistles, shouts, the barking of dogs, barracks, chimneys—and faces. Faces like stones, stones like faces revolved before my eyes like the dislodged cobbles of a disintegrating pavement. From predawn twilight until late into the evening the five hundred women of my barrack loaded stones onto lorries and transported them from one place to another. Even though I was tortured by hunger, I still felt vigorous. Hard labor had not yet broken my spirit. But I had another kind of trouble to torment me. In my lost former life—as close as yesterday and yet as distant as a dream—I had been vain of my statuesque figure and my healthy, well-developed body. Now my height became my greatest curse. It was not possible to hide or melt into the crowd. Whenever we marched in columns, I stuck out like an exclamation mark, which provoked in our guards an irresistible urge to smack me down to size. I suppose that my height irritated them because it disturbed the symmetry, the perfect harmony of the world they had created.

Never before had anyone raised a hand against me. Now I endured more slaps and kicks than any of the other marchers. Those slaps and kicks were the worst. I could not bear them. I was convinced that neither weakness nor hunger would destroy me—but those blows could. (Maybe this was why I was later so generous in meting out my own kicks and slaps to the girls under my supervision.)

In this way my life in the camp dragged on until the moment came when my despair prompted me to risk my neck on a gamble. I risked my life in order to save my life. I turned my very visibility to my advantage, as I did my proficient German. The language of my home had been Polish, but we had had a German cook. I also learned German in high school. I was just beginning to appreciate the true glory of German poetry when the war broke out. *"Mach deine Rechnung mit dem Himmel, Vogt."* "Settle your account with heaven, Vogt," Schiller's William Tell said to his oppressor. I settled my personal account with heaven one bleak dawn before sunrise as we were marching in our columns past the men's camp on our way to work. Usually I tried to place myself in the middle of the row, which consisted of five women, in order not to be quite so conspicuous. But this time I walked on the outside of my line of five, the closest to the barbed wire fence that surrounded the men's camp.

I knew that the shaven-headed kapo Albert, our overseer, would be waiting for us at the gate. Our column of women marched past him with eyes lowered and heads bent. According to camp rules, it was forbidden to so much as glance in the direction of the men's camp. I alone did not obey the order. I drew myself up to my full height, and when my eyes met Albert's I beamed my most bewitching smile in his direction, then took a chance on greeting him with my perfectly accented *Guten Morgen.*

Albert wore a green triangle on his striped suit, which meant that he was classified as a criminal. And he was German, a heartless brute who could strangle his victims with his bare hands. Not only was he incapable of smiling, but he could not even manage a facial expression that resembled a smile, and I am certain that in all that valley of death he had never once encountered a smile like mine. In the dark before dawn I could sense how deeply my chutzpah had shocked him.

That same bleak predawn he came up to me at our workplace. He caught hold of my arm and, without saying a word, dragged me to the far end of the sand field that surrounded us. There, behind a shack, stood a mountain of broken lorries, one stacked on top of the other. I was certain that he was about to kill me. He pushed me into an overturned lorry, and there he took me.

This was how Albert became my first man. I, who had been brought up to be so shy with men! The first great love of my life had had to be satisfied with stolen kisses on dark boulevards and in shady parks. But with Albert I forsook inhibition. In return he saw to it that I should become a *Stubendienst*, a supervisor in my barracks, and then an auxiliary kapo, and after six months in the camp I was made a full kapo. That was lucky because I was pregnant. As a kapo I could move about freely, and Albert could arrange things so that I was soon rid of my problem. Albert—my Teutonic god! He could do with me what he pleased. When he told me for the first time *"Ich liebe dich,"* while the smoke of the crematoria burrowed into my nostrils, my heart nearly stopped beating. Did not such words, spoken in an upside-down world, have exactly the opposite meaning? Might this not mean that he was ready to do away with me?

My god Albert knew well enough that he was committing *Rassenschande.* But this amused him and added fuel to his hellish love for me. He even promised to marry me as soon as the war was over. I stroked his shaved head and wondered if my god, the monster Albert, had ever been a child, had ever been dandled on a mother's knee, had ever absorbed even one drop of the milk of human kindness. Such a thing did not seem possible. My god Albert impregnated my soul with a demon I did not dare exorcise because it guaranteed every single day of my life. Thanks to that demon I evolved into the person that I became. I was proud of my Albert; I was proud of my position in the kingdom of death. In the camps, the word *kapo* elicited the kind of awe reserved in ancient times for the priests and priestesses who guarded the sacred flame.

The women inmates sucked up to me. If I said a kind word it was music to their ears. It made them feel more secure about the next few hours of their lives. They quarreled among themselves as to who should wash my underwear and clean my shoes. They trembled at each disdainful motion of my hand and anxiously read and interpreted every expression of my face. I, who before the war had blushed to hear language that was even remotely risqué, now became positively prolific in inventing entries for a lexicon of obscenities. I, who before the war had spoken the Polish language in the most elegant and refined tones, now took a wild pleasure in ranting like a bitch. And I, who once thought that my hands had been created for nothing but tenderness and caresses, now kept them clenched in rocklike fists, the better to pound them against hunched skeletal backs—and I did this with pleasure, with genuine sensual delight, orgiastically.

The newly born demon within me gave me a sense of freedom in the midst of slavery, a sense that one day of life was an eternity, that the concentration camp was the universe, and that there were no roads leading away from this point. Of course, we spoke and dreamed of real freedom, but no one really believed in it. The smoke rising day and night from the chimneys confirmed the finality of existence. It drugged my fear, intoxicated my senses, and made me wanton. All the restraints of civilized human conduct fell away from me. I had the impression of wandering about as if the skin had been peeled from my body and I was left to revel in an orgy of the most primitive impulses. The borderline between what is and what is not vanished, and the dividing line that distinguishes man from beast similarly disappeared. If an ember of humanity still glowed within me, it was no more than a spark.

But why am I tearing my hair trying to describe things that cannot be described? I had no intention of going off on this tangent. Even so, I must emphasize that it is false to think that not everyone could have been a kapo. It is a lie. In that world from which I miraculously escaped, every single person had the potential to be a brute, a thug, a murderer. When it comes to fighting for one's own life, moral laws cease to exist. You may ask, were there really no exceptions? To this I answer, of course there were—fools who risked their own skins in order to preserve God's image in their hearts. But I was not one of them. I did not want to put my life at risk.

Charitably, my memory has failed to preserve the face of Albert, my concentration camp god. All that I remember of him is the gray shadow of his shaven head, which looked as if it were covered with ashes from the chimneys.

My tragedy after the war stemmed from the fact that I could neither unburden my heart to anyone nor ignore the weight of the sins I carried within. I agree with the modern psychologists who claim such deep understanding as they dig into the psyches of the survivors, when they say that each survivor is afflicted by an immense feeling of guilt for the simple fact of having survived. If this is true, then what should be the extent of my guilt feeling? The trouble is that it is not so much guilt that I feel as it is disgust, an all-embracing disgust—mostly for myself—accompanied by a peculiar anxiety, a strange dread of the word *kapo*. The word has been stamped on my soul like the mark of Cain. I shudder whenever I hear someone speak it. This is why I ran away to this remote corner of the world, hoping the frost native to this land would freeze the word into oblivion or that the snow would erase it. I was mistaken. And the paradoxical result has been that I have remained passionately attached to life while constantly flirting with death, all the while waiting for the moment when someone would exclaim: "I know you! You were a kapo!"

This same suicidal impulse has kept me attached to Edgia. It was from her that I expected to hear the accusation.

* * *

It was during a roll call for selection in the camp. Edgia—I didn't know her name then—was on her last legs. Most likely she was afraid that she would be picked out of her row and sent for "scrap," as we called those who were selected for the crematoria. She did not respond to the roll call but hid in the mud between the broom box and the latrine. A silly place to hide. If not I then some other kapo would have found her. In my search for those who evaded roll call, it was not long before I discovered her there. She crouched in the black mud like a submerged sack of bones, while the bristly hair which had begun to sprout on her shaven head stood up like wires. Her face was as dark as the mud.

I grabbed her by the collar of her ragged dress. She fell forward onto all fours, and this was how I dragged her along like a recalcitrant dog.

"Have pity," she whimpered, digging her thin hands into the loose soil. I jerked her from the spot. But at that moment my eyes met her pleading gaze. Her dirty face, small and shrunken, was blotted from my sight, and all I could see were those eyes. I felt as if I were drowning in them, as if I were being sucked into an abyss. I saw the eyes of my little sister Maniusha looking at me imploringly as the SS man tore her from my arms.

I continued to pull Edgia after me. "No . . . no . . ." she squealed hysterically. I hit her a few times and ordered her to stand up. Then I wrapped my arm around her head, blocking her mouth with my hand. In this manner I dragged her into my barrack through the back way and into the corner that I occupied behind a curtain made from a blanket. I pushed her under my bunk—not a great place to hide either, but there was nothing better—and ran out of the barrack. By the time I got back to roll call they were already leading away the group of "chosen" girls.

I returned to my barrack and looked under the bunk. Edgia was no longer there. I did not know her number nor her name; I did not know who she was nor where she came from. I never saw her again inside the camp. Most likely she deliberately kept out of my way.

The smell of war's end hung in the air, and I sensed that my end too was drawing near. I began to fear what the Germans might do to us in the last moments, and to fear as well what the prisoners might do to the kapos if we survived our liberation.

On one of those last days I was sent out to the train station. I was supposed to assist with the loading of a transport of women who had been assigned to work at another camp, maybe one of those camps where the crematorium no longer functioned. I envied these women. In spite of all my good fortune I considered that they were luckier than I was because I had to remain behind.

I helped to pack the women into the roofless cattle cars, and that is how I suddenly saw Edgia clumsily trying to climb into a wagon. I grabbed her arm. She stared at me with a pair of frightened, mousy eyes as if she were looking at the Angel of Death. "Where are they taking us?" she gasped.

I did not answer but whispered into her ear. "Swear to me this very minute that if we manage to get out, and we happen to meet somewhere else in this world, you will never breathe a word to anyone that I was a kapo."

She remained frozen to the spot, one foot dangling in the air. My request must have struck her as idiotic. And, in fact, it was idiotic. Several hundred other women inmates knew that I was a kapo. I suspect that all I really wanted at that moment was one last look at Edgia, the beneficiary of my one and only heroic act in the camps.

As I stared at her I had the impression that at any moment her face might dissolve into a smile. "And must I also not reveal that you saved my life?" she asked, as it seemed to me then, with false humility.

"Not that either. Swear it! Swear by your life!"

"I swear by my life, if that is still worth something. Where are they taking us?" she asked again as she pulled her other leg into the wagon.

I could not bear the gnawing at my heart brought on by the sight of her, so without answering I ran off and busied myself herding the other women into the boxcars.

Not long afterward we were liberated. At one stroke I was freed from the Germans and from my god Albert. Instead I fell captive to my conscience and to the perpetual fear that somebody would recognize me.

* * *

As I said, I was happy to emigrate to Canada, which I considered a land "far from God and from people"—by which I meant former concentration camp inmates—where I would be unlikely ever to be confronted by an accusing finger. In fact, when I first landed, I was one of the few survivors to have reached these shores. Later I realized that I had only been among the first swallows. Soon the others started to arrive in the thousands. The entire American continent swarmed with them. Commemorations, memorial evenings, remembrance ceremonies were attended by masses of people. Books began to appear on the subject of the Holocaust, all of them providing detailed descriptions of the tragedy. There were so many books that they filled entire libraries. But nobody tried to get to the bottom of the particular tragedy of the Jewish kapos.

I did not read these books. I knew more than they could ever tell. I did not go to the various commemorations and memorial evenings. I needed no one to remind me of what had happened. I remembered on my own and only too well. Even if I had been tempted to attend a Holocaust memorial, I could not have given in to the urge for fear that someone might recognize me.

As soon as I arrived in Montreal, I went to work in a factory, and in the evenings I diligently studied English. With the first money I earned I went to a plastic surgeon and asked him to remove the tattooed number from my forearm. I did not see the point of advertising where I had been. Of course I knew that it was easier to remove the tattoo from my skin than to erase the mark of Cain from my soul. But what went on in my soul had the advantage of not being visible. Outwardly I inhabited

a new skin, a new identity, that could disguise whatever I found conve-
nient to disguise.

Because I was afraid of being alone, I tried to make contact with
the local Jews, but we had no common language. They knew almost
nothing about the Holocaust. What they did know they did not understand. I was drawn to my own kind of people, in fact to those very
people whom I should have been avoiding like the plague. And so I
made friends with other new immigrants. A few of these I suspected of
having been kapos, but most of the others had survived the war on the
Aryan side in Poland and after the war had made their way to Germany, where they feathered their nests by profiteering and trading in
black market merchandise. When the occupation forces began to wrest
some order out of the chaos of a devastated Germany, my friends found
themselves with nothing more to do, so they came here. I soon realized
that what tied me to these people mattered less than what separated me
from them. They were vulgar moneybags with base appetites. I longed
for culture. I needed it as a bridge to throw across the abyss of my war
years and link me to my home and my happy childhood. I needed culture as a form of purification.

It was at this time that I really began to suffer from insomnia.
During the course of the day I wandered about as if I were drunk. I
found myself inhabiting two worlds at the same time, tormented by all
kinds of visions and hallucinations. In the faces of people who passed
me in the street I saw the features of camp inmates. Every chimney
of every factory seemed to me to be the chimney of the crematorium.
In every dog that ran past me I recognized the German shepherds
and Doberman pinschers of the camps who had been taught to savor
human flesh. The sight of any man in uniform—a policeman, a fire-
man—brought the SS to my mind. And if I happened to be traveling
by train and the whistle blew, I imagined that I was again traveling
with my loved ones in the cattle car, drawing ever nearer to the station
of the concentration camp.

The worst of it was when I saw myself in flashback repeatedly strik-
ing someone who resembled one or another of the women I had known

in the camp. I would see my hand go up and down, up and down, like the hand of an automaton. I went about with an ache in the muscles of my right arm, as if I had been carrying a heavy weight. The palm of my hand burned. I had to quickly rid myself of these afflictions because they endangered my work at the factory and, just as important, my learning to write English. I found it difficult to hold a pen in my hand.

For these reasons I became a frequent visitor at the doctor's office. With a tactful little smile on his face, the doctor informed me that I was suffering from pernicious hypochondria, which was not amenable to treatment. But since the sleeping pills I had brought with me from Germany had long since run out, he kept me supplied with more. They helped me very little because I took them so sparingly. I had to be careful of maintaining a sufficient supply of pills against the eventual hour of my reckoning. Having my little stash of pills made me feel more secure.

And in order to feel still more secure I became obsessed with beautiful clothes. I had an urge to be constantly changing my garments, rearranging my appearance, but my earnings did not permit me the luxury of a constant change of clothing. It was the summer of 1950. I heard that JIAS was distributing used clothes for newly arrived immigrants. It was clear to me that a secondhand dress donated by a wealthy Montreal woman would look better on me than some cheap rag that I could afford to buy on my own, especially since I had a good figure, and even cheap clothing looked expensive and elegant on me. Yes, I looked good, despite my nightmares. I was like the proverbial apple, beautiful and healthy on the outside, wormy and rotten inside.

So one day I paid a visit to the JIAS storerooms. I walked into a room full of racks of clothing. There were dresses, suits, skirts, and blouses, all tightly packed together. The sight made me dizzy. I pounced on each full rack, moving rapidly from one to another, and this was how my restless gaze came to fall on the figure of a familiar-looking woman as she too rummaged among the clothes racks. My heart stopped. My first impulse was to get away, but my feet refused to move. I could not take my eyes off the woman's profile. The face of that monster Albert had been erased from my memory, but Edgia's face, which I had glimpsed only twice in my life, I remembered so well that it was not difficult for me to recognize her, despite her altered appearance. Although her complexion still had a sallow hue, her profile was rounded and her hair was of normal length. I felt myself drawn to her face—the face of my own kindness.

I broke away from the spot where I was standing and threw myself at her. I pulled her into a corner. The yellowish cast of her face turned white as chalk; her head sunk down between her shoulders, just as it had during the scene of our first encounter near the camp latrine. She acted as if her life were still in my hands, but this time we were both trembling with anxiety.

"Do you recognize me?" I asked her.

"Yes, I recognize you," she stammered.

"And do you remember that thanks to me you are still alive?"

"Yes, I remember."

It annoyed me that even now she refrained from thanking me. All of a sudden my voice assumed the shrill, harsh note of my camp days. "I hope you also remember the vow that you swore to me then."

She nodded, turned away from me, and with trembling hands resumed rummaging among the dresses on the neighboring rack, her head sunk between her shoulders. She hastily pulled a dress from a hanger and stuffed it into her bag. I realized that she was about to leave. I felt compelled to follow. I must not let her get away. I must keep my eye on her. I caught up to her and blurted out: "I've forgotten your name."

"I remember yours," she answered. "You are Black Rella."

"What's your name?" I insisted.

She told me her name. I ventured to ask for her address. To my astonishment she gave it to me, almost eagerly. Most likely she wanted to keep an eye on me too. Maybe she felt as drawn to me as I did to her.

* * *

I visited Edgia uninvited. I visited her again, and then again, and in this way I became a frequent guest at her home. She introduced me to her husband, Lolek, a handsome blond man, unusually amiable and extroverted. Edgia proudly told me that he had been a partisan and had survived the war years somewhere in the forests of Lithuania. This was one of the rare occasions when Edgia mentioned the war during our habitually awkward conversations. As a rule we talked about insignificant daily matters and never touched on our shared experiences, not even remotely. As for Lolek, I felt immediately at ease in his company. We were on the same wavelength. He was a cultured man with good manners, and I was very eager that he should think well of me. I needed to win his confidence in order to find out whether Edgia had not by chance been babbling the truth about me.

Edgia and Lolek introduced me to their circle of friends, who were all, like me, immigrants from Europe, cultured and intelligent. Fortunately none of them had been incarcerated in my camp. I was drawn to them like a moth to flame. The group's frequent get-togethers resulted in my seeing more of Edgia than either of us really desired. We were both trapped in a situation we ourselves had created but chose to regard as something that could not be changed.

And that is how I became Edgia's omnipresent representative from the past and she mine. I was her living nightmare, and she was mine. She symbolized my one and only moment of humanity, of kindness, and I symbolized her moment of humiliation. I reminded her of the time when she had crawled on all fours and pleaded for her life. She reminded me of how I had raised myself to the level of self-sacrifice. In this manner we became bound to one another in a singular friendship—our reward and punishment for having survived.

* * *

The first ten years of my life in Canada were financially difficult for me, but intellectually I accomplished a great deal. I mastered the English language. The only thing that upset me was my European accent. My teacher good-naturedly teased me with the assurance that I would never lose the accent, so I had better make peace with it. But for me this was not a laughing matter. The accent prevented me from becoming a new person.

Some time later I opened a small ladies clothes shop, and as if to spite myself I called it "La Boutique européenne." My European accent contributed to the continental ambience of the shop, which in turn appealed to the predilections of my customers. This made me realize how attractive Europeanness could be when it appeared in a non-European setting. My boutique grew even more successful a few years later, when I graduated from an evening school for dress design. After that I prospered to such an extent that my clientele included some of the wealthiest and most socially prominent women in Montreal. My financial worries evaporated, but not my discomfort with my accent, which remained an attribute I would gladly have done without.

My new circle of friends also made great financial advances. They too were in the process of fitting themselves into new identities. Like Lolek, none of them had any intention of crying over the past. We were, all of us, determined to be positively inclined toward life, and we prided ourselves on looking forward, not back.

* * *

Our group of friends—and this was especially true of the women—took particular pleasure in getting together at Edgia and Lolek's apartment on Esplanade Avenue, even though it was more modestly furnished than that of anyone else in the group. Socializing at Lolek and Edgia's place had the great advantage that there, the women could relax. Not only did they not have to cook in their own homes but they were also freed from the obligation of helping the hostess serve or clear the table. At these gatherings even the pretense of rising in order to help Edgia was superfluous. Dear Lolek's unusual amiability and hospitality expressed itself also in this—he issued a decree that no woman besides Edgia was allowed into the kitchen.

"Stay where you are!" he commanded in the barking tone of a theatrical general, snapping at any woman who attempted to help Edgia.

And if one of us, just for the fun of it, did approach the kitchen with a tray full of dirty dishes, Lolek would block the door with outstretched arms as if he were heroically guarding the entrance to a fortress. *"No pasaran!"* he would declare, playfully shaking his head as he sent the tray and its bearer back to the table. Or he would personally steer the miscreant back to her seat, his arm thrown over her shoulder in good-comradely fashion, as he added, "Really, it's not necessary. Edgia and I would be insulted. Edgia does it all with the greatest pleasure."

If, on the other hand, Lolek and Edgia paid one of us a visit, it did not take long before Lolek began winking meaningfully at his wife. The result was that her contribution to the success of the evening was to take over the hostess's duties in the kitchen. Edgia did not even take up an extra seat.

I don't mean to suggest that the members of my circle of friends were not supportive or helpful to one another. On the contrary. There was a warmth and caring in their relationships that is rarely found among groups of friends born in this country. The group was a sub-stitute for our closest family. But as far as Edgia was concerned, it was somehow not possible to have any serious regard for her. And it was Lolek, Edgia's wonderful husband, under whose spell we had all fallen, who saw to it that we should have no qualms about our treatment of Edgia.

Only once do I remember Edgia's name being mentioned at one of our gatherings. We were all a little tipsy and jolly, so we decided to play a word game. At that point, Pavel, the most reserved and quiet member of our group, suddenly asked, "Why don't we call in Edgia to join us?"

We all exchanged looks, and then, with a slight undertone of as-sumed guilt mixed with irony, we called out, "Edgia, where are you? Come and join us!"

Edgia's head peeked out from behind the kitchen door, and her thin lips stretched into a pathetic half smile. "Go ahead and play. It doesn't matter about me."

And this was the truth about Edgia. She did not matter. (Except, of course, in the special way in which she mattered to me.) Even among her closest friends, she was of no significance. With her characteristic pathetic little smile she served us so deftly at table that we hardly noticed when and how she did it. We turned to her with mechanical civility when we needed something from the kitchen, when there was a knife or a fork missing or when we wanted another cup of coffee. We often became excited and thirsty from our heated discussions on the subjects of modern art or literature—subjects that were as distant from Edgia's concerns as day is from night and that further caused us to forget there was an Edgia in the world at all.

I would not say that Edgia was a fool or an idiot, or even that she was ugly. Far from it. But there was something in her manner that canceled her out. She belonged to that type of woman who blends into her surroundings like an object to which the eye grows quickly accustomed and stops noticing. She was there and yet not there. It did not matter if what she had to say was clever or stupid. Nobody was curious about what she had to say. Her words swam past a listener's ears and dissolved in the air as if she had said nothing. Nor did anybody care whether she was beautiful or ugly. The pallor of her frightened, mousy face, the delicacy of her profile, and her opaque, absent gaze ensured that the eyes of others would glide past her as if she were a void. She left no impression.

In addition she made herself appear smaller than she really was. Thin, slightly stooped, she always carried her head tucked in between her raised shoulders as if she were afraid that something might at any moment fall on her. Even the tattooed number on her left arm seemed paler and more crooked than any other such number I ever saw. When I once advised her to have the number removed, she threw back her head in sudden anger and exclaimed, "Not that! Never!"

Her shadow never darkened the doorway of a beauty parlor, and her hair, which was the color of mud—as though she had dyed it for life in the mud behind the camp latrine where we met for the first time—dangled negligently from her head, stiff, dull, and brittle. Long, unkempt bangs covered her entire forehead to the eyebrows, as if she wished to hide her already small face behind a curtain of hair. She dressed without taste—although neatly—in dirty-looking clothes of indefinite shape, as if in that way too she were trying to erase her presence from the eyes of others.

I behaved toward her as the others did, taking care not to betray the role that she had played in my life. I was convinced that she expected such behavior from me. We were satisfied with one another. Basically, the way she looked pleased me. She looked just as I wanted her to look. I liked her very much. I told her so once when we were alone.

"I like you very much too, Rella," she replied with a comical little sigh.

* * *

Just as Edgia counted for very little in our circle of friends, so her husband Lolek counted for a great deal. In my opinion, it was only on his account that Edgia was even tolerated in our circle. The friends accepted her as if she were just a flaw in Lolek's character, a blemish on his personality. This made him, the hero of the partisans, appear more human in our eyes, nourishing both our respect and our compassion for him. There was no doubt in my mind that if Edgia had been single, as I was, she would never have been accepted by our group of friends. The group was very selective about who was allowed to join. We considered ourselves to be the intellectual elite among the new immigrants. If we decided to include somebody in our company, that somebody had to be capable of making a stimulating intellectual contribution.

We were immersed up to our ears in modern culture and its achievements. Most of us had lost the last vestiges of religious belief in the camps, and since we required some form of faith to hold on to after the liberation, we seized on the idea of modern culture and allowed that to take the place of religion in our lives. This was the luminous bridge we threw across the dark abyss of barbarous savagery that had once swallowed us. For this reason there were no greedier, more avid readers of the most recently published books than we were. We threw ourselves at every best seller as soon as it appeared on the best-seller lists. We ran to all the modern and postmodern experimental performances. We enthused over pop art and op art. We even had a few marijuana smoking sessions when that became fashionable. We practiced hatha yoga and regularly visited a guru in his ashram in the Laurentians.

In our zeal we tried to effect a spiritual escape not only from the outmoded Jewish shtetl but also from the Jewish mentality that had once inhabited the East European metropolis. If culture symbolized a bridge, it had to be a bridge that led away from the past, no matter how sweet the memories that still bound us to our childhood and youth. We were frightened of the dampening effects that such memories could have on our present positive attitude toward life. We wanted no part of the past. We were dying to be in tune with the progressiveness of modern times. We wanted to absorb everything new that had been created since the Second World War. By inhaling the winds of change we tried to fit ourselves into the present, to incorporate ourselves into modern society, to be energetic and optimistic, at least on the surface. It was the surface that mattered and nothing else. What remained crippled and wounded within each of us was nobody else's business; it was a burden we had to carry on our own.

The women of my circle were by no means less avid in their intellectual hunger than the men. We were modern women in the full sense of the word. And I would venture to assert that just as women are generally more devout than men, so our greed for culture was even stronger than that of the men (not counting Lolek). When you come right down to it, men's interests tend generally toward business and politics. For them, literary discussions or going to the theater were no more than weekend pastimes. But the women, especially those who stayed at home keeping house and raising children, felt acutely the dulling effects of being constantly imprisoned in their homes. Neither politics nor business offered them any spiritual sustenance. So for them culture became a breath of fresh air. No, more than that—it provided a forum where they could indulge their inclination to devotion, even to fanaticism. As for me, who had no husband and no children, my passion for culture was another means of jumping out of my skin and obliterating the nightmare of my sins.

Pavel, the cynic in our group, took pleasure in sarcastically labeling us "culture vultures." He would call us this in Yiddish. In the group we generally spoke either Polish or English, and it shocked us whenever, out of the blue, he burst out with one of his vulgar Yiddish expressions in order to lend spice to his critical opinion of us.

Pavel was a pharmacist. He came from Lithuania, but he had studied in Warsaw. He spoke Polish well, and his English was as good as mine, if not better, because his accent was not as pronounced as mine. He was a man of middle height, broad-shouldered and heavyset. He had a round, child's face and a pair of deep blue eyes, which when viewed behind his thickly rimmed glasses seemed even larger and bluer than they actually were. The childlike innocence of his appearance belied his personality. He was an unhappy, bitter man, stingy with words and without a spark of *joie de vivre*. I disliked him intensely. The mere fact of his unaccented English would have been reason enough for my dislike, but he was also a thorn in my side because of his penetrating gaze. His stubborn silences irritated me no less than the sickening philosophy of life he preached on the rare occasions when he did speak up. True, his sarcastic remarks often found their mark, but precisely for this reason they seemed tactless and offensive. Pavel resembled Edgia in having no burning passion for the achievements of modern culture.

But then it was not he but Lolek who was our spiritual guide. Lolek surpassed us all in his enthusiasm for everything that was new and stimulating. Like the other men in our group he was preoccupied with politics, but in contrast to the others, who did nothing but talk, Lolek was *engagé* and an activist. A humanist to the bone, he marched in all demonstrations and attended all rallies called in support of individual rights and freedoms.

Lolek was the heart and soul of our circle, its compelling force, even though his English was much worse than ours, worse even than Edgia's. He lacked the patience to acquire a thorough grounding in the language. Perhaps he had no ear for languages. His sentence structure was catastrophic, his choice of words horrendous, his idiomatic expressions unrecognizable. In later years he stopped speaking any language as it should be spoken. He mixed so many anglicisms into his ungrammatical Polish that it sounded like a new dialect altogether. But after all, what did it matter? The important thing was that we understood him perfectly well.

He was not only our inspirer but also our chief animator, book provider, and ticket buyer, a connoisseur of what was in and what was out, our resident expert on contemporary sexual mores. Unlike the other men in our circle, he never discussed business, as if this were a topic that was beneath his notice. And he was in fact beneath the others in business affairs, which is to say that in financial terms he was a failure and, in comparison to the others, a virtual pauper.

He owned a small leather goods shop where he manufactured purses. Edgia, when she was not too sick, helped him with the bookkeeping and performed the functions of an all-purpose errand girl. Whereas the others in our group had long since moved into comfortable new homes in other parts of town, Lolek and Edgia were still stuck on Esplanade in the district of the Mountain, as we Jews called the neighborhood near Mount Royal. This was the part of town where we greenhorns had settled just after our arrival in Canada.

According to Pavel our group was even more snobbish with regard to financial status than it was with regard to cultural status. Despite this, the sorry state of Lolek's pocketbook did nothing to diminish his prestige among us—a clear proof of the magnetism of his personality. He earned our respect for his idealism and contempt of material values, a respect that did not interfere with our own enjoyment of the things that money could buy.

We very nearly idolized Lolek. And to tell the truth, we preferred it when he came to see us without Edgia. When this happened we really were all on the same wavelength, although someone always asked him with feigned concern, "Where is Edgia?"

He would wave his hand dismissively: "She's not feeling her best today."

Edgia often did not feel her best. She suffered from migraines, stomach cramps, bellyaches, and all kinds of neuralgia. She was also prone to accidents. One day she slipped on the stairs to her door, another day she burned herself; one day she cut her finger, another day she fell and bruised her knee.

Another time when I asked Lolek where Edgia was, he shrugged, "You know Edgia. This won't interest her."

The "this" was usually a lecture about the most recent discoveries in sexual research, or an experimental film, or an exhibit of modern painting, or a concert of electronic music, or a nightclub, or even a day trip to the guru in his ashram in the Laurentians.

* * *

I found Lolek's appearance and comportment, in fact the style of his masculinity in general, very much to my taste. He had a fine, interesting face with a high forehead. After a time he took to adorning his cheeks with trimmed sideburns as was then the fashion. When his hairline began to recede he compensated by skillfully combing the long hair from the side of his head over the bald spots to form bangs and by growing a mane of thick blond hair at the back of the head, which curled charmingly around his neck. He was not too tall, but he wore shoes with elevated heels, which gave the impression of agreeable height. He dressed stylishly in shirts with open collars, a silken ascot of Oriental design tied under his chin. Often he wore tightly fitted jeans, and in summer he wore tight shorts beneath a shirt kept unbuttoned to reveal his hairy chest. Around his neck he wore a gilded chain or a velvet ribbon from which dangled a miniature Maori idol—a symbol of fertility and a good-luck charm. He was not overweight like the other men of our group, whose middles, after a time, began to look like mobile bagel stands, the rings of fat stacked on top of one another. Lolek looked much younger than any of them.

One day, about ten years after I first met Lolek, I happened to be sitting—much against my will—next to Pavel in a car into which we had all squeezed for a drive to the theater. Lolek was at the wheel. Pressed against my stubbornly silent neighbor, I tried to alleviate my discomfort by teasing him out of his reserve with a little verbal pinprick.

"It's hard to breathe in your company, my dear Pavel," I said, smiling at him. "If Lolek were sitting beside me I might have more air."

"No doubt about that," Pavel answered, with a glint in his blue eyes. "After all, Lolek is nothing but air."

"What do you mean by that?" I retorted, feeling offended for Lolek.

"Nothing more than what I said. I just wanted to explain to you why you would be so much more comfortable if you sat next to Lolek."

"I would be more comfortable because he is slim and you are as round as a barrel."

"Forgive me for that. I will do my best never again to be seated next to you."

I did not want him to take offense. I wanted to live in peace with all my friends, even with Pavel. "Don't take me so seriously," I said in a mollifying tone, as I patted his hand. "I only wanted to suggest that you might do well to lose a little weight." In order to change the subject, and since Lolek was always on my mind and I was very curious about every detail of his life, I broke my resolve never to mention the past and took the opportunity to ask Pavel for information. "Tell me, Pavel," I whispered in his ear, "you know Lolek from the old country, don't you? When did you actually find out about his participation in the Resistance?"

Pavel did not answer, so I repeated the question. He fixed his deep blue eyes on me while seeming to weigh his answer. Finally he whispered back in my ear, "I knew it all the time, from the very beginning; that is, if participating in the Resistance means sitting in a hiding place and not being caught."

I was stunned by Pavel's words. I could barely fathom what he was trying to tell me, but that he intended to blacken Lolek's name was perfectly clear. So I exploded: "Who needs enemies with friends like you? Couldn't you have invented a more plausible lie than that about your most devoted friend?"

"He really is a devoted friend. And believe it or not, I am devoted to him too. But that doesn't change the fact that I was the one who supplied him with money and food while he was in hiding."

"So you're trying to say that you were the hero, not he?"

"Hero, my foot! My heroism consisted of the fact that I looked like an Aryan and so could move about more freely and not be recognized as a Jew."

"But Lolek also looks like an Aryan. He's blond, after all."

"True, but he has brown Jewish eyes, while my eyes are blue."

"Edgia surely knows the truth about Lolek better than you do. She never stops babbling about his bravery."

"She needs to believe it. It makes her feel like a partner to his courage."

"So why don't you open her eyes for her and tell her your lying truth? Why don't you tell it to all of us? Why don't you confront Lolek with this particular truth?"

"You must be joking! Why should I do such a thing? Whom does he hurt? Whether or not he was actually a partisan, he still fought for his life tooth and nail, and he has had more than his share of suffering. He needs to feel that he is important and virile. Where is the harm in that? I would never have answered your question about him if I hadn't wanted to make you see Lolek in a more realistic light—for Edgia's sake. Your innocent flirtation with her husband must cause her pain. She is so sensitive, and she has suffered so much!"

I ignored his remark and asked angrily, "But how can you be close to someone who is such a fake?"

Once again Pavel fixed his deep blue eyes on me. "He and Edgia are the closest people in the world to me. But I worry more about Edgia than about Lolek. She cannot seem to get back on her feet, and no superficial distractions are of any help. And Lolek himself is certainly no help. But since I can't do anything for them, I have to content myself with just keeping an eye on them, which I do also out of curiosity to see what effect this so-called normal life can have on two people who have miraculously escaped from hell."

I did not react to his words. I was too bewildered and distraught.

* * *

In the course of the next few days I mulled over what Pavel had said. Despite the shock his words had given me, they did not really manage to penetrate my consciousness. I was incapable of seeing Lolek in any light other than the one in which I had always seen him, and my feelings for him remained unchanged. It did not take long before Pavel's words began to seem like nothing more than tasteless gossip that I had picked up in some indistinct place, and they dissolved into such a haze that I managed to convince myself I had never heard them. Once again I saw in Lolek the former partisan hero and wonderful human being, the same dear friend, affectionate and loyal.

It made a woman feel good to be seen with Lolek in a restaurant or at the theater. He did in fact often go out with us, his women friends, usually to places where the other men had no interest in going. I have no idea what he did with the other women after a theater performance or dinner downtown, but when he went out with me he usually ended the evening by coming up to my apartment for "a cup of coffee."

I considered myself a liberated woman, although before the war I would have been called an old maid. During the war I had lost my first and only love. Then that monster Albert had come into my life and robbed me forever of the wish to live with a man. His *Ich liebe dich* murdered my belief in romantic love. I never married—not because I had no opportunities, and not because I had completely rid myself of romantic illusions, but because I did not want to have any children, so what would be the point? True, I would have liked to carry on the hereditary line of my family, but I was haunted by the fear that I might bring potential kapos into the world—that's how neurotic I was! My sexual encounters with men gave me little pleasure, but my loneliness would not permit me to give them up. My heart was rent by a million anxieties; terrifying hallucinations tormented me throughout the day. My sins pursued me and instead of diminishing seemed to grow to colossal proportions. I had the impression that the moment of reckoning lay in wait for me around every corner. Most often it seemed to peer at me from the eyes of children, especially from the eyes of ten-year-old girls on their way to or from school. My sleepless nights were steeped in horror. And when sleep would not come, and I tossed and turned on my bed, I ached for the proximity of another human being and yearned to feel the touch of warm skin against my skin.

Lolek looked up to me with respect and admiration. "You are the only one of us," he would compliment me, "who has completely freed herself from our spiritual ghetto." He raved about my excellent English, my up-to-date expressions, and my fashionable style of dressing. My chameleonlike qualities pleased him no end. In him I had an enthusiastic admirer and attendant. It required no more than a wink from me for him to run and fetch whatever my caprice dictated. He was always at my disposal. Time was never an issue. He managed to get away from his shop for hours at a time, leaving Edgia, whom he had trained, to mind the business.

Since Lolek and I were not indifferent to each other, the coffee drinking at my apartment often dragged on until late at night. Becoming lovers was no more than a natural step in the development of our friendship. Lolek reawakened in me the distant memory of the poetic charm, the warmth, and heartfelt tenderness that had accompanied my first lost love. But no emotional scenes were ever played out between us, no jealous keeping of accounts, no reproaches, as often happens between two people who are as intimate with one another as we were. If Lolek ever unwittingly hurt my feelings, I forced myself to ignore the pain. My romance with him was my greatest treasure.

Lolek and I believed that we had no reason to be ashamed or to hide our conduct from our friends—or even from Edgia. As far as I was concerned, I did not see why I should be circumspect with Edgia, and this was not because she was so unaware of what was going on around her, or because I was afraid of hurting her feelings. Such niceties did not even occur to me, since I seldom thought of her as a full-blooded person but saw her instead as the symbol of my essential goodness. When it did occur to me to acknowledge her humanity, it was only to consider that she was more fortunate than I. Lolek put himself out for her. He would not abandon her, and it was to her that he actually belonged. I was jealous of her. So the reason I was not careful to hide my affair from Edgia had another source: I already knew for certain that Lolek knew nothing of what had happened between Edgia and me in the camp. He did not even know we had been in the same camp together. I kept silent whenever our group's conversation turned to those times. I never so much as mentioned the name of my camp, and if I was asked where I had been incarcerated, I always answered vaguely, "Oh, it was near some Bavarian village."

I was grateful to Edgia for not betraying me. She, who was otherwise so weak and helpless, displayed an odd strength of character in this instance. Because of this, and because of my feelings for Lolek, I felt even more attached to her. This was why I considered it my duty to do nothing behind her back.

I will not claim that this was easy for me. Vestiges of the old sexual morality still clung to me, and they made me feel sick with guilt, a guilt that merged with my other powerful feelings of sinfulness. As a result, it became clear to me that my behavior was no more than another form of flirtation with death. I realized I was playing games with Edgia in order to provoke her into accusing me. That was why my frankness with her required a great deal of courage.

As for our friends, they reacted to Lolek and me as we anticipated and made no comment. Our group was made up of couples who had gotten married after the war, some for the second time. Most of these couples clung to each other and were very devoted. But only one or two of them were really well matched. So I was convinced that the majority of our friends admired Lolek and me for daring to put into practice those freedoms we preached in conversation.

Only Pavel, the silent and embittered one—embittered possibly more against himself than against us—would occasionally direct venomous remarks at Lolek and me. But that didn't matter because Pavel did not spare the rest of the group either. He believed that we were a bunch of phonies, that we were not genuine or authentic in our feelings and behavior, that we were dilettantes who succumbed to foolish enthusiasms for every new fad—and all because we were afraid to face the truth. And that truth was that we felt alien in this new world, that we were so caught up with modernity because we found it so frightening.

But we were accustomed to Pavel's needling. His game was to cut everyone down to size, himself included. He too dragged behind him the baggage of the past. During the war, while he had been so preoccupied with caring for others who were confined to their hiding places, his wife and child had been captured, and he never saw them again. Throughout all the years he never lost the feeling that he had been responsible for their deaths. Fortunately he had Sylvia, his attractive, vivacious second wife. She would insist that he accompany her to our get-togethers. She held us in great esteem, and we, in turn, were proud to have her in our midst. She had come to Canada just before the outbreak of the war, but we considered her native born, a genuine Canadian. Pavel did not appreciate her. He made her life difficult. More than once Sylvia complained about him to our group, how he sadistically tormented her with the reminiscences of his first wife and child and with his habit of constant self-accusation.

But although we ignored Pavel's sarcastic remarks in the same way we ignored whatever Edgia had to say, Pavel was by no means a masculine version of Edgia. First of all, he had a university education, which we, whose university had been the concentration camps, envied. Secondly, although he lacked enthusiasm for current fashions, he nevertheless knew what was going on in the world. Moreover, he was capable of great kindness to others without making too much of a fuss. This I had to admit, despite my personal antipathy toward him. For instance, I knew from Lolek that it was Pavel who kept an eye on Edgia's health problems and that he did so in such a way that neither Edgia nor Lolek felt uncomfortable about it. This was why I felt a cold respect for Pavel at the same time as I disliked and avoided him.

And if Pavel was correct in his opinion of us, so what? Was not his opinion, especially about Lolek and me, basically superficial? How deeply, after all, could he peer into our souls? What did Pavel know about the real me, or the real Lolek, for that matter? The human tragedy—or better said, the human tragicomedy—harbors the sad truth that whoever nourishes a viper in his bosom and consumes a daily dose of poison is blind to the fact that his neighbor nourishes a similar viper and also subsists on a diet of poison.

Pavel did not know, nor did he suspect, that Lolek and I were like two drowning people who cling to each other. Even if this clinging makes the two sink faster into the whirlpool, at least it gives them the momentary illusion that they have found a support and are saving themselves. What did I, apparently strong-minded as I was, hard and shielded as I was, possess in this world besides my salvaged, lonely, neurotic life, a life that demanded so urgently to be lived and that forced me to seize with gratitude and without scruple upon every grain of pleasure that fell across my arid path? And Lolek, who loved life so enthusiastically and joyfully—did he not have days of deep depression?

* * *

Whenever I felt indisposed or in a bad mood, Lolek would call me ten times a day to find out how I was doing. In the evenings he would come over and stay with me. If something similar happened to Lolek, and he fell into one of his depressions, I reciprocated with the same solicitude.

If I called his home and Edgia picked up the phone, she would exclaim with exaggerated friendliness, "Oh, it's you! How are you, Rella?" And without waiting for an answer she would add, "Just a second. I'll give you Lolek straight away."

When Lolek got on the phone I would tease him. "You see," I would say, "your Edgia gives you to me." As I said this the receiver in my hand would grow strangely heavy. Calling Lolek at home, when my call had nothing to do with our group, always made me uneasy.

One time when Lolek was in a deep depression and had no energy to leave home, I felt it my duty to visit him in his apartment on Esplanade Avenue. As I made my way there I could feel my heart fluttering with joy and apprehension. I asked myself how Edgia would receive me.

A Montreal-style winding wooden staircase led directly from the street to the second-floor apartment where Lolek and Edgia lived and where our group's get-togethers so often took place. The apartment was long and dark. Only the living room possessed a large, wide window with a panoramic view, a view that gave out on a large sports field in the foreground and Mount Royal topped by its cross behind. The furniture in the apartment was the same that Lolek and Edgia had acquired in the early years after their arrival in Montreal. The passage of time had burrowed holes into the upholstery of the sofas and armchairs, sucked the vibrant color out of the curtains and left them an indeterminate hue. But the rooms were neat, arranged with modest means yet in good taste. I had no doubt that Lolek had had a hand in creating this agreeable effect.

Edgia received me with a shy half smile. She offered me a glass of tea, put some refreshments on the coffee table, and Lolek and I sat down, or to put it more accurately, sank into the deep sofa with the broken springs under the seat. I eagerly launched into a conversation, trying to cheer Lolek with my chatter about all kinds of cultural events, while Edgia served us. She forgot to bring lemon for the tea, an omission Lolek politely brought to her attention in a silken tone of voice.

She clapped her hand to her cheek and exclaimed, "How absent-minded I am! It's coming right away!"

When she returned with the lemon, Lolek good-humoredly remarked in her presence, "Edgia lives on the moon."

Edgia nodded her head in agreement. "Yes, I have a weakness for astronomy."

Lolek winked at me meaningfully. We waited for Edgia to disappear into the kitchen and take with her the black tomcat that rubbed sensuously against her thin, rather shapely legs. She called the cat Loverboy. Once she was gone, I resumed my conversation with Lolek, and in this way a few hours passed. I could hear Edgia's voice coming from the kitchen as she talked to her cat, and I found myself imagining that she was preparing some poisonous dish for Lolek and me. With feigned cheerfulness I called out to her, "Edgia, what are you doing in there? Why don't you come in and join us?"

Her head peeked out from behind the kitchen door, and she favored me with a crooked little smile. "I'll be right there. I just want to feed my Loverboy first."

I continued my chat with Lolek and waited for Edgia to join us. I expected—like one condemned yet brave—that at any moment she would appear before us with the poisoned dish, that she would fix me with a vengeful look and compel me to consume what she had prepared. That she craved vengeance—of that I had no doubt. I subscribe to the old adage that says that we resent most those whom we have the most reason to thank.

But Edgia did not emerge from the kitchen until just before I left. "Go in good health," she said. "Thanks for coming."

At this moment Lolek declared that my visit had so refreshed him that he felt ready to walk me home. We stepped out of the door onto the landing and remained standing in front of the winding staircase that led down to the street. Edgia and the tomcat came out to say another goodbye, and Loverboy began to rub against my legs. I was afraid he would start a run in my nylons. I had an abhorrence for this black monstrosity of a cat, this disgusting pussyfooting spying devil with its knowing eyes that crept all over me like two green searchlights.

Edgia was well aware of how repulsive I found her cat. When she saw him winding in and out between my legs, she broke into giggles, then gave him such a powerful kick that he let out a shriek in a voice so high-pitched that it sounded nearly human. In the blink of an eye the cat vanished into the depths of the apartment. I was stunned by Edgia's brutality. In that moment I understood how much more I feared Edgia than I did her cat.

I carefully descended the stairs, fighting the feeling that at any moment a hand would push me from behind and I would roll down onto the sidewalk. I turned my head back and saw Edgia on the landing above leaning against the doorpost with the tomcat in her arms. She pressed him against her breast and I overheard her murmur to him, "Oh, what have I done to you, Loverboy? Forgive me. I didn't mean to hurt you. Now hush, Loverboy, hush." When her eyes met mine, she waved her hand and called after us, "Go in good health and enjoy yourselves!"

* * *

I recall another time when I visited Lolek and Edgia alone and not with the rest of our group. On that occasion Lolek had not yet returned from work. I had arranged with him to drive to a restaurant for dinner and then to the vernissage of an avant-garde artist who experimented with various kinds of chemical reactions to produce color. Lolek's car had broken down, and I was supposed to pick him up in mine at his apartment. Edgia received me as usual with exaggerated friendliness and invited me to make myself comfortable on the sofa. After a few minutes she approached me, a smile both childish and cunning playing on her lips. She held a small, faded photograph in her hand and showed it to me.

"See what a relative has sent me from Argentina?" she asked in a solemn whisper. "The little girl that you see here is me. I was ten years old then. I'm holding an award in my hand. I was the best student in my class."

My little sister Maniusha had been ten years old when she perished. The little girl in the photo brought back her memory with painful clarity.

"As you know, when we got to Auschwitz they took everything away from us, the photographs too," I heard Edgia saying.

The name "Auschwitz" spoken aloud, and the memory of our arrival there, which Edgia's words so unexpectedly evoked, took my breath away. I wanted to block my ears, to stop her mouth with my hand, to run away. I grew stiff at the thought that at any moment Edgia might start to say more about Auschwitz, even though she had never done so before. Like me she never spoke about those days. Fortunately, she did not do so now either. As soon as we heard Lolek running up the outside stairs, she grabbed the photograph out of my hand and quickly hid it under the doily on the commode.

Lolek burst into the apartment like a tornado. Everything began to vibrate with excitement and expectation. He waved at me gaily and ran into the bedroom to change. I managed to avoid Edgia's glance, yet I did not want her to leave the room. Next to me on the sofa lay a book called *Epochs in Chaos* by somebody called Velikowsky.

"Are you reading this?" I asked Edgia with surprise.

Edgia bent her head to her shoulder and assumed the look of a moron. "I just look at the pictures," she giggled.

With a strange sense of revulsion I began to flip through the pages, just as Edgia stretched out her hand and took the book away from me. I noticed a small bandage sticking out from underneath her sleeve. Out of politeness, I asked, "What did you do to yourself?"

"Oh, it's nothing." She quickly pulled her sleeve over the bandage, adding in a whisper, "It's Lolek . . ."

I raised my eyebrows, ready to spring to Lolek's defense. "What do you mean?" I nearly shouted. "Does Lolek hit you?"

"Heaven forbid," she quieted me. "Lolek would never touch me. What are you thinking? He is the very embodiment of delicacy. You should know that by now. And the way he behaved as a partisan . . . Why, books could be written about that! He is too modest to talk about such things, but I know my Lolek. I'm the one who is the *schlimazl*. You know me. I cut my hand on the mirror, if you can imagine such a thing. It's my own stupid nature. Whenever Lolek makes the least remark, my head begins to spin. I've lived with him for so many years, and I still can't get used to his sense of humor. Whenever he calls me by his favorite nickname for me—he calls me 'holy Cunegunda'—I drop whatever I'm holding in my hands. You understand? I was combing my hair in front of the mirror. He was in a hurry to leave and wanted me to iron his pants. So he teased me. 'Why do you waste your time standing in front of the mirror? Do you think that the mirror will help your looks? Nothing can help a holy Cunegunda like you.' And he's right, after all. So I threw away the comb, but so clumsily that my hand bashed into the mirror. The mirror was cracked, so it shattered."

* * *

I remember particularly the "historic" occasion of my birthday, which for the first time Lolek forgot. His passion for me had by then started to cool, a fact of which I was ignorant at the time. That evening I could not bring myself to stay home alone and decided to mark my so-called celebratory day with a visit to Lolek and Edgia. I put on a new white dress and took along a box of chocolates, even though this was one day when I was the one who should have been receiving gifts.

Lolek was not at home. Edgia took the box of chocolates from my hand and put it on the table. "Lolek will thank you for this. He has a sweet tooth, as you probably know." She left me sitting on the sofa, disappeared into the kitchen, and did not come out again. I found it a little tedious waiting for Lolek, but mostly, on that particular day, I felt drawn to Edgia. In my mind, I went over all the birthdays of my childhood, and I was particularly oppressed by the memory of my birthdays in the concentration camp. I got up from the sofa and went over to the kitchen door. I saw Edgia standing in front of a basin filled with water. Next to her on the table lay a gleaming knife and a large turnip, which reminded me both of my days in the ghetto when turnip was the staple of our diet and of that monster Albert's gray, shaven head.

"Today is my birthday," I said to Edgia.

"Oh, you don't say!" she exclaimed, wiping her palms against her dress and extending a damp hand. She kissed me. "I wish for you everything that you wish for yourself." She pressed me so tightly to her bosom that I had the impression she would gladly have suffocated me.

I freed myself from her embrace and asked, "Why do you wash the clothes by hand and not in the machine?"

She began to titter. "These are not just any clothes. These are Lolek's shirts. Lolek likes me to wash his shirts with my own hands. This one, for instance . . ." She pulled a dripping shirt from the basin and showed it to me. "I'm washing this one for the third time. He wasn't satisfied with the way I tried to rub out the lipstick stains."

I had the feeling that at any moment Edgia would snatch the knife from the table and hold it against my throat. I left the kitchen and returned to the sofa in the living room. Edgia followed me without the knife, drying her hands on a small towel.

"I am so grateful to you," she whispered, before coming to an abrupt pause, as if she lacked sufficient air to finish the sentence. "Grateful for what you do for Lolek. Be patient with him. People like him require a great deal of patience. He will soon be here and then he will also wish you a happy birthday. Personally I don't celebrate any birthdays. I have too many dates of birth to remember. You were the midwife at one of my births, or rather rebirths, remember, Rella?" She stared at the black tomcat, who was rubbing against her legs as if she were addressing the question to him and not to me. Then she pointed her chin at the window, through which we could see the cross on top of the mountain. Illuminated by electric bulbs, it shone into the room through the navy blue darkness of evening. "Do you see that cross up there? Beautiful, isn't it? But I have the impression it's missing something. Guess what?"

"Jesus!" I exclaimed and burst into awkward laughter.

She nodded. "Yes, Jesus. Every cross should have its Jesus, and every Jesus should have his cross. Do you understand, Rella? The cross is the question and Jesus is the answer. Sometimes I believe that I am just such a cross and that I carry my Jesus on my back."

I looked at her inquiringly. Did she really mean what I thought she meant? But how could she, in her otherworldliness, ever have fathomed the depths of Lolek's tormented soul? I again gave an awkward laugh.

"Believe me, it's not a joke!" Edgia shook her head and put her hand to her breast. "I know Lolek's kindness, his generosity of heart. He would take the shirt off his back for you, for his friends, for all of humanity."

"But mainly for you," I ventured to give her a little prick.

"Certainly, mainly for me. For me he takes his shirt off so that I should wash it. He knows how I love to wash his shirts. It makes me so happy that he has chosen me to do this for him. You could search high and low and you would never find such another good man like Lolek. Why, he's practically another Jesus!"

She sounded so sincere that the laughter died within me as a chill passed up and down my spine. I was gripped by apprehension that at any moment she might start to extol my kindness as well.

* * *

Later that evening, when I finally went out into the street with Lolek, he began to complain that Edgia was the major cause of his depressions, that something was terribly wrong with her physically and mentally, that she was absent-minded, lost in her own world, that she talked to her cat as if it were a person—friend and enemy at the same time. She kicked and caressed the cat, laughed at him and cried over him. Lolek said that he had no common language with Edgia, that her mind was mired in the nineteenth century, that she read and reread Tolstoy's novels, sighed and lamented over Dostoevsky's victimized and degraded characters. On those nights when Lolek did not eat dinner at home, Edgia's own meal consisted of nothing more than a turnip, as if she were still living in the ghetto. And sometimes she did not even eat that. If she did not go into work, then she did not see another human being all day long, nor take a breath of fresh air. It was no wonder, then, that she was always sick and that her head did not function properly.

"She can sit for hours by the window and stare at the cross," Lolek complained. "When I ask her what she's dreaming about, she answers that she is dreaming of a time when all the world's Jesuses will climb down from their crosses, become astronauts, and move to other planets. Because here on Earth they don't fit in properly, and they do great harm without meaning to, and for this reason they are idolized. Those are the kinds of idiocies she tells me! As for the way she looks and the way she dresses, you can judge that for yourself. I know that all this is a hangover from the camps, and it's not that I am purposely impatient with her, but if a person behaves like a worm . . . She looks like such a martyr with her saintly Cunegunda face and her frightened, mousy eyes."

"Maybe if she had a child she would recover more quickly," I suggested hesitantly.

"What do you mean, Rella?" Lolek looked at me with reproach. "She herself is worse than a child, and certainly more helpless. Years ago she used to nag me about having a child. So I told her quite openly, 'First you yourself must grow up!' Do you understand, Rella? I could never have forgiven myself if such a thing happened. I don't want to have the responsibility of a child on my conscience. Fortunately, she no longer mentions it. But I still have the feeling that I don't treat her well enough."

"You treat her very well!" I jumped at the chance to defend Lolek against himself. "I see the sensitivity with which you treat her. I'm full of admiration for your patience and consideration. The very fact that you don't leave her . . . You sacrifice yourself for her."

Gratefully, he kissed my hands with cold, dry lips. Then he continued talking: "You have no idea what talent these broken people have for provoking feelings of guilt in those nearest to them. I would do anything to escape the guilt. I would run as far away as I possibly could." Lolek smiled sadly, like a little lost boy. "But how does a person escape from guilt? Can one escape from oneself?"

I felt an ache in my heart. I made an effort not to think of myself but to concentrate on Lolek instead, which was much less painful. "You don't have the least reason to feel guilty," I consoled him. "You say yourself, and rightly so, that this is all the fault of the camps. That's what broke Edgia, not you. On the contrary, you are what keeps her alive."

* * *

That evening Lolek was so serious, so immersed in his existential sorrow, that I gave up the idea that I had had earlier of going with him to a nightclub to celebrate my birthday. Instead we drove up to Mount Royal and took a walk around the lake and through the woods. The air was pleasant, mild and caressing. It was late in June, one of the first true summer evenings. But our mood was not at all summery. Lolek's despair was contagious. My heart overflowed with compassion for him—yes, for him, not for Edgia. For her I felt only jealousy mixed with contempt. Her pathetic behavior at once pleased and irritated me. I could not forgive the power that she had over Lolek—the brutal power of her weakness.

I turned Lolek's situation over in my mind until I came to this conclusion: "For you," I said, "it would certainly be better to leave her. No person has the right to poison the life of another. She is destroying you. I can see it clearly. She clips your wings. You will end by losing your *joie de vivre*, your interest in life. She might, heaven forbid, drive you to who knows what!"

Lolek waved his hand dismissively. "I'm a coward. I don't want to have her on my conscience. She would never be able to survive a single day without me. She is the cross I must bear."

"You call this cowardice?" I exclaimed, full of admiration. "I am speechless . . ."

I kissed Lolek by the light of the lamps on the mountain, kissed him with more tenderness than ever before, even though his lips remained dry and cold. We were standing under the illuminated cross on the mountaintop. I looked at Lolek's pale, suffering face in the glow of the electric lights that outlined the cross in liquid gold. I was ready to give myself to him right there in the dark shadows the cross threw over the blue bushes. More than at any time previously the torments of his soul made the blood boil in my veins, and I was overcome by a passionate longing for him.

After a while I succeeded in convincing him that we should go to my apartment—it would be his present to me on this special occasion. I found it humiliating to have to resort to this particular argument when not very long before he had been so eager to spend an evening at my place. But I also derived pleasure from my humiliation, which helped me to mobilize all my female charms. Thanks to them I even managed to talk him into staying with me the entire night! It was one of the most beautiful nights of my life, because if I still envied married women it was only for the reason that they spent entire nights next to the warm body of a man. Despite the fact that I had lived alone for so many years, I was still beset by a terrifying loneliness every night when I lay alone in my empty bed. It seems that, just like hypochondria, the craving to be with another person is an affliction for which there is no cure.

At the beginning of this night with Lolek, images frequently flashed through my mind of Edgia lying alone in her bed the way I usually did.

But after a while I imagined that she was not alone but lying together with Lolek and me, entangled in desperate proximity.

In the morning, after I had gaily chattered away an hour at breakfast, while Lolek sat across from me, sleepy and somewhat bewildered, the moment finally came when he had to leave me and face the harsh realities of life. He went home to change for work. Not long after he left, Edgia called. Her voice grated hoarsely.

"Is Lolek all right?" she asked.

"Why do you ask if he's all right?" I asked her back, in order to gain time while I decided what to tell her. The receiver in my hand seemed to weigh a ton.

"I understood that he is with you," Edgia went on. "This is the first time that he hasn't come home to sleep. I stayed up all night looking out the window for him. He didn't even phone, so I began to worry whether—God forbid—something might have happened to him." Suddenly she cried out in an exaggerated tone of childish delight. "Oh, he's just come in! Guess who I'm talking to on the phone, Lolek, sweetheart?" I heard her exclaim. Then she shouted into the receiver, "I must hang up! He won't let me talk to you. He says that you are a creative and productive person, and you are in a hurry to get to work." She hung up.

I was surprised when, late that same day, Edgia called me again. "Lolek wants me to invite you to our place for breakfast tomorrow," she mumbled. "Tomorrow is Saturday, and he wants me to tell you that you must on no account refuse."

"What do you mean?" I stammered. "What for? And why doesn't he come to the phone himself?"

"He says that he's in a bad mood. A deep depression . . . And he wants me to invite you myself in order to show that I am not angry at him and not at you. So I'm inviting you."

I understood what was at issue. Lolek needed this gesture on my part. So I suppressed the unease that I felt in my heart, and the next morning went off to take my breakfast with them.

As we sat down at the table in Edgia and Lolek's kitchen, Lolek—with extreme politesse—bade Edgia prepare a glass of hot chocolate for me. I usually drank hot chocolate with my breakfast every Saturday morning. Edgia had also prepared my favorite Saturday breakfast, pancakes with maple syrup. Lolek complimented me on my figure, telling Edgia that I never needed to count calories because I was a creative and productive person. I burned them off with all my energy and accomplishments.

The pancakes tasted heavenly. You could say what you liked about Edgia but not that she was a bad cook. As usual, somewhere in the back of my mind there nagged the suspicion that Edgia had put poison in the pancakes. And she looked so awful in that faded housecoat of hers—her pale face had a bluish cast, and her small mousy eyes were rimmed with red—that I almost lost my appetite.

* * *

That summer went by like a dream. It was a glorious, joyful time, followed by a long, golden autumn. I felt wonderful. The air around Lolek and me vibrated with something close to incipient love—at least I thought it did. I was looking forward to an interesting winter season. Lolek made sure to buy our theater tickets well in advance so that the members of our group would have good seats next to one another.

That winter began with a series of snowstorms followed by a spell of brutally cold temperatures. The outside staircases of buildings like the one in which Lolek and Edgia lived had to be regularly scraped clean of the accumulated ice and snow. Even then they were dangerous because they were very slippery, making it imperative to hold on to the railing. But whenever Lolek was with me, and even when he was in the company of other women, he would run down—virtually fly down—the stairs so skillfully that the neighborhood children would gape with admiration.

That was how the tragedy occurred.

Lolek slipped while running down the stairs, not of his own building, but of a building of questionable reputation in Old Montreal by the port. His head knocked against the iron banister with such force that he got a hemorrhage. His wallet appeared to have been stolen even before he fell because there were no identifying documents on his person when he was found. It took thirty hours before his identity could be established.

After Lolek failed to come home to sleep that night, Edgia called me the next morning to ask how Lolek was feeling. Stunned and deeply hurt, I told her the truth—that I did not know because I had not seen him. When she began to whimper and moan that her heart was full of foreboding, I first tried to calm her, then lost patience and banged down the receiver.

I was in turmoil myself. At first I thought that something had in fact happened to Lolek—that was the effect that Edgia's apprehension had on me. But then I calmed down. There was only one thing that could have happened to Lolek, I told myself: he had spent the night with another woman. But this was not a happy thought either. After all, the past summer and fall had had a particular emotional significance for me; it had been the time when my love for Lolek had started to germinate. His disappearance this night was proof that he did not take me seriously and had not been sincere with me. I recalled what Pavel had told me about Lolek and his attempt to fool the world into believing that he had been a partisan. It suddenly dawned on me that a man who was false about one aspect of his life could be just as false about any other aspect.

That whole day I kept to myself. I did not call Lolek and Edgia. The next day Sylvia, Pavel's wife, phoned to give me the news of Lolek's death with all the gruesome details.

Our group of friends was in shock. The guiding light of our small familial circle had been extinguished. Lolek, who had been so full of life, of curiosity and playfulness, of ideas and idealism, who had been so greedy for joy and pleasure, was no more. It was difficult to make peace with the fact. We felt orphaned. But whatever grief the others felt I felt doubly. With Lolek's passing from the world, fate had played me a spiteful trick. Lolek, dishonest and false though he was, had been a light in my life. I had never gotten to the point of actually loving him—

another proof that the camps had forever deprived me of the ability to love—but I had badly wanted to love him. I had taken delight in the pretense of being in love with him. Now the abyss of my loneliness yawned before me, and I was engulfed by darkness.

* * *

During those days of mourning, we all worried about Edgia. We were afraid she would have a complete breakdown. How would she ever be able to go on living without Lolek? She had worshiped him. And how, in practical terms, would she manage? She had never made the slightest move without Lolek. She had always lived in the clouds. Nor was she physically very strong.

But after a while, as often happens, our friends stopped calling or visiting Edgia. Nor did she keep in touch. Other dramatic events in the lives of this friend or that took priority, and our contact with Edgia was completely broken. The group hardly noticed this. Just as they had once hardly noticed her actual presence, they now did not notice her absence. She would, in any case, not have fitted into our group without Lolek.

As for me, I did remember her. I remembered her very well, and in a strange way I began to miss her even more than I missed Lolek. Deep in my heart I felt some satisfaction that Edgia, the living proof of my humanity, existed in this world, and I felt relief that the tragedy had occurred to Lolek and not to her. More than once I had the impulse to visit her but forbore because I could not predict her reaction to such a visit nor how I myself would handle it.

In this way more than a year passed. I heard from acquaintances that Edgia was beginning to return to normal, that she went to work at the leather factory every day and that somehow she was learning to master the handbag business. People started to say she had a strong character. Then I heard her factory was growing and that despite the recession she had been able to hire two more artisans. Word also went around that she was exploiting her workers.

Time went on. I found myself thinking often of Lolek, yet more often of Edgia. I still intended to call her. More than once I already held the receiver in my hand when a warning voice ordered me to put it down. What should I call her for? What would I say to her? Should I ask her to forgive me? Did I really regret my conduct with Lolek, even if strictly speaking it had not been morally kosher? Did I not hold dear all my memories of the hours that we had spent together? And why willingly throw myself to the wolves? I expected that now Edgia would point her accusing finger at me—and so take her revenge.

So things went until one evening I suddenly found myself face to face with Edgia during an intermission at the theater. She was standing in the middle of a group of men and women, total strangers to me, holding a glass of liqueur in her hand. Of course I did not have the slightest doubt that I was looking at Edgia, although the sight of her stunned me. Before me stood someone entirely different from the person I remembered—a blooming, attractive woman, an apparent reflection of myself.

She was wearing an elegant suit, and my professional eye immediately discerned that it was made of the most expensive imported fabric and was cut in the style I myself had introduced into fashion. In her high-heeled shoes, which were very similar to mine, with her thin shapely legs, her perfect posture, with the head carried proudly above the shoulders, she seemed taller than the shrunken Edgia I had known. In fact she seemed almost as tall as I was. Her small face, with its delicate features, its short nose and tiny mouth, was framed by a halo of wavy hair, dyed black—my hair color—and it was combed in my style. She reminded me of an unfurled flower. Only a few deep wrinkles on her forehead, which I noticed beneath the strands of hair, bore witness to the fact that it had not been easy for the flower to straighten herself.

The odd thing was that despite our strange resemblance it took Edgia a long time to recognize me—or perhaps she only pretended not to know who I was. But when she noticed that I remained rooted in one spot gaping at her, she gave a gasp of surprise and hurried toward me with a radiant face. She threw her free arm around me and pressed me so tightly to her bosom that, just as in the past, I was afraid that she would crush me. She then ordered a liqueur for me and introduced me to her companions. She praised me so effusively to her friends, with such eloquence and humor, that the blood rushed to my face, and I felt embarrassed and uncomfortable.

"Rella is a creative and productive person," she concluded. Then she asked me what I thought of the performance. "Pinter really gets to me," she said. "He's as powerful in his way as Tennessee Williams is in his, don't you think?" She discoursed enthusiastically on Pinter, displaying such erudition that I was overcome with envy. Her eyes glistened with delight.

"Why don't you ever come to our get-togethers anymore?" I felt prompted to ask.

She answered defensively that she had no time. "The days are too short now that I have to manage the factory, and I have no end of things to catch up on. But let me know the next time you go somewhere. I will gladly join you. I haven't seen you all for so long!"

Our group of friends began to meet with Edgia again. After all, there was so much that tied us—and especially me—to her. And every time we met with her she rose another notch in our esteem. Of her former giggling, stammering self not a trace remained. On the contrary, she was forceful and convincing in what she said. She was clever, profoundly knowledgeable, and had a wonderful sense of humor. She contributed the salt and pepper to our table talk. Even the reticent Pavel took her seriously and because of her began to participate in our discussions. We started to sense that without Edgia our get-togethers lacked luster, even more than had been the case with Lolek. Somehow Edgia's presence added weight and meaning to the friendship of our group.

I would say that the only obstacle to our getting along harmoniously with Edgia was the fact that she was a woman. What an irony! We women noticed that she bewitched the men—and especially Pavel—with her cleverness and charm. This meant that a gradually lengthening shadow of jealousy fell across our admiration for Edgia. We were ashamed of this feeling. After all, this was the same Edgia as of old.

As for me, I felt even worse than the other women. Edgia humiliated me by usurping my position in the group. I certainly did not lag behind her in intellectual matters, especially not when it came to contemporary issues. But just like Pavel, Edgia mocked modern culture and the group's tendency to be swept up by the latest trends in books, paintings, plays, and music. She thought all this flimsy and irrelevant, just passing fancies, the result of the postwar confusion of values in all spheres of human endeavor. She held fast to her Shakespeare, her Tolstoy, Dostoevsky, Thomas Mann, and the like. And the upshot of it all was that I, who had once taken such an active part in our discussions, was now afraid to open my mouth. I was afraid that at the least provocation Edgia would contradict me with some devastating argument, that she would discredit me in front of everyone or that in the heat of discussion she would point an accusing finger in my direction and exclaim, "How dare you speak! You were a kapo!"

But the mysterious power of attraction that existed between Edgia and me ensured that, despite all complicating sentiments, it was precisely at this time that she and I should become truly intimate friends. In addition to the past, which bound us so closely, we now had a business connection through my fashion boutique and her handbag factory. We understood each other's business problems, and we inspired one another in matters of style and advertising. I was flattered as well—although I sometimes suspected that she was mocking me—that she religiously followed my advice on how to dress and on fashion in general.

Edgia was in the best of health both summer and winter. I never heard her utter so much as a sigh. When I once mentioned her former illnesses, she replied as if she herself were surprised: "Yes, they have all disappeared. Maybe I was too spoiled." She winked at me. "Taking up sport must have done me some good."

Edgia had become a disciplined sportswoman, displaying an unexpected skill in whatever she attempted. She tried tennis and talked me into playing with her. She and I also met first thing every Saturday and Sunday morning, rain or shine, at the top of Mount Royal, just below the cross. Dressed in our sweat suits, we would jog the few kilometers down to the lake and then up again to the cross. This done, content and perspiring profusely, we would set out for my apartment, take a shower, and busy ourselves in the kitchen. Edgia prepared her famous pancakes and I prepared my specialty, a delicious cup of hot chocolate. Then we stretched out on the bed, put on a record of classical music to please Edgia and another of modern music to please me, and chatted and joked, sometimes also discussing more serious matters of the heart—but we never touched on anything remotely related to the camps.

If the topic of Lolek came up, we did not try to avoid it. On the contrary, we both became very involved in the conversation. There was not the least hint of reproach in Edgia's attitude toward my relationship with Lolek. At times I had the impression that his memory was dearer to me than it was to her. When we spoke of him my voice sounded less steady than hers. At such moments, I felt more than ever that I was in her power, but somehow this no longer bothered me. And so our conversation would flow on in a tone of heartfelt regret. We would analyze Lolek's complicated tragic personality and then let him swim away on the current of our words while we concentrated on people and events more closely connected to our present-day lives.

I began to need Edgia more and more, and she seemed to need me. I felt acutely not only Edgia's intellectual superiority but her superiority as a person of clean conscience. I was always alert to what she might say or do. I became her echo. I copied her wisecracks and witticisms. I craved her praise and gave in to her in everything. For her part, she seemed to copy my mannerisms and my style. She copied my appearance, my bearing, and my attempts to keep up with the times in matters of fashion. From time to time we felt the urge to needle one another with sarcastic questions or remarks, but I was always careful not to arouse her anger.

One day when I was at her apartment I suddenly realized that the black tomcat was nowhere in sight. So I asked her, "Edgia, I don't see your Loverboy anywhere. What happened to him?"

She stared at me as if she did not understand what I was talking about. Then my meaning dawned upon her and she burst out laughing.

"Oh, my tomcat, you mean? He's been gone for three years. I accidentally scalded him with a kettle of boiling water."

I shuddered, as if she had at that very moment poured a kettle of ice-cold water over me.

* * *

Every year the pages of the calendar seemed to flip by with greater speed. My complicated friendship with Edgia flourished, but her friendship with the other women in our group faded because of her aggressive behavior and the attraction that she held for the men.

This was how things stood when we discovered that Pavel had fallen head over heels in love with Edgia. Pavel was in every respect Lolek's opposite. Despite his many good qualities, he had never occupied the same position as Lolek in our esteem. He did not possess Lolek's charm and boyish attraction. He was too sober, surpassing Lolek in one particular only—his honesty. He was, in fact, too forthright for my taste. More than once one of his remarks threw cold water on the group's spontaneous enthusiasms.

It was not long before Pavel separated from Sylvia, a separation quickly followed by a divorce. Pavel went to live with Edgia, and as day followed night, they soon got married.

This dramatic romance in the midst of our circle of friends brought to the surface undercurrents of antagonism against both Edgia and Pavel. We stopped meeting with them.

As for my own reaction, I felt a double dose of that peculiar pleasure that one feels at the misfortunes of others. It always gave me a secret satisfaction to hear that a couple had separated. This was proof to me that I had sacrificed very little by not marrying. But I was also pleased that Edgia had married again. I hoped this would diminish her uncanny hold over me. I believed I knew human nature well and could predict people's behavior. Edgia, according to my ideas, belonged to that type of woman who automatically assumes the same role with regard to every man with whom she has a relationship, even when the men are such contrasts as Pavel and Lolek. In my imagination, I saw Edgia stop imitating my looks and manners—which made me uneasy—and gradually revert to the servile, pathetically smiling little mouse I remembered from the days of her marriage to Lolek. It gave me pleasure to fantasize how she would look in her shapeless clothes. In my head I dressed her that way, adding a new black tomcat at her feet to complete the picture.

For a long time I heard nothing from Edgia and Pavel, nor did I run into them. Not that Edgia had ceased to occupy my mind or that I did not have the impulse to call. On the contrary, I could not stop thinking about her. But for my own good I forced myself to keep a distance in order to breathe freely in an atmosphere where no one knew of my past as a kapo and no one could point an accusing finger at me. I remained loyal to my group of friends. Anyway, I disliked Pavel. I even began to believe that I had finally freed myself of Edgia, despite my obsessive thoughts about her.

But the day came when I could no longer restrain myself. I managed to convince myself that the demands of business made it imperative that I get in touch with Edgia. I called her, but a strange voice answered in Greek, and I understood that Edgia had moved away from Esplanade Avenue. I searched the phone book and discovered that Edgia now lived in the elegant residential district on the other side of the mountain. I called her. She was very friendly—too friendly. She invited me to her house, or more accurately, I saw to it that she should invite me. After all, she had done me no harm, nor I her. At my age and in my loneliness I could not afford to lose good old friends. It was so difficult to find new ones.

So we stepped back into our friendship as if it were a pair of comfortable old slippers. I could once again keep an eye on Edgia. I was even more concerned than I had been with Lolek that Edgia should not reveal my secret to Pavel. I still felt a cold regard for him, and I was still frightened of his frank, penetrating gaze. I also saw to it that our group of friends should again begin to socialize with him and Edgia. Edgia, by virtue of her relationship with Pavel, had been neutralized, and the women's jealousy of her had evaporated. Besides, Sylvia, Pavel's former wife, had moved to Florida, where she had remarried.

As soon as we began to meet again at Edgia and Pavel's house we noticed that between these two there bloomed a late and ardent love—although mainly this appeared to be Pavel's love for Edgia. It radiated from him with an intense glow, a flame permeating the entire atmosphere of their house.

Every time that we visited—they invited us quite frequently—Edgia sat at the head of the table and led the conversation while Pavel served us, smiling with pleasure. Later, whenever we decided to meet at their place, we stopped saying that we were going to Edgia and Pavel's but said only that we were going to Edgia's. And that was how it was. Edgia dominated our get-togethers. If the always cheerful Pavel did venture to say something, Edgia jokingly finished the sentence for him, which amused all of us, including Pavel. And if Edgia held forth at the table, Pavel nodded his head encouragingly at her. If he made a remark to give her support, she tenderly put her hand to his mouth and said lovingly, "Don't help me out, dearest."

I became a frequent guest at Edgia's. She felt at ease in my presence, had no secrets from me, and only wanted to know how I would do certain things if I had been in her place. We used to relax in the alcove off her bedroom, sprawled in comfortable black leather armchairs that stood next to the window. On the window ledge was arrayed a row of flower pots. Edgia hated cut flowers. The mountain, topped by its large cross, loomed just outside the window.

"That cross follows me everywhere," Edgia complained. "It pierces my eyes. Maybe if I could hang a Jesus on it, it would leave me alone."

She said this in a whisper as if she were afraid that Pavel, who was busy in the kitchen preparing tea, should hear her. I never knew what she meant by this, but I was afraid to ask.

* * *

Edgia often discussed Pavel with me. She poked fun at his appearance and his negligent manner of dressing. Once when the subject of masculinity came up, Edgia asked me, "What would you do if you had to deal with a loverboy who was constantly melting with tenderness and affection at the same time as he was shockingly shy and inhibited?"

She never raised her voice when she spoke about Pavel, but she developed the habit of speaking in a hiss whenever she was irritated with him, which she often was. She called him "loverboy" in the same grating tone she had once used for her cat.

Since I was under Edgia's spell, I viewed everything through her eyes. Her attitude toward Pavel appeared to me quite normal, and I was pleased with it. After all, I had never liked him myself. It now seemed to me that he acquired the look of a moron whenever he was in Edgia's presence, that he had become a mere rag of a man without a shred of self-respect, a nothing, a zero.

So I nodded in agreement whenever Edgia hissed out her complaints against Pavel, which occurred whenever something in their house was not in order, or when Pavel did not bring something she requested quickly enough, or when the photos he had taken of her did not turn out well. I consoled her as best I could. I sympathized with her. I understood her despair and the extent of her existential malaise.

"He hasn't got the faintest idea what I am all about," she would complain. "Not who I am nor what I am. He never stops living in his own masochistic fantasies, beating his breast for having abandoned his wife and child forty years ago. He poisons my days. He clips my wings."

"You must break free of him," I advised her.

She stared at me with astonishment. "Break free of him? How can I? I would never forgive myself if I took such a step. Can't you see for yourself how attached he is to me and how much he loves me?"

* * *

I usually managed to avoid meeting Pavel, but one time I dropped in when Edgia had not yet returned home from the handbag factory. In order to have something to say, I asked him how Edgia was doing. His face twisted into a pained grimace. "Not too well," he answered, leading me into the living room. He turned to face me, and the deep blue of his eyes poured over me with bottomless sorrow. "That is"—he seemed to be forcing himself to speak—"that is, superficially, everything is fine, but deep inside her nothing has changed. Once she was servile, now she is aggressive, and it all springs from the same source, from her feeling of worthlessness. I had hoped that my love would cure her, but it seems that not even love can repair the wounds she suffered in the camps. Maybe if she could just bring it all out from inside her . . . But she refuses to talk to me about it. Did she ever tell you anything about her experiences in the camps, Rella? You are such close friends."

"Never!" I said sharply, feeling my throat tighten.

"Not one word, eh?" He shook his head, and as if he had grown tired of the tension, he sank into an armchair and motioned me to sit down as well. So we sat in silence for a long time and looked at each other. I felt very uncomfortable. I longed to hear Edgia's steps on the landing. I was about to jump to my feet and run out of the room when I heard him say, "She did once tell me about a strange dream she had. In that dream she saw herself in the role of a kapo. She even described how she looked and—forgive me for telling you this—but the figure in which she saw herself resembled yours. I tell you this, Rella, not in order to pain you, but in order that you should understand her better. She picks the closest people, those most devoted to her, to avenge herself on for the wrong that was done to her. Basically we are all like that." Now the blue of his eyes embraced me with sudden touching warmth. "We must stand by her, Rella. She is dear to both of us. And who can know as well as we what goes on in the dark corners of her soul?"

I don't know why, but I started to cry. The first and only time in my postwar life that I ever cried was in front of Pavel, of all people.

* * *

A short time later I learned from Edgia that Pavel had high blood pressure and a weak heart. Edgia insisted that he give up his work, and she became the only breadwinner. Pavel took care of the house. He bought food, cooked, and prepared the meals. Needless to say his cooking could not be compared to Edgia's. I know this for a fact because I frequently took my dinner with them. Edgia often forgot that Pavel was forbidden to eat heavily salted foods.

"You put on too little salt, Loverboy," she playfully caressed the top of his balding head. "What's the matter, don't you love me anymore?" Usually Edgia turned such incidents into a joke, and more than once when I was eating dinner with them my sides nearly split with laughter as Edgia comically mimicked her cook Pavel.

When we—I mean our group—drove out to the Laurentians for the weekend, Edgia proved the most energetic mountain climber among us. She would insist that for Pavel's good health he should climb with her on this or that moderately steep slope, which she had picked out beforehand to suit his capacity. She believed that he exercised too little and that mountain climbing would fortify him. When they returned from climbing and Edgia sat down to rest, she would send Pavel on errands—she required another pair of shoes, a cold drink, a handkerchief with eau de cologne to wipe away the sweat. When, panting, he finally sat down next to us, Edgia would describe how clumsy Pavel was at climbing. She did this with so much bubbling humor that the tears came to our eyes from laughing—and they came to Pavel's too.

When we vacationed in the Laurentians, Edgia did not neglect our usual routine of jogging in the morning. Seven o'clock sharp she would knock at the door of my motel room and at eight o'clock we would meet on the road that passed through a pine forest. Pavel waited for me along with Edgia. He ran beside us for part of the way, and when he got tired he sat down on the stump of a fallen tree to rest and wait for us.

As we ran, Edgia took pleasure in every blooming bush and every majestic tree. The sight of wildflowers awakened her enthusiasm. I nodded my head as she spoke, but I did not share her pleasure. When it came to the beauty of the Canadian landscape I might as well have been blind. I looked but I did not see. It was better for me that way. The landscape reminded me too strongly of the district that lies at the foot of the Carpathian Mountains, where I had used to spend summer vacations in my childhood. One time as we were running, Edgia pointed out a cluster of particularly colorful wild flowers and said, "In Auschwitz no flowers grew, remember, Rella? But when I was there, in order to keep up my courage, I would conjure up just such clusters of flowers in my imagination, and I would decorate the entire globe with them."

* * *

The last time we drove out to the Laurentians was on the eve of a hot summer weekend. When I opened my eyes the following morning I was drenched in sweat, and I could feel how heavily the air weighed on me. It was going to be an unusually humid day; the sky was preparing to storm.

That same morning, even before we began our jog, Pavel collapsed on the road, and Edgia and I could not rouse him. I ran back to the motel to call a doctor. When I returned to the road I could hear Edgia's wailing from the distance. I saw her sitting in the middle of the road, Pavel's head and part of his body cradled in her lap, as if she were the Pietà and this was to be her last comment on the theme of the empty cross.

"What have I done? Oh my God, what have I done?" she cried.

Pavel was driven to the hospital. Edgia never left his side. Whenever I entered the hospital room to visit Pavel, I saw Edgia sitting in the same position, bent over her husband's body, swaying over him, mouthing half phrases and broken words. As soon as she saw me she would stop talking and stare at me through red, swollen eyes. All the sorrow of the world screamed at me through those eyes. I realized that I had yet another Edgia before me, a completely new person with a new emotional makeup, a new knowledge, that had no connection to the sort of knowledge I and our friends had so eagerly pursued. Who was this new Edgia? I was very much afraid of her.

The last time that I came into the hospital room, Edgia stared at me for a long time with those same eyes. A strange worshipful expression smoothed and relaxed her face. She straightened herself, came out from behind Pavel's bed, and approached me. So we stood, eyeball to eyeball. That was when I heard her dry, heavy voice speaking these fateful words: "I thank you, Rella, for having saved my life. I thank you for everything. I have decided that we two, you and I, should never in our lives meet again. I no longer want your friendship, and I no longer want to give you mine. It was a sick, a poisonous, an impossible friendship."

Her words shattered my heart like an explosion. A pall of darkness fell over me. Edgia's sentence seemed to pulverize me, to reduce me to dust. The end flashed before my blinded eyes, and ever since that day I have peered into the depths of that end.

* * *

I never saw Edgia again. From acquaintances I learned that Pavel was out of danger. Edgia brought him home, took care of him day and night, watched and trembled over him. Friends told me of the atmosphere that permeated their house, and in my imagination I visited them, sensed the heavy silence, the expectation, as if someone were constantly praying. Then I heard that Pavel was much recovered, that he was walking around the house. Carefully, not wishing to betray the fact that Edgia had thrown me out of her life, I continued to seek out news of them. This was the thread that I tried vainly to hold on to. In this way I learned that Pavel could go out of the house and that he was well on his way to a full recovery; that in their home there was now an atmosphere of peace and calm, that from both Edgia and Pavel there radiated joy and serenity. I was told that Pavel had become more talkative than he had been before and that Edgia's humor was no longer so aggressive and biting but had grown milder and gentler.

Not long after these events I began to lose the desire to join the others at our get-togethers. I hardly noticed how distant I had grown from them, nor how I was losing my passion for things that had once interested me. I no longer possessed the drive or the eagerness to chase after the always-changing times. Time became for me a stagnant water that had crystallized in one spot. I peered into it and saw that all that remained to me was the nakedness of my guilt, which I no longer had the means to dress. My loneliness no longer troubled me. I avoided people and at the same time took a dislike to my beautiful apartment and my *boutique européenne*. I ate my meals in restaurants and sat there for long hours staring straight ahead and seeing nothing.

After a time I heard that Edgia and Pavel had also lost contact with the group. Like stars drawn toward different orbits, we had finally managed to tear ourselves away from the constellation of the friendship which had held us together for so many years. The last news I had of Edgia and Pavel was that they had liquidated all their assets and set off on a long voyage around the world.

* * *

And now I too am about to embark on a long voyage, a voyage which Edgia precipitated by removing herself from my life. With this she canceled my only moment of humanity, which I had thought would cleanse me of all sins. She had never pointed an accusing finger at me, and so she left me with the feeling that I must point the finger at myself, that I must let all the world know that I was a kapo.

This was Edgia's revenge. So be it. I am, in any case, sick and tired of the fear of being found out, sick and tired of myself. So I sit here and stare at my medicine, my vial full of sleeping pills, brightly colored like beads.

Every criminal craves the moment of judgment, no matter how afraid of it he might be. I sentence myself willingly. I return to the camp, to the scene of my crime. The slice of life I managed to sandwich in between the two camps—the camp that was forced upon me in the past and the one that I am about to force on myself—was not tasty, nor worth the price I paid for it. I remove the lying inscription above the entrance to Auschwitz, *Arbeit macht frei*, work makes you free, and replace it with another, "Death makes you free." I take the hand of my little sister Maniusha and promise her that I will never betray her again.

Little Red Bird

It has not stopped snowing for three days. The snow falls so lightly that it seems motionless, as if it were gossamer suspended in mid-air. But a closer look reveals snow petals floating playfully through the air or whirling weightlessly within shifting spirals before dissolving on the ground.

Manya is standing by the window, peering out at the snow. A little girl is playing in the street among the mounds of snow. The child is about five years old. She wears a red coat and a red hat, just like Little Red Ridinghood, the child the wolf tried to devour in the story by the Brothers Grimm.

Manya's child was in fact devoured by the wolf—a wolf who was, in a sense, a grandchild of the wolf in the Grimm brothers' story. Manya's child had been destroyed by the Germans when she was five years old. Her name had been Faygele, Little Bird. She too had had a red coat. When she wore the red coat her parents called her *roit faygele*, little red bird. Her parents delighted in the sight of Faygele wearing her red coat. The color suited her. It harmonized with the dark brown hair her mother would roll in tissue paper to form curls. The curls peeked out charmingly from underneath Faygele's red hat. It did not occur to Faygele's parents to associate the color red with the color of blood—Faygele's blood.

"It says here in the paper that Pakistan has most likely acquired the atomic bomb," Manya hears Feivel say. Feivel is her husband. Since it is

Saturday, he is not working. For many hours he has been sitting in the armchair near the fireplace, reading the double edition of the Saturday paper.

Manya and Feivel met after the war in the displaced-persons camp of Feldafing in Bavaria. Both had been members of the Bundist youth organization in Poland; he in Kracow, she in Lodz. They had discovered each other during those confusing post-liberation days of hope and despair. Neither of them had any surviving family, so their need for closeness and intimacy with another human being was great. The quality of the air around the DP camp in Feldafing near the enchanting Starnberger See—a former vacation spot for the Nazi brass—was conducive to the flowering of awkward romances between former concentration camp inmates or those who had arrived from exile in Soviet Russia. The surroundings infused their conversations and expressions of affection with an air of unreality.

From his previous life in prewar Poland, Feivel has retained a great interest in politics. He still worries about the world, and so does Manya. They devote a lot of time to reading newspapers, listening to the news on the radio, and discussing the world situation. This habit is a holdover from their socialist upbringing, when they were both members of the Bund. There are people who suffer from professional deformations; Manya and Feivel suffer from a political deformation that shows itself in their passion for politics and in their adherence to the Bund, a left-leaning political party most of whose membership had perished in the crematoria. They are both upset about the direction the postwar world has taken, about the fact that the sacrifice of millions has been in vain. But in Manya's case, there lingers beneath the surface of her general sorrow over the fate of the world an additional, more intimate pain, which translates into a longing to have another child.

* * *

"The world weighs heavy on my heart all day long," Manya hears Feivel say, half in jest.

Usually on such a Sabbath day, Feivel is very active around the house. He arranges whatever needs to be arranged, working with his hammer, fixing things that need fixing. Energetic and active by nature, he is what has come to be called a workaholic. When he can find nothing useful to do around the house he spends his time constructing toys for children. In fact, a large part of the garage is taken up with cartons full of the miscellaneous parts of broken appliances. He refuses to throw anything away. From these scraps he skillfully, magically creates toys. He nails, hammers, files, saws, carves, then paints and decorates every finished creation until it assumes an identity of its own, becoming "something out of nothing," ready to start a new existence in the service of some child's imagination. Feivel is amazingly inventive. He is a magician enchanted by his own magic, which transports him into another world.

Whenever there is a celebration at the home of one of his and Manya's acquaintances, Feivel always has a toy ready to take along for the children. He is embarrassed by the fact that he finds it difficult to part with even the most insignificant plaything, but he cannot help it.

This morning, despite the laziness that has crept into his bones, Feivel decides to light a fire in the fireplace. It will chase away the gloom, he announces. When the fire flares up, he contentedly rubs his hands together and says to Manya: "Look, Manya, how brightly the flames dance around inside." Manya does not turn her head to look at the flames cavorting in the fireplace. She does not want to miss even one second of watching the child in the red coat playing outside.

She finds no beauty in the sight of the fire blazing in the fireplace. On the contrary, it horrifies her. It reminds her of the crematorium fire that swallowed her Faygele. Of course, she does not say so to Feivel. She never objects to his lighting a fire in the fireplace. He likes to do this, so let him enjoy it. After all, he has never been incarcerated in a concentration camp, and he was not Faygele's father, so he cannot be troubled by the associations that disturb her.

Faygele's father perished in the crematorium at the age of twenty-five. Manya and Faygele's father had loved each other with a young couple's love—a joyful, innocent, and naive love. When the Germans invaded Poland, Manya and her handsome young husband tried to save themselves. They wanted to begin a new life and find a safe home for Faygele. So they ran to the border, intending to steal across it into the Soviet Union and there search out a place to live. But they ran out of luck. The Russians caught them and deported them back to the Polish side. The Germans packed them off to the ghetto. From the ghetto they were herded into boxcars, along with their families, and transported to Auschwitz, where all perished except for Manya. The fire did not swallow her. She was destined to live, and after the war, fortune rewarded her when she met Feivel, her second husband.

Feivel had spent the war years in the Soviet gulag. For him, the seasonal frigidity of Montreal was just a minor nip compared to the intense cold of Siberia near the Arctic Circle. Feivel had suffered tortures from the frost, which froze the big toe on his left foot so that it had to be amputated. He is still persecuted by visions of vast frozen deserts, as well as by visions of lice. Even today, so many years after his incarceration, he has the ugly habit of scratching himself when he thinks that Manya is not looking. She knows that whenever he is alone he scratches himself. Every day he stands under the hot shower for an hour or longer. Every day he washes his hair with a pungent liquid that gives off an ugly smell. Then he rubs his skin with a rough towel, as if he were his own torturer. The cupboard in the washroom is piled high with bars of soap, which he constantly replenishes as though in fear that the supermarket might run out.

He likes to poke fun at himself. One day he even joked to Manya that he would gladly swallow a bar of soap in order to cleanse his inside, which he felt was just as dirty as his outside. She understood that this was one of those meaningful jokes that signifies a feeling of guilt, most likely for having abandoned his first wife and their two small children. When the Germans entered Krakow, Feivel was forced to escape, since he had been a leader of the Bundist youth organization and had served as a Bundist city councilor. The Germans had his name on their list of those they would round up first, so he ran away. His wife and children were supposed to follow, but he never saw them again. When he returned to Poland at the end of the war he found out that they had perished in the death camps.

Manya has another suspicion about Feivel's mental state. She believes he also feels guilty for having betrayed Bundist comrades in Soviet Russia. Being a Bundist in the USSR meant a death sentence. During one of his interrogations, the NKVD interrogator placed the muzzle of a revolver against Feivel's temple. Feivel told Manya about these experiences when they met for the first time in the DP camp in Feldafing—she a Bundist from Lodz, he a Bundist from Krakow. Even today Manya thinks she sees the fear of death peering out of Feivel's eyes.

This fear of death strengthens the bond of love between them; it keeps them bound to one another in many complicated ways. It plays a role even in their lovemaking, in which their former spouses somehow seem to be participating. Manya and Feivel's life together is a dual conspiracy, a futile means of effecting an escape from the constant threat of unbearable, unspeakable memories. This is why Manya can bear, without even a twinge of disgust, the sight of Feivel scratching himself. Nor is she repulsed by the offensive odor emanating from his scalp. On the contrary. She is attracted to him. They desire each other with desperate passion. They have nobody else in the world but each other—and this sad, pitiful happiness of theirs.

It is a sad, pitiful happiness because a curse hangs over it. Ever since Manya and Feivel first met they have been dreaming of establishing a family and having a houseful of children. But in all the years of their marriage Manya has been unable to conceive. She is barren and is consumed by the burning desire to hold a child in her arms, to caress it, fondle it, press it to her bosom, and imbibe with her kisses the balm of consolation over the loss of Faygele. In the past ten years she has tried many times to adopt a child through the Baron de Hirsh Foundation but has constantly been refused. Her war experiences are still too powerful, they impinge too strongly on her mental condition, say the psychiatrists to whom the foundation has sent her.

The doctors cannot understand why Manya is unable to conceive. She, however, does understand it. It is on account of Faygele's father.

He will not permit her to become pregnant. He considers her a traitor. So do the murdered members of his and her families. They surround Manya's bed whenever she and Feivel make love. She feels them shadowing every step she takes and sitting in judgment on everything that she and Feivel do. They are all on the side of Faygele's father.

"First love is a sacred love," they tell her, as though she did not know this.

She *does* know it, and she knows as well that Faygele's father is jealous. He begrudges her the sad happiness that she enjoys with Feivel. But mainly Faygele's father will not permit Manya to conceive on account of Faygele. "Faygele's memory requires all your devotion," she hears him say.

He is right, of course. But how can he ever imagine that her memory of Faygele would fade? Even if she brought a houseful of other children into the world, would not Faygele still have Manya's eternal love? How could it ever be otherwise? How is it possible that Manya should not carry Faygele's name sealed on her lips forever, even though she never utters that name aloud? Even after Manya's death, the memory of Faygele would hover in the air above Manya's grave. Such a powerful, indestructible longing can never be erased. The voice of Faygele's father, which echoes in Manya's head, talks nonsense. It has become the voice of an irascible person, a severe, vengeful voice.

In order to escape that voice and to calm her grief Manya frequently goes for walks on streets where she will pass shops with children's clothing. She stops in front of them and peers in through the window, looking at the bibs, or the tiny socks and shoes, or she admires the displays of little girls' dresses adorned with flowers and ribbons. The coats and hats attract her, especially when they are red. She has never yet been able to pass such a store without entering. She looks around, moving from one rack to another, touching one tiny outfit, then another. She seldom leaves the store empty-handed.

At home she plays with the tiny outfits. She sees them inhabited by soft, living bodies. She imagines the delicate limbs, the round faces, and hears the echoes of gurgling laughter. An entire drawer of her bedroom cupboard is filled to bursting with these miniature ensembles. Whenever one of her acquaintances gives birth to a girl, Manya has a ready gift to give her. And every time she wraps the gift in pink paper, she feels an ache in her heart. To part with a never-worn little dress, one that has absorbed the warmth of a mother's never-expressed caresses, is not an easy thing.

Feivel, who is busy wrapping a gift of his own, understands her very well.

* * *

The snow has not stopped falling. Peering through its white, frosted curtain, Manya can see the little girl's red coat vibrate slightly, as if it were both real and unreal, as if it possessed hypnotic power. She feels herself attracted to the child. She longs for it so badly that her entire body quivers with the desire to touch the small figure, to hold it in her arms, embrace it and press it to her bosom.

"Is something wrong, Manya, my dear?" she hears Feivel ask.

"Heaven forbid," she responds.

"Are you angry at me?"

"Why should I be angry, darling?"

"Because when I said that there are rumors that the Pakistanis have the atom bomb you didn't answer me."

"What is there to answer, Feivel dear? I'm looking at a beautiful little girl playing outside in the snow. Such a delight to look at her."

Feivel sighs. "I'm afraid that I'm the one with the problem. I don't feel right in my skin today," he says. "I don't know what's happening to me. A laziness has crept into my bones, and I feel as if a rock were sitting on my chest."

* * *

Although he has never said so, Manya suspects Feivel of holding her responsible for the emptiness of their home. Of course he knows that it is not her fault, but he cannot help himself. It is because of her that he has not become a father again. She once proposed to him that they separate so that he might find another woman and have children with her. But Feivel scolded her for saying that and warned her never to bring up the subject again. In her opinion, this was the best proof that he was thinking just such thoughts but did not dare allow them to rise to the surface of his consciousness. Manya believes that his preoccupation with constructing toys is another indication of the same thing.

* * *

The glowing logs crackle in the fireplace as if they are about to explode from Manya's tension. She cannot bear the silent reproach hovering in the stillness of the room. The air is so stifling that it is impossible to breathe. Manya sees herself running out of the room. Where is she running? She is running toward the child in the red coat who is playing outdoors in the fog of snowy whiteness. She is trying to break through the curtain of dizzying, frosty light to reach the little girl and say to her, "Come for a walk, Faygele."

She sees herself walking with Faygele, who hops along playfully by her side. Manya hands her a toy clown Feivel has made. When Faygele pulls at the string, the toy clown bends his legs and blinks his eyes roguishly at her.

Manya and Faygele enter the park, where there is a joyous commotion. The park is full of mothers and children who slide on their sleds, glide by on their skates, or tumble down mountains of snow. Faygele runs around and Manya runs after her, trying to keep up. Manya cannot shake off the tension she feels. She is afraid that Faygele might get lost, afraid that the flames of the crematorium, or the fallout of an atomic bomb, might destroy her. Manya grabs hold of Faygele's soft, plump hand. What a sweet feeling to hold a child's hand in the palm of one's own! Manya feels the warmth of the small, tender hand with its soft-boned fingers. The warmth spreads all over her body. How could anybody destroy a creature who has such soft, plump hands, such small, delicate fingers?

Manya cannot let go of the hand. She will steal the child! Yes, she will kidnap her, and together they will hide from the world so that Faygele can once again resuscitate Manya's soul. Manya has such a powerful impulse to take the child, an impulse that she cannot control, but which she must control, because she could never hurt the little girl's mother by depriving her of her child. Oh, she knows very well the bitter taste of that pain. To this day she feels the violent wrench at her heart and the unbearable weight of her suddenly empty arms. To rob a mother of her child is the greatest sin imaginable, even if one has not the slightest intention of harming the child. On the contrary. Manya wants to raise the little girl on the milk of love that has gathered in her breast to the point of bursting.

Suddenly the little girl bursts into tears, as if she were frightened by Manya's thoughts. "I'm scared," she cries. "I want to go home to my Mama. I want my Mama."

"I am your Mama."

"No you're not. My Mama's hand is softer than yours."

"There's a strange pain in my right arm," Feivel mutters. He is sitting in the armchair beside the fireplace, bent forward as if he were being pulled to the floor. The creased newspaper rests in his lap under a hand limply rolled into a fist.

* * *

Manya is smiling at the little girl who is playing in the snow in front of the window. She waves her hand at her. The child does not see. Manya imagines how the little girl would have looked when she was smaller, when she was three, for instance, or two. Manya sees her own Faygele learning how to walk, taking her first steps. She thinks back to Faygele's birth and feels in her nipples the pain and delight of nursing Faygele for the first time.

"I'm having trouble moving my right arm," Feivel moans.

Did Feivel say something? Manya sees herself riding a bus in the direction of the Jewish General Hospital. In the past she has gone there to visit, just as a pastime. She feels at home at the Jewish General Hospital. In that magnificent building there is a constant struggle with death—but in the obstetrics wing, life is constantly renewing itself.

Manya would gladly strike up a conversation with the nurses of the maternity ward. But she dares not accost them, although in Poland she had been a nurse. In the concentration camp she worked in the infirmary, performing the most unproductive of all medical functions, that of putting the patients back on their feet so that they could march to the death chamber under their own steam.

Manya takes the elevator up to the maternity ward. As soon as she enters the bright corridor she sees a nurse coming toward her. This time Manya cannot restrain herself and speaks to the nurse: "This ward is the exact opposite of the infirmary where I worked in the concentration camp. There people suffered from hopelessness, while here they give birth to hope."

The nurse stares at her, unable to grasp Manya's meaning. After a moment she breaks into a knowing laugh. Her laughter mingles with the sounds emanating from the open doors of the many rooms; it mingles with the cries of the newborn babies and the delighted squeals of the new mothers. Manya regrets having accosted the nurse. She has no right to be here. They might expel her before she manages to steal some joy for herself.

She sneaks into the small room where the nurse, standing behind a glass partition, holds up the newborns to show to the family and friends of the parents. Envy grips Manya's heart, an envy so powerful that it demolishes all scruples. She is unable to stop herself as she spreads four fingers at the nurse on the other side of the windowpane, asking to be shown the baby in crib number four near the window. And so the miracle happens. To Manya's delight, the smiling nurse appears at the window with the swaddled baby in her arms. She lifts it very close to Manya's face on the other side of the pane so that Manya can have a good look. It is a beautiful baby! Such a sunny face that Manya screws up her eyes in order not to be dazzled by the light. "Faygele!" Manya exclaims and smacks her lips at the baby.

"I once had a little girl like this one," she says to the woman standing beside her by the window. "The Germans killed her when she was five years old." The woman casts a piercing glance at Manya and steps back in fear—or so it seems to Manya. "I would have been a young grandmother by now, and my Faygele would have given birth, perhaps in this very same ward, and become a young mother . . ."

The woman standing on Manya's other side inquires, motioning with her eyes at the baby in the window, "Your grandchild?"

"Yes," Manya replies. "My daughter Faygele's daughter."

* * *

Manya finally steps out of the room into the corridor of the ward. She notices that no one is at the nurses' station that adjoins the waiting room. The nurses are busy making the rounds of the ward, carrying babies to their mothers for nursing. Manya takes off her coat and hangs it up on a coat rack in the waiting room. She removes a white coat from a peg on the wall behind the nurses' station, puts it on, and makes her way boldly from one patient's room to another. A divine radiance emanates from the flushed faces of the mothers. Trembling slightly, they clumsily busy themselves with the tiny bundles of life cradled in their arms. Manya assists them. With respect and gratitude in their eyes, the new mothers listen to her instructions. She teaches them how to hold the babies closer to their breasts and how to suckle them. As she does so, she plays with the babies' tiny fingers, allowing them to grip her own. She kisses the soft-boned fingers and allows them to wander into her mouth.

She walks from one room to the next until she comes to a room where a pretty young mother, one of her breasts exposed, is reclining on a white bed. In her arms she is cradling the baby Manya had seen through the glass earlier. The pretty young mother is at a loss. Saliva bubbles on her lips as though she herself were a newborn infant.

"What's the matter?" Manya asks her.

"She doesn't want to suck. She doesn't know how to take the nipple." The young mother is near tears.

"Nothing to worry about, my child." Manya strokes the mother's shoulder and smiles reassuringly at her. "She'll learn the trick in no time. Instinct will teach her. But now, my dear, please forgive me for disturbing you in your pleasure. I must take your daughter away for just a few minutes for a blood test. We'll take no more than one tiny drop of blood. She won't lose a single hair from her head, I assure you. After all, how could anybody want to hurt such a magnificent little creature?"

Carefully, delicately, Manya lifts the baby out of its mother's arms and carries it into the corridor. She jerks her coat off the coat rack in the waiting room and covers the baby with it. Walking rapidly past the elevator, she heads for the exit door to the stairwell, then she runs down the stairs with the precious bundle in her arms. So many stairs, going down, down, down! At last she is in the street. Only now does she realize that she is still wearing the white nurse's uniform.

* * *

As soon as Manya brings the baby into the house and deposits it on the bed, a brightness fills the entire room as if the sun in full radiance had burst through the snow that is still falling on the ice-cold world on the other side of the window.

Manya hears a strange sound, a pounding, a groaning sound, like an aborted screech. She has probably shut the door too loudly, despite her extreme caution. Now it is quiet in the house. She has not had a chance to look around, but she is aware that Feivel is not at home. This surprises her. Where can he have gone on a Saturday, leaving the fire untended in the fireplace? But she has no time to look into the matter right now. She has to hurry. The life of a baby is in her hands.

She leaves the sleeping baby on the bed and rushes out to the supermarket to buy some milk formula. She also buys a large number of bottles so as never to run out of milk for the baby, no matter what. She buys a supply of diapers, pacifiers, baby powder, Vaseline. This chore accomplished, she hurries to the shops of children's clothing and purchases an entirely new wardrobe for the baby girl. True, she has a drawer full of baby clothes at home, but for this occasion she must have something special. She also buys a red coat and a red hat. She will save them for when Faygele is five years old. But she does not buy a single toy. There can be no prettier toys than the ones Feivel makes. After all, he constructed them all for their daughter.

* * *

Manya keeps no secrets from Feivel. He is her only friend. As soon as she can she shows him the baby, and as she had expected, he clicks his lips at it. Only later does he reproach Manya with the hideous crime of breaking a young mother's heart. But as he scolds her, she reads tenderness and gratitude in his eyes. After all, he too is dying to have a little Faygele, a little bird in the nest. He has suspected that Manya might one day concoct such a plan, even though it is a criminal act. He knows that she is capable of risking her life in order to brighten their sad home. He loves her too much to divorce her, and she loves him too, very, very much. Nevertheless, neither their love for each other nor the well-being of their home can justify the crime that has been committed. It is a horrible crime, horrible in particular because the perpetrator is a former concentration camp inmate.

But it does not occur to Feivel to go to the police. If he did so, Manya would have to go to prison for a long time. And what did he do to deserve being deprived of his beloved Manya? No, he would rather become a partner to her guilt. They would share the punishment and together be incarcerated in the prison of their consciences.

* * *

Manya and Feivel, nervously, anxiously, pack their belongings. They are getting ready to leave the country. The police will very soon be on their trail. Feivel is full of energy. He looks younger and healthier than ever. His muscular arms, with their swollen blue veins, bulge out from beneath rolled-up sleeves as he carries the suitcases to the car. He sits down at the wheel and soon, forelocks flying in the wind, he is heading down the highway. Manya sits beside him, holding Faygele on her lap.

The highway stretches into an infinity that seems to be without horizon. The police are in hot pursuit of the two criminals who hide in museums, where Feivel takes the opportunity to study the maps of the world. They sleep in public libraries, where Feivel pores over thick tomes of world history. But search as he may, he cannot find a single spot on the entire globe where Faygele could enjoy a safe peaceful future. Interpol, Scotland Yard, the CIA are after them. Nobody is willing to give refuge to the child abductors. All ports are shut tight, all borders are off limits.

"No admission to child stealers!" scream the posters hanging at the entrances of all the borders.

"Turn back! Turn yourselves in to the police!" voices blast from the loudspeakers on ships.

It is not the first time in their lives that they have heard these injunctions. This is how they were shouted at in the past, when they were innocent. The newspapers are full of pictures of the kidnapped child's mother. Her tear-stained face appears on TV. Weeping, she appeals to the public to help her find her little girl. Manya sobs along with her, and along with her, she appeals to the public.

* * *

At the Mexican border the traffic of illegal crossings is flowing in the opposite direction—out, not in. This is good. There is nobody guarding the entrance. And so the three of them cross the border and travel until they reach the Yucatán Peninsula, former home to the ancient kingdom of the Mayas, a land of majestically hovering pyramids that dominate their surroundings. Feivel, Manya, and the child mingle with the crowds of tourists climbing the pyramids. Everywhere they find traces of the old civilization, along with traces of the brutality that was

part of ancient religious rituals. A stone altar where humans were sacrificed to the gods decorates the entrance to one of the ruined temples.
One can still see the sports arena where the sportsmen competed fierce-
ly with one another, each team vying for the honor of being proclaimed
the winner because only the victors were granted the privilege of being
sacrificed to the gods. From time immemorial the gods have thirsted
for blood. In every corner of the globe humans have built altars of one
sort or another to sacrifice victims of their own species. To search for
peace is futile. There is no choice but to continue living in the shadows
of these altars.

A year earlier Manya and Feivel had visited the Yucatán as tourists. They had come to celebrate their twentieth wedding anniversary.
They had spent unforgettable days here, and for this reason they have
now returned and set up house in the hacienda on the other side of the
main pyramid.

* * *

Manya dresses like a Mexican Indian so that no one should recognize
her. Feivel grows a bushy Mexican mustache. He wears a poncho and
hides his head under a sombrero. He looks very virile and attractive.
At night they dance in the shade of the pyramids by the light of the
enormous stars. Mariachis strum on their banjos, singing melancholic
tunes interspersed with hot rhythms that heat the blood in their limbs.

Faygele grows fast. She is five years old. She is already wearing the
red coat and the red hat that look so becoming on her. She is a beautiful child. The tourists visiting the pyramids are enchanted by her and
cannot stop staring. Manya's heart is full of pride at the same time as it
freezes with fear, in case one of the tourists should become suspicious.
Feivel suffers from no such qualms. He abandons himself to his delight
in Faygele. He is the tenderest of fathers. He tells Manya that he has
only just begun to realize how badly he had wanted a child. At times
he even forgets that the child is not his. Manya and Feivel are delighted
with their stolen Mexican happiness.

But not Faygele. Faygele is unhappy. She is growing up with the strange feeling that Manya is not her mother.

"Don't call me Faygele," she says to Manya.

"Why not?" Manya asks, as a shudder creeps down her spine. "Aren't you my child?"

"No, I'm not."

Faygele bursts into tears, as if she were frightened by Manya's fear. "I'm scared," she sobs. "I want to go home to my Mama. I want my Mama."

"I am your Mama."

"No you're not. My Mama's hand is warmer than yours."

Every time that Manya hears these words she panics and her heart pounds in her ears.

* * *

Faygele dreams of the land of snow, about which Feivel has told her many stories. So the three of them prepare to return to that land in order that Faygele can see the snow for the first time and go for a sleigh ride. It is a joyful trip. Manya is lighthearted and playful. As soon as they reach their destination one snowy afternoon, Manya dresses Faygele in her red coat and cap and seats her on a sleigh Feivel has made.

Manya trudges through the snow-covered streets, pulling the sleigh in the direction of the Jewish General Hospital. They leave the sleigh at the hospital door and take the elevator to the maternity ward. Manya leads the little girl to the desk in the brightly lit corridor and pins a small note to her collar.

"Wait here," she says to the little girl. Cheerfully she plants a kiss on the child's forehead and turns away. She takes the elevator to the lobby and goes outside. There she sees the sleigh that Feivel has made. She does not want to part with it, so she slides it along behind her. She walks back home, pulling the empty sleigh through the snow of the street.

The maternity ward nurses at the Jewish General Hospital notice the child in the red coat and the red hat who stands at the desk, waiting for someone. They smile at her and she smiles back. They notice the note pinned to her collar and read: "I am the child who was taken from my mother's arms five years ago. I vanished from this hospital and this ward. I want to go back to my Mama."

* * *

Manya turns her head away from the window. As her eyes slowly focus on the room, she sees Feivel sprawled in the armchair, his head resting on his shoulder, his arms dangling limply above the floor. The creased newspaper lies between his oddly turned-in feet. He looks as if he were asleep.

Outside, the snow continues to powder the street. The little girl in the red coat and red hat glides through the white fog. The fire crackles in the fireplace.

François

François was born and died suddenly. He was born in his finite form as a Parisian Frenchman living in Montreal, a man of nondescript age clad in a checkered suit made of English tweed, a pair of reading glasses tucked into his breast pocket. Underneath his jacket he wore a turtleneck jersey. His head was covered with thick, wavy, chestnut-brown locks, and he sported a bushy, rectangular mustache over his full upper lip. His brown, suntanned face was covered with wind-etched wrinkles, while his brown, dreamy eyes hinted at the concealed longings of his soul.

* * *

It all started on a winter's evening during a raging snowstorm. Mountains of snow blocked the lower half of the view from the windows of the house. The white snow seemed to be reflected in the navy blue darkness of the sky. Like gleaming kernels of ice, the frozen moon and stars swam in and out of the web of white, transparent clouds. Thin strands of smoke, disturbed by the wind, rose from the chimneys on the neighboring roofs. They looked like columns of steamy breath exhaled from large stone mouths. There were fires going in the fireplaces of most of the houses.

Leah peered out through the living room window. She was waiting for Leon to return from work. The house was quiet. But to her it seemed that the howling wind was inside the room, augmenting the mute howl that escaped from her heart. "What is it that weeps inside me and gnaws at me so stubbornly?" she asked herself. Was it that she had been all alone in the house the whole day, just as she had been alone the day before and the day before that? For the past two days, the raging snowstorm had piled mountains of snow in front of her door and windows.

Not so long ago a snowstorm would not have kept her from venturing outdoors. On the contrary. She had found it exhilarating to march against the wind and driving snow and to stubbornly resist the onslaught of the elements. But neither today nor yesterday nor the day before had her willpower been functioning properly. In fact, her willpower had recently entered an irresolute state. For certain physical activities, such as housework, which she performed mechanically, she still had some stamina left, but her will to engage in any kind of intellectual activity had long since deserted her. Instead a strange howling had settled within her. "What is it that gnaws so at me? What do I crave?" she asked herself.

The rumble of a car's engine reached her from outside. The glare of headlights shone into her face through the window like the eyes of a black panther. After a few minutes Leon entered the room. He gave her a frozen peck on the lips and stroked her cheeks with ice-cold hands. His glance rested on her for a moment.

"You should start tinting your hair and go for facial massages," he remarked, giving her a comradely pat on the shoulder. "Every woman your age does it nowadays."

Leah set the table. The evening meal was sitting on the stove ready to be served. She served it, surveying Leon closely as she did so. His black hair was beginning to acquire a silvery sheen at the temples, but he was still a robust and fit man. Hungry and talkative, he sat across from her at the table, still wearing his white shirt and tie. He was telling her about his day at the office. His black eyes jumped back and forth between her face and his plate. The movement of his facial muscles and the definite way he had of eating attested to both his vigor and his restlessness.

In the first few years after his arrival in Canada, as soon as he had earned some money, Leon had begun to deal in real estate. He had such success that soon he was able to buy a house of his own. He could afford to send his children to the best universities in the United States and to take pleasure trips with Leah to Israel and the rest of the world.

Leah understood little of real estate matters, but she usually paid great attention to what Leon said about his business so that she would not blurt out any silly remarks. Once in a while she interjected a comment or asked a question in order to create the impression of a cozy, domestic atmosphere in the house, of a husband and wife sitting together at the kitchen table engaged in interesting conversation during dinner.

Tonight, however, she neglected to follow the train of Leon's talk and instead continued the conversation that she had been carrying on with herself at the window. She tried to conceal her inattention from Leon by murmuring a word or two during his talk until, of course, she blurted out something silly.

He burst out laughing. "You haven't got the least idea what I'm talking about. Where is your head, my dear wife?"

Where was her head? "I lost it!" She joined in his laughter.

They finished dinner in a cheerful frame of mind. Leon patted Leah affectionately on the arm and asked her to bring his glass of tea over to the telephone. He picked up the newspaper—he was a keen follower of current events—and sat down at the telephone table. He had the habit of talking on the telephone while simultaneously leafing through the newspaper. A substantial part of his business was conducted in the evenings, on the telephone. Sometimes Leah would think of him with a sense of compassion and guilt. He was such a busy person, so overburdened with work, while she was a lazybones who did practically nothing all day long. Sometimes when he was feeling hostile toward Leah, Leon would burst out in a reproachful tone of voice, "Who the hell am I slaving for if not for you and the children?"

No wonder that she felt indebted to him, although she did not see things in quite the same way as he did. In her opinion it was not a case of self-sacrifice at all but of compulsion. He was driven by a strange inner force to chase after a chimera that had taken the form of dollars, although she was convinced that money was not really his primary goal. What, then, was his primary goal? What was *her* primary goal?

While Leon sat at the telephone, Leah cleared away from the table. Recently she had lost all interest in watching television. She went up to the bedroom, put on the FM music station, and stretched out on the bed. Very quietly the notes of Wieniawski's violin concerto drifted into the room. Ever since her children had left home to study at the university, she had had more time to listen to music—and more time to listen to herself as well; that is, to her thoughts about herself and about Leon.

Now, as she lay on the bed, she also thought about him. Caressed by the notes of the violin, her thoughts of Leon grew warm and affectionate. She recalled how she and Leon—he had called himself Leibel then—had met after the liberation from the concentration camps. They had both been left all alone in the world. They clung to each other—two orphans facing a cruel, alien world. Leibel wanted badly "to stand on his own two feet and begin to live," as he put it. He moved heaven and earth in order to get a visa to the United States for himself and Leah. Failing in that, they decided to settle in Canada. From his first day on Canadian soil Leibel began laying the foundation for their new life, a new life he inaugurated by changing his name from Leibel to Leon. At first Leah had worked too. She was fortunate enough to find a job as a saleslady in a department store. She had retained some French from her high school years and had started to learn English right after the liberation. Her knowledge of the two official Canadian languages was an asset. But as soon as Leon began to climb the ladder of success he would not permit her to continue working. Her role was to manage the home and bring up the children.

Leon was a good father and a good husband. True, he was not a man given to overt expressions of affection or tenderness. His kindness was expressed in his deeds. He never failed to buy flowers for her birthday, or for the anniversaries of their wedding, or for Valentine's Day; sometimes he even bought her a piece of jewelry as a gift. During all the years of their marriage it had only happened three or four times that he had forgotten one of these important dates.

He was generally an amiable and friendly man. People liked him and enjoyed his company. On the trips that Leah took with him he was the first to make the acquaintance of their travel companions. He had an enormous fund of jokes and anecdotes stashed away in his memory, which helped him to win the friendship of strangers. Moreover, as an expert on current events, he was capable of carrying on a knowledgeable conversation on serious political subjects. People sought out his company and enjoyed socializing with him at restaurants. He was also a good dancer. Not overly tall, he was sturdy and agile and moved with the graceful steps of a panther.

Leah appreciated her good life with Leon. She had nothing to complain about. On the contrary. During all the years she had spent with Leon she had managed to educate herself. She studied her children's school subjects. She also soaked up some of the modern youth culture. With its screaming music and wild dances, it was not exactly to her taste, but she wanted to be on the same wavelength as her children and thus strengthen her spiritual bond with them. Indeed, her bond with them had never weakened; it had only become somewhat unraveled. It was there still, although it existed perhaps more in her heart than in theirs—but such were the laws of life.

After the children left home she tried not to become overly depressed by the sight of the empty nest. She read a lot, read and read, making her way through entire shelves of books. Mostly she was interested in Romantic poetry, the kind of poetry that was the least fashionable; although to tell the truth, people in general rarely read poetry anymore. Poetry was studied in the universities. So she enrolled in university courses in order to complete her education and sharpen her understanding of poetics. But very soon she stopped attending the courses. She felt that academic analysis destroyed the emotions that the poems awoke within her. So she attended concerts instead or listened to music at home. She hardly noticed when and how she had grown tired of reading, or was overcome by revulsion whenever she saw a book lying around.

She then began experimenting with painting. She bought watercolors, oils, pastels, and canvases. But nothing came of it. She tried to write and began keeping a diary, but she cast that aside as well. She obviously had no particular talent for anything. Her heart was swollen with feelings to the point of bursting, but she could not find an outlet through which a fraction of all that she felt might seep through and give her some relief. Then it occurred to her that the routine of a regular job might perhaps relieve her. It would give her the sense of being a useful citizen who participated in the forward march of society. So she resisted Leon, who believed that she ought to stay home and take care of the house, and eventually she found a job as a substitute kindergarten teacher for one year. Then she volunteered at a hospital. She was also active in the Jewish community and threw herself heart and soul into a variety of community projects. There could, of course, be no talk of her becoming politically involved. Unlike Leon, who thought of politics as a chess game writ large, with the entire world as chessboard, she was irritated by politics. It brought her to the verge of despair. Political events after the Second World War had disillusioned her too much.

At length she realized that all the activities that she had undertaken had done nothing to cure the rip in her soul. They had only plunged her deeper into pits of boredom and despondency. She gave them all up. She frequently asked herself whether what she needed was not, simply, a friend. Of course she had various so-called friends, friends of the family, with whom she and Leon would spend time during the weekends. But then it was he who would carry on the conversation.

Their group of friends were postwar immigrants like themselves, people who enjoyed the same kind of conversation that Leon enjoyed. Their conversation made for a pleasant few hours spent on gossip or a discussion of local events or international intrigue spiced with jokes that Leah, as a rule, knew by heart. These conversations deepened her sense of alienation not only from society but also from her own self.

Perhaps the wisest thing would have been for her to strike up a conversation with Leon himself and open her heart to him. After all, he was the person nearest to her heart. True, he had the habit of talking down to her, sometimes quite roughly. But of what significance was that when set against his essential kindness toward her? And he was smart, intelligent, involved in life. But what would she tell him? How could she find the words to explain the ache inside her? Even if she succeeded in expressing what she felt, he would not understand what she was talking about—precisely because he was so clever. Most probably he would tell her that she was spoiled, that her life was good and she shouldn't complain.

For a friend she needed an intimate, sensitive soul mate. Leon, kind though he was, was not her soulmate. Perhaps she needed a lover? She was still quite attractive when she dressed herself up; sexual impulses still vibrated within her, perhaps even more today than in former times. But to take a lover would be to cheat on Leon. And it would require too much energy. She would need to fix herself up, become coquettish, fake good cheer when she did not feel cheerful, be false—false toward Leon, false toward the lover, most of all false toward herself. She did not want it.

Something seemed to have gotten stuck in her throat. She rose from the bed and went down to the dining room. She heard Leon talking animatedly on the phone. She took the bottle of whiskey from the cupboard. For the last few days, when she had been cooped up in the house, she had been drinking more than usual. She took the bottle and a glass and went back upstairs. Leaning on her elbow, she lay on the bed and sipped at the burning liquor as she listened to the music rise to a crescendo of rage and despair. She conducted the music with rhythmical jerks of her head. The walls of the room seemed to revolve around the bed. Hot tears burst from her eyes and she wept, smiling at the light that circled round and round the ceiling.

Somebody was standing in the doorway. A familiar figure. A pan-therlike creature. Who was it? It was Leon, of course. She was drunk, but in her head a little island of sobriety still held its own against the sea of drunkenness. She always tried not to become intoxicated to the point of losing control. Her tearful eyes attached themselves to the circle of light on the ceiling, and in an exaggeratedly loud voice she exclaimed, "Francois!"

The dark figure stood a while longer in the doorway. "So you've got yourself good and soused, my wife?" she heard Leon say before he burst into harsh laughter. "Who is this fellow François all of a sudden?"

"François!" she exclaimed louder still.

"Which François? Who is François?" He repeated the question in a grating tone of voice. And as she repeatedly called out the name François, Leon swept down on her with the speed of a hawk. He gave her cheek such a hard smack that she thought an entire whiskey bottle had shattered against it. "Bitch!" he snarled.

That was how François was born.

* * *

The next day the temperature rose and hard icy kernels of freezing rain pelted the windowpanes. Leah and Leon ate their breakfast in complete silence. He peered into the newspaper while she peered into the blackness of her coffee cup. Suddenly he raised his head and asked, "So you have a lover, do you, my virtuous wife? So, all these years, you've been carrying on with someone behind my back while I slaved away to provide for you?" He stared at her with such open hatred that her breath caught in her throat. Was Leon capable of hating her so much?

Keeping her eyes buried in her cup of coffee, she said quietly, "I swear to you, Leon, I do not have a lover. I never did."

"What do you mean you have no lover? And who is this François?"

"I haven't got the faintest idea. I drank too much last night. Perhaps . . . Oh yes . . . Yesterday at noon, I heard a broadcast on the radio about François Mitterand . . ."

A heavy silence followed. Suddenly Leon's facial expression changed as if he had put on a cheerful mask. He burst into hearty laughter. "*Oy, gevald!* What stupid ideas can pop into my head! What an idiot I am! You with a lover? Good heavens, how could such a suspicion have entered my mind!" He got up from the table, walked over to her, and gave her a cheerful pat on the shoulder. "Forgive my craziness. Forget it."

Normally she would not have reacted to his poking fun at her or to the raw language he used while talking to her. She would tell herself that he meant nothing by it. After all, he treated her very well. His coarse language was a leftover from the war; it was the psychological deformation of a former concentration camp inmate. Perhaps there was still something in her demeanor that reminded him of those years he so badly wanted to forget. As long as he did not offend or invade her shielded inner world she did not mind. Let him talk. It was only her external form—the part of her that he called "my wife"—that was unprotected from his stare. And that part of her was of secondary importance.

This time, however, she raised her head from the cup of coffee and looked at him with hurt in her eyes. "I don't know whether I will ever be able to forget the slap in the face you gave me last night, or what you said to me. I don't know whether I can ever forgive you for making my life so bitter after all that we went through during the war. My happiness should be sacred to you, as yours is to me."

He did not grasp what she was saying. "Oh, for heaven's sake, don't preach to me. What do you expect? That I should carry you around on my arms?" He blinked teasingly at her. "Lose some weight; then maybe I might do that for you." He grew thoughtful, and after a moment of silence he said, "Do you know what? I'm going to leave the car with you for the day and take a taxi to the office. Go for a ride. It will refresh you. Yes, pull yourself together, my wife. Enjoy life a little!"

* * *

He left in a taxi, just as he promised. Leah got dressed and went to the garage. She started the car and began driving through the icy rain that fell on the snow-covered street. Ice pellets tapped against the roof and windshield of the car as it slowly slid down the street past the houses with the mountains of snow piled in front of their windows and doorsteps. The accumulated snow was still fresh, and the icy frosting on its surface, created by the rain, shimmered like crystal. The freezing rain pounded the road with hard white pellets, causing the middle of the road to shimmer like a carpet encrusted with diamonds.

At first there were many cars in front of her. People were driving to work, incessantly honking their horns. Truck and car wheels groaned and squealed against the slippery snow and ice. But after a while the road became freer, quieter, until it transformed itself in front of her eyes into a broad, nearly empty highway of shiny whiteness. Silvery ice-covered pine trees appeared by the roadside. The freezing rain encased them and everything around them in a misty spiderweb of icy threads. Then Leah noticed François sitting beside her on the front seat.

She heard him recite the verses of Verlaine: "It rains in my heart, as it rains in the street. What is the name of the longing that gnaws at my heart? It rains for no reason in the heart without a heart. What, no betrayal? Sadness without a name? This is the worst kind of pain. Not to know why. Without love, without hate, my heart is full of woe."

She smiled at him through misty eyes. "True, *l'amour est morte, l'ame est morte*. Love is dead, the soul is dead. Is there a meaning to it all?"

"The soul lives on in the death of love," he replied.

He was dressed in a checkered jacket with the rolled top of a turtleneck jersey visible above the lapels. His eyes, hot with longing, caressed her face, drying the tears on her cheeks. "Aren't you cold, sitting like that with no coat on?" she asked.

"I'm hot," he smiled broadly at her, a smile of exactly the right amount of sweetness to erase from her memory the bitter taste of Leon's cynical grin. "By the way, I have regards for you."

"You do? From whom?"

"From God."

She waved her hand with playful dismissiveness, "He's a dream, just like you are."

"But you believe in me, don't you?"

"Just as much as I do in Him. Basically I'm an atheist. And let me tell you another important fact about myself, François. I was an inmate in a concentration camp. In the camps, you see, all the gods perished together, along with those who believed in them."

He drew a pair of glasses from the breast pocket of his jacket and inclined his body toward her face, as if intent on reading it. "I get the impression," he said, "that you talk about your stay in the concentration camp as if you regarded yourself as both a heroine who deserves praise and a victim who deserves to be pitied."

She shook her head. "Oh, that is not what I meant to say . . . No, not at all. I meant to say that I expected something more from life after the liberation."

"Expectations are seldom fulfilled, except in dreams. That's why it is good to dream. In dreams hopes come true; in dreams they become more beautiful and precious than one ever anticipated, and one comes to realize how good it is to be alive in this world."

"These are all clichés! It is only when your life is threatened and you are about to lose it that it becomes beautiful and precious. So very precious."

"That's how you feel right now, isn't it? You still can't see any meaning to your life. But if there were no meaning to your life I would not be sitting here beside you. I am the answer to your yearnings for happiness."

"Happiness!" she exclaimed. In her agitation she lifted her hands from the steering wheel. The car skidded from side to side. François put his hand on top of hers in order to help her recover control of the car. But the opposite happened. The car began to spin. Fortunately there was no other traffic nearby. She clasped the wheel more firmly in her hands and, maneuvering carefully, finally succeeded in making the vehicle straighten itself as it continued along the road. "Where are we? Where are we going?" she asked. "Do I want to lose my life?"

"Heaven forbid!" François laid his warm hand on her forehead.

"Don't cover my eyes! I can't see the road! Where does it lead?"

"It leads to the Laurentians. I own a cabin on Mont Tremblant, the trembling mountain, the mountain for those with tremors in their souls."

"You too have tremors in your soul?"

"Yes, tremors very similar to yours, *ma chérie*. But I am a skier. Skiing binds me to nature. I am a believer in nature. Summertime I go for long boat rides on the lake. I've got a rowboat. But mostly I like swimming. Then I feel at one with nature, as if I were still in my mother's womb."

"Even nature can lose its charm."

"You've just told me that your heart has swollen to the point of bursting, so how can nature lose its charm for someone like you?"

"When did I tell you this? Did I also tell you that I don't know who I am, what I am, or why I am? That I've lost my 'I' and don't know where to look for it?"

"Look for it in me."

"An illusory 'I'?"

"A consoling 'I'—expansive, rich, and closer to the truth than truth itself."

"You are telling me tall tales, my hot-eyed bluffer, aren't you? I think that I'm about to fall in love with you."

* * *

The following day Leah chatted cheerfully with Leon at the breakfast table. She pleaded with him to again leave her the car and take a taxi to work. He could afford it. He could see for himself how driving about town had refreshed her. He had in fact noticed this and conceded the point. He promised to buy her a car for her next birthday. Until then he would leave the car for her use whenever he did not need it.

That day François appeared on the seat next to Leah as soon as she drove the car onto the road. "Yesterday you almost made me crash on this highway," she reproached him.

"You're not in danger of ever crashing. You are *une survivante*. You know, I visited your concentration camp immediately after the war. I was with the French resistance under the leadership of the *Maquis* commander François Mitterand. We saved a number of Jews from death."

"And now you've come to save a Jewess from life?"

"That's the reason why he brought us together, *ma bien aimée*."

"Who is he?"

"The Supreme Commander."

"Yours, not mine."

"Both of ours."

"What do you mean by both of ours? You're not a Jew. That's your only fault."

"But I am not a non-Jew either."

"You're on the side of the Quebec separatists, aren't you?"

"I support none of the 'ists,' with the exception of the fantasists."

"The optimist fantasists, or the pessimist fantasists?"

"I belong to the movement of the escapists, of the seekers after love, of the pursuers of meaning. You should know this by now."

"I do, but you must be making a living somehow."

"I make a living from you."

"That doesn't mean that I understand you any better. You must be doing something in this nonexistent life of yours."

"Of course. I work at the Université de Montréal as professor of Romantic poetry. This term I'm teaching '*Le bateau ivre*' by Rimbaud. I am your *bateau ivre, mon amour.*"

"Do you intend to perish by drowning and take me with you?"

"People like you don't drown. You've paid too high a price for your life."

"Is that so? And what about Paul Célan or Primo Levi or Adolf Rudnicki or Jerzy Kosinski? They all committed suicide after the war. Is it only writers who are capable of ending their dearly bought lives? Don't I have a talent even for that?"

* * *

Every day François sat with Leah in the car for a couple of hours. She never invited him into her home, although she was there alone all day long. She was afraid that, once inside, François would not have enough air to breathe. So she preferred to drive around with him through the outskirts of town. At first she experienced no physical desire for him. It was only the festering wound in her heart that needed him as a balm, nothing else. But soon she felt a greed for him rising along her limbs, a greed that grew stronger with time. As soon as she had the city behind her, she rented a motel room for a couple of hours. François was with her. His body was beautiful, like Michelangelo's David grown middle-aged. François was very affectionate with her. His words sounded more beautiful than any love declaration she had ever heard in a French film. He spoke in a language that was beyond language.

"You are beautiful, *mon amour*," he told her.

"How can this be?" she wondered. "If Leon heard you say this he would explode with laughter. He doesn't think that I am capable of attracting a lover, let alone a lover like you—the best of lovers. You have wonderful hands, François."

"They're suited to your tears. You can weep into my cupped palms."

"The tears might overflow your fingers. I haven't wept for such a long time."

François stroked the graying strands of hair on her head. "Eyes overflowing with tears speak to me of the deepest depths of human loneliness, depths filled with a music of their own. Your mouth absorbs my sadness, while my love for you dissolves the darkest, most indifferent silence of the universe."

"It is you who have made me beautiful," she answered. "The wounded stag jumps the highest, I heard the hunter say. Are you familiar with that line, François? It's from a poem by Emily Dickinson."

He gathered her into a protective embrace. "Let me be your sanctuary. Let us pray to the beauty of our nonexistent love."

* * *

A few weeks passed. Leah sat across from Leon at the breakfast table. Leon could not bear her false cheerfulness. He could not get used to her changed behavior. It made him nervous.

"You look awful," he said to her. "What happened to your eyes? They're red and swollen, all puffed up. You ought to make an appointment with the eye doctor. And why don't you tint your hair a decent color to cover the gray? It would refresh you." He grew thoughtful and reached out to pluck a large shiny apple from the bowl of fruits on the table. As he peeled the red skin, he seemed to be weighing something in his mind. Finally he said to her, "Do you know, an idea has just popped into my head. It's obvious that you need a change. Why shouldn't we go on our trip to South America now instead of waiting for spring? We'll aim for real adventure. We won't follow the tried-and-true tourist track; we'll seek out what other people rarely get to see."

She stared at him in astonishment, unable to make out whether he was serious or merely amusing himself at her expense. Was it possible that he too was seeking something? What did he hope to find?

* * *

They were seated in a small, shaky airplane with twenty other passengers, flying over Maracaibo Lake in Venezuela, on their way to the famous Angel Falls. The airplane was half empty. On one side of Leah sat Leon, and on the other François.

"I am with you," he whispered in her ear. "In case you need me." He wore the same checkered jacket that he usually wore for their encounters.

"Aren't you too hot?" she asked him.

"I am always hot," he smiled softly. "But I'm not in the habit of perspiring."

The leader of the excursion, a youngish-looking woman with bleached blonde hair, wearing a navy blue summer suit, busied herself energetically about the airplane. She peered out through the windows, giving explanations to the tourists in a heavily accented English, an accent that was not Spanish but sounded rather Slavic.

"And now, ladies and gentlemen," she pointed a manicured finger at the window, "we're flying along the Orinoco River basin, which extends to the foot of the Andes. The Orinoco River is the longest river in Venezuela. The Angel Falls release their waters into one of its hundreds of tributaries. The Angel Falls are 3,212 feet high—the largest water-falls in the world!" The woman was standing beside the passengers who sat behind Leah and confessed to them, "Every time that I leave this paradise, this Eldorado, I burn with impatience to return as soon as I can." Leah decided that the woman's accent was Polish beyond a doubt. She was convinced that the woman was Jewish, that she was a Jewish woman from Poland.

Leon made fun of her: "What brilliant ideas pop into your head!"

"I'm sure that she's a survivor. She's my age. She probably has a number tattooed on her arm. Why else would she wear a jacket with long sleeves on such a hot day? Go ahead and ask her, Leon. You've got more nerve than I do when it comes to speaking to strangers."

Leon shook his head. "Leave me alone. Maybe you can forget your Jewishness and your concentration-camp madness for a while? We've come on this trip for a bit of pleasure, haven't we?" He indicated the blonde woman with his eyes. "She may be your age, but she looks twenty years younger than you do."

Suddenly the tour leader leaned toward another window and called out with hysterical exaltation, "Canaima! Down there is Canaima!"

"Canaima?" The passengers stared at her.

"There in the vicinity of Canaima National Park are the Angel Falls! One of the greatest wonders of the world!"

"When will we be there?"

"We shall be landing shortly," the woman nodded excitedly.

A few minutes later they disembarked onto an enormous empty field in the middle of a thick jungle surrounded by mountains. The out-door air embraced them with its hot, subtropical breath. On one side stood a number of low wooden cottages. A dozen half-naked Indians and Mestizos of mixed Indian and Spanish blood busied themselves amid an assortment of donkeys, dogs, and horses.

"We've now arrived at my *penzione*, ladies and gentlemen, my El-dorado, my corner of paradise, far from both God and people." The blonde woman chattered on excitedly as she led the small group of tourists in the direction of the dark wooden cottages. She wiped the perspiration off her forehead with a piece of tissue paper. "Here are your cabins, ladies and gentlemen. The dining room is in the next cottage."

"When do we leave for the Angel Falls?" one of the tourists asked.

The blonde woman did not answer immediately. Soaked in perspiration, she kept wiping at her forehead with the tissue paper, then burst into giggles. "Oh, the Angel Falls?" She waved her hand dismissively. "To get there from here, my friend, you would need a journey of six days on foot through the jungle. But I have my own waterfalls. Five of them! They are small, of course, but no less phenomenal . . . No less breathtaking, believe me."

"Did you hear what she said?" Leon cast a stupefied glance at Leah and said to her in Polish, "Do you realize what's going on here? Swindle! We've been tricked!"

The blonde woman turned her head sharply at him. Did she understand what he had said? With assumed cheerfulness she exclaimed, "Get organized, my friends. Deposit your things in the cabins, wash up, and change. We'll meet back here within an hour. Then I'll show you my natural treasures. Take along your cameras, of course, and your bathing suits, those of you who want to have a dip in my beautiful lake."

In their cabin Leon could not shake his disappointment. He took off his shirt and wiped the sweat from his face with it. "I'm not ready to let her get away with this deception so easily, oh no!" he raged. "She's got no idea whom she is dealing with here, the thieving bitch! Imagine, six days' walk to the Angel Falls through the jungle! She had nerve to organize such a hoax! According to our itinerary, we're supposed to spend our holiday in the jungle of Peru, not here. We'll have enough to do with the jungle as it is! The moment we get home I am contacting the travel agency to demand my money back. We live in the twentieth century. People involved in such shenanigans pay for it or they go straight to jail! Such chutzpah!"

"Hurry up!" Leah urged.

Washed and wearing fresh clothes they stepped outside, bathing suits in hand. Leon took his camera along. He never parted with the camera when he was on a trip. He was a good photographer, and he liked to take photos of everything he saw. "It's the only way to halt the progression of time and immortalize the moment," he liked to say.

The blonde woman, clad in white shorts and a white cotton blouse with long sleeves, was waiting for her visitors. On her bare feet she wore a pair of sandals. She waited until they had gathered together, and then, chattering nervously, she led them off in the direction of the jungle.

"What do you call this place?" one of the tourists asked.

"We don't call it anything," the woman answered, grinning enigmatically.

"Hasn't it got a name?"

"No, there is no name for a place like this. My private name for it is Eldorado."

She brought them to the edge of the forest and gestured with her hand. "Here is the path. Follow it as far as it goes. After a five- or ten-minute walk you will reach the waterfalls. There is no danger. I must hurry back to check on the preparations for dinner."

It took more than twenty minutes to walk to the falls. Even though they were skirting the outer edge of the jungle, the vegetation grew so thick that little could be seen but darkness and nothing could be heard above the deafening chatter of the birds—a humming, singing, a cheerfully soothing yet deafening noise. It mingled with the pleasant, splashing sounds of waterfalls and the burbling brooks.

At length they were greeted by the sight of five magnificent waterfalls. White and foamy, the falls rushed down the surrounding cliffs into a small lake that reflected the sun like a yellow pupil in a sky-blue eye. It seemed to Leah that this eye was blinking at her, calling to her, enticing her. She hid behind a tree and changed into her bathing suit. Then she entered the lake. Leon was right behind her.

As soon as she reached the middle of the lake she noticed François swimming beside her, naked. "I can't stop thinking of the blonde woman," Leah said to him. "What vitality! What daring! Taking chances as if she were still struggling for her life, no price too dear for her to pay.

Should I envy her this talent for experiencing life on the edge of danger, a talent that I no longer possess? Do you think that she has really found herself here?"

He did not answer the question but whispered with watery lips, "You see, *mon amour*, we are swimming together inside nature's womb. Listen to the hum of the waterfalls. They're playing the sweet lament of Sibelius's doomed Swan of Tuonela."

She turned onto her back, face up to the sky, and stopped working her arms and legs. She let herself be carried by the water, supported by the caressing, fluid touch of François's hands. She listened to the music of the Swan of Tuonela. The foam of the bubbly water at the foot of one of the waterfalls sprinkled her face with droplets that tasted like her tears but were sweeter.

When the group of tourists returned to the cottages the blonde woman came out to greet them. "So? How did you like it?" She stared at Leon with such eyes—as if her life depended on his answer.

He did not reply, pretending not to have heard, or perhaps he really did not hear her. He was involved in a conversation with one of the tourists, a young German whose acquaintance he had made in the water. Leon's command of German was excellent, and he enjoyed showing it off.

To make up for her husband's silence Leah answered the blonde woman. "An enchanting spot," she said. She moved close to the woman and walked in silence beside her for a while. Then she gathered her courage and asked her, "Do you live here all alone?"

"As you see, I am not all alone. I have a staff," the woman answered coldly.

"And family? A husband? Children?"

"Without a husband or children."

"You're from Poland, aren't you?"

"What difference does it make where I'm from?"

"How strange! In what remote corners of the world we survivors show up."

"I did not 'show up'!" the woman exclaimed in a harsh tone of voice. "This is my home! This is my happiness!" She cast a short fierce glance at Leah and walked away.

Dinner was very tasty and reminded Leah of long-forgotten yet never sampled dishes. For the next five days the blonde woman did not appear, not even once. The tourists were left to explore the region on their own. It had become increasingly obvious to them that coming here had been a put-up affair, a swindle that consisted of luring naive tourists to this spot for the sole purpose of supporting the business of the hotel owner.

But every time that the tourists went out to bathe in the lake between the falls the delightful coolness brought a wonderful, peaceful stillness to the mind, an enchanting sense of well-being. Even Leon surrendered to the spell. When, after five days, the time came to leave, he was reluctant to depart. "An Eldorado, far from God and far from people," he repeated the blonde woman's words before they boarded the small airplane. His face expressed genuine regret as his eyes swept the landscape with a sorrowful look.

The flight back to Caracas was made without the blonde woman. On one side of Leah sat Leon, immersed in reading the *International Herald Tribune*, which, despite all his leisure time, he had had no chance to peruse. On Leah's other side sat François.

"'Where did you disappear to after we met in the middle of the lake in the blonde woman's Eldorado?" she asked him.

"I did not disappear. I've been keeping an eye on you all the time," he answered.

"Then why didn't I see or hear you?"

"Because you avoided me, *mon amour.*"

"Why do you think so?"

"Your imagination stopped in mid-flight on the threshold of God's splendor."

"But François, why don't you understand? The hollowness in my heart made my need for you all the greater. That spot in the middle of the lake between the waterfalls was too beautiful to compensate for the sense of loss that never leaves me."

* * *

The next stop on Leah and Leon's itinerary was Peru, where they were to spend an entire week in the jungle. After two days of travel they arrived to Pucallpa, a dusty, desolate town not far from the Amazon River. From the small, sandy airport a massive jeep took them on a ride along a road that was actually not a road at all but rather a track of parallel furrows dug into the brown grass by vehicles that had passed that way before. These furrows wound along the shores of the lazily flowing river. Across the river, on the other side, the jungle spread its tentacles of branches and roots in all directions.

"Do you know why it is called the Amazon?" Leon asked Leah. He was wiping his sweaty face as he leafed through the pages of the tourist book. "In the sixteenth century a traveler here came upon a militant tribe of large, powerful women. He called them by the name of the Amazons of Greek mythology. And that's where the river gets its name."

The guesthouse was located by a bay of the river. A large wooden house with a neat backyard bordered the river's shore. Leah and Leon were given a bungalow to themselves. The furniture was made of raw planks. There were two hard beds, a table, a cupboard. The room was spartan but neat. There was even a shower. Through the window one could see a brown, sun-baked square of ground and the brown water of the river. Now Leah and Leon were truly in the wilderness.

Leon changed into shorts and a cotton shirt and went into the main house to finish checking in. Leah lingered outside the cabin door. She looked around, listened, and wiped at the perspiration that penetrated her eyes and burned her lids. A vague unease permeated the atmosphere. The jungle beckoned mysteriously from across the river. Brown waves beat against the shoreline of the brown river, scrubbing the sand with rushes and weeds. Huge water lilies floated between the gnarled roots of trees growing into the water. The sun, hot and inhospitable, cast its dazzling light over the river's rippled surface, as if it were scattering mocking smiles through the floating mouths of thin waves.

Leon emerged from the main cottage and approached Leah.

"Imagine," he exclaimed cheerfully, "the owner speaks German! We won't have to break our tongues trying to communicate. Dinner is at seven."

"Are they Germans?" Leah asked.

"Of course. So what? They've been living here for the last twenty-five years. I had a chat with them. Very simpatico. They told me that we can swim in the river. At the shore the water is shallow, but farther out it is quite deep. We'll go for a swim before dinner, won't we? Tomorrow we leave for an excursion deep into the jungle."

When the flaming sun began to sink behind the tangle of treetops across the river, Leon and Leah went for a swim in the Amazon River. Leon, superb swimmer that he was, sliced the water's surface energetically with his arms. Soon he was far away from Leah. She could barely see his head bobbing over the surface of the water. She commenced her own rhythmical stroke. She reached the middle of the bay, where huge water lilies floated all around her like sailboats. The trees cast dark shadows over the entire bay. The water was mild, caressing, and crystal clear. It was the brown, sandy bottom that made the color of the water appear to be brown. In the distance, far away from Leah, swam Leon—and nearby, very close, swam François.

"It's a delight, isn't it?" she heard him whisper.

"Yes," she answered, "but I can't bear the thought of the German owners. Perhaps they're Nazis? There are many Nazis hiding out in South America. We are alone with them here. Leon has, I'm sure, told them that we are former concentration camp inmates. He loves to boast about it to everybody, despite doing everything he can to forget the fact. How strange it is! The places where both we and our murderers have wandered, and how destiny keeps entwining our fates with theirs."

François did not react to her words but whispered to her through moist glistening lips, "I can see an entire school of fish beneath us. Look into the water." His voice delicately caressed her ear in rhythm with the lapping of the waves. "And there, have a look, by the trees, a mother turtle is playing with her baby. Look how their limbs embrace." François floated very close beside her, and as he spoke, he ever so lightly took her into his arms. "Elsewhere time swims on, but here it has stopped moving. Eternity stands still as it slips through our fingers. Who knows for how long these turtles and these generations and generations of fish—the same and yet not the same—have been swimming through these same waters, waters that are the same and yet not the same. And you, *mon amour*, in this instant of eternity, are magnificent to look at! Can you hear the sweet lament of Sibelius's Swan of Tuonela, the lament of the doomed swan that accompanies you?"

"Fear gnaws at my heart, François," she said in a whisper, stepping out of the water.

She and Leon returned to the cabin and took a shower. Then they dressed for dinner. Leon glanced at her. "Is that how you dress for dinner, my wife? You look like a plucked chicken. Can't you do something about your hair?"

"What can I do about it? It's wet."

"You look like a witch. You would frighten the dead."

He looked both cheerful and strangely dissatisfied with her. She was upset when she answered him, "After all, we're in the wilderness. What difference does it make how I look?"

"The owners are civilized people, and so are we."

"Then I'll wait until my hair is dry."

"We can't wait. Dinner is at seven o'clock sharp."

The dining room was located in the main cottage. It was plainly decorated but was neat and cozy, arranged in the manner of dining rooms in European guesthouses, with beer mugs, brass pots, and frying pans hanging from the walls. There were no other tourists present. The owners of the guesthouse, Herr and Frau Sterbe, asked permission to sit beside Leon and Leah for dinner. They badly missed the company of Europeans, they declared, casting contemptuous glances in the direction of the dark-skinned servants.

Leon nodded enthusiastically. All four of them seated themselves at a table covered with a spotless white tablecloth, on top of which the sparkling dishes were neatly arranged. Leon immediately launched into a friendly conversation with the Sterbes. Frau Sterbe made an effort to involve Leah in the conversation. With her massive figure and threatening self-assurance Frau Sterbe seemed to Leah to resemble an SS woman, an SS woman who had flexed her muscles at a concentration camp somewhere in Poland or Germany. Leah discouraged her advances saying in English, "I do not speak German."

Frau Sterbe fixed her with a pair of metallic gray eyes and refrained from speaking to her again. After this the conversation proceeded without Leah. No one seemed to notice her presence. The other three were busy talking as they ate. Leon cracked jokes. The owners did not understand the jokes perfectly well but they laughed anyway, their merriment enhanced by the wine. The husband and wife constantly exchanged meaningful glances.

Leah drank down one glass of wine after another. The owners were not stingy people. As soon as one bottle was empty they ordered the servants to replace it with another.

Leah said to François, who sat in an empty chair at the neighboring table, "Something is gnawing at me. I am afraid of these two. They are both the same age as Leon and I. Did you notice their behavior, the military air they have? I could swear that she was an SS woman. Those muscular arms, those hard, masculine hands. Only the whip is missing. Look how they exchange glances. Are they scheming something? Maybe they've become suspicious that we have guessed their identities and might betray them? Who knows how many Jewish lives they may have on their consciences?"

"So you do tremble for your life," François interrupted Leah's thoughts. "And I had the impression that you did not care for it."

"I don't want to perish at their hands. This I don't want to happen, François."

* * *

The next day Leon and Leah left for an excursion deep into the jungle. There they encountered endless varieties of trees, each one different from the next, intertwined with one another, tied together with vines,

interwoven with huge, fingery ferns. The protruding roots were so entangled that it was impossible to tell where one tree ended and the other began, as if they were all simultaneously involved in both a deadly
struggle for life and a supportive embrace of love. Nothing moved on
the ground, which was thickly overgrown with vegetation and filigrees
of roots. But up in the air, amid the tangle of treetops, there buzzed
and hummed and shrieked entire metropolises of living animals, mostly monkeys. The air was hot with heavy equatorial heat and a stifling
dampness.

There were four in their party, Leah and Leon and two dark-
skinned mestizos with long, sharp knives in their hands and firearms
suspended from their shoulders. Leah asked them in sign language
why they needed the firearms. "Jaguar! Cougar! Puma!" Laughing,
they pointed into the darkness between the trees. Their naked bodies
shining with sweat seemed to have been formed from smooth pillars of
bronze. With their long knives they cut a passage through the density
of vines and knotted branches. They nearly hit their heads against the
suspended nests of insects or against sleeping bats, which hung upside
down from the branches, their heads toward the ground.

"They'll slaughter us with those knives on their bosses' orders,"
Leah whispered to François, who was suddenly beside her. "The farther we go into the bush, the more frightening are the heat and the
humidity. You see, a mosquito has again landed on my arm. It's suck-
ing my blood." She was covered with mosquito bites from head to toe.
Some bites were so deep that blood oozed from them.

"You have sensitive skin," François remarked. "Leon's skin is thick-
er than yours. That's why the mosquitos bother him less."

It was impossible to establish any sort of communication with their
dark-skinned companions. Even sign language yielded no results. Instead of answering they laughed and chatted among themselves. Leon
took photos of the men, the forest, and the monkeys. At length the
group arrived at a village in the middle of a clearing between ferns and
trees. A semi-savage tribe lived there in huts on wooden stilts that had
no walls and were covered with straw roofs. Dark-skinned, bare-breast-

ed women, some of them holding suckling babies to their nipples, ran out to greet the visitors, as did swarms of naked children. Their necks were adorned with beads and necklaces made of colored peas. Intricately woven grass hats decorated with pea beads covered their black, stiff hair. They giggled childishly when Leon took pictures of them, and they followed him with great curiosity wherever he went.

* * *

When they returned from the jungle Leah's whole body was flecked with splotches of blood. There was not a spot on her arms, feet, or neck where a mosquito had not sampled her blood. The bites burned and itched.

"Don't scratch," Leon warned her. "It will leave you scarred for the rest of your life."

It was easy for him to talk. The itching drove her mad. She put on her bathing suit and ran out to throw herself into the river and allow its waters to soothe her outraged skin. François appeared beside her.

"Why don't you help me, François?" she asked him reproachfully.

"I can't help you, dearest. I'm so sorry. I may have some expertise in treating the wounds of the soul, but I have none in treating those of the body." The water cooled the swelling and soothed the itching, but the turmoil in her mind was beyond the soothing capacities of either the water or François.

 The following day the marks from the mosquito bites had not diminished nor had the itching stopped. Leah felt feverish. She shivered in the heat of the day. As they were about to enter the dining room for dinner she said to Leon, "I don't feel well, Leon. You will have to eat by yourself."

He instantly agreed. "I'll bring something back for you to eat in the cabin."

Instead the owners had her dinner sent directly to the cabin. By the time Leon returned it was dark outside. He called her to the door. The night was heavy with heat and restlessness. Amid the buzzing of insects one could sense the loud pulsations of the jungle's midnight heart. The calls of night birds rang out through the trees.

"Look at the swarms of bats!" Leon pointed to the skies. "Whole clouds of them. Frau Sterbe told me that some of them are called vampire bats because they suck human blood."

Lying that night on her hard cot, Leah shivered with fever and listened to the pulsations of the dark. The sharp, rattling song of the cicadas sounded like the noise of a distant freight train, a never-ending chain of boxcars rolling on and on, on countless wheels—boxcars loaded with people.

* * *

In the morning Leah felt better. Nevertheless she decided to stay in the cabin. She stood in the cabin doorway and stared outside and listened. Multicolored parrots flew overhead, as did wide-winged vultures. Leon had left on an excursion by himself. When he returned he spent the time that remained before dinner in the main cottage, talking with the owners. Leah understood that he was finding it difficult to be in her company without interruption, that he needed other people around. At home in Montreal, leisure time during the weekend was spent with friends, either visiting or receiving guests. It had been a long time since he had spent entire days alone with her—or she with him. She was glad to be by herself now. She spent the entire afternoon with François.

She had gotten into the habit of sharing her thoughts with François, but as a rule she communicated with him through silence rather than through talk. It was enough for her to feel the touch of his soul. What passed between the two of them needed no words, not even poetic ones. Although she melted with pleasure on hearing his tender, caressing words, she absorbed even more deeply the music of his unspoken declarations of love. There was power and truthfulness in not using words to express feelings. At such moments she no longer saw him clearly. He had become love itself, a love that wound itself through her senses and liberated them. And so she spent the afternoon with him in the cabin, where it was so very quiet, despite the buzzing of the insects and the chattering of the birds, that François could hear the sound of her tears dropping onto his fingers.

Later that evening Leon returned with news. "Tomorrow we are scheduled to go on a hunting expedition on the Amazon. Would you ever have imagined, Leah, that the two of us would one day go crocodile hunting?"

During the whole of the following day Leon waited impatiently for the hunt to begin. Frau Sterbe had declared that the crocodiles only appear after sunset. So they waited for darkness to set in. Then the servants prepared the motorboat, loading lanterns and ropes. They were to be five people altogether. Frau Sterbe led the expedition. Dressed in men's slacks and a man's brown shirt, she took the seat across from Leah, resting the rifle across her lap.

"And where is *my* rifle?" Leon asked Frau Sterbe in a tone of polite reproach.

Frau Sterbe chuckled her dry staccato chuckle. "I'm sorry. It is against the law to arm tourists."

"Are we on the way to our execution?" Leah asked François, who was sitting beside her. "Now, at night, she can do it with her own hands. How could they have permitted us to swim in the river if there are crocodiles in it?"

The boat drifted along with the river, ever deeper into the jungle. Hours seemed to pass. The motor cackled like an impatient hen. Frau Sterbe had forbidden them to talk too loudly. The night was hot, as usual, dense with humidity, with anguish and expectation. Not a single crocodile swam into view.

"*Donnerwetter*, I must find at least one crocodile for you!" Frau Sterbe said with determination. But there were none to be found.

"Look," Leah whispered to François, "she's reaching for the gun. She's going to shoot us instead of the crocodiles and feed us to the fish."

On their way back, Frau Sterbe launched into a complicated explanation of why the crocodiles had begun to avoid this section of the Amazon River. "Not so long ago we had plenty of them. The local population made a good living selling their skins. But we did not bother. We used to shoot them just for pleasure and for the pleasure of our guests."

Later, when they were back in their cabin, Leon said to Leah, "Before the war we used to believe that Germans were incapable of lying. The war proved how wrong we were. Do you know what I think? I think that Frau Sterbe took us for a ride in the true sense of the word, just like that blonde woman did with her Angel Falls. This is how the tourist trade works in these places. Frau Sterbe knew perfectly well that there are no crocodiles in the river. That's why she allowed us to swim in it."

A few days later Leon and Leah were back at the airport in Pucallpa. For two days they waited for an airplane to take them to Cuzco and Machu Picchu in the Cordillera Mountains. They had to sleep over in the guesthouse. Back at the airport two ragged, barefoot youths strummed their beat-up guitars, singing the same Spanish songs over and over again, songs in which the word *corazon* featured prominently.

* * *

In order to get to Machu Picchu, Leon and Leah had first to fly to Cuzco, a city located eleven thousand feet up in the Cordillera de Vilcabamba Mountains. Cuzco, the ancient capital of the Incas, was full of fortresses and temples, as well as the houses where the present-day descendants of the Incas lived. All these structures bore witness to the excellence of Inca building techniques, as well as to the Incas' skill in stone-relief carving and in sculpture. The pyramid forms of the structures seemed to mimic the shape of the surrounding mountains. Cuzco had been destroyed a number of times both by humans and by nature. The Spaniards, led by Francisco Pizarro, had conquered and destroyed the town in the sixteenth century. Then it was rebuilt only to be destroyed again by two brutal earthquakes.

Despite these catastrophes Cuzco had retained the spirit of the Inca epoch. Modern dwellings were constructed on top of the ancient stone walls, which consisted of huge rectangular rocks seemingly designed to demonstrate the endurance of a world without modern technology. The smooth stones massed at the foot of the walls seemed to be awaiting some new natural disaster or some new conquest in order to demonstrate again their powers of endurance.

Cuzco attracted swarms of painters, sculptors, jewelry makers, and chiselers of ornamental wood carvings. No wonder. The town exuded a picturesque charm and yet seemed enveloped in an air of mystery. A profusion of colors seemed to brighten the otherwise destitute appearance of the local inhabitants, who lived in extreme poverty and misery. Leah and Leon joined the flocks of tourists, who like themselves had stopped to spend the night in Cuzco before taking the train the next day to the mountaintop fortress of Machu Picchu—the lost city of the Incas.

But the next day's trip up the mountains was canceled. There had been terrorist activity in the region, and saboteurs had precipitated a landslide, which buried under rubble the train tracks leading to the top of the mountain.

So Leah and Leon found themselves stuck in Cuzco. Sheep, llamas, and alpacas grazed on the hills surrounding the town. A chinchilla hopped over the crumbling stairs that led to the ruins of the Temple of the Sun. It was New Year's Eve, and the spirit of protest mingled with the spirit of celebration well into the night. Over the cobblestone marketplace towered the old, majestic cathedral with its wide stairs surrounded by a number of decrepit cottages. These cottages housed tiny shops that seemed to have been made for dwarfs. They remained open at night and did business by the light of small, colorful lamps, selling a variety of gifts and souvenirs: sweaters knitted from the local untreated wool, with multicolored Indian symbols embroidered into the design, or baskets made of painted straw, or straw shoes, or sheep bells, or wood carvings and paintings, as well as picture postcards.

Leon bought some postcards and a painting from a local painter. The painting was of a Cuzco street. The painting was intended as a substitute for taking photos. He had left the heavy camera at the hotel. The air in Cuzco was very thin, and they were finding it difficult to wander about the town. Both Leon's and Leah's *corazons* felt uncomfortable and fluttered wildly inside their bosoms.

Leon and Leah talked very little to one another, except about mundane matters. They seldom shared their impressions with one another. There was no need. Leah knew that Leon was dissatisfied with the entire trip, that it had disappointed him and he was impatient to return home.

"How can we be happy," she asked François, who accompanied her wherever she went, "if we each carry our own anguish luggage with us wherever we go?"

"At least you have me," François whispered back to her. "We feel happy with one another, don't we?"

"Yes, I have you," she smiled bitterly.

"Have you something to reproach me, *mon amour?*"

"I certainly have. Yes, I have a great grudge, a profound regret, my consolation, my bright darling. I shall never forgive you for being nothing but a dream."

"Nevertheless, I will accompany you to Machu Picchu, in case you need me."

* * *

Late that night Leah and Leon returned to their hotel room. The hotel looked as if it had originated before the times of the Spanish conquest. They climbed up to their room, which had a slanted floor and peeling plaster walls, and there sank heavily into their narrow, sunken beds.

"I'm tired," Leon sighed. It occurred to Leah that he had intended to say "I'm tired of you" but had thought better of it.

A modern oxygen tank stood in a corner of the poorly lit room in case it was needed. Leon had taken along a bottle of champagne to be opened at midnight, but when the church bells began to toll, announcing the new year, Leon and Leah gave up the thought of toasting the moment with a glass of champagne. In that thin air their uncomfortable *corazons* would have reacted badly to the alcohol, or so Leon joked. They slept badly on their sunken beds that night. Their pounding hearts perched like birds of prey on their chests and weighed them down.

In the morning, the first day of the new year, they found that the train tracks had not yet been cleared. So Leon and Leah again went out for a walk around the town. The tourists mingled with the brightly dressed locals who were in turn surrounded by swarms of brown-skinned, colorfully clothed children as they all strolled through the marketplace. From hamlets in the surrounding mountains groups of Indians could be seen descending in festive serenity. The men wore sombreros, the women black hats. The women's shoulders were covered with colorful shawls; the men's chests sported colorful vests. An avalanche of color came tumbling down the mountainside. The marketplace became crowded. On top of the profusion of colors floated a sea of brown, sadly smiling eyes, of faces creased by the sun, the wind, and the misery of life, faces that seemed to belong to the bygone time of the Incas, faces that bore witness to the eternal attachment of man to the soil and to life.

A fat, bald priest in a ceremonial soutane appeared on the wide, front stairs of the cathedral and raised his outstretched arms over the heads of the crowd. A band of musicians dressed in military garb grouped themselves in formation behind the priest, stroked their mustaches, then blew a deafening fanfare on their trumpets. The crowd quieted. Then the priest's voice boomed out through a bullhorn above the sea of heads while an echo reverberated along the sides of the mountains.

Leon and Leah stood at the foot of the broad stairs of the cathedral. They did not understand a word of the priest's sermon, but they recognized the name of Karl Marx and such words as *democracia sociale* and *justicia.*

Leon was amazed. "A socialist priest!" He shook his head in disbelief. "Obviously the leftists are ready to take power in this region."

The crowd was calm but seemed not to be attending to the priest. The faces, with smiles chiseled in place, looked stony, brown, and as dry as the rocks of the ruins. The crowd seemed to listen with its inner ear not to the voice of the priest but to the voice of its distant and forever present past, a voice that could never be silenced.

* * *

A day later the train tracks were finally cleared, and the tourists set out in a rickety old train to travel up the mountain on a track that climbed forever higher toward one of the world's great wonders: Machu Picchu.

As soon as they reached the summit they came face to face with a reality that surpassed even the loftiest flights of imagination. The gigantic top of the mountain seemed to have been lopped off to leave a plateau, flat like a plate under the canopy of the sky. It looked like God's open palm cradling the last vestiges of a vanished civilization. The air was even thinner here than in Cuzco. Yet somehow breathing was less of a problem, as though an umbilical cord had been cut and the heaviness of the world had floated off into oblivion.

"Do you realize, my beloved," François whispered into Leah's ear, "that the memory of the blonde woman and of the two Germans on the shores of the Amazon River, that the memory of the various upheavals of life down in the valley, have faded from your mind?"

"Not at all, François," she whispered back. "They have not faded, but here, at this moment, I can see my entire life in perspective. I find myself face to face with all the riddles that ever troubled me and for which I could never find an answer."

"Try to solve those riddles with the name of our splendid, wondrous love and see whether you have guessed right."

Guides were leading groups of tourists through the ruins of ancient market stalls and public baths, through an amphitheater and residential quarters. The tourists marveled at the intricate sewer system carved in stone alongside the stone houses. The huge sun clock still showed the time—of the past or the present? Or was it the time of eternity?

Leah, her imagination aflame, could not stop talking to François. "All these temples, the altars, the Inca gods. Tell me, how do they differ from what we have today? What needs did men and women seek to satisfy with such things in those times? What gnawed at their hearts? Did they too experience the fear of death and the fear of life? Perhaps they were busy just getting through the day, so caught up in trying to survive that they had no time for such thoughts? And yet these ruins bear witness to people's longings, to their existential nervousness, to their search for something. Did they build all this because they were happy or unhappy? It is nothing more than an illusion, François, that up here we are cut off from the earth. These mountains that practically touch the sky are just as distant from the answer to the great questions as are the valleys below in which these mountains are rooted."

She did not wait to hear what François had to say. She and Leon were excited, overcome by wonder. They climbed up and down the rocks like experienced mountaineers, feeling no fatigue but an extraordinary resilience and lightness of heart. Leon admired the intricate style of construction. He bombarded the guide with questions, without ever stopping to take photos of the things that excited him.

Leah heard François's tender voice, but it seemed to be coming from far away. Her own voice as she spoke to him prevented her from hearing what he had to say. Except for one moment when, anxious to keep up with the other tourists, she had seated herself on a rock in order to dislodge some stones from her sandals. Then she felt with all her being that François was sitting beside her, reading her face through the glasses covering his eyes.

"You've begun to separate yourself from me, haven't you, my dearest?" she heard him whisper.

"Don't be silly, François," she whispered back. "I have no patience right now. I must catch up."

"Catch up with what?"

"I don't know myself. For the first time I feel . . . I've got no idea what to call it."

"The breath of life? Just as when you stepped out of the concentration camp?"

"Yes, a reattachment to life, just like then."

* * *

Most of the tourists returned to Cuzco the same day. But Leon could not tear himself away from Machu Picchu. "Do you know what, Leah?" he said. "Let's spend the night here. We'll be able to see the sunrise."

She stared at him in amazement. Leon watch a sunrise! Of course she agreed. There was a guesthouse on the mountain for those who wanted to see the sun rising over Machu Picchu.

There was an oxygen tank in their cabin in the guesthouse, just as there had been in Cuzco. But neither Leon nor Leah needed it. They slept surprisingly well, and even before dawn had begun to turn the sky gray they dressed themselves warmly and went outside. Overhead the navy blue cupola of the sky spread out all around them, its border made jagged by the zigzag tips of the surrounding shadowy mountains. But to the east, from between a slit separating the mountaintops, there suddenly sliced through a reddish-orange streak of light. In an ever widening semicircle the light spread over the sky, gradually transforming the dark blue dome into a sea of brilliant crimson in whose middle emerged the round hump of a fiery leviathan—the sun itself. The sun's rays cascaded over the mountain cliffs and the rocky mountain walls with a reddish-golden glitter.

Leah and Leon stood beside each other and observed the spectacular display of colors in front of their eyes. They said not a word to one another. Leah glanced at Leon's face, which, in the light of the sun, had acquired a pinkish cast. As she looked on him a grimace of sadness and grief distorted the line of his mouth into a strange grin. His eyes stared into the distance as if searching for something. What is bothering him? she asked herself. Does he too feel as if he were suddenly face to face with his entire life?

"What are you thinking of?" she asked him. He stared at her in surprise, as if he had only then noticed her standing beside him. "What are you thinking about?" she asked again.

He wiped his face with the palms of both hands and burst out, "What business is that of yours? Can't I keep my thoughts to myself?

Do you have to creep into my soul?"

"Forgive me," she mumbled, and said nothing more.

So they continued to stand in silence beside each other as if they had turned to stone, as if they had become part of the ruins. They stared straight ahead, letting the mild, warm light of the rising sun illuminate their twisted faces as well as the surrounding masses of stone. Their eyes wandered over the real and unreal sights of a world that existed and did not exist, but now they were hardly capable of absorbing the sights. Then Leah spoke again: "Do you see those two mountain peaks over there, straight across from us, Leon? They are so close to one another and yet they never reach each other."

"Will you stop chattering for a moment?" Leon snapped. He sighed deeply. "If you only knew, my wife, how very tired I've grown of you." He turned his head away from her.

"I've grown tired of you too," she replied. After a moment of silence she added, "I think that when we return home we should separate." She turned and walked away from him.

A group of tourists passed them. Leah joined them. The sun's rays were pouring over the surfaces of people and rocks. Leah felt herself permeated by the light. Such brightness took hold of her that it almost brought her to the border of joy. She noticed a narrow, high rock protruding from the ground in the distance. It was the tallest rock in the vicinity and towered over its surroundings. People wandered all around it. Some tried to climb to its top in order to get a better view of the panorama beneath. The rock was pointed and somewhat slanted. There was room for only one person at a time to stand on its summit at the edge of the precipice. Leah put herself in line.

She was surprised at the strength she still felt within her. Sweat poured down her face; her heart hammered wildly. Her hands were growing painfully sore from clasping the protruding tips of stone as she climbed higher and higher. Soon she reached the top. She straightened herself and squeezed at her pounding heart with both her hands. Panting, gasping for breath, she smiled, proudly turning to look at the mountains all around her, gazing up at the sky and down at God's palm, where the ruins of Machu Picchu basked in the sun. At her feet lay the abyss. She had to be careful. One careless movement and she would fall from the cliff. She had to stand firmly on her feet.

She felt François's presence beside her. She saw him in his full form, wearing his checkered jacket with the reading glasses in his breast pocket. She saw his wavy chestnut forelock and the chestnut mustache above his upper lip. A bottomless longing called out to her from the depths of his eyes.

"There is no room for you up here, François," she whispered as her head began to spin. She inhaled deeply.

"Have you found yourself at last between heaven and earth, *ma bien-aimée*?" he asked her, smiling sadly.

"Oh, not yet," she answered, sadly smiling back. "But I'm on my way. You see, Paul Célan, Primo Levi, Adolf Rudnicki, and Jerzy Kosinski should not have done what they did. Nor must I. I must not even lose myself in your arms, my handsome, soothing darling."

"How will you manage without me?"

"I've no idea. It breaks my heart to part with you, my impossible, dazzling dream." She gathered together the tatters of her shredded courage. "Adieu, François!" she exclaimed, and with the sudden strength of will that had taken hold of her, she thrust his figure over the precipice.

That was how François died.

Serengeti

The plains of the Serengeti are located to the east of central Africa. A small part belongs to Kenya, while the rest lies within the borders of Tanzania, reaching almost to the belt of the equator. From the Serengeti's northeastern border protrude the rocky peaks of Mount Kenya, which the local inhabitants, the Kikuyu, believe to be the seat of their omnipotent god. From Mount Kenya a valley opens up like a gate toward the southeast, where the Serengeti's border extends to the huge volcanic crater of Ngorangora. Nearby rises majestic Mount Kilimanjaro, wrapped in the splendor of everlasting snow, its crown of rocks twinkling like diamonds. Across the western border of the Serengeti spread the waters of majestic Lake Victoria, the largest lake in the world, notorious for its diabolical storms that dissipate almost as suddenly as they materialize.

There are no seasons on the Serengeti. The suffocating heat lasts the full twelve months of the year. There are long periods of rain in April and May and shorter periods in November and December. Here, sunrises and sunsets are spectacles of short duration. Before one can turn around, day has changed into night or night into day.

The breath of eternity hovers over the Serengeti plains. The relentless progression of time seems not to belong here; instead a certain noble rhythm is apparent in everything that is in motion, like music steadily rising and descending, proceeding neither forward nor back.

An encounter with both the two-legged and four-legged inhabitants of the Serengeti resets the clock of imagination to pre-Genesis, to that pre-mythical time before God planted His paradise on Earth for the benefit of Adam and Eve. Such an encounter with the Serengeti is liable to lead one's thoughts backward to those days before God had sown the seed of contradiction in the hearts of Adam and Eve. This same seed of contradiction had been implanted, countless generations later, in the mind of the man who now stood on the Serengeti's primeval soil, Dr. Simon Brown—the grandson of a Talmudic teacher from New York's East Side—and it had led him to choose psychiatry as his profession.

Dr. Simon Brown was a man in his mid-fifties, not overly tall, with a professorial goatee at the tip of his chin and the beginning of a moon-shaped pate on the top of his head. He was slightly overweight, but sportive looking; the compactness of his body betrayed the wealth of vitality and energy with which he was endowed.

During this twilight hour of a day in early January, when wintery, damp, cold New York was bathed in the neon glitter of the not-yet-cleaned-away Christmas and New Year's decorations, Dr. Simon Brown, dressed in a khaki shirt and shorts, stood in front of the window of his room in a guesthouse in Kenya at the border of the Serengeti plains. He was looking out to the west at part of the copper-hued sky where the sun was about to set.

The window stood open, the wooden Venetian shutters were hooked up on the outside, but a wire mesh covered the window casement. There were also mosquito nets suspended above the beds in the room. On top of the beds lay two opened valises. Dr. Simon Brown's wife, Dr. Mildred Brown, stood nearby, her slim body wrapped in a silken slip. Her bare left arm was covered with oddly arranged plasters that protected the scars from her typhus, cholera, malaria, yellow fever, and sleeping sickness inoculations. She was in the middle of unpacking.

The Browns' luggage contained very little clothing. Mostly they had packed books, miscellaneous files, cameras, tape recorders, and a variety of additional equipment. They had arrived by bus from Nairobi an hour earlier. Simon Brown had just entered the room after inspecting the guesthouse and checking on the accommodations of his colleagues. He was the head of this expedition of psychiatrists, and he considered himself responsible for the comfort of the participants.

On his way through the lobby Dr. Brown had made the acquaintance of Mr. Mashada, the Indian gentleman who was the supervisor and general manager of the guesthouse. Dressed entirely in a white Nehru suit, which harmonized pleasantly with his white hair, the highly cultured and extremely polite Mr. Mashada gave the impression of a peculiar sort of eccentric. His expressive brown face with its black, dreamy eyes gave the impression of belonging to a different time and a different world. In his lilting English he extolled the plains of the Serengeti, telling Dr. Brown that in these surroundings a person could enter into a rare state of grace and thus find himself included in the circle of the Great One's radiance.

Simon Brown had also received from Mr. Mashada some general information concerning the guesthouse and the neighboring coffee plantation.

Until the end of the First World War, this large house with its many rooms, as well as the neighboring coffee plantation, had belonged to German colonists, who had grown rich not from coffee beans but from the trade in elephant tusks, leopard skins, and rhinoceros horns, which were highly valued by Oriental men as aphrodisiacs. After the German defeat, when England took over the rule of North Africa, the German owners sold the house and the plantation to some Dutchmen, who continued with the same kind of business.

After the Second World War, when Kenya obtained its independence, a law was passed against killing animals on the reservations. The house was then officially transformed into a guesthouse for tourists and nature lovers, who used it as a base from which to set out on photo safaris to the Serengeti plains.

Nevertheless, there was no dearth of hunters among the guests even today. These were men of ample means who came in search of adventure. They came to the Serengeti yearning to indulge for a time in the discomforts of primitive living and to return home with trophies of lions' heads, which would confirm their bravery and masculinity, qualities about which the Second World War had obviously failed to reassure them. There had been a number of prominent diplomats and politicians among those guests, as well as movie stars and international personalities of the caliber of Ernest Hemingway. In most of these cases the hunts were staged, that is, some local black hunters would tie a wounded zebra or antelope to a pole and drag it along as they ran so that the lion or leopard, enticed by the smell of blood, would appear within range of the white hunter's gun. More often than not the decisive shot came from the skillful hand of one of the white hunter's black-skinned companions. Then the white hunter would triumphantly place his foot on the back of his prey and be photographed, thereby immortalizing his act of heroism for all eternity.

"Do you understand, sir?" The expression on Mr. Mashada's face conveyed both irony and sadness. "The new countries that have just sprung into existence are in dire need of money, and to get this money they must maintain good relations with rich foreign governments. And so the killing of lions, rhinoceroses, elephants, leopards, and antelopes continues, although illegally. The African governments look through their fingers. The smaller the herds of elephants, the higher the price of ivory on the world markets. Fortunately, now that the Grzimeks have raised the alarm all over the world, and now that air travel has become less expensive, more people of average means are arriving here not to kill, but to observe the animals in their natural habitat. So perhaps tourism will end by assisting the African countries in fulfilling their mission to protect this sacred treasure of the Serengeti and save it from destruction."

* * *

The ball of the purple sun descended with surprising speed toward the tops of the thorny acacia trees, which together with the gigantic mimosas and eucalyptuses were dotted around the yard of the guesthouse in an irregular circle. The branches of the trees did not point upward but spread out horizontally. This gave them the appearance of a circle of opened umbrellas.

Two yellow blotches blocked the view of two acacia stems. At first Simon Brown thought that the blotches were a reflection of the setting sun. But as the sun sank deeper behind the crowns of the trees he began to discern the contours of two barefooted men whose dark faces and dark limbs merged with the color of the tree trunks. The two yellow blotches were two yellow blankets that the two slim men wore like Roman togas tied over one shoulder. Each man held on to a spear that lay across the back of his shoulders and protruded from either side. Motionless, the men leaned against two tree trunks, balancing on one foot, the other foot raised and wound around the standing leg's calf. They stared at the guesthouse. In the sudden onset of dusk they looked like tall plants. As he stared at them, Simon Brown suddenly realized that the men must be Masai tribesmen, the only representatives of the human race to inhabit the plains of the Serengeti.

A half-dozen young monkeys cavorted on one of the tables and the chairs that were scattered over the stone terrace in front of the guesthouse, hopping lightly as they chased each other. Another group of older monkeys sat closely entangled atop another table, delousing one another. They seemed to be casting mocking glances in the direction of the white-skinned creature whose torso protruded from behind the mosquito net covering the window. Their laughing mouths emitted high-pitched squeals.

A vulture, its huge wings extended like two black patches of cloud against the purple sky, lowered itself onto the very tip of an acacia to await its prey.

Simon Brown wiped the perspiration from his face and from his neatly trimmed goatee. The droning fan in the center of the ceiling sent a hot wind in his direction, a wind not at all related to the stifling, smelly gusts of New York's summer evenings. This wind carried with it the hot breath of pre-biblical times, when the world was still fresh and young. Although sweat was streaming down his body, he was still capable of breathing and savoring the cleanliness of the Serengeti air.

He inhaled deeply, as if to confirm with his nostrils and lungs the fact that he was really there, in the heart of Africa; that this project of conducting a conference of psychiatrists who supported his theories of marathon group therapy sessions—a project on which he had worked for an entire year—was about to become a reality. Would he be able to go through with his program exactly as he had projected it? How would the confrontation between this world of primeval simplicity and the complex, intricate world of the neurotic human psyche affect his own and his colleagues' therapeutic approaches? Would his carefully formulated thesis about the cure and rehabilitation of the neurotic personality stand the test of this strange African reality and remain as rational as he had once thought it to be?

* * *

The sun completely vanished behind the acacia trees. Suddenly the air turned pleasantly cool, permeated by a pungent, sweetish fragrance, although except for the mimosas and some brownish clumps of grass there were no other flowers or plants growing in the yard.

Mildred had finished unpacking the valises. Her humming could be heard in the washroom, punctuated by the periodic spurting of the shower faucet. In his imagination Simon Brown saw his wife's perfectly sculpted body delighting in the caressing streams of water that enveloped it. He seemed to feel the waves of cool water cascading over his own body.

There was not a trace of resentment in his heart against Mildred for having opposed his idea of coming to Africa. She believed that going to Kenya, and in particular on an excursion to the Serengeti, would contribute nothing to the success of the seminar. Quite the contrary: the strangeness of the surroundings would hinder the participants' ability to concentrate. Unrested, exhausted from the heat, people would be too distracted. Their irritability might aggravate frictions between colleagues whose collegiality, even in the best of circumstances, was rather superficial and often full of rivalry and envy. Perhaps Simon himself would be unable to master his feelings and accept with equanimity his colleagues' criticism of his theories—criticism that was to be expected.

This would put the success of the entire enterprise in jeopardy.

Truth to tell, Mildred saw no sense in coming to the Serengeti even for a vacation alone with Simon. "I wouldn't have done it even if I were paid for the pleasure," she told him, laughing. As far as she was concerned, Africa was a wasteland, a cesspool of stagnation and apathy. She was a child of the big civilized city, raised in a country where comfort and the achievements of technology were part and parcel of everyday life. She saw beauty in the forests of Manhattan's skyscrapers and was intoxicated by the noisy rhythms of Broadway and Sixth Avenue. Nature never spoke to her heart. She always said that if she wanted nature she could watch the animals at the Bronx Zoo, where she occasionally enjoyed spending a few hours. Nor did she dislike taking a stroll in Central Park or leaving town for a day or two. But a longer stay in the country usually bored her.

How could Simon hold this against her? After all, he was himself not a great nature enthusiast. Coming to the Serengeti was not, for him, a simple matter of loving nature. It had a much deeper significance. He was hardly able to explain it to himself, but for some strange reason he looked on this trip to the Serengeti as a kind of pilgrimage.

As he stood by the window immersed in thought, he allowed his eyes to wander around his strange surroundings while Mr. Mashada's remarks about the Serengeti reverberated in his head. He felt himself obliged to admit that Mildred might be right after all. She often was right. His project might turn out to be a fiasco. The thought made him feel insecure. He grinned crookedly at himself. She, the Boston-born shiksa, whose ancestors had belonged to the Puritan elite of New England, had a cool, down-to-earth frame of mind, a WASPish frame of mind, in contrast to his own passionate Hasidic nature, which often prompted him to "climb the straight walls."

* * *

Mildred had been his student at the university. He had lost his heart to her almost at first sight. Tall, blonde, graceful, and slim, she had conquered him against his will, breaking down all his defenses as if he were a fortress. She had robbed him of his willpower. She had forced him to break his resolve never to become romantically involved with his female students, a resolve that most of his colleagues had ridiculed. But Mildred proved to be the only exception to this hands-off rule, because he married her. After the publication of a series of articles established his reputation in psychiatric circles, women had begun to pursue him. This had occurred during the liberated decade of the sixties, when unrestrained sexual expression had become the fashion among the young. In order to put himself on an equal footing with his colleagues, Simon had pretended to be having affairs with dozens of women and to be deceiving his wife just as they did.

In reality he felt no need for other women. He loved Mildred, and through her he loved America. Thanks to her he not only felt himself more of an American but also more of a citizen of the world. The unfamiliar and mysterious aspects of Mildred's nature were not only part and parcel of her femininity but were also something more embracing, more existential, which lured and attracted him. Every time that he held her in his arms he had the feeling of coming home after a long voyage. The history of America that he had mechanically absorbed in his childhood and youth became, after his marriage, as familiar and near to him as Mildred's heartbeat. She gave him strength and pride and an awareness of his power. He worshiped her. He had moments when he was overcome by a desire to devour her, to devour her alien, peculiar qualities, to become her. He also experienced moments when, in a surge of tenderness, feelings of intense humility took possession of him, when it seemed to him that he had no right to her, as if he had been pilfering from somebody else's garden. This sentiment had hardly undergone any change in the course of all the years during which he and Mildred had settled into their home, brought children into the world, and established their professional positions, which meant mainly his professional position.

Simon considered that marrying Mildred had been a stroke of good fortune. She was faithful to him and managed their home with a firm hand, while she taught him—her distracted, dreamy, nervous, idiosyncratic Jewish husband—how to dress and conduct himself in the proper manner. She introduced him to various fashionable sports and saw to it that every morning before breakfast he went jogging for half an hour. She awakened his passion for skiing and made certain that he regularly practiced his relaxation exercises.

Just as dutifully as she devoted herself to managing their home, she devoted herself also to the management of his professional life and that of the institute he had founded. She saw to it that everything ran smoothly. She kept order in his papers, managed the calendar of his appointments, lectures, and speeches. Refusing to rely on his secretary, she herself typed out his manuscripts for publication. She helped him to disentangle his thoughts and to express lucidly those ideas that jostled and clashed against one another in his head. She helped him to crystal-lize even those thoughts that were beyond her grasp. She was both his most ardent follower and his fiercest critic.

So, despite the fact that she had expressed her strong opposition to his "African adventure," she had seen to it that everything would run smoothly, that every detail of the project would be taken care of. As was her habit with whatever task she undertook, it was executed with efficiency, care, honesty, and order.

Even Mildred's beauty had an honesty and orderliness about it. Her blonde hair was always arranged in the same style; her face—with or without makeup—always wore the same expression of composed seriousness, while her voice was even-timbred and crystal clear. Only when she and Simon went out on the town would the primitive and childlike qualities of her nature come into play. She liked to adorn her slim body with loud colors, to wear huge earrings and shoes on stiletto heels. It was easy to entertain her. The merest display of flashiness, the presence of a crowd of wildly screaming people, any joyful hullaballoo delighted her. She would laugh fullheartedly, her bright blue eyes re-vealing her joy in being alive.

Her naivete and innocence, her trust in people and her acceptance of whatever they said at face value without fishing for a hidden meaning—a quality totally alien to his Jewish habit of always trying to figure out where the "legs were growing from"—went hand in hand with a certain lack of discrimination that extended into her simplified appreciation of the arts. It was also expressed in her lack of acuteness, in her lack of genuine insight and effectiveness as a therapist. But these qualities heightened her charm as an American. She personified the best in the American character. Simon needed Mildred as he needed air to breathe. He could not imagine life without her.

His Jewishness played no significant role in Simon Brown's life. His parents, born in America, had torn themselves away from the Lower East Side so as to assimilate as quickly as they could. Their family name had been Brownstein, but they had discarded the "stein" and become Brown. As the children of immigrants who had experienced the pogroms in Russia, Simon's parents flaunted their American patriotism. The only aspect of Jewishness they cherished and preserved was the cooking. They joked that their palates were unable to accommodate themselves to any goyish dishes. So, for as long as Simon's mother was alive, Mildred dutifully learned how to cook Jewish dishes from her mother-in-law. Mildred was accepted into the Brown family with a tolerant matter-of-factness, perhaps even with a tinge of pride at having acquired a daughter-in-law of such pure-blooded American descent.

Simon himself saw no reason to deny his Jewishness, although he could hardly define what this Jewishness meant to him. Like his friends, who were Jewish intellectuals born in America, he considered himself just as good an American as people of Irish or Italian descent. Mildred, however, a descendant of the first Puritans who had arrived in America with the intention of building a New Jerusalem in the New World, appreciated Simon's Jewishness very much. She thought it added an exotic touch to his prestige, although her parents were considerably less impressed with their daughter's misalliance.

As for such cataclysmic events in Jewish life as the Holocaust or the establishment of the State of Israel, Simon considered the first a colossal tragedy and the second a positive event in Jewish history. But he saw neither one nor the other from a purely Jewish point of view, but rather from a broader humanistic perspective.

When America had entered the war with Hitler's Germany he had been an officer of the medical corps. He had more than once been exposed to direct artillery fire. After Hitler's defeat he and the other medical men had visited some of the liberated concentration camps and were shaken to the core by what they saw there. Simon could not accept the fact that the human spirit was capable of such moral depravity, that human beings could be responsible for such unadulterated evil. He was revolted by the thought that the highest attainments of science and technology could be used in the service of the basest, most bestial, most debauched of human instincts. The impression that the Holocaust made on him influenced his choice of psychiatry as his medical specialty, a choice he made after the end of the war and his discharge from the army. About the Holocaust itself there had been little talk during the years immediately following the war. If the press mentioned it at all, it was as a sporadic phenomenon, a by-product of the war. There seemed to be a taboo about seriously discussing the subject.

Both Simon and Mildred were liberal-minded freethinkers and had given their children no religious instruction whatsoever. Nevertheless, just as he had done as a young man before the war, Simon Brown ascribed everything that he disliked about himself to the disheveled little Jew who dwelled within his well-groomed, sportive, modern American body.

* * *

As if in answer to his thoughts, Dr. Brown noticed a young woman appear on the terrace of the guesthouse and with a light, brisk step approach the table where the monkeys were hopping about. She sat down on one of the chairs and took out a camera from a cloth bag that dangled from her shoulder. The monkeys became even more playful as she began clicking the camera, trying to catch the small creatures in their various positions as they leaped into the air. When she had finished snapping photos and put down the camera, she noticed Dr.

Brown looking out from the window of his room and waved to him.

"For my daughter," she called out, pointing at the camera.

He did not know that she had a daughter. And what about a husband? A few years ago he had known everything there was to know about this young Polish woman called Marisha Vishnievska, the daughter of a widowed Polish peasant woman. Marisha had studied psychiatry at the University of Warsaw. When she arrived in America she had had to take her exams again and be recertified. Toward this end she spent four years in psychoanalysis with Dr. Brown.

Those were quite stormy sessions. More than once he had had to fight off the urge to stop the analysis because of her ability to drag him into the quagmire of bitterness and hatred in which her soul wallowed. To make matters worse, the obnoxious, wordless way she had of teasing him kindled a feeling of repulsion within him. She was capable of spending the entire fifty minutes of the session lying mutely on the sofa in his office. Her position as she lay there was outwardly decent and decorous, but he nevertheless found it vulgar and provocative. Or she had attacks of compulsive volubility. Sometimes she even tried to take over, to turn everything around and analyze him! Her critical remarks, delivered in a heavily sarcastic tone of voice, cut him to the quick so that he was hardly able to maintain his composure.

It was difficult to tell whether Marisha Vishnievska was pretty or not. She had a large, wide scar on her forehead that ran along the entire length of her left temple. It was the scar of an unhealed wound she had received as a two-year-old, when she had fallen against a rock. The scar seemed to erase the vividness of her other facial features. Only the glow of her large brown eyes resisted effacement. Those eyes could light up with such fury that he had to turn his own eyes away from the sight of her face. At such times the cut on her forehead also seemed to flare up and take on a furious, throbbing redness.

Similarly, nothing complimentary could have been said about Marisha's figure. There was an awkwardness in the massive roundness of her body that did not harmonize with her thin arms and slim legs. Her light brown hair was plaited into a thick braid that was wound around the top of her head in old-fashioned style. What's more, she dressed without the slightest sense of elegance or élan, like a true member of the Beat Generation, a fact that added to her repulsiveness. It was only his determined professionalism that made possible the completion of her analysis with relative success.

Marisha had gone on to become a rising star in the world of psycho-analysis. Moreover, she became an ardent supporter of Simon Brown's theories. Fearing that someone else might snatch her from him, he had invited her to join the institute he had founded. Mildred protested. Marisha's appearance and bad manners would bring no honor to the institute, she warned. The dress and comportment of a doctor consti-tuted, in Mildred's opinion, a major factor in sustaining the proper distance between doctor and patient. Mildred nagged Simon to at least call the young woman's attention to her dress. Mildred was right, as usual, and he had agreed to talk to Marisha.

Greatly embarrassed, he once said to her casually, "I would much appreciate it, Dr. Vishnievska, if you would pay more attention to your attire when you are at work. You surely know that the dress of the doctor is a basic factor in establishing proper relations between him or herself and the patient."

"What's wrong with the way I dress?" Marisha asked calmly.

"You look like a bag lady, like a vagrant!" he burst out in sudden anger, avoiding her eyes.

"Well, that's what I am," she smiled at him forgivingly. "And let's not kid ourselves, Professor, that's what you are too. Perhaps it is you who should change the way you dress."

Such nerve she had! He actively disliked her. However, in a strange way he also needed her, and if it happened that she failed to come to work—she never bothered to telephone to give the reason for her absence—he would become irritable. With her unusual ideas and her eccentric remarks she was a refreshing and stimulating presence in the daily routine of the institute, although he avoided all face-to-face contact with her. Because of something in her behavior, or perhaps because of her unpleasant looks, he always felt nervous and dissatisfied with himself when he was alone in a room with her. Sometimes the air around them would become loaded with tension. Her perplexing practice of suddenly quizzing him would often leave him open-mouthed, unable to think of a response. Nor could he ever decide whether her questions were clever or stupid.

Once, after one of his lectures had made a strong impression on his listeners and been followed by a storm of applause, Marisha had nearly made him jump out of his skin. During the question period she took the microphone and launched into a rambling tirade against psychotherapy, which according to her twisted reasoning suffered from a lack of moral values. She ranted on about how in helping the patient find in his or her childhood years the psychological origins of his or her neurotic, antisocial, or even criminal behavior, the therapist was giving the patient a tool with which to whitewash and justify present behavior. No matter how hard one then tried to awaken in the patient a sense of moral responsibility, he or she would inwardly feel free from it.

"This is because," she exclaimed excitedly, as the scar on her forehead glowed a fiery red, "because psychiatry puts a negative emphasis on the individual's sense of guilt, disregarding guilt's positive role as a potential corrective to behavior. The reproach 'You are making me feel guilty' has even entered day-to-day speech and become a protective incantation for those who have every reason to feel guilty."

Because of this tirade Dr. Brown wrote a lukewarm evaluation of one of Marisha's papers when a journal editor submitted it to him for an opinion.

* * *

Now as Dr. Brown looked at the young woman playing with the monkeys, anxiety took hold of him because she was sitting so close to the animals. How could she be so reckless? The older monkeys might attack her. What did she know about monkey behavior? Was she a total stranger to fear?

"Be careful!" he called out to her. After all, he bore a certain responsibility for her safety.

"Don't you worry about me, Professor!" she called back exuberantly. "The monkeys consider me as one of their own."

It was strange, almost paradoxical, that Marisha Vishnievska had been the moving force behind the realization of this "African adventure," as Mildred had labeled the trip. Simon Brown recalled how about a year and a half ago, as he was in the middle of writing an article, an excited Marisha had burst into his office and without great ceremony exclaimed, "Professor Brown, I've got a great idea!"

His first impulse had been to send her out of the room. He feared her great ideas. Besides, her interruption had broken the thread of his thoughts. But her hot eyes burned right through him and the red scar on her forehead pulsed like a crackling flame. Somehow he lacked the heart to turn her away. The only way to be rid of her was to hear her out, then send her off with the excuse that he needed time to think her idea through. So he waited for her to continue, his eyes fixed on the red cut on her forehead.

"I want to propose to you that we hold our forthcoming conference in the Serengeti." She smiled at him with a mouthful of strong white teeth.

"Where?" He wrinkled his forehead as though he had not heard her well.

"In the Serengeti, the plains that lie on the border between Kenya and Tanzania."

"In Africa?"

She undid the strings of the cloth bag suspended from her shoulder and drew out a booklet that she placed on his writing pad. "Read this, please. Perhaps there is a possibility . . ."

He glanced down at the cover of the booklet. The title read *Serengeti Shall Not Die*. The authors were Bernhard and Michael Grzimek. "Poles?" Dr. Brown asked.

"I'm not sure," she answered. "Dr. Bernhard Grzimek is the director of the Frankfurt Zoo as well as of Tanzania's national parks. His son Michael perished in an airplane crash during the first head count of the remaining animals in the Serengeti. Serengeti is threatened with extinction. The animals are being slaughtered." She bent over the desk, her head so close to Dr. Brown's that it blocked his view of the cut on her forehead. He felt only the silken touch of the strands of hair that dangled loosely from her head. She recited to him the quotation from Ecclesiastes II, 19–21, printed on the first page of the book.

For that which befalleth the sons of men befalleth beasts; even one thing befalleth them: as the one dieth, so dieth the other; yes, they have all one breath; so that a man hath no preeminence above a beast: for all is vanity.

All go unto one place; all are of the dust, and all turn to dust again.

Who knoweth the spirit of man that goeth upward, and the spirit of the beast that goes downward to the earth?

That day Simon Brown did not finish the article he was in the middle of writing. The seed Marisha Vishnievska planted in his mind had begun to germinate. A sweet longing suddenly overcame him. He recalled the passion with which he had absorbed Stanley's account of how he had found Livingstone. "Doctor Livingstone, I presume," had been Simon's jocular way of greeting his friends when he was young. He also remembered reading Conrad's *Heart of Darkness* and Hemingway's short stories: "The Hills of Africa," "The Snows of Kilimanjaro," and "The Short Happy Life of Francis Macomber," as well as the stories of Isak Dinesen, in which she described her life on a coffee plantation.

Yes, deep within Simon Brown's heart there lay a longing for Africa. He was attracted to the continent as though his primordial, eternal, ever-longing self were calling out to him. True, he had been unaware of such an inner voice up to then, as if some thick membrane of distraction had barred it from his consciousness. But the repulsive Marisha Vishnievska had accidentally pierced that membrane by appearing before him with her proposal, and she had made this proposal at precisely the moment when he was planning the next psychiatric conference. Perhaps there were no accidents, and all the unexpected things that occurred in one's life had their own hidden logic.

As he stood peering out of the window of the guesthouse, Simon Brown was overcome by a sense of expectation, as if he were awaiting some miracle to happen. This earth, this spice-scented air, the Masai tribesmen who were still standing motionless on one leg leaning against the acacia trees, the playful monkeys, and the young woman with the scar on her forehead all seemed to partake of the fragrance of miracles.

* * *

Simon Brown slept badly during his first night in Africa. The hard, narrow bed of the guesthouse was uncomfortable in its unfamiliarity. The light of the night sky outside, densely canopied as it was with a net of gigantic, twinkling stars, shone in through the cracks in the wooden shutters and irritated his eyes. The night knew no rest. It throbbed with life. There was a constant crackling and creaking. He could hear a dull stampede of galloping feet, an endless hooting of owls, the wailing of jackals, the whining and chattering of hyenas, and now and again the roar of a lion, all of it against the incessant background buzzing of the night insects.

When Simon Brown finally closed his eyes and fell asleep, the red scar on Marisha Vishnievska's forehead sailed into his dream. The scar resembled a red-lipped mouth. It spoke to him, called out to him, invited him to touch it with his finger. He felt an impulse to do so but was afraid that the mouth might burn or bite him. He tried to move away from the scar, to withdraw to such a distance that he could no longer see it. But the mouth followed him until he escaped into wakefulness. He opened his eyes. Mildred was peacefully asleep in the neighboring bed. Her soft, regular breathing seemed to infuse the room with a feeling of peace and calm. Simon felt a strong impulse to climb into her bed. He knew that holding her in his arms would help him drift off into a good, deep sleep. But he was reluctant to wake her. There was also the danger that one of them might fall off the narrow wooden bed.

The gray light of dawn had barely begun to brighten the air when a light tapping was heard on the door: "*Jambo . . . Bwana macumba . . .* Please, safari." The deep, hoarse voice of a black servant traveled from door to door waking the guests in the guesthouse.

An hour and a half later the twenty members of Dr. Brown's group, all of them loaded down with cameras, sat in two quaint-looking vans that were painted with zebra stripes. In place of windows the vans had narrow openings under the roof, wide enough to look out and take pictures.

Mr. Mashada had probably sensed a kindred soul in Dr. Brown because he decided to make himself available and take over the leadership of the excursion. Armed with a rifle, he boarded Simon's van. With his radiant brown face and large sparkling black eyes, he resembled a mischievous boy who had run away from home. He had no sooner boarded the van than he began to give instructions to the passengers on how to conduct themselves during the safari. The day before he had advised them not to wear brightly colored clothes and to have their heads covered because the sun of the Serengeti was treacherous.

Now Mr. Mashada added, "Please, ladies and gentlemen, refrain from making any hasty movements, from talking or laughing too loudly, and in general be attuned to the pulse of the plain and try to feel yourselves into its rhythm. Then perhaps you will become more than observers; you will become participants in the enchanting world of the Serengeti. And please remember, under no circumstances are you to leave the van."

Two armed black guards, clad in shorts, boarded the vans and shut the doors. The motors started and the two vans slowly emerged from between the trees that surrounded the yard and, shaking violently, chugged down the sandy road. Soon they swerved onto the endless expanse of brown-green land, which extended as far as the eye could see. The grass-covered sandy flatland was not so much flat as it was undulating, full of valleys and hills. As if planted by a reckless hand, thorn trees, eucalyptus trees, and acacia trees grew helter-skelter all over the enormous tracts of land. Between the trees and all around them for miles on end lay the red soil dotted by clusters of tall brown grass, all awash in the pale, nebulous light of the rising sun. Gigantic clouds swam by very low above the plain. Like monstrous animals the clouds lazily stretched and recoiled, melting into one another as they floated along a sky whose horizon had been erased by the purple morning fog. The earth took on a copper hue. Masses of birds of all sizes and colors circled in the air as if trying to decide where to have breakfast—either up in the sky or down on the ground.

All that the tourists could see during their first fifteen minutes in the jostling vans was this majestic expanse of space. Far in the distance the smooth horizon was punctured by the sharp outlines of bluish mountaintops that seemed to have torn themselves away from the coiling cloud formations. Then something strange rose up before their eyes: a multitude of conical clay structures were scattered all over the plain, each structure the height of a human being. These architectural marvels resembled archaic temples, their walls densely pockmarked, as if covered by filigrees of spiderweb.

"What's that?" asked one of the astonished therapists.

Mr. Mashada chuckled as proudly as if he were personally responsible for the structures. "Termite nests," he declared. "After the rains, the termites come flying out of the holes and swarm around the nests. That's when my friends, the Masai people, rejoice. They race over to gorge themselves on the termites, which fly straight into their mouths. To the Masai termites are a most tasty delicacy, just like chocolate is for us."

"Phoo! That's disgusting." Mildred made a face as she held the camera next to her eye.

All the passengers were now crowded together at the opening beneath the roof of the van, energetically clicking their cameras. Simon Brown draped one arm over Mildred's shoulder while his free hand played mechanically with the camera suspended from his neck. As he turned his head, he noticed Marisha Vishnievska standing beside Mr. Mashada, absorbed in what seemed to be an intimate conversation. He knew that she had spent some years in India and assumed that they were discussing the subcontinent. Soon he heard Mr. Mashada compare the elephants of India with those of the Serengeti. Simon Brown felt a compulsion to move closer to the two speakers so as to be included in the circle of their confidentiality. A mood of festive expectation had taken hold of him, and he had the feeling that by standing at a distance from them he was missing out on something very important. Mr. Mashada, who was probably Simon Brown's age, no longer appeared either odd or eccentric. On the contrary, he seemed to have acquired a kind of superiority over Simon by displaying something essential in his nature that he, Simon, lacked. Marisha pointed at something in the distance.

"Don't stretch your hand so far out, Miss," Mr. Mashada warned. "It's dangerous."

"Dangerous? And what about the Masai who live here?" she asked. "Two of them are walking over there, and here stand two others. Why do they move about so freely, so fearlessly, Mr. Mashada?"

Two Masai men, tall and slender, stood on one foot by the edge of the sandy road, leaning on their long spears. Their raised feet were wound around the calves of their standing legs. They resembled the two men whom Simon had seen the day before at the far end of the guesthouse yard. Their earlobes were completely deformed by huge earring holes, which contained two gleaming red Coca-Cola cans. The outlines of the men's faces and bodies resembled Egyptian figurines painted on ancient frescoes. They exuded an air of simple innocence and noble dignity. In the distance far behind them a Masai woman was gathering dry branches for firewood. Mildred snapped photos.

"The Masai are the only humans tolerated by the lions," explained Mr. Mashada.

"Why is that?" one of the passengers asked.

"That is one of the Serengeti's mysteries," Mr. Mashada smiled enigmatically. "Perhaps because the Masai are part of the hierarchy of the Serengeti, the hierarchy of death. The lion knows his place. He is at the top of the ladder, yet he is not exempt from danger. In the same way the Masai rule over these plains but are not free from danger. Nothing living can escape danger. So perhaps there exists an intuitive agreement between these two groups of rulers to tolerate each other. Generally both groups obey the agreement, but exceptions do happen."

The shaking vans penetrated deeper into the plain. As they moved forward a large gray mass of moving, rounded boulders approached from the distance. As the van drew closer Marisha solemnly announced, "Here they come, Mr. Mashada."

The gray mass turned into a herd of about twenty elephants. A forest of triangular ears flapped back and forth like huge fans. The long trunks swayed massively right and left. The vans pulled over to the side of the road.

"The elephants have right of way," Mr. Mashada explained excitedly. "After all, the elephants stomped out this road in the first place. Oh, the elephants, my friends! They are the philosophers of the plains. They need no radios or telephones to communicate with each other. They're capable of transmitting information at a distance of miles and miles. If they do produce any sounds for the purpose of long distance communication, our ears are incapable of picking them up."

With heavy, slow steps and great dignity the elephants moved past, seemingly oblivious to the two vans, which seemed small and insignificant next to them. A cluster of baby elephants, the size of gigantic bears, trotted clumsily behind their mothers. Every step the herd took raised a cloud of dust and left deep imprints in the ground behind them.

When the elephants had passed, the vans returned to the middle of the road and began to climb uphill. The sun was already burning hot. Drops of sweat appeared on the foreheads of the travelers below their sun hats. As the van reached the top of a hill, an immense panorama suddenly opened before them, so that they all simultaneously gasped with wonder. On the plain below them they could see hundreds upon hundreds of antelope, wildebeests, buffalo, zebras, impalas, and gazelles. Grouped in a semicircle, they stood motionless, one animal next to the other. They remained rooted in place, their heads all facing the center of the semicircle so as to observe the slightest motion of the animal lurking there all alone—a gigantic lioness.

The vans stopped. The drivers turned off the motors. There was silence inside the vans, just as there was silence outside them. The clouds seemed to have stopped swimming across the sky; the grass seemed to have stop swaying. Something stirred in Simon Brown's heart. He grew tense; he was awed and anxious. He clutched Mildred's waist and, deeply moved, whispered in her ear, "I love you, Mildred."

The silence grew tense, both inside and outside the van. Just then the travelers, as if simultaneously woken from a dream, remembered their cameras and began clicking furiously. Mildred kept her eye glued to the viewfinder of her camera.

"Why don't you take any photos?" she asked Simon between clicks. "Isn't this what we have come here for?"

Simon mumbled something into his chest. Was this what they had come here for? No, he had come for something entirely different, something much more important, although he hardly knew what it was. Yes, perhaps he was a kind of Stanley who had gone into Africa to find Livingstone in the wilderness of his soul, who had gone into Africa to participate in a miraculous encounter with his own self. He had made this trip in order to seize a moment of enlightenment that would help him reach that unreachable spot within himself, the point when his heart had become entangled into a knot. Only a minute earlier he had told Mildred, for God knows the how-manyieth time, that he loved her. Why was it that these words had escaped his mouth at exactly this moment? Did he really mean to say them? What did he really mean to say? It seemed that he had really wanted to say, "I'm frightened." Was this the meaning of his love for her? What was the proportion of egotism to altruism in his feelings for her? Would he still have loved Mildred even if he were—like one of those thousands of animals out there—in danger of losing his life? Simon Brown stared at the sight before his eyes and suddenly his heart began to pound heavily, as if he remembered the scene from another, more familiar place.

A hand touched his free arm. Marisha Vishnievska stood beside him. Her eyes were riveted on the multitude of hypnotized animals as she whispered in his ear, "The moment of judgment."

He was surprised at the feeling of satisfaction it gave him to have her beside him. As he stared at the horrific sight he began mechanically to tug at the short sleeve of Marisha's blouse. "I saw a similar scene in a photograph of a concentration camp. A *selection*, they called it. What was his name—that famous selector?" he asked in a whisper.

"Don't insult the lioness, Professor," replied Marisha with bitterness.

The frozen scene in the distance lasted another five long minutes. Then the lioness turned her back on the half-circle of animals that surrounded her and whose eyes were focused on her every movement. With soft, graceful steps she slowly wandered off in the direction of the acacia trees.

"She's obviously not hungry," Mr. Mashada remarked. "Lions eat every three or four days. The other animals know that. They sense it. But for security's sake they are on the alert. The lioness might suddenly have a caprice to sample a small zebra or the thigh of a gazelle—just for a snack, you understand. Usually lions are lazy when they have fed. They can sleep for fifteen out of twenty-four hours. But a hungry lion is truly dangerous, especially the one who is rarely seen, who lurks secretly and hunts at night."

The lioness vanished from sight. The animals dispersed over the plain as if nothing had happened and resumed grazing. The young antelope and zebra colts, wildebeest and gazelles were soon frisking on the grass. Colors and forms shimmered peacefully in the warm air; a leisurely neighing interrupted the silence. The drivers started their motors and the vans moved ahead. They crossed the border from Kenya into Tanzania. The smiling, dark-skinned border police waved them through from the distance.

One of the therapists broke the silence as if on purpose to dispel the impact of the scene with the lioness: "A high school teacher I once had looked exactly like one of those buffalo we saw."

"I had a teacher who resembled a horse—or maybe it was a zebra!" a woman giggled nervously.

"I have a neighbor who looks like a monkey!" a corpulent woman chimed in.

"But you, my dear, are as slim and graceful as a gazelle," came the rejoinder.

"And you look like an elephant!" harrumphed the corpulent woman. "Your elephantine philosophies are just the thing for this place."

"So we've come on this safari to take photos of our own selves!" another voice intruded, half in jest, half in earnest.

"That which befalleth the beast befalleth the sons of men," Simon heard Marisha reverse the quote from Ecclesiastes for Mr. Mashada, who stood on her other side. "But man is worse than any animal. Man kills. Not because he must but for his own perverse pleasure, simply out of a passion to destroy. We humans are scandalous squanderers of nature's resources."

Simon could not bear her moralizing tone. Nor could he tolerate the fact that she had glued herself to their Indian host and would not leave him alone. Suddenly he heard Marisha burst into laughter. "Look at them, Mr. Mashada!" she exclaimed. "Just look at them!"

At a distance of a few yards two big-bellied ostriches raced by on agile, sticklike legs, parallel with the vans as though they were racing the drivers.

"The largest birds in the world!" Mr. Mashada exclaimed with pride, as if the size of the ostriches were his own doing. "The one to the right, with the black and white feathers, is the male. Look how arrogantly he holds his head, how he puffs himself up so as to display the elegance of his muscular thighs. The idiot! On account of their beautiful feathers male ostriches used to be killed by the thousands, especially during those times when it was the fashion for our women to decorate themselves with ostrich feathers. We humans disparage the ostrich for hiding its head in the sand. But in truth there is nothing ostrich-like about ostriches. They sit down and bury their heads in their plumage or in the sand because that is how they rest. This protective position makes them appear from a distance like mounds of sand. But they make self-sacrificing parents and loving couples. Both the male and the female sit on the eggs, and together they protect their young from the sun by spreading their enormous wings."

"Are they monogamous?" one of the women asked.

"That, Madam, is something that nobody has yet managed to discover. That is an ostrich secret."

The two racing ostriches finally overtook the vans, which had reduced their speed because of a herd of giraffes coming into view in the distance. The faces of the perspiring passengers lit up with childish curiosity. They felt as if they were witnessing a solemn procession of unearthly creatures, a slow, graceful queue of long-necked ballet dancers advancing on toe. The giraffes' tall necks seemed to reach the clouds. With their lofty heads crowned by abbreviated horns that resembled small coronets, their golden skin set off by large brown spots as though their bodies were clad in ermine, and the white patches on their slender legs, they looked like the capricious invention of some wild-eyed eccentric. Silken dreams seemed to float by in the gleam of their large brown eyes. Negligently they nibbled at the leaves at the tops of the acacia trees, as if food were the last thing on their minds. And so they proceeded forward—a herd of noble philosopher kings who, although their feet walked the earth, had their true kingdom in the sky.

"They are docile, affectionate, and not at all aggressive," Mr. Mashada whispered respectfully, moved by the beautiful sight as if he were seeing a procession of giraffes for the first time in his life.

One of the passing giraffes appeared to look Simon Brown straight in the eye, as if her wise, warm eyes had something important to say to him. What did she want to tell him? Most likely nothing pleasant. She was probably wondering with compassionate reproach: "Why do you make such a fuss about yourself, Simon Brown, my relative from the human race? Basically you're nothing but an emotional impotent. What are all your passions, all your loves, if not an egotistical bluff by which the tiny Jew within you feeds his enormous ego? You love no one, least of all yourself. That is the saddest fact about you. What attracted you to psychiatry if not your self-serving ambition to make a name for yourself, coupled with your compulsion to search for yourself, while praying to God that you never be found? As for your coming here to this wilderness, this too is a self-serving act, not meant for the benefit of either your colleagues or psychiatry as a whole. Mildred was right."

Simon glanced at the perspiring faces of his astonished colleagues. How strange it was that ever since they had arrived in the Serengeti no one had ventured to make a psychiatric comment, crack a psychiatric joke, or use psychiatric jargon. Of course Mildred was right. The Serengeti was capable of shaking up the mind, of rearranging the furniture in one's head and putting the totality of one's rationalized worldview under a question mark. It seemed that they had all regressed to the primitive state of their childhoods, while at the same time they had the wisdom to realize how irrelevant their academic knowledge was in the face of this strange vastness with which they were awkwardly trying to familiarize themselves. It was as if they had torn themselves away from the cycle of life and had allowed their intellects to lead them so far astray that they no longer knew the way back.

It suddenly occurred to Simon that Mildred had something of a giraffe about her. Her graceful body, her tall neck, her head proudly raised as if she were wearing a crown, and the reproachful mildness of her manner when she criticized him had something giraffe-like about them. Only the giraffe's eyes were unlike Mildred's. Instead the giraffe's eyes had reminded him of Marisha Vishnievska's brown eyes. He looked across at Marisha in order to verify the comparison.

Marisha looked back at him. Something very compelling peered out from her brown giraffe eyes. It seemed that her eyes were calling him to her.

"Look, look, my friends, over there!" Mr. Mashada suddenly exclaimed, pointing with his chin. Three colossal lions, two females and a male with a streaming mane, were racing in the direction of a herd of kudu antelope whose twisted horns resembled the branches of a menorah. Confusion and panic spread all over the plain. A stampede. A dusty whirlwind. The earth turned into a drum vibrating to the pounding of escaping feet. The drivers stopped the motors. The dark-skinned guards held their guns ready.

"Don't move," Mr. Mashada ordered. "As long as we don't leave the van there is no danger. The lions know that we can harm them.

And they hate the smell of gasoline. What's more, they don't consider us to be particularly tasty. But you never know. A hungry lion is not finicky."

The three lions raced by with such speed that they seemed to be soaring through the fog of dust that they raised. The panicked herds shimmered in the distance, as if their outlines were reflected in the waters of a far-off mirage. In an instant one of the lionesses uncoiled her graceful body and, with paws extended, leaped onto the back of an antelope. All the other animals in the vicinity darted away in a mad panic until they disappeared beneath the line of the horizon, leaving the three predators and their victim to their unequal struggle. The deadly fangs of the lioness sank into her prey's neck. The antelope's twisted, menorah-like horns fenced with the empty air. Then the horns stopped moving.

"Finished!" proclaimed one of the women therapists.

"Hard to know for certain," Mr. Mashada replied. "Some animals become paralyzed at such a moment. Some instinct tells them to play dead as a last resort in order to save themselves. That's because the lioness sometimes drops her prey and there is a slight chance of escape. But in most cases this hypnotic state anesthetizes the victim not to feel the bite of death."

The male lion, his mane shaking, was already tearing chunks of flesh from the still-jerking antelope. The two lionesses joined him. It was not long before all three lions were treading noiselessly over the grass, large chunks of antelope flesh dangling from between their teeth. Their departure was followed by the arrival of those garbage cleaners of the plains, the hyenas. Cunning and cowardly, their rounded ears shaped like bow ties, the hyenas had come to check whether there were any bones left on the carcass to munch on. Usually they kept an eye out for the lions, who treated them with hatred and tended to persecute them. But now, with the lions gone, the hyenas could fill the air with their chattering laughter. Above their heads the vultures flew low, fanning the air with outstretched wings.

Gradually, the herds returned to their leisurely grazing as they again spread out all over the plain. The vans now drove past hundreds of zebras. Meek as tame horses but restless and hungry, the zebras neighed disconsolately, raising a great noise. Monkeys with red posteriors danced from tree to tree as if a leopard, their greatest enemy, were not slumbering on a branch nearby, lazily awaiting the sunset, when he would go in search of supper.

"How quiet and *gemütlich*. As if nothing had happened," Simon heard Marisha mutter.

Mr. Mashada nodded in agreement. "That is the rhythm, the music of the Serengeti. Life and death, death and life, fear and hunger, hunger and fear. Up and down, down and up, and in between—the state of oblivion. Forgetting helps one to continue with the business of life, and yet forgetfulness is life's greatest enemy." Mr. Mashada noticed something move outside the van. "Really, my friends, the Serengeti is giving you a royal welcome. To encounter so many lions in one outing is a rarity!"

A few yards away a pride of lionesses lay in the shade of an acacia tree busily enjoying a meal. Between their paws lay the remains of a zebra, its insides open and bleeding. The lionesses' faces and paws were smeared with blood. As they gnawed on the carcass, they licked the blood from their whiskers with fat, salivating tongues. The cubs gamboled on their mothers' backs and sides like so many kittens, trying to squeeze into the center of the feast. They rubbed up against the bodies of the adults, but their mothers pushed them away, occasionally licking them with their rough, blood-red tongues or slapping at them with a bloody paw as if in punishment for bad manners.

"Obviously the principle here is that for the well-being of the child the mother's needs must be satisfied first," Mildred commented drily, clicking away with the camera.

"If a Jewish mother saw such a scene she would scream with indignation," commented one of the younger therapists, a wise smile fixed to his face.

"True!" Marisha Vishnievska confirmed with a nod.

Simon Brown looked at her with surprise. "Do you know any Jewish mothers, Dr. Vishnievska?" He insisted on calling her by her family name and title even though he addressed all his other colleagues by their first names.

"Two of my mothers were Jewesses," she answered with feigned nonchalance.

"Really? How many mothers did you have in all?"

"Three."

She was teasing him. "Most of us have only one mother," he replied with an edge in his voice.

She did not respond.

One of the lion cubs finally ventured to bite into a chunk of meat that was protruding from the muzzle of the only male lion in the pack and tried to extract it from between the lion's teeth. The cameras clicked and whirred. Only Simon and Marisha held their cameras away from their faces, fingering them absentmindedly. The other therapists in the van were fascinated by the family scene being played out before them; they smiled at each other and blinked meaningfully. They were all becoming used to the sight of death, which was simultaneously the sight of life. It was becoming commonplace, trivial. The scene before them was so recognizably human, so homey: a family gathering for a picnic, a shared meal around a table covered with a green tablecloth.

The drivers started their motors. But this time the wheels of the van carrying Dr. Brown and his group spun ineffectually in the sand. They were stuck.

The lions, still busily chewing, turned their blood-stained muzzles in the direction of the two vans, whose presence they had up to now ignored. Angry rumbling sounds filled the air. The lions were obviously upset at having their feast disturbed. Inside the vans the heat became suffocating. The passengers' faces were red and glistened with perspiration.

"Don't move from your places!" Mr. Mashada shouted. For a moment he took counsel with the dark-skinned driver, after which, guns in hand, he and the driver jumped out of the van. They were soon joined by the two armed guards. The driver of the second van suggested using his own van to push the immobilized vehicle from the rear. Mr. Mashada firmly rejected this proposal. He was afraid that the increased noise would only irritate the lions further. So the second van's driver and its two guards carefully got out of their own van and, using their van as a shield, approached Dr. Brown's immobilized vehicle with slow, gingerly steps, guns at the ready. The seven men pressed their bodies against the immobile van and heaved. Then, placing their shoulders and hands against the sides of the vehicle, they began rhythmically rocking the van back and forth. Inside the van the tension increased. The passengers huddled together.

Simon Brown gave Mildred a reassuring pat on the shoulder and squeezed his body in behind the wheel of the driver's seat. The men outside were in danger. Would he increase the danger if he started the motor? Two lion cubs approached playfully, curious about the big striped thing swaying back and forth. Their mother let out a bellow. There was no more time to lose. Simon started the motor. He took a minute to sense the rhythm of the swaying vehicle and pressed his foot down on the gas. The startled cubs stopped in their tracks. The van jerked forward and immediately rolled back into the sandy ditch it had dug beneath itself. His hands hot and sweaty, Simon gave a sharp, sudden jerk of the wheel and the van, like some large lazy animal, began slowly to inch up the sandy mound it had itself created.

The men hopped in. Simon yielded his seat to the driver. Clumsily, in jerks and jolts, the van moved away from the pride of lions whose uninvited guest it had been. In a few minutes it was back on the gravel road. The excited passengers thanked Mr. Mashada, the driver, and the guards and praised Simon for his driving skill and composure. There was a lively clamor in the van fueled by a sense of relief that the danger had passed. The passengers wiped the perspiration off their faces and repeated to each other the details of the ordeal they had just lived through. They were proud of their experience and felt heroic for having been stuck in the sand just a few feet away from a pride of lions.

Mildred dabbed Simon's forehead with her handkerchief, gazing at him with devoted, loving eyes. He glanced at Marisha. She was standing a short distance from him, her back turned to the other passengers. Although sweaty, her face was pale. Her lower lip trembled. So she knew the meaning of fear after all.

A few minutes later, as one of the guards was distributing paper cups filled with drinking water, Simon took the opportunity to move closer to Marisha. It was odd that he, who had used to avoid her so determinedly, should be suddenly gripped by a desire to stand beside her. "Are you still upset by what happened?" he asked her.

"No, not by that." She shook her head, but her lip trembled.

Mr. Mashada apologized for the loss of time caused by the incident and ordered the drivers to turn back toward the border. A small, isolated guesthouse stood amid a few acacia trees, with tables and benches scattered about in the shade. There the passengers consumed their lunch, which they had brought along with them on the road. There was also a garage nearby to check the motors and fill up on gas.

* * *

A cluster of jacaranda trees stood like a bouquet of purple flowers at the entrance to the Masai village toward which the vans had headed as soon as they crossed the border back into Kenya. The cluster of trees stood near a protective enclosure of thorn branches used to fence in the herds of cattle.

"The Masai used to be proud warriors," Mr. Mashada explained. "During the slave trade the slave merchants avoided this entire territory, and no Masai was ever sold into slavery. But since they no longer go to war and are not even permitted to hunt, legally that is, the only honorable occupation left to the men is to be the herdsmen of their cattle. Cattle are their greatest treasure. They drink both the milk and the blood of their cattle, and this is their main source of nourishment."

Inside the village the travelers noted the rounded, cone-shaped huts built by the Masai women out of twigs and cattle dung and covered with animal skins. These were laid out in a circle around a large yard. The huts were so low that it was impossible to stand upright inside them.

Slim, narrow-hipped men sat around in the yard. Conforming to their ideal of beauty, none of them was muscled or heavy-set; instead their bodies were lean and graceful, with smoothly textured light-brown skin. The women wore strings of beads suspended from the huge holes in their earlobes. Some were dipping thin twigs in shells filled with paint and painting delicate designs on the men's faces, arms, and backs while others braided the men's hair into long, thin braids they arranged on their heads, smearing them with a claylike red paste to keep them in place. Still other half-naked women busied themselves inside the huts.

"The Masai don't tolerate anyone ruling over them," explained Mr. Mashada. "Only old people and medicine men have any authority over them. And just like any democratic society, it can take them weeks if not months to arrive at a decision."

Mr. Mashada introduced Simon as the leader of the group of visitors to the few old men who appeared before them. One of the old men brought a leather gourd from his hut and in a show of hospitality offered Simon a drink of milk from the gourd.

"Pretend to be drinking, Professor," Mr. Mashada whispered in Simon's ear. "They have a habit of washing their gourds with urine."

Simon bowed before the old man and moistened his lips with the milk. Mildred, who stood beside him, wiped his mouth with a piece of Kleenex. "Disgusting," she muttered under her breath.

Mr. Mashada continued speaking: "The Masai themselves observe a sort of dietary law, not unlike the dietary laws of the Jews. They don't drink milk if they know that they will be eating meat later on."

The crowd of men, women, and children surrounding the visitors grew. What intrigued and amused the Masai most was the hair growing on their male visitors' arms and legs and peeking out from their chests beneath their unbuttoned shirts. The bodies of the Masai were smooth and hairless, and they could not understand how hair could grow directly on the body. They began to pull at the hair on the white arms of the men in order to see whether it was natural or fake. One curious Masai stuck his finger into Simon's ear, trying to pull out a hair that was growing there. The joyful laughter of adults and children echoed all over the yard and between the huts. They found the white people very amusing.

In response to an order from the gray-haired old man, the painted Masai men, spears in hand, formed themselves into a column and began to dance with short, hopping steps, round and round the yard, to the rhythm of a monotonous chant.

"This is all that is left of their former glory," Mr. Mashada explained. "Once they were invincible warriors. They come from the north; they arrived in hordes from Egypt and caused the local tribes to flee. But they never became rulers over any conquered tribe. Instead they merely conquered and moved on. They were fearless, skillful in the use of the spear, but they never resorted to covering their spears with poison like the warriors of other tribes. Such tricks would have been beneath their dignity. It is interesting that although they never part with their spears, they consider the spear makers to be unclean and ugly; they wash their hands after greeting them. What's more, they're forbidden to marry into a spear maker's family, and whoever sleeps with a spear maker's daughter is sure to die soon. Today the Masai live only with their traditions and with the symbols of their past. These traditions enhance their self-respect; without them they would perish. Their proud laziness may seem ridiculous to you, but they are more active than they seem. When they are not tending their cattle they are dancing. But this is not merely dancing. Their dancing is part of their religious ritual and gives them spiritual gratification. They believe in one God and consider themselves to be God's chosen people. They are familiar with the stories of Adam and Eve, the flood, Cain and Abel. They look down their noses at the darker-skinned tribes as well as at the whites. They believe that God created the world exclusively for them. They think that love and brotherhood exist only among themselves, so they don't consider it a sin to cheat or steal from members of other tribes. They have their own language, but they can make themselves understood also in Swahili, and they are starting to acquire a facility with English."

"Maybe they're one of the lost tribes," one of the Jewish therapists mused. "Maybe they built the pyramids in Egypt and escaped from slavery at the same time as the children of Israel but then got lost in the desert? Or maybe they rebelled against Moses because he forbade them to paint their bodies?"

Mr. Mashada did not smile at the remark. "As a matter of fact," he said, "they circumcise their boys. The ceremony takes place once every three years, and a most important ceremony it is too. All boys of the same age are circumcised together, on the same day. This collective circumcision remains a bond between them for the rest of their lives. When they reach marriageable age the young men leave their homes and are forbidden to return until they have killed a lion as proof of manliness. They practice this skill even today. They don't consider themselves obliged to obey the law forbidding hunting on the Serengeti. If caught, they pay the required number of cattle as punishment for having broken the law, then they carry on as before. Afterward the young men and girls leave for the forest and mate indiscriminately. Upon their return, each young man builds a hut for himself and the girl he has chosen to be his wife. If there is a death in the hut, the hut is burned and a new one is built. The corpse is arranged in a fetal position and deposited on the open plain to be eaten by the animals. If the corpse is not eaten by the animals it is considered a bad omen. The Masai feel themselves to be a part of the circle of life and death on the Serengeti. Nothing must go to waste here."

As the dance of the warriors continued, a group of old men and women brought over a calf and forced it to its knees in the middle of the yard. A few young warriors left the group of dancers and approached in order to bind the calf's neck with thin twigs. One of the old men shot an arrow into the calf's neck and a jet of blood burst forth, which the women caught in clay dishes. The old man spat on his finger, mixed the spittle with soil, and rubbed the paste into the open hole in the calf's neck. The blood stopped oozing. The old man took a bowl of blood from one of the women's hands, stirred it with a stick, and was about to touch it to Simon's lips when Mr. Mashada stopped him, explaining in Swahili that the visitors did not drink blood.

"We white people spill blood just for the hell of it," Simon heard Marisha Vishnievska comment behind his back.

* * *

By the time they left the Masai village the sun had begun to set. Simon Brown sat in the van, his mind dwelling on the Masai in the village they had just left. He did not trace them back in his imagination to ancient Egypt, nor even to more remote times. Yet he felt as if here on the Serengeti he had come face to face with his own ancestral origins.

The van grew cooler and airier. In the west the sky was bathed in the pink of the descending sun while at the same time a pinkish shimmer danced through the air to the north. The vans were approaching Nakuru Lake, the shores of which were trimmed by the feather-pink of hundreds upon hundreds of flamingoes. Once more the tourists beheld an image of perfect harmony, the resplendent interweaving of color and form. Nature smiled a pink smile and sang a joyous song of praise in tune to the pastel-pink flutter of wings and deafening clatter of beaks as the beauty of the sunset was reflected in the pink mirror of the lake.

A short distance from the lake stood the plant queens of the plain, the thorny acacia trees. On a thick branch of one such tree, exposing her graceful splendor to the onlookers' awestruck eyes, lay a long-whiskered female leopard. Like an indolent odalisque, the solitary night huntress lay luxuriantly stretched out along the branch of the tree. Her long, flecked tail with its black tip dangled lazily above the ground. She was not hungry. From the branches of the surrounding trees were suspended chunks of zebra and gazelle carcasses that she had deposited there to keep them safe from thieving hyenas or jackals.

* * *

The tree house on the northern border of the Serengeti stood on an elevation at the foot of Mount Kenya. It was hidden inside a forest of massive trees. The tree house was really a hotel built up in the air around an ancient fig tree. It provided nocturnal lodgings for guests, who seldom slept during the night. Nobody went there in order to sleep. People came instead to observe the nightlife of the animal world. The tree house had a long balcony that ran like an apron around the tree's black trunk. There were no stairs leading up to the tree house. Instead there was a sort of stepladder, and it was to this ladder that the armed guards led the guests as soon as they emerged from their vans. Remote and old though the tree house was, it had made its mark on modern history as the place where Britain's Princess Elizabeth had spent the night when she first learned of the death of her father, King George VI.

Here the night was cold. The huge stars glimmered as if they had been polished by frost. The moon resembled a brilliant chunk of ice. The place exuded an air of ghostly secrets and bloody horror.

Wrapped in their sweaters, the group of therapists sat on the hard bench that encircled the tree trunk like a gallery in a theater. The best seats were those that faced the huge water hole where the animals came to drink. Mildred had, as usual, thoroughly studied the tour brochures and had had the foresight to take along sweaters and an old knitted plaid. Now she sat on the balcony cuddled up against Simon's arm, both of them wrapped in the warm plaid.

Mr. Mashada made his apologies to Simon and the other guests, requesting that they leave him alone for the time being. Solemnly he explained to them that his greatest pleasure was to spend the night on the gallery of the tree house in total silence, listening to the music of the forest's wakeful darkness. He advised his guests to do the same.

The moon dipped its reflection in the water hole while the reflections of the stars sparkled above it. It seemed as if the hippopotamuses swallowed a mouthful of stars every time they raised their heads over the lake's surface to blow jets of water into the air with heavy snorts. A variety of animals came to drink at the water hole. Their watchful eyes ever on the alert, they lapped up their share of water while keeping an eye on their young. As soon as they sensed something suspicious in the air they disappeared into the depths of the forest.

A leopard padded to the water's edge for a drink, followed by a cheetah. Then came a shaggy-maned lion accompanied by an entourage of lionesses and their cubs. They were followed by foxes and jackals, which were in turn chased away by a pack of wild dogs. Water mongooses, like huge rats, crawled out from their muddy nests on the shore and wandered around the water hole.

It was after midnight. Mildred was sleepy. She left the knitted plaid with Simon, kissed him, and returned to their cabin to lie down. The other guests too, exhausted after the long hot day full of impressions, found themselves unable to keep the vigil any longer and retired for the night.

It seemed to Simon that he had been left all alone on the gallery. If Mr. Mashada was still sitting somewhere, Simon could not see him. Then he noticed someone approaching. He knew who it was—Marisha.

"Oh, you have a plaid, Professor," she said in a whisper. "I'm freezing. I washed my hair in the cabin, and it hasn't dried yet." With a sweeping movement of her head she shook out her hair as if she were unfurling a huge black fan before his eyes. Her hair was astonishingly long. She rubbed some long strands with her hands.

The scar on her forehead was invisible. It seemed to Simon that her face was pale and very beautiful. He drew the plaid out from behind his back. "Here, take it." He held out the plaid to her.

"Not for the world!" she shook her mane of wet hair. "Unless you wrap yourself in it next to me." He hesitated. He did not want to share the plaid with her. But he did not want her to leave either. He indicated the seat beside him, which she took, and he threw the plaid over both their shoulders.

A mother rhinoceros with her offspring by her side approached the water. The rhinoceros's two horns cut into the darkness like elliptical slices of moon. Night birds rode on the backs of the two animals, cleaning the vermin from their leathery skins. Mother and child looked like two large, clumsy pigs. There was something awkward yet endearing about their movements. Simon burst out laughing, not really knowing whether he laughed because of his pleasure at the touch of Marisha's hip and arm or because the rhinoceroses were so quaintly amusing.

"If you ask me, these are the ugliest creatures on God's earth," he remarked.

"Ugliness is a question of personal taste," she answered dryly. He stared at her, surprised to see her observing the mother rhinoceros and her calf with such gloomy earnestness. "I miss my daughter," she added after a long moment of silence.

"How old is your daughter?" he asked.

"She's eight."

"Eight? You never said a word about her during all those sessions of psychoanalysis."

"I did not have her then, Professor. Besides, I cheated more than a little during my psychoanalysis." She laughed unpleasantly.

"What do you mean you cheated? I don't like such jokes."

"Remember what Schopenhauer said? There exists in this world only one creature capable of cheating, and that is man. All other animals are straightforward and honest. They show themselves for what they are and don't pretend to emotions that they don't have. Almost nothing I told you during our sessions was true, my dear Dr. Brown, not even the contents of my dreams, which so intrigued you. To put it more correctly, there was just enough truth in my babblings to make my lies sound truthful. My actual life, Professor, the life I really lived, is still lying submerged within me. It suffocates me. It keeps me from catching my breath."

He could not decide whether she was joking or really meant what she said. "You wouldn't have dared . . ."

"Why not? I wanted the right to practice."

"If what you're telling me now is true I will take that away from you."

"Why are you threatening me?" She softly stroked his hand. "We both know that you will do no such thing because it would discredit you more than it would harm me. A man of your standing and authority, with your psychoanalytical skills, not to have detected my lies? And then you wouldn't harm me because of solidarity. Somewhere deep inside you have known all along that there is Jewish blood in my veins, although you deliberately blinded yourself to the fact, just as you've blinded yourself to many other things. And I suspect that there is also a third reason . . ." She snuggled closer to him.

"I refuse to believe it. What about the tears, the spasms, the hysterical explosions of anger? And then those endless hours when you lay on the sofa in my office and refused to say a word. Was that too a put-on?"

"The tears, the spasms, and the rage came upon me without much effort, and the stubborn silences were the easiest part. It all goes to prove, Professor, that our profession hangs by a hair, suspended between lie and illusion."

"And what about the story of having fallen face down on a rock at the age of two?"

"That was true."

"Bravo!" he snapped. He edged away from her, letting the plaid slip from his shoulders.

He felt her hand sliding in under his arm. "Don't give up on me. Don't give up on yourself, Professor. I did fall on a rock when I was two. That was true. But how this came about I did not say, because then I would have had to confess my Jewishness. Talking about it meant that I would have had to touch upon a wound festering inside me. And I was not ready for that yet."

"Are you ready now?"

"I think so."

"How do I know that you're telling the truth now?"

"We are in the face of truth here; we are in the land of truth."

"But we are only tourists in this land. As you said yourself: man is a liar. Woman is a liar. You are a liar. A pathological liar."

"So are you, Professor. You lie about yourself. You deny the truth about yourself, the truth that is within you."

"What truth is that?" Simon could not understand why, despite his bitter words, he felt no stirring of anger against her. On the contrary. He felt instead a sense of humility and tenderness that brought him close to tears.

It seemed so simple, so natural, when she put her arms around his neck. Spontaneously, unthinkingly, he embraced her, feeling the dampness of her hair between his fingers. He rejoiced at being able to hold her like this. Her face was close to his, a white rising sun in the middle of the night, a sun that exuded a caressing, familiar, much-longed-for warmth. He noticed the glint of her sparkling teeth between her smiling lips and heard her whisper: "Put your finger on my forehead. Touch the scar. This scar represents the truth about you just as it represents the truth about me. This cut on my forehead I received on an early spring night in 1943, when my mother threw me from the speeding cattle train that was transporting us from Warsaw to Treblinka. I was wrapped in a shawl, but my face was only partly protected. I hit against a rock lying on the edge of a field."

The mother rhinoceros and her child were slurping the silvery water of the pond. Simon put his hand on Marisha's head and let it slide down along the silk of her hair. He stroked her hair not with his hand but rather with his heart, which no longer felt balled up like a fist but was open, as if waiting for an offering—or ready to make one.

"I often have nightmares like that. I dream that I am a child wandering in a field all alone on a dark night." The sound of his own whispering voice surprised him. "I can hear myself calling, 'Where am I? Who am I?'"

"I wandered and wandered through that field in the dark," she continued. "That is all that I can remember. A poor peasant woman who lived in a cottage near the rails found me. Her husband had left to join the Polish army when the war broke out, but he never came back. Barbara Grzimek was her name. That's why when I came upon the name Grzimek two years ago, that is, the father and son who sounded the alarm about the deplorable situation in the Serengeti, and when I read their appeal to the world to save the animals, I became curious. But I never succeeded in discovering whether there was a link between them and Barbara Grzimek, my second mother, who gave me life for the second time. She had left her hut that dawn to fetch water from the well, and she saw me lying in the next field, my face smeared with blood. She took me into her home. She understood where I had come from and was afraid to take me to see a doctor. So the wound on my forehead was never sewn up. Barbara had two children who were older than I, but they were still too young to understand much. So she simply told them that I was their newly found sister. The neighbors from the distant village had no idea how many children she really had."

"So you didn't lie to me completely. You used to tell me so much about Barbara, your mother, the kindhearted peasant woman who raised you on herbs during the week and on sorrel with potatoes on Sundays."

"How well you remember my confessions, Professor. But you're mistaken. My real mother survived the war. She escaped from Treblinka during the uprising in the camp. Right after the liberation she began to search for me in the region where she had thrown me from the speeding train. And she found me in Barbara's cottage. She tore me out of Barbara's arms, tore me out of my home, tore me away from my sister and brother and brought me to Warsaw. When I was about six years old and began to go to school, I started to torment her about the disgusting scar on my forehead. And so she would tell me horror stories about my Jewishness, about my father who had been shot in the forest, about how she had thrown me out of the speeding train in order to save me. She told me about a concentration camp with gas chambers, and she told me that my real name was Esther. At first I hated that name; I hated my mother and did not believe her stories. Nor did I believe that I was Jewish. I suspected my mother of telling me lies in order to frighten me. She would tell me that thanks to me she had survived, that the thought of me had given her strength. She fed me wonderful food and fed my soul with the sweet melodies of Yiddish songs. Her eyes were two caverns full of sadness, but with me she was playful and merry. And so she finally won my heart, and I grew very attached to her. I adored her smile and her sad beauty. She became the dearest, most precious person I had in the world. Our single room was always full of visitors, my mother's comrades. They drank a lot, they ate and sang, in order to dull their memory, in order to make themselves forget the horrors they had witnessed. There was a couple among the visitors. They were my mother's best friends, who had worked with her after the war organizing children's clubs all over Poland. Stefa and Karol Vishnievsky were their names. They both had degrees. Mother told me in secret that they were Jews just like us, and that they had taken on the name Vishnievsky when they were hiding from the Nazis on the Aryan side of Warsaw. On account of her work, my mother traveled a lot over Poland. When she had to be away, she left me with the Vishnievskys, who were childless. The Vishnievskys adored me and did not mind if I turned their entire apartment upside down. They bought me toys and spoiled me with sweets. I was a happy, pampered child. Both my mother and the Vishnievskys found comfort in me, but at school my life was full of bitterness. The children poked fun at me because of my ugliness. The scar on my forehead became a sort of mark of Cain. It gave me a twisted sense of guilt for having had the bad luck to be born a Jew."

Simon Brown felt a stirring in his heart. He too considered his Jewishness a sign of shame, a cause for guilt, a scar on his soul. The veil that he had drawn over his consciousness was related to this shame. Because he felt the crippling burden of his Jewish fate he never saw himself as a complete person.

"So this is the truth about you . . ." he murmured.

"Not the entire truth yet, Professor. Another chapter is still to follow, or better still another two or three chapters. The joy of having found my mother lasted no longer than two and a half years. In June of 1946, a year after the liberation from the camps, there was a pogrom against Jews in the town of Kielce. And there were assassinations of Jews in many small Polish towns, to say nothing of anti-Semitic attacks on trains and buses. To protect themselves some Jews started carrying weapons concealed in their clothing. On the fifth of May 1947, my mother was traveling by train to another town on business. Hoodlums from the N.S.Z., a Polish nationalist organization, stopped the train. They took out all the Jews and shot them, my mother included.

"After her death, the Vishnievskys adopted me. They sent me to the *gymnasium* and to the university. They were fanatically committed to communism, and they believed in the communist future of Poland. They loved Poland. They continued to hide their Jewishness and thought that I had forgotten about mine. I acted like an ordinary Polish girl and began to believe in the part I played. So began my career as a liar. I became quite good at it. But I could not forget my Jewish mother. When I heard people talking about Jews and complaining that so many of them had returned from the camps, rage erupted within me. Rage and despair. If Treblinka, if Auschwitz were not enough—then what was enough? I was glad when the State of Israel came into being. But I did not believe that it had the power to obliterate the hatred toward us. The roots of that hatred run too deep. I wanted to understand where the hatred came from, from which source in the human soul. And so I was drawn to psychiatry and decided to make it my medical specialty. But to tell you the truth, I've not come very far in my search.

"As for the Vishnievskys, they were proud of me. I graduated from medical school with honors. I was sent to India, as you know, in order to complete the research for my dissertation on the influence of Hindu philosophy on psychiatric thinking. There, one day in 1967, I got a letter from Karol Vishnievsky, who had been so delighted with my achievements, telling me that he and Stefa had lost their jobs. He indicated that the communist government had embarked on an anti-Jewish campaign and that the remainder of Jewish survivors were fleeing Poland. He implored me not to return home. As for himself and Stefa, he wrote that they were too old to emigrate.

"That's how my wandering began. I wandered from one university to another, taking all possible jobs, living on pennies, until finally my luck changed. I was awarded a grant to study in New York at your institute."

"And so you finally had a happy ending?" Simon was deeply moved and wiped his face with his hands. "At last," he said, "I know the truth about you."

"Still not the whole truth, Professor. Three years ago Karol Vishnievsky died, and after him Stefa. I left for Poland to visit their graves, and I also paid Barbara a visit. She was raising a Polish orphan girl in her cottage. The little girl was five years old. I adopted her and brought her to America. I am raising her as a Jewish child. We celebrate the

217

Jewish holidays together. We learn Bible stories together, and she knows by heart all the Yiddish songs that my mother used to sing."

Simon continued wiping his face with his hands. "How stupid, how idiotic," he whispered. "I don't know what's come over me. I haven't shed a tear since my mother died."

"These are good tears," Marisha said softly, embracing his head and pressing it to her bosom. "I sensed that they were about to come, that you were beginning to realize that you are attracted to me. Touch my forehead. Don't be afraid. Kiss me."

He touched her forehead and kissed her scar.

"Kiss me on the lips. That's what you want, isn't it?"

"I mustn't. It's dangerous."

"But you are brave."

"I love Mildred. She is my home."

"I am your home. Your real home. Call me Esther."

The tears still flowed from Simon's eyes. "I must get away from you, although it's true that I'm attracted to you. But I also hate many things about you. I hate what you are doing to me."

"You hate the reflection of yourself that you see in me, and that's why you love me even more."

He jumped to his feet and, mumbling a cold good night, walked quickly away to his own cabin, leaving behind Mildred's plaid.

* * *

The following day, on their way back to the guesthouse, the vans traveled faster than they had on their outbound journey. But they again stopped to observe the herds of animals grazing peacefully on the plain. And so the travelers saw again the scenes they had witnessed the day before, when hundreds of animals were hypnotized into paralysis by the sight of a skulking lioness a few meters away. Every time that Simon Brown saw this scene he turned his head automatically in Marisha's direction. He had made sure to sit as far away from her as possible in the van. He stayed close to Mildred, chatting with her about writing a letter to the children and making arrangements for the "marathon" session that was due to begin the next day. Mildred answered him in her clear, matter-of-fact tone of voice, chuckling occasionally at some amusing thoughts she related to Simon as they occurred to her.

The sun burned mercilessly, and perspiration streamed down the faces of the travelers. The longer they drove the more the sun's rays burned through the roof of the van. There was no longer any protection against it. The tourists tried to cover their limbs and fan themselves with whatever material was at hand. Again they passed the chilling sight of lions devouring their prey. This time the victim was a giraffe. The flesh had been peeled away from the giraffe's long, slim neck, exposing the vertebrae, so that the two lions chomping on the carcass looked like they were sounding out a mellifluous hymn to brutality on the harmonica of the giraffe's neck.

A hot, suffocating wind lifted the tangled manes of the two gorging lions and blew into the van. Suddenly something white flew out of the van and shot through the air. It was Marisha's sun hat, which the wind had blown off her head. The hat came to rest just in front of the two feasting lions. The therapists in the van collectively gave vent to a half astonished, half fearful, "Oh!" and exchanged uneasy glances.

"Sorry, Miss," Mr. Mashada said to Marisha in a whisper. "I'm afraid you must say goodbye to your charming sun hat." He made a sign to the driver to drive on.

The hot winds filled the air with dust and made it difficult to breathe. The travelers' dust-covered clothes fluttered in the breeze, but the ventilation gave no relief from the heat. They all held on to their sun hats with their hands, except for Marisha who had lost hers. They were seated now, jumping to their feet only when Mr. Mashada pointed out something of interest. Only Marisha stood the entire time, gazing out. Her thick braid had slipped from the top of her head and was now hanging down her back. The wind and the continual shaking of the van caused the braid to undulate like a snake in motion. The sun shone directly onto her forehead, making her scar even more fiery and prominent than usual.

"I must not let her stand like that in the baking sun," Simon thought to himself. "She might get a sunstroke. I'm responsible for her." As if the scar on her forehead had hypnotized him, he stood up and made his way over to her, taking the hat off his own head and putting it on hers.

"It suits you," he said to her with tenderness.

"You mustn't," she raised her hand to remove the hat.

"Leave it! That's an order!" he exclaimed. Feeling satisfied with himself without really knowing why, he laughed at her. And so, laughing, he went back to sit down beside Mildred, wiping the sweat off the top of his head with his handkerchief.

Mildred was angry. "How could you do such a thing? She has enough hair on her head to protect her, while you have hardly any."

"Her hair is dark; it attracts the sun's rays. I am responsible for our expedition, my dear."

"Then take my hat," Mildred removed the hat from her head. "I have light hair." She smiled at him maternally.

He put the hat back on her head. "Leave it! That's an order!" He looked at his wife tenderly. Even now, in the suffocating heat, in the general disorder of appearance caused by the heat, she looked beautiful, neat. Her sweaty face seemed to project coolness. "I love you, Mildred," he whispered, planting a kiss on her moist cheek.

The salty taste of her sweat evoked a cloudy recollection of a kiss he had once planted on his grandfather's sweaty hand. During the sweltering heat of a New York summer his grandfather would sit on a deck chair on the porch, a large open volume of the Gemarah on his knees. Grandfather wore a red hanky, its four corners tied in knots, over the yarmulke on his head.

Simon made four knots, one in each corner of his handkerchief, and tried to pull it onto his head. But it did not hold. His head was too big. His colleagues offered him their handkerchiefs. He felt ridiculous and irritably asked them to leave him alone.

One of the guards distributed paper cups with lukewarm water to drink. Simon sipped from his cup. The water in the cup reminded him of the lake where he had sat the previous night beside Marisha. "I love you, Marisha"—he drank in the refreshing words. When the guard later offered him another cup of water, he noticed a small black fly inside it, swimming in circles. It circled round and round the edge of the cup—a little black fly, a tiny Jew, a "Yidele" who was trying to make order in his heart, who was trying to save himself. Simon stared at it for a long time—until he stopped seeing it. The turmoil inside the cup had transferred itself to his head as the sun lashed him with its hot rays.

* * *

Simon was unconscious when he was taken off the van. Waves of water were whirling around in his head. For a moment the thought that he was dying from sunstroke pierced his consciousness. The sun of Serengeti was too hot for him. Mildred was right. Mildred was always right. What would now happen to the seminar? What would turn out to be the fate of psychiatry? Was it doomed never to find its way in the wilderness of the human soul?

Suddenly he saw an image before his mind's eye. He saw Mildred fighting with Marisha over him. One pulled in this direction, the other pulled in the opposite direction. They were like the animals of the Serengeti, fighting over their victim, tearing chunks from his body as if he were a zebra in their hungry mouths. To whom did he belong? Where did he belong? How good it would be if Mildred and Marisha made peace with each other. Why shouldn't they? After all, Marisha had cured him of the disease of seeing himself as a pitiful little Jew with a dozen diplomas. She had done wonders for him. She herself was wondrous. He was a partner to that wondrousness. He was by no means emotionally impotent. It had only seemed to him that he was because his love had been one-sided, incomplete. Now, however, he loved both women equally. He carried them both within himself. Had he only allowed himself to offer each one what belonged to her his head would not be spinning so badly. He was unable to continue in such a turmoil. In such chaos he was doomed to be ground down, leveled, annihilated, reduced to zero, to a large, round, empty zero.

A zero? Heaven forbid. He was a human being. He was very happy that he had given Marisha the hat. He was responsible for her. And he was responsible for Mildred and their children as well. He was responsible for his colleagues and for his patients, and for Mr. Mashada, and for the Masai people, and for every single human being populating the globe. He had his human dignity, the dignity of a proud Jew and a proud American, the dignity of a small fly that had drunk from the waters of the infinite and had not drowned in their depths. Of what importance was it to whom he belonged? He belonged to no one except to the global Serengeti. He belonged to the sun, the queen of life and death. That was enough for him. *Dayenu* . . . That was plenty.

The Masterpiece

There is almost no spring in the province of Quebec. One fine day, the abundant snows of winter, which lie welded to the ground for half the year, disappear, and during the days that follow the naked trees stand ready to don their new leafy dresses. Before long, the trees welcome the world clad in flickering green, as if flocks of tiny green birds were resting on them. And so spring makes its short-lived appearance like a lackey preceding his mistress, the Queen of Summer, in order to announce her imminent arrival. In no time at all summer arrives and the hot days begin.

Such is the climate of Quebec, which cheats on spring in order to pay back double in fall with the splendor of Indian summer. It is then that the trees, bushes, and shrubs begin to glow with the colors of sunset, a blazing array of yellow, orange, red, brown, but mainly gold. The towns and villages with their gardens, as well as the city of Montreal, with its parks, its long avenues, and narrow residential streets adorned with rows of trees, bask in the sunshine as if dipped in a painter's palette, or as if someone had hung them with garlands of gold. The falling leaves circle in the air like dancing gold coins. They accumulate on the sidewalks in golden heaps. Pedestrians stir up the gold dust with every step.

When Indian summer is at its peak, the Laurentian Mountains, which begin north of Montreal as rolling hills dotted with cool, clear lakes and endless tracts of forest, take on the magic of a fantasyland. Nature lovers come from near and far to admire the marvelous colors of the foliage. For the inhabitants of Montreal, the Laurentians are a favorite year-round vacation spot, because during the winters the mountains assume an altogether different kind of beauty, one that is both dramatic and soothing. There is drama in the contrasting interplay of the black trees and the icy, unblemished whiteness. And there is something pleasing to the eye and soothing to the soul in the white stillness spreading beyond the horizon.

* * *

Sonia and Victor were born in Lodz, the Polish Manchester. Both were concentration-camp survivors who had lost their families, friends, and neighbors during the war. They had arrived in Canada carrying the substantial psychic baggage of horrific nightmares and tragic recollections, but aside from these, they had—in a manner of speaking—nothing else to declare.

In their memories, the prewar childhood vacations that they had taken in the sub-Carpathian regions of Poland stood out like images of a paradise lost. The Laurentian Mountains reminded them of those enchanted spots, and so, even at a time when they could scarcely afford it, when their children were still small, Victor and Sonia had rented a cottage in the Laurentians when the summer heat made Montreal unbearable. They had borrowed money and renounced small luxuries so that they could rent a small cottage near *Le petit lac mirage*, which was located in a remote area far from the bustle of the more fashionable vacation spots, an hour and a half drive from Montreal.

Later, when their financial situation improved, they bought the cottage. Victor, who was a Yiddish writer, had been offered a teaching position at the Jewish Teachers' Seminary in Montreal, while Sonia, also a teacher, was hired by a Jewish high school. It was then that they began to spend not only their summer vacations but also their weekends in the Laurentians.

During all the years that they owned the cottage they invested little money in renovating it, and it remained the same old wooden shack it had been when they first rented it. After all, how much time did they actually spend inside the cottage? Didn't they really go there to enjoy the splendors of nature? The main thing was that the roof of the cottage did not leak, the stove and the fireplace functioned well, and there was never a lack of firewood. And perhaps both Sonia and Victor harbored a subconscious wish to retain as much as possible of the cottage's resemblance to those ramshackle huts in which they had spent their childhood holidays.

Every visit that the entire family paid to the cottage was a festive occasion. Sonia and Victor felt themselves infused with a sense of gaiety and renewal, which was largely attributable to the feeling of freedom that the generous beauty of the location gave them. The open sky, like an enormous canopy, unfurled an ongoing spectacle of colors and cloud formations, while the surrounding mountains, covered with dense forests of maple and fir trees, whispered of enchanting secrets buried in the womb of the crystalline lake. They kindled a craving in Sonia and Victor's hearts to fit themselves into the harmony of nature and to come in direct contact with everything alive and present in God's magnificent world. In order to recapture their own simplicity and innocence, the couple tried to emulate the friskiness of their children as they frolicked around the cottage like young squirrels.

Of course, more often than not, both Sonia and Victor failed in their attempts to be joyful. The burden of their city cares, the weight of their pasts, and the aftertaste of recurrent nightmares were not always easy to discard, not even in the country, not even in the company of their carefree children. And yet, despite these hindrances, the very fact of being at the cottage at *Le petit lac mirage* had a refreshing effect on them.

* * *

When Sonia and Victor's children reached their teens, they stopped accompanying their parents to the country house. They had grown tired of always spending their holidays in the same place and so were packed off to summer camps in various locations throughout Canada and the United States.

Only the youngest son, Danny, continued to feel an attachment to the cottage. Danny had been a sickly child. But during puberty, when physical prowess is so important to boys, he had ambitiously taken up swimming and racing with a self-discipline matching that of his father. In this way he had managed to build up his strength. He grew in height and weight and developed into a good-looking young man.

While still a child, Danny had loved music and had talked his parents into funding violin lessons. Violin playing became the passion of Danny's life. His love of music made his father feel an affinity with him that he shared with none of the other children. Father and son were bound to each other by a shared sensibility, a shared spirituality, and by their love of things artistic. At the age of fourteen Danny was accepted into the Montreal Youth Orchestra.

* * *

Sonia and Victor had triumphantly maintained their love for each other through all the years of turmoil, hope, and despair after the Second World War, and they were both proud of it now.

Sonia was a charmer. She had a dark complexion and an abundance of glistening dark hair that framed her open, smiling face. Her eyes were lively, curious, even mischievous, although in their darkest depths there smoldered a barely discernible reflection of a never-healed pain. Her figure was both shapely and sturdy. She had successfully conquered tuberculosis and typhus, the illnesses of a concentration camp inmate, and was now in perfect health. Blessed with a sharp mind, she had both a practical sense and a fine critical taste that went hand in hand with her great vitality and joie de vivre. She overflowed with such energy and zest for life that the very air about her seemed to vibrate with her restlessness. She craved compensation for the youth she had lost to the war; each day had to have the value of two, at least as far as achievement and enjoyment were concerned.

Victor, on the other hand, was a perfectionist, punctilious, a grinder, both in his teaching and in his writing. With a judicious eye he weighed and measured every step he took, both in his literary and in his day-to-day life. A skillful observer of human nature, he knew how to winnow the genuine and sincere from the pretentious and superficial. He was capable of forgiving people their weaknesses but only up to a point. Yet he was hardest on himself.

Along with his self-imposed discipline, which seemed to have found its expression in his tall, lanky figure and pale rabbinic face, went an inborn softness of heart, which was reflected in his warm, dark, glistening, sad Jewish eyes. His orderliness and self-control were a form of armor that he had forced upon himself in order to contain his inner fire and protect it from the destructive forces of reality. Perhaps this was his way of defending his mad optimism, his faith in the redemption of the human spirit through love, a faith the brutality of war had not had the power to destroy, a faith without which—or so he believed—he could never have been a teacher or a writer.

Sonia and Victor had five children, four boys and a girl. They had planned to have more. Victor would sometimes remark with a regretful smile, "The Jewish people need children. As a good Jew I must satisfy that need to the best of my ability." It seemed to him that the more children he had, the more his home deserved to be called a home. He was a committed family man, the more so since neither he nor Sonia had any other surviving relatives.

Sonia, for her part, shared Victor's desire to have a large family. She was an enthusiastic mother. She felt best and looked best when she was pregnant. To her, the pregnancies, the caring for the children and the home, had an additional significance. They expressed her own effort at self-discipline, at taming her unquenchable passion for life. She looked on her family as an exercise in harnessing her greed for experience and adventure. And so she and Victor, despite the differences in their personalities, harmonized with each other and led a life of peace and contentment.

Every day for sixteen years Victor rose at the first light of dawn and worked for two to three hours at his desk before eating breakfast and leaving for work at the Teachers' Seminary. He often wrote in the evenings as well as on the weekends in the Laurentians, where some of his most inspired pages were written. He was writing a novel, an epic about the Jewish tragedy in Europe during the Second World War. The backbone of the plot was the love between a man and a woman. Sonia and he served as his models.

When he worked on the novel—which had begun to look as though it would never come to an end—Sonia never disturbed him. On the contrary, she did all that she could to put him in the right frame of mind and to give him some peace and quiet. She watched over him like a guardian angel. She had the necessary qualities of mind to appreciate his undertaking, to grasp the vastness of the literary panorama that he was painting, and she valued his artistic achievements.

She had come to appreciate the importance of Victor's work because she had, in a manner of speaking, sinned against him throughout all the years that he had been writing his novel. Whenever Victor was not at home, she would sneak into his room and read the chapter that he had just written. She read it with a frisson of guilty pleasure, as if she were tasting a forbidden fruit. Victor, the perfectionist, was reluctant to show the unfinished product of his labor, even to her.

But she was so overcome by curiosity that reading his chapters as they were being written became a compulsion that she could not subdue. She was particularly thrilled by the manner in which Victor described the character of his female protagonist, since she knew that this character was modeled on herself. She was fascinated by the way in which this character developed over the course of hundreds of pages into a magnificent portrait of a woman. She was flattered by the light in which Victor saw her and adored the reflection of herself in the book—although at the same time she was also greatly ashamed of herself. Sometimes, in her enthusiasm, she was beset by an attack of spasmodic laughter that brought tears to her eyes, so ludicrous did the situation seem.

When the children grew older and left in the evenings for their various activities—Danny, for instance, to his music lessons—Sonia and Victor remained alone in the house. These were the most peaceful hours of their day, when they forgot their cares and devoted themselves to their own activities, taking delight in each other's presence. Victor sat down to work at the desk in his small office, while Sonia, still full of energy, threw herself into her housework, cleaning, sewing, and fixing whatever needed to be fixed. When she was done with that she corrected her students' papers and then devoted herself to reading various books related to her current interests. Sometimes these interests were in the field of zoology, at other times in the fields of history, or music, or medicine, or psychology, or Buddhism, or even astrology. She wanted to know everything, to devour everything, as if she were still on the threshold of her life, ready to discover the world. Rarely did she have the patience to sit down to watch television. When her restlessness became uncontrollable, she grabbed her coat and rushed off to spend some time with a girlfriend, or she went to see a movie. Once a month she attended a ballet performance. This was an especially festive occasion for which she dressed as elegantly as if she were going to a ball.

Victor accumulated a great deal of remorse on account of his neglect of Sonia, of her being forced to go everywhere alone. Still enamored of her fiery temperament, he regretted every moment that he was not in her company, taking delight in her vitality, in her bubbling intelligence and charm. He always felt torn between Sonia and his desk, and he looked forward to the day when he would complete his novel and be drawn only to her, his eternal beloved.

When she entered his room to say goodbye before leaving for the ballet, she would be dressed in her most elegant attire, her feet encased in high-heeled shoes and her purse and gloves held in a manicured hand. Enveloped by the delicate fragrance of her perfume, he would look at the black wavy hair that framed her dark, radiant face, drink in her hot, dark look, and his heart would ache at the sight of her beauty. He was jealous of the many strangers' eyes that would be glancing at her, and he kissed her greedily, guiltily, and gratefully.

"Do you forgive me, Sonichka?" he whispered on one such occasion. "I have only a few more episodes to write, and I'm afraid that if I don't do it tonight, I will forget them and they will be lost forever."

Sonia's ringing laughter sounded no different than her laughter from the times after their liberation from the camps. "It's I who must ask your forgiveness, Victor, for not being able to help you in any way."

"What do you mean by not being able to help me? You help me all the time." He took her hand into his. "Can you imagine my undertaking this project without you? This is our joint endeavor, darling. That's what it is. It belongs to both of us. Just let me get this text into some kind of order . . ." She left. He turned back toward the desk. The dog, Lord, made himself comfortable at his feet.

When Sonia returned late in the evening and the children were already asleep, Victor forced himself to push away the piles of paper. He insisted that Sonia, tired and sleepy though she was, go out with him for a walk. They took the dog along. As they walked they talked about their home and children, discussed their teaching projects, and made plans for their forthcoming trip to the Laurentians.

* * *

The day of Danny's first solo performance with the Montreal Youth Orchestra was approaching, and the entire family anticipated the event, making whatever arrangements were necessary to be present. Even the eldest of the children, who was studying at Columbia University in New York, came home for the occasion. Danny was everyone's darling.

But two days before the performance Masha, the only daughter, came home with the news that she had broken up with her boyfriend, and the atmosphere in the house changed to something resembling that of *tisha b'av*, the day of mourning over the destruction of the temple in Jerusalem. This had been the girl's first love, a great love, and Masha was devastated to the point of making herself sick. She refused to eat and wandered about the house in her housecoat, sobbing. Sometimes she stared out the window, oblivious to what was said to her, as if a wall had risen between herself and the rest of the world so that nothing could reach her. Sonia, silent, absent-minded, looking somewhat guilty, hovered near her constantly.

There could be no talk of Masha's attending her brother's concert. Then, on the very day of the concert, Sonia declared that she too would stay home in order to keep her daughter company.

"I feel the hand of fate in this," she said to Victor and Danny. "It has not been granted to me to hear you play, Danny. But I have no doubt that, no matter what, you'll surpass yourself tonight."

Neither Victor nor Danny understood Sonia's decision. After all, Masha was not in danger. True, she was suffering the pains of a great loss, but time would heal the wound, and Masha would resume her normal life. She took after her mother. She was a strong, active person, a true fighter. Moreover, Masha's closest friend had volunteered to spend the evening of the concert with her, and Masha herself believed that her mother should attend the concert—for Danny's sake.

But Sonia stubbornly persisted in her decision. Victor patted Danny on the shoulder, a half-hearted grin on his face. "What do the French say? The human heart has its reasons that the reason does not know. That's especially true when you're talking about a mother's heart."

Victor told himself that he understood the heart of this particular mother and accepted Sonia's decision without much protest. But deep in his heart he knew that the evening was spoiled for him as well. He had been eagerly anticipating the pleasure of sitting beside Sonia in the concert hall and sharing with her his pride in the achievement of their son. As a rule, his pleasure doubled whenever she joined him at a concert, or theater performance, or an exhibition. This would have been especially true tonight.

But his son the musician, warm-hearted, lovable Danny, smiled at his mother and pretended that he was only slightly upset by the turn of events. "Not to worry," he said to her in an overly loud tone of voice. "Your and Masha's ticket will still be valid for my real concert, next year at Carnegie Hall!"

Victor remarked thoughtfully, "A waste of two tickets. We could have offered them to somebody."

Sonia, busying herself at the open refrigerator, said, "That's exactly what I did. I gave our tickets to Berger."

"Why to him?" Victor asked, astonished.

"So that he could appraise Danny's playing," she answered.

Simon Berger was a musicologist, the conductor of the choir of which Sonia had been a member for many years. He was a passionate chess player, and years earlier he had been a frequent guest at Sonia and Victor's apartment. This was at the time when Sonia had set her heart on becoming an accomplished chess player and had studied chess manuals written by the masters. Until late into the evening Berger would sit with her in the kitchen, explaining the intricacies of various strategies. When Sonia transferred her interests to anthropology and mythology, Berger stopped his visits.

Sonia was not overly fond of Berger. She considered him conceited, an arrogant boaster. Victor, although influenced by Sonia's dislike of the man, nonetheless defended him against her criticisms, minimizing Berger's shortcomings while stressing his intellectual ability. Had not Sonia herself raved about Berger's unusual talents both in the field of music and of chess?

* * *

Hours later Victor found himself sitting in the concert hall. Three of his children sat to his right, while Berger and his wife—a svelte, flashy middle-aged matron—sat to his left. Berger was a corpulent man with an elongated, deeply creased face. Unruly strands of graying black hair stood out from his head, pointing in all directions. He had greeted Victor with a firm, friendly handshake. But after they had run through the standard questions and answers—they had not seen each other for a number of years—a silence fell between them, which Berger interrupted just before the beginning of the concert.

"How is the masterpiece coming along?" he asked Victor. "Sonia told me the other day at choir rehearsal that you're about to finish the first draft. How many drafts do you intend to write?"

Victor noted the sarcasm in Berger's question. He smiled, more to himself than to his neighbor. Accustomed to the respectful disdain of noncreative people, especially those intelligent and gifted who tried to conceal their envy behind such acerbic remarks, he replied amiably, "Very soon you'll see how it is coming along. "

"What do you mean?" Berger asked.

"Danny is my real masterpiece."

Berger's face flushed a sudden red. He tried to answer Victor with a smile of his own, but instead his mouth twisted into an ugly grimace. He gave Victor a strange look, then turned his head away and began to chat with his wife.

The concert began. During Danny's solo, Victor was so tense, so acutely attentive, that his ear lost its discernment, and he could no longer make out the shades of tone in Danny's playing. His heart hammered in his chest and he missed the feel of Sonia's hand in his during the moments of almost unbearable joy that overflowed his heart. When Danny's violin began to ascend the final crescendo, Victor cast a triumphant glance at Berger and, to his amazement, noticed that the man's wide-open eyes were overflowing with tears. That moment Victor forgave Berger for everything. He felt closer to him than to a brother.

* * *

There was still a considerable amount of work to do before Victor could finish the first draft of his novel. Masha had long since been cured of her broken heart and had left for Toronto to continue her studies. Her departure had been preceded by a period of much discussion at the dinner table of the various universities and their respective merits. Victor and Sonia's other two sons were also within a year or two of applying to university. Sonia, vivacious and cheerful as ever, continued with her daily routine. She had just started on a new interest. This time it was botany. And as usual when her enthusiasm for a new passion reached its peak, she would expound on it for hours. This time she went on and on about the development of plants, their "moods," and their sensitivity to such things as music.

The day finally came when Victor completed the first draft of his novel. In order to celebrate the end of this important phase of his work, he and Sonia decided to play hooky for a day and drive out to their cottage in the Laurentians. They took along Lord, the dog, who had grown up along with the children and had been everybody's best friend, but whose primary attachment had always been to Victor, whom he followed everywhere.

Golden autumn reigned in the mountains; the forest surrounding the cottage was ablaze with color. The road down to *Le petit lac mirage* was covered with a carpet of leaves in all shades of gold. On the mirrorlike lake, the fallen leaves sailed about like tiny golden gondolas in an imaginary Venice.

No sooner had they arrived at the cottage than Victor busied himself with his usual country chores, which gave him the opportunity to move his limbs and put him in a leisurely frame of mind. He chopped wood for the kitchen stove and prepared thick logs for the fireplace to be lit that evening, since he and Sonia had decided to stay overnight and return to town early in the morning. Humming a little tune to himself, he raked up the piles of leaves in front of the cottage and gathered them into large stacks. He tried not to think about his work but to give his mind a rest in order to fully enjoy the peaceful moments. He was also determined to concentrate his attention on Sonia. Such solitude à deux would strengthen their bond, contribute to their intimacy, and bring them still closer together.

Sonia too seemed to be in a cheerful frame of mind. Nevertheless she was preoccupied, walking about absent-mindedly. She was silent and her languorous smile seemed not her own. She observed every tree and shrub with a mystical tenderness bordering on piety. Victor, as he watched her, ascribed her strange behavior to her absorption in her botanical studies. But he detected a vague nervousness in the air about her. He asked her whether there was anything troubling her.

After a moment of silence she responded, "You know very well that I hate being completely cut off from the children. Every year we talk about installing a telephone, and we never do anything but talk."

"I give you my word of honor as an absent-minded professor," Victor playfully pounded his chest like Tarzan, "that come next summer, it shall be done. If you like," he added softly, "we could walk over to the village this evening and call the children."

"And I will keep on reminding you . . ." She smiled back at him with that same enigmatic smile. "Because once you set your mind to forgetting something, Victor, no amount of reminding you will have any effect. Don't we both know that?"

"When did I ever set my mind to forgetting anything having to do with a wish of yours?"

She pretended to think hard, as if she were trying to remember. They laughed. In truth, when it came to Sonia or the children, Victor was never stubborn or forgetful. If he was, it was only in matters regarding himself. But it was also true that he was not too enthusiastic about installing a telephone in their cottage. He considered the telephone a scourge, even in the city, but he had to tolerate it there. In the country, however, he preferred to be completely isolated from the rest of the world. When it was absolutely necessary to call, it was always possible to walk over to the village. What was more, the farmer who lived fifteen minutes away also had a telephone, and in an emergency the children could always get in touch with their parents.

Sonia and Victor took their lunch on the veranda, which was draped around its borders by the climbing vines that grew over the entire cottage. This meant that on a fall day the cottage appeared to be immersed in flaming gold and red, while the veranda seemed to be surrounded by walls of fire.

The veranda was free of vines only on one side, the side facing the lake. As Victor and Sonia sat at their rustic table consuming their lunch, they looked out on the dazzling panorama of the mountains and the lake. A light haze rose slowly from the placid surface of the lake. Sonia's eyes were just as misty as the lake. There was a strange and unfamiliar something lurking inside her gaze as she listened to Victor talk about his feelings for her. He was capable of formulating these feelings with admirable precision. She could not detect a single banal note. His words moved her so that she stopped eating.

That day Victor's words of love were exceptionally beautiful. He was composed and satisfied with himself after the completion of his first draft, the first stage of his work. At last he had the entire novel laid out on paper. No longer was it in danger of being threatened by the vagaries of uncertain memory, no longer could any scenes fade into oblivion and slip out of his grasp. He could now visualize his work in its entirety as a reality that had not existed before and was now present. This gave him a great sense of relief, almost of bliss.

He considered the moment ideal to finally talk freely to Sonia about his work. He could question her about her approach to certain issues and compare her answers with the views of the most important female character in his book. He also told her which incidents in their life together had inspired some of the scenes in his book and why and how he had transformed them in his narrative. The character of his female protagonist was not intended as a faithful reproduction of Sonia, as Sonia doubtless knew. What he was trying to do was to capture the essence of her personality.

"My purpose," he remarked, "is not to portray our lives during the war as they were but to place them in an altogether different context. How should I put this? I wanted to come closer to the meaning of our tragedy's meaninglessness . . ."

They had finished eating and were now sitting at the veranda table, sipping hot coffee from their cups, as Victor continued with his monologue. He was totally absorbed in what he was saying. Her cheeks aglow, Sonia listened to him. She was aware that he was presenting her with the gift of his soul balanced on the palm of his hand, that he was offering her all that his intellect possessed, as if he were clearing out the most hidden recesses in the workshop of his mind and revealing all the secrets he had been hiding inside.

Sonia looked up at Victor from beneath the strands of wavy black hair that dangled over her forehead and eyebrows. Her eyes were strangely troubled, and sparks of acute suffering shot up from their depths. She could not tolerate the frequent allusions he continued to make to his love for her. They made her ache all over.

"How well I understand Hemingway," Victor continued, "when he says that he writes best when he is in love. Without my love for you, Sonitchka, I would never have dared to aim so high. It was the power of my feelings for you that gave me wings."

"You're exaggerating, as usual." She frowned impatiently. "Do you realize how long we have been living together? Do you keep count? It's been ten years since I began dyeing my hair to cover the gray."

"You talk nonsense, darling." He moved closer to her. "A love such as mine for you takes no account of years. As far as I'm concerned time has made no changes in you, and I'm not joking when I say that you are a partner in my work just as you are a partner in my life."

She sipped her coffee, and he wondered whether it was the steam from the cup that moistened her face or whether those were tears.

* * *

In the afternoon they went for a walk around the lake, following a path carpeted with yellow leaves. The dog ran ahead, chasing squirrels. He pounced on the heaps of leaves and barked playfully. Every few minutes he raised his leg to pay his respects to a tree trunk or a pile of leaves that he had disturbed and then raced on, leaping into the air with great abandon. The vacation cottages that dotted the road at a considerable distance from one another were almost all vacant.

A solitary boat sat in the middle of the lake; the person inside was catching fish. From the distance the contours of man and boat resembled the anchor of a large invisible ship. An air of something primeval and mythical hovered over the lake, as if the story of its genesis were still in its making. As if purposely disturbing the silence, Victor and Sonia held hands and trod noisily over the leaves. In their free hands each held a walking stick that Victor had fashioned out of dry branches. They talked very little. Sonia seemed so deeply immersed in her thoughts that her dark eyebrows were arched and her forehead was wrinkled. Victor was reluctant to disturb her. He assumed that she was mulling over what he had told her at lunch.

As a matter of fact, Sonia was thinking about what Victor had said over lunch. She was thinking about him, about herself, about their life together. She felt particularly sensitive to her surroundings this day and found herself drawn to Victor by the secluded intimacy of the lake and the forest. She was grateful to him for the words of love he had said to her—grateful and at the same time deeply ashamed.

She had not been happy with Victor for a very long time. She was glad he was so absorbed in his work that he had failed to notice how false her good cheer had been, how he bored her to tears, and how torn she felt. She was not really troubled by the fact that she cheated on him every now and again. Once he had ceased to touch her soul, she no longer felt any bond with him. She had lost interest in him, and she did not in the least care for what he had to say outside the framework of his novel. It had all been an act she had put on for the sake of convenience. And yet she was constantly troubled by a sense of betrayal. It ate into her like poison. It aroused in her a feeling of guilt toward him, a guilt that had corroded her life for many years. Her natural vitality enabled her to mask it all with an air of assumed candor, but not even her vitality could erase the self-disgust from her heart. And for that she could forgive neither herself nor Victor.

Today, however—she did not know why or how, perhaps because the magic of the autumn landscape moved her so deeply—her heart suddenly recaptured the love she had felt for Victor during the first years of their life together, during that time after the liberation, when she had been a very young woman. Now she conceived a passion for him at the same time as she experienced a great need to merge with the atmosphere of their surroundings and partake of the innocence and honesty of nature. She had to recapture her purity of heart. She was exhausted from the effort of decorating her external self with all manner of artifice; she was even tired of her artificial hair color and of the makeup that enhanced her false, golden smile. Just as Victor had finished a phase of his work, so she longed to finish this phase of her life and to start a new chapter along with him, her husband and lover. He would rewrite his work while she would redo her life. She needed this remodeling in order to save herself, save her soul, and be rid of the devastating hatred that she felt for herself.

She walked on, her face lowered over the heaps of dry leaves as she punctured them with her walking stick. Then, with sudden decisiveness, she stopped and turned to him. "I must tell you something, Victor. And please forgive me for doing it today, such an important festive day for you."

"For both of us," he corrected her softly.

"First I must tell you," she continued, "that I love you . . ." He raised her hand to his lips to kiss, but she jerked it away. "I never loved you as much as I do now . . ." She was about to proceed, but suddenly she recalled a scene from a war film that she had recently seen: a Nazi aiming his rifle at a child who laughed playfully as it gamboled through a pasture full of flowers. Sonia recoiled from the memory. Her head still lowered, she moved slightly away from Victor and neglected to take the hand he held out to her. "But I must tell you this . . ." She broke off for a moment to catch her breath. Her heart pounded violently.

"Go ahead," he smiled encouragingly.

She flung up her head and stared straight into his eyes. His smile pierced her heart, but she held straight to her course. "This is going to hurt," she warned him. "I hope you're strong enough. I hope you'll forgive me."

"Shoot!" He spread his arms theatrically.

She waited for him to drop his arms. "Danny is not your son!"

The smile did not leave his face. "What do you mean, not my son?"

"I mean to say that you are not his father."

"Then who is?"

"Berger is."

"You're crazy."

"This is my first moment of sanity, Victor. I've been leading a double life for the last fifteen years. You were so deeply buried in your mountains of paper that no suspicion ever entered your mind. What did you expect me to do? I needed some intimacy, a soulmate, or even just a companion. I wanted to live, to enjoy myself, to go places after the daily drudgery at work and at home. You were always at your desk, always scribbling away, day in and day out, week after week, year after year. What did you expect? I'm not an angel. I wanted a little happiness for myself, just as you got yours for yourself. You found your thrills in your work, while I found mine in other men. You made love to paper people, and I made love to people of flesh and blood. Yes, you deceived me too. You forgot that I really existed outside the confines of your imagination, as a living woman who loves life—real life, Victor!" She had not intended to hurl reproaches at him. She was not certain that even if her reproaches were not true, she might not still have deceived him. Yet the only way that she could defend herself was to make an attack.

His face had grown gray. He looked helplessly in all directions, then leaned his shoulder against the nearest tree. She hovered near him. They stood face to face. She continued talking as she observed her victim wince and writhe against the tree trunk like a snake in agony. Soon she would revive him with all the loving words that overflowed her heart. Soon she would tell him how powerfully her love for him had returned to repossess her soul. Soon she would throw herself into his arms and kiss the despair from his pale face, kiss the protruding eyes that stared at her blindly and full of despair. Soon she would smother him with the most transporting caresses and reinstate herself in his heart, where she would reign forever. She could achieve this so easily. He would never be able to live without her. But first she had to drain the last drops of venom that had accumulated in her heart over the years. She had to mitigate her own guilt by accusing him. They had sinned, both of them. They were partners. He had said that she was a partner to his work; then let him be a partner to her guilt.

"I could have gotten rid of the pregnancy, Victor," she continued in her hard, metallic voice while struggling to dam the tears that welled up behind her eyes. "But then you would have found out everything, and I was not yet prepared to let you know. I wanted to protect our home and the children, and that's how it happened. Now I don't regret it at all. I have Danny. You have Danny. You are his father. Can you imagine our life without Danny? And Victor, later on . . ." The tears finally overflowed her eyes, but her voice remained clear and sharp. "In later times, when the children were grown, and I felt so unhappy in our relationship, I did not leave you—not because of the children, and not because I did not want to break up our home, but because of you. I wanted to spare you; I wanted you to continue with your work, your great work. I wanted you to succeed, to become famous. I sacrificed myself for you more than you can imagine."

"But . . ." he mumbled. "How could you have found . . . have found . . ."

"How could I have found the time to have affairs? Is that what you want to know? Ask the blood in my veins. My compulsion was so strong; my craving was so powerful . . ." She ran out of breath, and she too failed to complete her sentence.

Victor said nothing more. He slumped down to the foot of the tree. After a long silence he said to her, "Go back to the cottage. Let me sit here for a while." The dog snuggled up beside him, and Victor patted him with rapid, mechanical strokes. His dull gaze followed Sonia's figure as it edged away from him through the sea of golden leaves.

"My beautiful Sonia, my beloved, my only one," he muttered aloud, his voice hoarse. "You are so powerful, more powerful than the Nazis. They tortured my body, but they could never reach my soul. You alone managed that. You have destroyed me, and destroyed the image of yourself within me . . . Danny!" He let out a prolonged howl and burst into sobs.

* * *

As he followed Sonia's receding figure through misty eyes, he suddenly recalled how they had met for the first time. He saw vividly the infirmary of the Neuengamme concentration camp. It was a gray, rainy afternoon. A salty sea wind danced between the infirmary walls, penetrating his bones to the marrow. That day he had been assigned to scrub the floor in the corridor of the infirmary. There he noticed a young female inmate sitting on a bench, shivering in her striped camp outfit—a scrawny, ugly creature whose skeletal face, twisted with cold and suffering, seemed to consist only of a pair of fierce black eyes overflowing with tears of pain and rage. She had been brought to the infirmary from another smaller camp that had no infirmary. Her feet were wrapped in wet rags, and she held a pair of wooden clogs on her lap. She had stubbed her toes so badly during the marches to and from her workplace that her toes had become infected and covered with boils.

As he knelt with the scrubbing brush in hand, Victor felt that the girl's eyes were calling to him in desperation from her corner. He glanced at the SS guard who stood at the door, his rifle at the ready. Moving his scrubbing brush vigorously back and forth over the floor, he managed surreptitiously to move closer to the girl. As a member of the inmates' underground at the camp, he was used to doing forbidden things under the noses of the SS men.

The moment he was within an arm's length of the girl, he heard her rasp out between chattering teeth, "Have you got anything to eat?"

Yes, he did. He had on him the second half of his daily bread ration, which he had put aside to eat in his bunk that night, so that the pangs of hunger would not keep him from falling asleep. He carried the small chunk of bread around with him so nobody would steal it from him. He kept it inside his striped pants, wrapped in a rag, tied with a string, and attached to the cord of the pants. He got it out and placed it quickly in her palm. Saliva dripped from her mouth onto his hand like a kiss, like a hot seal. As soon as the SS guard turned away, Victor managed to tell her that he came from Lodz. She said, "So do I." He told her his name, she told him hers. He asked whether she had met any women inmates with his name. She asked the same about her male relatives. That moment they knew everything there was to know about one another; their bond was sealed.

The next time they met was after the liberation, in the displaced persons camp in Feldafing in Bavaria. She recognized him among a crowd of survivors. From then on they were inseparable. Both of them were alone; they had no one in the world but each other. They moved in together into a tiny cubicle in a mansion that had formerly housed the SS brass. The mansion was crowded with DPs. Victor and Sonia slept on the same cot since there were no extra cots available. It was not a question of love at that time. It was fate.

It did not take long before Sonia recovered from her various illnesses and blossomed into a beautiful, life-loving charmer, bubbling with energy and greedy for pleasure. Victor's demeanor changed in the opposite direction. In the concentration camp he had been sociable, active, involved with his comrades in various dangerous activities. Now, as he began to write, a distance sprang up between himself and his comrades. Sonia would often run off alone to meet her friends while he stayed in their tiny room whose window faced one of the most beautiful lakes in Bavaria. It was during this time, surrounded by the most romantic landscape imaginable, that Victor and Sonia's passion for each other took root.

It was Sonia who supplied them both with food. She organized escapades into the countryside, sneaking into German farmhouses and making off with delicious, freshly baked bread, rolls, and succulent chunks of ham. She would bring them back to their cubicle for their mutual delectation. It was she who also organized their illegal crossing of the border into France and from there, assisted by the UNRRA, arranged their departure for Canada. They were married just a few days prior to boarding a cargo ship called *Patagonia* and set out on the long, stormy sea voyage across the Atlantic.

As he slumped against the tree, Victor could not tear his eyes from Sonia's disappearing form. As he looked at her, he had the impression that the cottage, whose roof was visible in the distance, was receding, floating away from him like a boat that he had failed to board. He knew that when he saw Sonia's face again it would no longer be the same face he had loved.

A few hours later they returned to the city.

* * *

Victor lacked the capacity to forgive Sonia, although he tried to understand her. Sonia was right; he must have been a terrible bore. He made an effort to justify her in his mind. He had been wrung dry, devoid of liveliness. He had nothing to offer her. All the riches of his soul had been invested in his work. Whatever sense of adventure, whatever flights of fancy and sparks of humor were left in him, he had kneaded into his text in order to render more digestible the essential brutality of his story.

But despite his best intentions, he found himself unable to live with Sonia any longer. What was more, he felt himself incapable of going on with his life at all. All the scaffolding that had supported his existence seemed to have collapsed. Like an automaton he went about his daily routine. When he was at home, he no longer sat down at his desk. He wandered about the house, chatted with the children or even with Sonia, but he did not really see them. A dull pain nagged at him, as if he had taken too weak a dose of chloroform. When he felt himself choking in the apartment, he went out into the street. Several times he considered visiting a brothel or just calling up one of his literary women friends. But he had no taste for women. He loathed the very idea of touching them. He desired no one, desired nothing. Every impulse within him was dead. He walked about like a sleepwalker.

Danny was the first of the children to notice the strangeness in his father's behavior. He tried to strike up a conversation with him; he volunteered to play Victor's favorite pieces of music on his violin. He proposed that they go somewhere together. But Victor was unable to look at Danny without tears coming to his eyes. The sight of the boy made him feel weak. He avoided him even more than he avoided Sonia.

As for Sonia, he talked to her about practical matters, about the children, the home and expenses, but he looked at her as if she were a stranger and treated her as if she were a neighbor with whom he was obliged to discuss certain necessary housekeeping details.

* * *

Sonia comported herself with no particular pride. Nor was she more humble or servile than before. She could not change what had happened, but she was willing to change what she could in the future. She was tormented by guilt for the suffering she had caused Victor but knew that she could not alleviate it. She too suffered. She came to realize that much as she wanted to she could not shake off her feelings of guilt toward Victor, and she began to think that she was doomed to carry them to the end of her days. But if it was not given to her to win Victor back, she still preferred the present situation to continuing with a life of lies.

It never entered her mind that Victor might leave her. She knew him too well, and knew the power of his love for her, even if he never again acknowledged it. She also knew how strong his sense of responsibility to his family was and how attached and devoted he was to their home.

So she kept herself composed and patiently waited for a change in Victor's attitude. In the meantime she abandoned her scientific pursuits. She lost interest in them but promised herself to take them up as soon as Victor came back to her. Every once in a while, when she and Victor happened to be alone, she would whisper softly to him, "Remember, Victor, that I love you." Or she would reprimand him: "For heaven's sake, Victor, cheer up. You're exaggerating the whole thing, as usual. Times have changed. Your rigid puritanical approach toward infidelity was outdated even at home, before the war."

He did not react to her words, as if he had not heard them. He continued to sleep with her in the same bed. After all, during the war, he had slept in the same bed with total strangers. He was as unresponsive as a rock. Nothing mattered to him. Whatever he did was transitory, temporary—he was certain about that. Not that he intended to commit suicide, although he thought of it quite often. But these thoughts of suicide, detached and logical though they were, brought him always to the conclusion that he must not grant the Nazis such a victory.

Finally the day came when Victor knew clearly what he had to do. He told Sonia that she should prepare to live her life without him, that he could no longer stay in the house, that they ought to make certain practical decisions. The main thing was not to upset the children any more than was necessary.

"When?" she asked.

"I don't know yet," he answered woodenly.

Sonia did not believe him. She was convinced that he would not have the courage to go through with his plan. She could not imagine him packing a valise and walking out of the house never to return. Even if he were capable of such an act on her account, he would never have the strength to walk out on the children. His conscience, the severe and rigorous demands he made on himself, would never permit this to happen. His home was sacred to him. This was not a pose, nor a pretense.

She was, however, convinced of another thing as well: that he would not go back to work on his great book, of which their mutual love had been the backbone. This she deeply regretted. She regretted it not only because she knew that his work was a masterpiece in the making but also because she loved his work just as sincerely as she had hated his continual absorption in it, and she loved herself in the image that he had created of her. She wanted to have his work at her side for her own pleasure to admire at will, as she would when looking into a mirror, regardless of the outcome of their marital upheaval. She wanted to be able to refresh her heart with the image of the magnificent Sonia of the book. She so detested the real Sonia.

And so, gradually, without Victor's knowledge, Sonia took each chapter to be copied. When it was all done, she put the huge manuscript into a cardboard box, put the box into the car, and drove alone up to the cottage at *Le petit lac mirage* in the Laurentians. There she wrapped the copy of Victor's work in many layers of silver foil, put them in cellophane bags, and stacked them in a metal safe she had bought for that purpose. She hid the safe in the cellar between the piles of firewood that were stacked in a corner. She intended to come up to the cabin whenever she felt like reading the book.

* * *

Sonia was correct in her assumption that Victor would never resume his work on the novel. Coming home from work one afternoon, she was confronted on the landing by a disheveled Victor, his shirt unbuttoned, throwing the last of his manuscript into the incinerator.

"What are you doing?" she cried, pretending to be both angry and desperate. Inwardly, she congratulated herself on her foresight in predicting Victor's behavior. This strengthened her conviction that he would never leave her. Moreover, she was glad that she had saved his work, and she was convinced that Victor himself would thank her for it one day.

"It's gone! Burned! Burned!" he exclaimed in a frenzy. Instead of returning to the apartment, he ran down the stairs and out the door. He stayed away for many hours. Soon after this incident Victor rented a room, packed a trunk of his personal belongings, and went to live on his own.

The first sleepless night he spent in his rented room he told himself that this was the beginning of a new, long night in his life. Thereafter he went to work as usual, and as usual contributed to the support of Sonia and the children, but he never again set foot in the apartment. He met with the children, but after the initial shock of their parents' separation had worn off, they concealed their confusion and resentment, claiming to be too busy with their lives and with their plans for the future to devote much time to their father. At length Victor remained close only to Danny, who was very attached to him. The two of them maintained the same affectionate contact that they always had, although Victor could hardly look at Danny without tears coming to his eyes.

When Danny learned from his mother that Victor was not his real father, their relationship, despite their genuine love for each other, underwent a change caused by the uneasiness of diverging emotions and thoughts. Danny, the gifted young musician, was the most innocent victim of his parents' frailties. His soul was forever scarred by the sins of the two adults who were responsible for his well-being. This truth peered out from his bewildered, questioning eyes. Victor felt he should sink to his knees before Danny and beg his forgiveness for not being his father.

Fortunately Danny had his violin. This was his salvation. Before long, he was accepted at the Juilliard School in New York, and with the beginning of the school year he left Montreal.

* * *

Victor's physical and emotional disintegration continued. He sank deeper into depression, became lackadaisical in his professional work, negligent in his appearance, and ever more eccentric in his habits. Neither his students nor his colleagues at the Teacher's Seminary could restrain the inclination to make jokes at his expense by recounting anecdotes about his absent-mindedness. Victor knew he was being mocked behind his back, but he did not care.

He regarded his experience with Sonia as the pivotal point in the dark night that engulfed him. There was now a total absence of light, of hope, in his outlook on life. One day, when he found himself in the very depths of despair, on the verge of a complete breakdown, he had a sudden impulse to leave for the cottage in the Laurentians. He and Sonia each had a key to the cottage. It was the beginning of winter. The first heavy snow had fallen.

When he got to the cottage he went for a walk. Thick snowflakes dotted the air between the trees. The snow descending on the lake brought to mind the image of a continuous fall of white curtains sprinkled with small, white cotton balls. The stillness was occasionally broken by a bird's cry. In the whirling whiteness, Victor watched the flapping wings of birds, black as inkblots, sawing through the air.

As he plowed through the snow, he felt as if he were a black rock frozen in one spot, while the snow whirling through the air seemed to be moving slowly ahead. He smiled at himself. A black rock? And why not a black bird about to rise into the air? He was only weary and exhausted. All he needed was to rest for a while before soaring into the flight that Destiny had decreed was his.

All of a sudden a craving began to stir in his heart. He wanted to write! "In spite of yourself, you must write!" he called out in the white stillness.

Writing was his destiny, his assigned function in life. This was how he was meant to contribute to the singing of the birds, to the slashing hum of waterfalls, to the howl of the wind and to the soundless fall of the snowflakes. It must be so! It was for the sake of his calling that he had needed this tremendous crash in his life. What a wealth of suffering he had discovered in the dark abyss of his soul! Too soon had he forgotten the suffering that he had endured in the depths of a former horror. He had abused the entire supply of knowledge he had gleaned from his former trials. He had squandered it almost entirely with a naivete of heart that bordered on stupidity! Only now, enriched by a completely new kind of torment, did he see himself standing one rung higher on the ladder of experience. Now he had a better view of the panorama of human fate, of the human comedy. During the time between that other storm and this new one he had become fossilized, stagnant in his fool's paradise; he had lost contact with reality.

He was spoiled. Writing had become a game for him. True, it was a serious game, but it was a game nonetheless. Having described people starving from hunger, he had sat down to a feast at his dinner table. Having described a character's terrifying loneliness, he had gone to bed with his wife. Having describing executions by firing squad, he had plunged into the lake to frolic with his children. Only now did he have his finger on the pulse of life's mystery. Only now did he taste the sting of its simultaneous banality and brutality. Now was the time to sit down and write his book. He must! This was his calling!

Although there were no particular ideas forming in his mind, he was overcome by the longing to write—just to sit down and write. He felt himself possessed by this passion. He forgot that he had barely any strength left as he marched through the forest at a quick, heavy pace in order to catch up with the swiftly running currents of his mood. Suddenly he turned back.

Two hours later he was sitting at his small writing table in his little room in Montreal. On top of the table he had placed a sheaf of clean, white, lined writing paper. Each sheet was a field waiting to be sown. The perfectly straight parallel lines were furrows; they were elongated mouths ready to swallow the seeds. The pen in Victor's trembling hand swept forward toward the top line on the first sheet of paper, and before long he was racing along the lines like a farmer rushing to sow his field before the sun set behind the horizon.

* * *

From that day on Victor worked feverishly in his room, writing with a quick hand. He wrote in the gray hours of dawn and during the late evening until long after midnight. He went to work as usual but hurried home every day like a mother racing home to nurse her baby. He ate while writing, drank while writing. He clung frantically to his pen. The first draft of the novel he burned had had a well-organized plot as its backbone. How ludicrous and false! Life was devoid of backbone. It resembled a coiled snake, rings collapsed inside rings. This being the case, he would represent life in these pages in just such a haphazard form. As far as Victor was concerned the disjointedness of life was none of his business. His business was to allow the ink to flow from under his pen in time to the flow of blood in his veins, to let words, like leeches, suck the pain from his soul. That was all he had to do.

Occasionally he stopped to check himself. What about his pain? Was it gone, or was he still drowning in it? What did it matter as long as he was himself again. He had his dignity.

And so he continued to write, not rereading what he had written, not knowing what he was writing about, not once glancing back. The crooked mirror in his mind had to remain crooked. His memory had to be cleared of the refuse of words in order to be refilled with new clutter, with new mountains of words. He had to pile them higher and higher. They would divide themselves into paragraphs on their own according to the tempos, to the tides and ebbs, of his passion. Let the words fall where they would. The only thing he would permit himself was to number the pages, number the chapters, and divide them into sub-headings. This was the only concession he would make to conventional form.

His pen sped on. Eight hundred pages lay in front of him, densely covered with the black pepper grains of his handwriting. He put a clean sheet on top of the pages and wrote "Volume One." He pushed away the pile and reached for a new sheet of paper. The second volume was begun.

He still had not read what he had written. He would read it later. Now he had to grab his inspiration by the hair. It was enough for him to know that he was writing a work of art. He was an artist. He felt it in his bones, felt it in the intoxicating intensity of his moods, in the ferocity of the blaze that roared within him—an all-consuming fire, the rage of a tormented, creative spirit. He was not conceited. He had never suffered from any megalomaniacal tendencies. But neither ought he to be overly modest. He was fully aware that what he was now creating breathed the breath of eternity. Only now, after he had found the strength to destroy his previous work with its deceitful construction, had he reached true greatness.

"Hemingway was a dwarf of a writer. That's why he needed to be in love in order to write at his best," Victor mumbled to himself. "But I'm not like that. I write best when my soul is sick, just as the world is sick. I write best when my soul hurts, just as life hurts."

Onward he galloped with his pen. He must not stop. He had a routine to which he must submit. Every free moment of his time must be crammed with words. He must pile them up, allow them to speak, to sing, scream, mumble, and groan so that the knottiness of existence should find its reflection not within them but between them, around them, in the chaos that they create as they hit against each other. James Joyce wanted to achieve this with his *Ulysses*, with his *Finnegan's Wake*. But Joyce did not go far enough. He lacked the courage, lacked the experience, lacked the trials of horror.

"I," Victor mumbled to himself. "I have survived the camps. I have faced the unspeakable, the inexpressible . . . and I've got the courage. I certainly have!"

* * *

A year went by. Sonia and Victor had not seen each other for a very long time. The cottage in the Laurentians was their only point of contact. But they never met there. Sonia drove out mostly during the week, when she had a morning free from work, while Victor drove up for the weekend. She knew that he had been there by the mess that he left behind. He, however, knew nothing of her visits, never noticing the order she restored to the cottage. But he sensed her presence nonetheless. It permeated the air.

They had still not made any formal arrangements with regard to their separation. He refused to bother about it. He did not care about such matters. He fulfilled his financial obligations as usual. Sonia, for her part, did not abandon hope that he might come back to her. She continued with her free way of life just as she had always done and derived even less pleasure from her adventures than before. She yearned for the warm and intellectually stimulating atmosphere that Victor had created in their home, despite his constant preoccupation with his work. She would have gladly reverted to the life she had led before she told Victor the truth about Danny. Obviously, in life, just as in art, the truth was not always the best choice.

Time went on. One winter's day Victor found to his amazement that the thread of his narrative was running out. He took it as a sign that he was about to finish the last volume of his work. A dybbuk seemed to have entered his mind in order to tease him. "You're coming to the end of the line," it squeaked. "The thread is breaking. Soon you'll have nothing to hold on to!"

He stopped writing. Glancing at the tabletop, he saw that it was covered with piles of paper filled with his handwriting. There was only a small space left for his arm, for the hand holding the pen, and for a sheet of paper. He could not understand how he had come to fill all these sheets of paper. Here were the completed volumes arranged all in one row, paginated in perfect order. The drive to make order is no doubt innate in human nature. It cannot be avoided. That was why he had to make the meaningless concession of paginating. Now all that was left was to add the conclusion, and number that as well. Perhaps there was something intrinsically positive about numbering?

The little devil sitting in his head teased him. "Soon you'll have nothing to number but blank pages . . . blank days."

Victor chuckled wisely. "But I have to start writing all over again— from the beginning! I must rewrite! There is no writing without re- writing! That is the writer's duty and his privilege! It is only life that happens once and cannot be repeated. You cannot restart it from the beginning. But the work about life can be started over and over again. That's why the Romans said '*Ars longa, vita brevis.*' Art is eternal, life is short."

Once again he was zealous. He wanted to keep his mind fresh for the conclusion of his book and forced himself to get up from the table. It was the end of the week. A thick snow had fallen outside. Never mind. One way or the other he would make it out to the cottage in the Lau- rentians. There he always rested best.

He looked at the table once again. His entire work lay there unpro- tected. He turned down the heating, checked if the burners on the gas stove were turned off, and unplugged all the electric appliances so that no spark could chance to fall on his work. At the foot of the bed lay a heap of newspapers. He never read newspapers, but bought one every day in order to glance at the headlines. Now he clipped those articles he thought might help him relax in the country. He carried the remainder down to the garbage dump. Once back in his room he put on his winter jacket and boots. He was still worried, fussing like a mother who was forced to leave her child alone for a little time. After he locked the door, he checked to make certain that it was well locked.

He drove as quickly as he could through the snow-covered high- way. Soon the mountains loomed ahead, the snow on their peaks un- dulating like puffed-up blankets of white eiderdown. He began to feel calmer. What a peaceful world!

The countryside was hushed, quiet. A wall of snow covering half of the window had transformed the cottage at *Le petit lac mirage* into a small fortress. Victor began to dig a passage for himself to the front steps. Exhausted, he climbed onto the snow-covered veranda and shook the clumps of snow off his clothes and boots. He kicked away the snow from the door and entered the cottage. The first thing he did was light a fire in the fireplace. Then he took off his heavy, wet winter jacket and hung it up to dry on the back of a chair so that it faced the fire. He threw himself on the cot that stood nearby. It was already late afternoon. Soon night would fall and trap the world in darkness. Tomorrow morning he would go for a long walk on the frozen lake. There it was the easiest to walk. He stared at the snowshoes that hung on the wall near the door. He would put them on tomorrow.

He lay on the cot with his eyes open and saw the night slowly creeping down the frozen windowpanes. Soon the melting panes would begin to weep. The fireplace was loaded with wood. The room was warming up quickly. Before long the panes, completely cleared of frost, would let the darkness of the night invade the entire room. Victor did not think of his work. It was enough for him to know that he would not stop writing it. The flights of his imagination would never cease. It did not matter that at that very moment he was too tired to do any work. It occurred to him that it must already be late. The wind howled inside the chimney. The wolves howled outside. Or perhaps this was the sound of Danny's violin wafting through the room? Victor wondered how it would feel to write to the accompaniment of the wind's laughter, to the accompaniment of the howls of the wolves, and to the sobbing of Danny's violin. But he had no energy to get up from the cot and sit down at the table. In any case, he had to have his entire work beside him when he wrote. There had been a time when he had worked well in this cottage no matter what. Then he had been surrounded and supported by his family, by Sonia and the children—at least he had thought that they supported him. Now the piles of paper filled with his own handwriting had become his family. Their presence strengthened him. They supplied him with spiritual fortitude. But he had left them in his small room in Montreal. So now he had no option but to lie on the cot and dream—just dream.

He drifted off to sleep. His winter jacket hung on the back of the chair very close to the fire in the fireplace. The rolled-up newspaper articles that he had brought along to read poked out from the pocket.

He snored heavily. Outside, the wind's fierceness increased. The wolves howled. The fire in the fireplace gorged on the wind and gagged, its flames flailing as if they were arms. A long red tongue shot out to the chair and licked it avidly. Another tongue reached the jacket pocket and wound itself around the protruding roll of newspaper. At first it licked the paper, as if just to get a taste, then the flaming mouth clamped down until it had got the entire jacket in its craw. Crackling triumphantly, it swallowed chair and jacket in one fiery gulp

* * *

That was the last night of Victor's life and of his and Sonia's cottage in the Laurentians. The fire burned the cottage to the ground. It also entered the cellar, and through the cracks between the stacks of wood, slipped into the place where Sonia had negligently hidden the metal safe containing the copy of Victor's manuscript. She had often come out to the cottage. She felt that this cottage and Victor's work complemented each other in some way. She had more than once grown so immersed in her reading of the novel and wept over it for so long that it had grown late and she had had to hurriedly hide the safe.

The flames had a difficult job with the metal safe. But eventually they broke through. Fortified by their consumption of the cottage, the fire melted the thin metal of the safe until it yielded, causing a crack that permitted access to the stacks of papers hidden within. In a wink the flames swallowed them all, down to the last white page, which had held only two words written in Victor's hand: *The Epilogue.* And so his creations shared the fate of Victor, their creator.

When, for the first time after his death, Sonia entered Victor's small, one-room apartment in Montreal, she was struck by the sight of the stacked sheets of paper covered with Victor's handwriting that were piled on the table in neatly arranged, numbered volumes. The first thing that occurred to her was that Victor, whose death had devastated her, had played a trick on her; that he had discovered the copy of the manuscript negligently hidden in the cellar of the cottage in the Laurentians and had made a second copy of it without letting her know.

This would have been an indication that he still loved her and that he had begun the definitive version of his novel.

Everything had happened as she had foreseen it. He had not been able to stop loving her. She had known it all along. In his heart he had never left her. This awareness alleviated Sonia's sorrow at the same time as it deepened the pain of her loss. She congratulated herself for foresight in saving his masterpiece for posterity by copying it. She noticed that there was no title on the cover page of the first volume and thought that Victor had probably wanted the two of them together to think up a title. Now she would have to do it alone. Now more than ever was she a partner to his work, and she would remain his partner forever. This work would become their joint offering to the world. She now had a purpose to live for; it might perhaps awaken in her a renewed zest for life.

A number of times Sonia felt an impulse to glance at Victor's work. But she did not dare do it so soon. She feared that this might lead to her complete breakdown. So, with trembling hands, she tied all the volumes of the manuscript with string, packed them into a large cardboard box, and took them home. Before long the box assumed a presence of its own in her apartment. It seemed to be calling her, tempting her to open it. Immersed in her mourning as she was, it occurred to her that the soul of the living Victor was to be found inside the box, between the lines of his novel; that inside, in that box, she could also rediscover her own soul, the soul of the real Sonia, the beautiful and innocent.

One autumn day, nearly a year after Victor's death, when Danny was home on vacation, Sonia proposed to him that they drive out to the ruins of their cottage in the Laurentians. She wanted to take Victor's manuscript along and there introduce Danny to Victor's work. But Danny would not hear of it. Ever since Victor's death a change had come over him. He was his own man now. He answered her with such a categorical "No!" that it sounded like a clap of thunder. Sonia did not dare to broach the subject again. So, after Danny's return to New York, she carried the box with Victor's manuscript by herself down to the car. For a moment she thought how good it would have been to take along the dog, Lord. But Lord had died not long after Victor.

And so Sonia left alone for the Laurentians. After she arrived at the ruins of the cottage she spread a blanket on the grass amid the nearby pine trees, facing *Le petit lac mirage*. She removed the box from the trunk of the car, placed it on the blanket, and laid out all the volumes stacked inside, arranging them neatly in front of her. She had the feeling that this was the most suitable place for her first thorough reading of Victor's work.

With a reverential tremor she reached for the first sheets of the first volume. She was stunned by their strange appearance. The handwriting was unrecognizable and barely legible. It took her a while before she realized that the thousands of handwritten pages were full of thousands of nonsensical disjointed paragraphs—a meaningless scribbling without beginning or end, a hodgepodge, a mess, a diarrhea of phrases, a disgorging of words . . . words . . . words . . . a heap of garbage.

She wondered if Victor had gone mad. This, at least, provided an explanation for his suicide at the cottage. His insanity had prompted him to destroy himself along with the sole copy of his earlier work as well as the cottage where he, Sonia, and the children had spent the happiest moments of their lives.

In the distance, the contours of the mountains resembled a chain of question marks hooked into each other, seeming to guard a mystery locked in their midst. A curtain of haze fell over the mirror of *Le petit lac mirage*. Golden leaves of autumn soundlessly detached themselves from the trees and slowly circled in the air before they touched the ground. There was stillness in the air, such a great stillness!

Originally published in English under the title "A Cottage in the Laurentians" in the Exile Book of Yiddish Women Writers, *ed. Frieda Forman. Exile Editions, 2012. Pp. 197–238.*

Letters to God

Lord, it is time. The summer has been very long . . .
Drive the last sweetness into the heavy wine.
Whoever has not yet found a home builds a home no more.
Whoever is now alone will remain so for a very long time
Will stay awake—will write long letters . . .

So wrote the poet Rainer Maria Rilke in "Autumn Day," a letter in verse addressed to you, dear God. So many letters have been written to you, so many people crying out to you with so many words, expressing their longing in prayers, in sighs and lamentations.

Why then do I regard my own writing to you as something tasteless and cynical? Is it because my summer has been devoid of the sweetness of heavy wine, or because I doubt your existence altogether? In my desolation and loneliness I clutch at you despite my perception of your nonexistence so that you might, at least, serve me as a companion, as a comrade, or—forgive the thought—as a crutch.

I read somewhere of the publication of a book of letters to God written by children. And what am I, after all? No more than a child—a child who has failed to learn how to write, a lost child with prematurely graying hair and a nervous heart, an adult child who still carries his immaturity around within him like a shield against life. Because it is false to think that You have created us in your image. It is we who have created You in our image, Immature God. Maybe this is why You come into my mind, Great Absent One, whenever I think of fatherhood, whenever I think of my own father, or of myself as a father.

* * *

Tateshie, you are dying. I expire before the fact of your imminent desertion, right now, this very minute, even as you linger on your sickbed in the room on the other side of the corridor of my house.

I remember how you carried me on your shoulders when I was three years old. You twisted your head around to look up at me from between my small shoes. "How do you like riding on top of your father, my son?" you asked, laughing. You took me on outings to the amusement park. You held me on your lap, strapped us both into the seat of the carousel, and we flew round and round the globe. It was a familiar globe, embraced by your strong paternal arms. The word "loneliness" had not yet come into existence.

I also remember another day, Father, when you boarded the green streetcar with me and we set out for the Green Market to buy the raspberries that had just ripened on the shrubs growing in the fields near the villages. I remember the raspberries' cheerful dark-red color, their bittersweet taste, and I can still see in my memory your mustache spotted with grains of raspberry red as we sat in the tram on our way home, both of us picking raspberries from the basket and popping them into our mouths. The moment we entered the apartment, Mama smiled at us with her raspberry lips. She poured white cream from a white jug into the white bowl full of dark red raspberries and sprinkled white sugar on top so that the raspberries became still sweeter, tastier, juicier, and redder beneath the cream.

I also remember the day, Father, when like an avenging God you spanked me—for having told a lie instead of confessing to playing hooky from school on that day in early spring when I skipped classes and went to the park to watch the ice breaking up on the lake.

I remember many other days with you, Father—the good days and bad days of my childhood—when you were like God to me, and both the bitter and the sweet days were happy ones. But what of that if I did not recognize them as such at the time?

* * *

You reproach me, Father, for not coming into your room often enough, for not sitting by your bed once in a while. "You cannot bear the sight of me . . . It's been taking too long, hasn't it?" your wise, faint smile seems to ask. You slide your pained, watery eyes along my right arm, trying to ascertain whether I've come in just to be with you for a while or whether I'm hiding the syringe with morphine behind my back to give an injection. You know as well as I do that the syringe is the head of a snake, that its prick is the snake's sharp tongue injecting you with deadly poison.

Should I tell you that I so rarely enter your room to sit by your side because I am too afraid of your suffering? I am afraid that in a moment of despair I will fulfill your secret wish and put an end to your life—out of pity, out of my own painful helplessness. I avoid coming in because I love you so much, and so childishly. It is the power of that love that chases me away from you. I am so attached to you, Father—*Tateshie!*—that the attachment feels like a rope wound tightly around my neck, choking me with such force that I feel I will lose my mind.

That is why I cling to you, you who know everything and nothing. You are my antigod, you who are so sick and helpless, you who are dying. That is why I cry out to you from the depths of my cursed confusion: help me now that there is no help to be had.

I haven't got the faintest notion why you planted this idea in me of trying to "write" to you the way Kafka wrote to his father, nor why I should feel the need to do so right now, from my bed, at this cold, nightmarish hour before the dawn. Don't you know that my inability to hold a pen in my hand means that I am unable to bring to the surface of my mind all the emotions boiling inside me? That is your fault. Or God's fault. Because a father must be obeyed. It was He who wanted me to become linguistically impotent. That is why I've never written anything. It just doesn't work. All the sluices have been slammed shut inside me—for life. I know that this does not matter to you, Eternal One; my literary lameness has no meaning *sub specie aeternitatis.* But to me it is of primary importance. To be an unfulfilled writer means to choke on one's soul as if it were a bone that cannot be swallowed.

* * *

Do you remember, Father, how you used to plan my future for me? According to your blueprint I was meant to become a famous scientist. I remember when I was eleven or twelve years old. We were on our way home from watching a soccer match in Polesie on the outskirts of town. You went from talking about the brilliant goalkeeper to speaking of a more important hero—me, the brilliant future benefactor of mankind. Yes, with dogged determination you tried to implant highly ethical ambitions in me. You encouraged and exhorted me; you overflowed with enthusiasm as you explained why knowledge is power. You told me about Kepler, about Newton, about Robert Fulton, about Edison, about Pierre and Marie Curie, and, of course, about Albert Einstein. You lit one cigarette after another, puffing with enthusiasm, pushing your cap back so far on your forehead that it almost fell off. And so, keeping your other hand on my shoulder, you talked to me.

"Remember, Yankele my son," you advised solemnly as the cigarette smoke spiraled out of your mouth, linking one word to the next. "If you're struck by an interesting idea, write it down. If you come across a clever thought in a book, copy it immediately. You never know from where a sudden spark of inspiration might come."

"But Papa," I tried to argue, "I want to become a writer, a poet, not a scientist."

"Of course." You patted my shoulder affectionately. "Becoming a scientist will make you a writer or a poet. The sciences are full of poetry. They penetrate the secrets of life and discover the basis of existence, they resonate with the music of the spheres, pointing toward the mystery of the beyond and toward a symbiosis with God Himself. It is not a coincidence that Albert Einstein is a first-rate violinist."

So we walked along the paths of the suburban fields engaged in this dreamlike argument until, suddenly, a gang of hooligans appeared from behind a cottage and began pelting us with stones. A stone struck my forehead and immediately raised a bump. I still have that bump. It has grown into my brain. No wonder that I carry no *tselem elokhim*, no sign of God on my forehead, but bear instead the mark of human hatred. Later I learned that those whom the Nazis did not permit to join the army, either for political reasons or because they were shlemiels, were called *Waffenunfähig*, which meant that they were unfit to bear arms. As for me, until I entered the concentration camp I was *Lebensunfähig*, unfit for life. Perhaps it is this shortcoming of mine that has attached me so powerfully to you, Father.

So powerfully attached to you was I that in order to spite you, when I reached my majority, I insisted on becoming a poet and not a scientist.

"Knowledge is not power but weakness," I argued. "Science knows nothing. Poetry knows all." This was how I explained my philosophy of life to you.

I liked to play with words. I derived great pleasure from the sounds produced by certain conjunctions of syllables and by the rhythmic harmony of certain lines when they were juxtaposed. And so I brought myself up on poetry, playing father to my own self. I grew up on literature. I sought refuge in literature from you and from your power over me, from your inescapable godliness. I ran to literature to escape my fear of life, my fear of the Gentiles. I lived more within the confines of books than in the real world.

I remember there was one particular day when I realized for the first time how liberating writing was. This happened on the morning when my high school teacher asked us to write a composition in class. "Walks with My Father" was the title of what I was supposed to write. Up to then my walks with you had been casual and leisurely, of no particular significance. But this very informality assumed an astonishing dimension once I set about transforming it into a literary text. Nothing came of the composition. I did not write it, because as soon as you entered my mind, I—pen in hand—made a broad, clumsy gesture over the white sheet of paper and knocked over the inkstand. The black ink spilled all over the white sheet of paper, and the teacher threw me out of the classroom. Ever since then I have been an outcast, an outsider in the world of those who are able to manage with words. I grew up a frustrated writer.

* * *

We were wonderful comrades in those days, Father. And yet, during those first years of my manhood, I imperceptibly began to despise you, to hate you with a profound hatred for the sin of being imperfect. I could not forgive your weaknesses. I labeled them hypocrisy, double-facedness, narrow-mindedness. I believed that despite your liberal outlook on life and your lofty preaching about knowledge and science you remained intellectually undeveloped, that your intolerance of me matured along with my own physical and mental ripening. You made no effort to understand me. You did not even attempt, you were not even curious, to see the world through my eyes. I could not abide your dry practicality, your desire to clip my wings, your habit of disparaging my dreams. I could not accept the pettiness of your authority.

Moreover, you were the king who begrudged me my privileged position in the heart of the queen, my mother, whose crown prince I was. I was the light of her eyes—as she was of mine. With your insistent practicality you brought us both down to earth and kept us there; you trampled on the joy that existed between her and me. I could hardly bear the sight of you.

How ridiculous all this seems to me now, Tateshie, how senseless and silly. All my resentment has been voided before the gigantic shadow spreading its black wings over my world. I cannot find the slightest speck of meaning in the dazzling darkness that threatens to blind me as it descends upon us. During those green, hopeful years, when you accompanied me through life, it was easy for me to invent a purpose for myself, a destiny—whether in agreement with you or in opposition to you—and to cling to the illusion that my existence in this world had significance. Even in the concentration camp I clung to this belief. But now, after so many golden, post-liberation autumns have passed, as you lie on your sickbed in the next room as if it were a raft about to depart while the rope that binds me to you slips from my hand, I feel hollow inside, empty throughout my whole being. The fear of your suffering, Father, is the only proof I have left that I am alive.

* * *

Which brings me finally to the truth about myself; namely, that I have become incurably neurotic. The psychotic neurosis of a schizophrenic personality is my diagnosis, formulated primarily by my wife, Malka.

I am shaking. I am attacked by spasms of terror that at any moment the door will burst open and the Doctor of the Universe, my wife, Malka, will make her appearance. She will pierce me with her burning and caressing green eyes and encircle me with the pitch-black strands of her silken hair. She will gather me into the embrace of her smooth, plump, viselike arms, which are so deceptively tender. I worship her. She is all that I have. She is my destiny, and there is no help for it.

Daylight is turning the sky gray. The first rays of sunshine have dappled the windowpane. I can see Malka approaching. She plants herself beside me and I can hear her say, "Good morning, my treasure. I am going to give you an injection so that you will not feel the electric shocks. Today is Friday. The electroshock therapy will bring you a peaceful Sabbath."

She ties the sleeves of my straitjacket and straps me in with the silk of her endlessly long black hair. She grips my shoulders with her soft hands, which have the clenching power of pincers; the loving eyes of her lovely face pierce me with the desire to destroy. She brings a deadly cure with her electroshocks. The electrodes press against my temples, my head is ringed with straps. She touches the switch. Save me, Father, save me!

* * *

Dr. Yacov Sapir woke with a scream and sat up on his bed. His wife, Malka, who slept beside him, also sat up with a start.

"What happened?" she asked.

Yacov fell back onto the pillow and emitted a deep sigh of relief. He rubbed his forehead with both hands.

"Nothing . . . nothing at all, sweetheart. I dreamt something, although I had the impression that I was awake. A nightmare. I dreamt that I was one of my patients." He stared at her absently for a while, as if he did not recognize her. Then he took her hand and laid it on his chest. Her face seemed to be floating above him. He looked up at her and smiled sadly. "You were in the dream too, my dearest. Your eyes were green instead of black." He caressed her fingers tenderly as her hand slowly crept over his hairy chest. "How is he doing?" he asked. "He's slept through the whole night, hasn't he?"

"He's still asleep," she whispered back. "After the injection you gave him last night . . ."

"As long as he's not in pain."

"I know. I also feel better when he's asleep. As soon as I hear him moaning I'm ready to run to the other end of the house."

Yacov searched the dark warmth of her eyes for a ray of encouragement to help him face the oncoming day. The black, silken strands of her hair were scattered, Medusa-like, over the bright skin of her neck and shoulders; they lay entangled in the shoulder straps of her nightgown, tempting his lips to a touch. For a moment he imagined himself gathering her passionately into his arms. Instead he gave her only a quick peck on the cheek and got out of bed.

As soon as he emerged into the corridor his youngest son, Sammy, barefoot and half naked, came running out to greet him. Grabbing hold of his father's knees, the four-year-old exclaimed in his ringing little voice, "Papa, I love you!"

Yacov gathered his son into his arms, then, raising him onto his shoulders, hopped around the corridor with him. He looked up from between the child's bare feet and repeated the question that his own father had used to ask him: "How do you like riding on top of your father, my son?"

He glanced quickly down the corridor at the closed door of the sickroom, then turned back.

* * *

Half an hour later he was dressed in the skin of Dr. Yacov Sapir, wearing his workday outfit of spotless white shirt, brown tie, and freshly ironed brown jacket and slacks. The shiny brown tips of his freshly polished shoes peeked out from beneath the cuffs of his slacks. He sat at the breakfast table in the kitchen hurriedly gulping down his cereal and milk. At his side sat Malka in her carelessly buttoned pink housecoat. Sammy sat on her lap, trying to construct something out of the teaspoons on the table. The spoons clinked loudly between his plump fingers. The other children had already left for school.

"You'll have to increase the dosage today," Malka said to Yacov as he wolfed down the spoonfuls of cereal. The grains cracked unpleasantly between his teeth. He was trapped in the same desperate tension that had not lifted since the day he had brought his father home from the hospital. "I thought I heard him groan a few times at dawn," Malka continued. "I know that you're pleased to have brought him home from the hospital, but if you want to know my opinion . . ."

Yacov had a vague sense that he was beginning to be afraid of her. Perhaps this was merely an aftertaste of his horrible dream of the night before. He pretended not to hear what she said and buried his face deeper in the bowl of cereal, eating faster. He sensed she was waiting for an answer and eventually felt himself obliged to speak.

"They refused to keep him any longer. You know this."

She nodded. "Of course. It made no sense. There's nothing they can do for him anyway."

It seemed to him that he had to appease Malka, as if she were a lioness ready to pounce. Any moment now he would put his arms around her and close her mouth with his lips. He softly stroked her arm, as if to pacify her.

"You are an angel, my love, to have agreed to it. You have no idea how grateful I am to you. I don't know how I would have managed without you. The children are taking his presence in the house better than I thought they would, don't you agree?"

"Yes, it might seem so on the surface."

Sammy clinked the teaspoons more loudly to keep up with the emphatic conversation he was having with himself. Malka continued in a whisper: "But what impact it's really having on them is hard to know. Even if they forget his presence, it doesn't necessarily mean that their subconscious doesn't register the atmosphere in the house."

"What's wrong with the atmosphere in the house?" Yacov asked, barely able to control his annoyance. "Aren't we carrying on with our normal routine?"

"How can you say such a thing? How can you speak about any kind of normalcy at all?"

"Perhaps you're right."

"Of course I'm right. The door of the sickroom is closed shut, but on the other side of that door it is deadly quiet . . . The whole thing horrifies me. I don't know how much longer I'll be able to bear it. I still think that it would have been much wiser to place him in the palliative care unit."

"Understand . . ." Yacov's voice caught in his throat and he coughed. He pushed away the bowl of unfinished cereal. "I cannot do this. I must not. He wants it this way."

"Which way? He hasn't got the faintest idea of what's happening to him."

"He knows, and so do I."

"But you don't have to obey him. You're not a child."

"He's my father."

"And he's still a despot."

"Don't talk like that."

"I'm sorry. But you'll inject him with a larger dose today, won't you?"

"Say something pleasant to me, Malka."

"I love you. Do it for me, Yacov, for the sake of my nerves. When he's asleep I feel calmer."

Yacov turned his head toward the window as if he were seeking an escape from the discomfort within him. A sumptuous maple tree with a wealth of leaves spread its regal branches over the entire backyard as if it were a dappled umbrella. The branches of the tree pressed against the kitchen window with the autumnal brightness of gold and red leaves—a cheerful announcement of decay—and blurred Yacov's view. The dull pain in his heart overwhelmed him.

"Autumn in full splendor," he declared, motioning with false cheer in the direction of the bright outdoors. "At least you, Malka, ought to be enjoying these last sunny days. Take Sammy and go to the park as soon as the nurse arrives. I have to hurry." He stood up, took both of Malka's hands in his, and made her stand too. He pulled her toward his chest. "Look at that autumn splendor outside. Just look at that tree."

They both observed the tree longingly until it seemed to Yacov that Malka's dark eyes were swimming toward the tree on tearful drops of sorrow. He was grateful to her for participating so deeply in his suffering. He embraced her more forcefully and desperately kissed her lips, as though determined to inhale hope from her mouth, or as if he were afraid that as soon as he removed his lips from hers she would open her mouth to plead with him, or to insist that he . . .

Hastily he detached himself from her. "I have a hard day ahead at the hospital," he said quickly.

She followed him into the corridor. "Don't come home late, please. I dread having to stay here alone all day. And give him the injection before you leave. Please, don't forget."

He nodded and entered his office to prepare the injection for his father.

* * *

Days passed, and the scene in the kitchen was repeated every morning. This morning, too, Malka sat by Yacov's side at the breakfast table while Sammy played on the floor. Yacov gulped down his breakfast cereal, trying to dull his private pain by concentrating on the public anguish reflected in the headlines that caught his eye from the front page of the newspaper. Now and then he raised his head and looked around. Sammy sat on the floor next to Malka's bare feet. A red velvet slipper dangled carelessly from her toe. The autumn sunlight shimmered through the entanglement of gold-and-red maple leaves and fell on Sammy's brown ringlets and on the shiny silk of Malka's black hair.

Yacov felt Malka's insistent eyes and glanced up from the paper. An expression of sadness and pain was etched into the net of fine, thin wrinkles on her face. He realized how poorly she looked. Her face seemed not to belong to the rest of her body, which radiated an attractive feminine warmth and freshness even now, as she sat with her disheveled hair spread in all directions over her carelessly buttoned pink housecoat. Without cosmetics, without powder, rouge, or lipstick, her face took on a pale yellow cast that seemed to change the color of her eyes from black to green. The deep furrows around her eyes and mouth pricked at his heart like the thin needles of a syringe. They seemed to inject a poisonous guilt into his bloodstream.

She put her hand on his knee. He covered her hand with his and they looked at each other silently. A multitude of inexpressible thoughts and feelings traveled between them. Then she moved her lips and he grew frightened at what she was going to say. He quickly covered her mouth with his hand.

"Hush, don't say a thing," he muttered. "Don't think that I don't know how unjust it is that I am away from home all day long while you carry the burden of this all alone. But, after all, he doesn't take up much of your time, and . . ."

"And what else, my dearest?"

"The nurse does everything necessary."

"That makes no difference. It is the atmosphere in the house, the fear, the . . . I don't know myself what to call it."

"I know what you mean."

"The children will be home from school very early today. It will be hard. Give him a larger dose."

"Why? He's asleep all the time as it is for quite a few days now."

"Yes, but he wakes occasionally. I beg you."

"I mustn't."

"A slightly larger dose. Do it for me, dearest."

"He won't be able to take it."

Sammy jumped to his feet and ran out of the kitchen as if he sensed the nature of his parents' secrets. Malka seated herself on Yacov's lap. He stroked the long, black hair that flowed over her shoulders, highlighting by contrast her pale, anxious face. The morning sun cut like a narrow surgical scalpel into the pink housecoat that lay against her breast. She caressed his head and sighed as she whispered into his graying hair: "The sight of that closed door terrifies me. It tears my heart apart. I am ashamed to smile at the children."

There was a knock at the front door. Yacov straightened himself with a start.

"It's the mailman," Malka said in a tone meant to calm him.

She stood up and straightened her housecoat. She made this movement in graceful innocence, ignorant of its enticing effect. Yacov was startled. He recognized in her the witch he had seen in a dream not long before. Suddenly he realized how much he hated her. He could scarcely breathe in her presence. He was afraid of her, afraid of what he felt. No! It was impossible! This must not happen! He must love her! She was the only light in his life. He must not run away from her. She supported him with her love, so devotedly, so magnificently. How could he be so brutal, so ungrateful?

He went out to the mailbox and returned carrying a pile of letters in his hand, with which he entered his office. He opened the letters but did not read them. They did not interest him. He was thinking of Malka and looked about him as if he were looking for her. He remembered how much she liked his office. His father had liked it too.

The walls of his office were specially insulated so as to prevent any external sound from entering the room, which was divided by an Oriental screen. On the far side stood a comfortable, black leather sofa with a matching black leather armchair and footstool nearby. Four evenings a week he conducted here his fifty-minute therapy sessions with his patients. On one side of the divider stood his mahogany desk, flanked on either side by two bookcases that stood against the walls. Nearby stood the locked glass cabinet with glass shelves upon which were arranged various medicines, including a small bottle of morphine.

From the very beginning Yacov had disliked the elegance of this room. It did not really suit his taste. But he had decorated it this way for the sake of his patients, since this was the style of the times. It conformed to the business side of his profession. This was the decor that his father and Malka had argued for when they assisted him in setting up his office. Actually his father never insisted but merely suggested what his son should do. He gave no orders to an adult son with a medical diploma; he was merely thinking aloud. So too Malka; she was only thinking aloud.

Yacov unlocked the door of the cabinet and prepared the injection for his father.

* * *

There was an unpleasant, acrid smell in the sickroom. The nurse who daily washed the bedsores on the sick man's body applied to them a soothing cream that left a heavy medicinal smell in the room. Yacov was used to the smell. He never minded it at the hospital, but here, in his father's room, he could hardly bear it.

"I have no relation to the man lying here on this bed. He's just another one of my patients, that's all," Yacov told himself, trying to believe in his self-imposed indifference. In fact there was no resemblance between the face he saw before him and the familiar face of his father. And yet the face was so familiar, so intimate, as if he himself were lying prostrate on the bed.

The sick man snored heavily. With careful movements, so as to avoid waking his father, Yacov removed the blanket that covered the sick man's body, revealing the yellowish pajama-clad torso that lay as flat against the bedsheet as if it were a two-dimensional cardboard cut-out. The wheezing snore seemed to be coming from somewhere deep inside the body. Yacov had the impression that he was snoring along with his father, that he had joined him on this voyage of no return.

Suddenly he felt an enormous desire to see his father's eyes open, to see his mouth move, to hear words issue from between the cracked, brownish lips. It had been many days since his father had been able to keep his eyes open or had uttered anything resembling a word. Yacov rolled up the sleeve that covered his father's arm and quickly jabbed the needle into the loose flesh. The body on the bed did not react, and yet the entire room was suddenly invaded by a stifling heat that buzzed with hissing, sizzling, never-expressed painful words.

Yacov's knees buckled. He sank into the chair beside the bed and allowed his eyes to rest on his father's scorched brown mouth, the source of the rasping, struggling breath—the only remaining sign of life.

* * *

"It seems to me, Father, that we are still in the concentration camp. I remember our relief that we had both survived the horrifying trial of the first selection. Now I see you going alone to the last selection—the one that awaits me too somewhere, sometime, at some future date. Of course there is a moral difference between a selection based on the brutal movement of a human being's hand and the selection conducted by a faceless fate. But the horror is the same, Tateshie, my brother in fate!

I see the two of us in the camp, and I recall how our roles changed. I began to act the father to you and in the process became your consoler and your consolation. In the camp it was impossible to argue with a treasure so miraculously saved as one's own flesh-and-blood father. We clung to each other. We nursed each other's wounds. We shared every crumb of food.

I remember how during the long marches in the winter I carried you on my back and shoulders like Jesus carried his cross to Golgotha. And that was how I got you across the river, followed by a spray of bullets. In this way we escaped from the camp a day before the liberation. It was then that I repaid you, Father, for giving life to me.

How painful it is to recall our happiness after the liberation. It consisted of more than the mere fact that we were no longer hungry, and more than the simple fact that we were free, or that we could finally indulge our own painful memories, or argue freely about anything in the world, but mainly about politics. It consisted of an inexpressible sense of elation, as if the coming of the Messiah were at hand, an elation that, unfortunately, gradually evaporated—at least as far as I was concerned. Because you began again to cling to your prewar ideology about the infinite potential for human redemption, whereas I refused to hear such hogwash. I, the former dreamer, had sobered up for good—or so I thought. In truth, I began to see myself as suspended in a void—and, just as in prewar times, I waited in vain for the salvation of poetry, of a new kind of poetry, to open the dams of unshed, hopeful tears and bring about my redemption.

I recall how your salvaged life demanded, in time, that it should be lived, and you suddenly grew jealous of my youth. Here I look at you, Father, and I can hardly believe that you are the same man who was then so vernal, who had so much vitality and virility and craved so actively the bodies of my young girlfriends. You used to steal the letters that I received from my fiancée Malka in order to read them in secret. In your love for me you acted with the greed of King Saul who had grown afraid of the young David—while I began to feel that you had become a burden and an obstacle to me.

My former campmates, those who had survived the war, envied me for having saved my father, while I burned with shame that your devotion to me caused me discomfort. I was annoyed by everything you said. Every remark you made grated on my ears, driving me to the edge of distraction, just as Malka's words today irritated and exasperated me, making me feel two times, three times, a thousand times more disgusted with myself. I feel like a villain, like a Nazi.

Forgive my tears, Tateshie. This is the only place I can weep freely. I can see you carrying me on your shoulders toward that day when I will be lying on such a bed as you are now—while my son Sammy says similarly distracted and distraught words of goodbye to me wordlessly in his mind.

I remember how triumphant you were, Father, when I decided to give in to you and become practical. I embarked on the study of medicine. How proud you were when I received my medical diploma! You even accepted with good cheer my specializing in psychiatry. That was my compromise choice. I told myself that psychiatry, like poetry, tackles the mystery of the human soul and heals its wounds in its own way. I deluded myself with the thought that I would be capable of alleviating the pain in the hearts of my former campmates, and I pretended ignorance of the fact that for the experiences of the camps there is no therapy, not even the passing of years.

You lived with my projects, Father; you identified with me. Thanks to me you imagined that you had finally lost your sense of alienation as an immigrant and become a co-participant in the strange tempo of life in Canada. Whenever you felt the urge to tease me a little, you, who could barely pronounce correctly a single English word, jokingly called me "Mister Shrink." To my ears this epithet, coming from your lips, sounded not like affectionate teasing but rather like a dismissive curse. "Mister Shrink!" It seemed to me that what you were really saying was "Don't grow so far beyond me; don't efface me so completely!"

Until this very day you have a weakness for Malka, Father. You love her. I know it. The harmony between the two of you used to both please and irritate me. You both took delight in my achievements, you boasting of your gifted son and she of her gifted husband. Together you worried about my working so hard, and together you made me feel eternally in your debt.

In debt? Here you are lying, your life dimming, ebbing away, my dear Tateshie, and I can do nothing for you—except to kiss your limp hand, except to avenge myself on you for the sin of having loved me with such devotion, except to liberate you from your suffering and curse myself for it—as your beloved Malka's pleading eyes demand. (Or does it only seem so to me?) Oh, God, how I hate her—and myself. How can a person, especially someone who was an inmate of a concentration camp, flirt with such thoughts?

* * *

Yacov barely knew how he managed to steer the car through the traffic in the center of town as he drove to work. At the hospital he forced himself to act normally, a normality that required so much effort and concentration that he felt as if he had been hypnotized.

After work he could not bring himself to go home. Instead he went for a stroll in the park. The trees displayed the full splendor of Indian summer; each was a brown, red, orange, and yellow bouquet of color basking in the sunshine. Falling leaves floated like flakes of gold in the air and soundlessly fell upon the ground around the trunks of the trees. The paths and the grass were littered with piles of leaves that crackled pleasantly under every step. Solitary, bright leaves danced in the air, swaying on the arms of a light-footed breeze.

Yacov caught sight of the bright outfit of a young kindergarten teacher on an outing with her young charges. He approached the class and observed the youngsters burying themselves in the mountains of leaves, rolling with squeals of delight over the colorful heaps or skipping around them. The blonde teacher gathered armfuls of leaves and laughingly allowed them to fall over the heads of the children. Golden leaves stuck to the wool of her sweater and caught in her hair, where they sparkled like pieces of jewelry.

Yacov moved still closer to the group of children. The teacher stared at him with her blue eyes, dilated in surprise and apprehension. He bent down, picked up a pile of leaves, and copying the teacher's movements sprinkled the leaves over the children's heads.

"A golden rain of leaves," he said to her. And in order to relieve her anxiety he introduced himself as a doctor who worked at the neighboring hospital. He felt foolish, yet at the same time he was overcome by a feeling of playful intoxication. "Such a bright, radiant world!" he exclaimed.

The blonde teacher had obviously decided that the stranger posed no threat; her blue eyes cleared and she smiled back at him. He noticed the sparkle of her two rows of white teeth. The sight of them dazzled him. He was convinced that he was dreaming because only in a dream could everything around him appear so luminous. And in the midst of that luminosity shimmered the brilliance of the teacher's two rows of white teeth, like two rows of tiny lightbulbs lit by the sun.

As if in a trance, he began to recite Rilke's "Autumn Day" to her:

Lord, it is time. The summer has been very long.
Spread your shadow over the sun clocks
and let loose the winds over the plains.

"How beautiful!" the young teacher sighed when he had finished. The sigh was a sad, dreamy exhalation, as if he had enchanted her.

"My father is dying." He was surprised to hear himself proclaim this, as if the news were an additional line to the poem he had just recited.

The light from the young teacher's teeth was extinguished behind the pursing of her narrow lips. She looked at him with compassion. "Oh, I'm so sorry. . ." She whispered this with sincere regret.

"Do you love your father?" he asked her as one asks in a dream.

She shrugged her shoulders. "I have no father."

"What do you mean? How old were you when you lost him?"

"I never knew my father, never laid eyes on him. He abandoned my mother when she was pregnant with me."

"Then you don't know what it means to have a father, and you don't know what it means to lose one," he said as if to himself. "And you don't know the guilt trailing after you like a heavy weight."

"Why guilt?"

"For having sinful thoughts."

He felt himself incapable of absorbing the entire picture of the young woman with the children against the background of the golden garden. Yet he felt love streaming into all his limbs. A tender love of spring, of youth, in the very middle of autumn. There was such a healing wisdom in life.

He felt a sting as he thought of Malka.

* * *

It was about nine o'clock in the morning. A gray, autumnal morning; there was no sunshine. Yacov left his breakfast unfinished and left the kitchen. For a while he listened to the children chattering with Malka at the breakfast table. It was a holiday. Thanksgiving. Yacov had no consultations that day, nor did he go to the hospital.

"No school today!" the childrens' joyful exclamations echoed in his ears.

"No school today!" he murmured to himself as he entered his office. He glanced at the other side of the divider. How glad he would be to stretch himself out on the couch right now, this very Thanksgiving morning, and make a confession before someone, before some nonexistent psychiatrist. But this he could not allow himself to do! He must not confess to anybody, not even to himself—because there was something he must do now despite his cowardice, despite the horror that engulfed him—he must do it . . . he must!

He was aware that a day more steeped in darkness than today would most likely never again occur in his life. The stifling darkness in his mind sank deeper and deeper into his body, into his limbs. But just as a cloud descending into a valley leaves behind a mountain peak basking in light, so from somewhere above him a thin ray of brightness forced its way through: the image of the kindergarten teacher with the children. The image established a relationship between light and darkness. He saw himself in the *katzet*, the name they gave to the concentration camp; he saw himself wearing an SS man's uniform over the striped rags of an inmate's clothing. From the other side of the fence Malka smiled consolingly, imploringly, promising, "Soon you will be free."

"Free? Idiot!" His face contracted with pain. "This is the moment when I really put on my chains."

His loneliness howled so desolately within him that he had to rush back into the kitchen in order to have another look at his children and fortify himself with the sight of them, at least for a moment. There they were, sitting on the kitchen floor, playing dominoes. At the table sat Malka in her housecoat, her hair disheveled. Her glistening face looked sticky. Her tired eyes looked out at the maple tree, which stared back through the gray windowpanes. Without sunshine on it, the maple tree looked pale, less significant. As soon as Yacov entered the kitchen, Malka transferred her gaze to him.

"Get dressed and go down into the park with the children," he told her calmly. He looked at her intently. Did she understand? She did. Her eyes caressed him tenderly. She stood up from the table with what seemed to him an ugly smile of gratitude lighting up the corners of her mouth. He would never forgive her for this. He felt his fear—and his hatred. She was the snake. She sat inside him like a dybbuk, entangling him in the nets of her poisonous Medusa hair.

He drew near her, put his arm tenderly around her, and felt the warmth of her loose breasts through the thin fabric of her housecoat. "I love you, Malka, remember that," he whispered. He bent down to the children, and a longing overcame him to stretch himself out on the floor beside them.

"Papa! Papa!" Sammy clasped him by the sleeve. "Let me ride on you a teeny-weeny bit!"

Malka went to get dressed. Yacov hopped round and round the kitchen table with Sammy on his shoulders. Soon Malka was back, carrying the children's clothing. With determined haste she and Yacov dressed the children, after which she ushered them out of the house, closing the door behind her.

The house sank into frightful stillness. Yacov went back into his office, unlocked the cupboard with the medicines, and removed the small bottle of morphine and the syringe from the shelf. He prepared a package of cotton and started to fill the syringe, dipping the needle in the bottle. The glass tube of the syringe sucked in one centiliter after another. Slowly the fluid jumped the indicator lines on the glass, moving ever higher. For the last few weeks those lines had become the ladder that his fluttering heart had climbed toward the precipice of the present moment. His father's astonishingly strong heart had behaved normally for the past ten days, but four days ago the pulse had begun to show certain signs . . . The heart was starting to acknowledge the losing battle; it was beginning to surrender.

A strong heart is a matter of heredity. A strong heart is the heart of a giant. Yacov heard his own heart hammering against the walls of his veins, hammering in his temples. A huge heart beat inside the room, taking up the space of the entire world, dulling the senses. It pounded in Yacov's steps as he left the office and opened the door of his father's room.

* * *

The bed. Yacov's eyes take in the sight of it, along with the barely visible elevation in the middle of the blanket. His eyes travel along every fold in the blanket and finally up to the pillow, where the head is resting. The head is strangely bare and round; a pair of gray hairs protrude from the scalp. The color of the skin mixes with the gray light from the windowpanes; the face is like a yellow autumn leaf. The eyes are shut. Good that they are shut. The dark-brown mouth is the only living point. It rasps. It rattles. It fights for a breath of air.

The arm rests limply on top of the blanket. Blood of my blood, flesh of my flesh. Father's sickbed is suspended in space like a hammock. In the hammock lies a little boy of three, and his father is swinging him back and forth.

A boyish voice cries: "Papa . . . forgive me for the estrangement between us. Forgive me for the closeness . . . forgive me for having to be your liberator . . . forgive me for the sins that cannot be forgiven. Here am I, your son Yacov, watching with my eyes open—as I pierce your skin with the needle for the last time. I can see liberation trickling into your body while your illness trickles into me drop after drop. Jews take leave of each other with the blessing 'Be well, go in good health, come back in good health.' Not we two, Papa, not we too. We don't take leave of each other. I am frightened. God, I am calling you from the depths of despair . . . I, your son Cain. I, your murderer who loves you, Tateshie."

He clasped the wrist of his father's hand in his. The pulse was gone. He kissed the hand, which was still hot with the life that was no more. It seemed to him that Sammy had thrown his little arms around Yacov's stiff legs. "I love you, Papa."

Originally published in Arguing with the Storm: Stories by Yiddish Women Writers, *ed. Rhea Tregebov. Sumach Press and the Feminist Press, 2007.*

April 19th

Hersh was lost within himself like a traveler in a foreign city. He did not know whether he was moving forward or back, whether he was dreaming or wide awake.

It was Passover, the night before the ghetto commemoration. In his sleep Hersh saw Rivkele, his blonde, light-footed first wife, who had never actually looked as beautiful as she did in his dream. And he saw their two children, Mirele and Yossele, who along with Rivkele had been taken away from him during the selection on the ramp at the Auschwitz train station, a selection conducted by the infamous Dr. Mengele. Hersh tossed and turned on his bed, entangled in a mass of half-seen images and disjointed thoughts. He thought of the happiness he had lost and of the happiness he had found after the war.

Hersh had been incarcerated in Auschwitz for two years during which time he had worked at the Union munitions plant as a slave laborer. There he had joined the secret resistance organization that had stolen dynamite from the plant for the October 1944 bombing of the crematorium at Birkenau, the extermination camp that adjoined Auschwitz. By some miracle his participation had escaped notice, and he was not punished when all the others were rounded up and executed. In the camp Hersh had been a daredevil, a desperado; he had felt no fear.

After the liberation in 1945 Hersh's personality underwent a transformation, at least on the surface. He became a devil of a different kind, a devil-may-care, fun-loving, happy-go-lucky young man. He made a tremendous effort to enjoy his painfully acquired bachelorhood. Since his memories were tortured, he tried to remember the past as little as possible, compensating for his former suffering by indulging in all the pleasures that the postwar world had to offer. But in this he succeeded only superficially. He did not really have the personality of a bon vivant. Nights posed a special problem. He slept badly or not at all.

And so his life continued in a kind of dreamlike intoxication, a painless vacuum, until he met Bronia, who was bright and enticing and also a survivor. Bronia had the look of an Asian beauty. When Hersh first met her, her dark hair was still in the process of growing back after having been shaved off in the concentration camp. She had dark, burning eyes that occasionally glimmered with a tormented rage. She had lost her first husband, her parents, and siblings at Auschwitz.

Hersh and Bronia got married and had two children, a boy and a girl. In order to make a fresh start they decided not to name their children after Hersh's first two perished children, even though in his head Hersh continually confused the names.

In his youth, when he had been married to the dreamy, silken-haired Rivkele, Hersh had had ambitions for a career in music, which he indulged by writing songs, mostly love songs. But once liberated, he suppressed these impractical aspirations. Soon after immigrating to Canada, he decided to train as an accountant. Before long he had a job and was making enough money to live a comfortable life with his family.

Once he had ensured the stability of his new family, Hersh's personality underwent another change. He became a fearful man, ceaselessly preoccupied with health, especially the health of his children and his wife. Their health worried him more than his own. He trembled especially over the well-being of his children, who personified his newfound happiness. He did not simply love his children, he worshiped them.

Hersh took delight in the normality of his uneventful marital existence. He hated change and made a continual effort to shelter himself and his good fortune behind a fortress of immutability, to protect everything he held dear by a set of rules and disciplined behavior. He doggedly pursued the stability of the everyday, rejoicing in the regular rhythm of his working hours, in the unexceptional transition from work to relaxation to vacation and back to work again. Any deviation from established routine filled him with dread, with a sense of foreboding and impending doom. The shell he had erected around his small world had to remain forever firm and inflexible. Once he had his new family, he wanted nothing more.

Bronia understood him well and went along with his idiosyncrasies, which were not much different from her own. She was even more stubborn and persistent than he in her effort to maintain a routine sameness in their lives. Bronia knew of Hersh's longing for his first wife, even though he rarely spoke of her. Bronia was sure that Hersh had loved Rivkele with all the passionate intensity of youth. She made no effort to drive Rivkele from Hersh's mind, and she did not try to emulate her. She was determined instead to emphasize her own uniqueness.

It was Bronia who had talked Hersh into taking courses in accountancy. In this way, she reasoned, Hersh would be able to solidify the financial foundation of their lives and at the same time find an escape from the forlorn sense of displacement he felt in the chaotic postwar world. Bronia had always known how to comfort Hersh and soothe his pain. He had grown to love her deeply, and through her, he had continued to love Rivkele.

In time the two women merged in Hersh's imagination, despite the fact that they did not resemble each other physically and despite the fact that their voices were not similar and their laughter was not alike. But he continued deluding himself that in all essentials they were the same, never remembering the differences between them. In his mind Bronia and Rivkele merged into the same person, despite the fact that Rivkele had used to cry a great deal, while Bronia never cried. He had come to consider Rivkele as a kind of fairy-tale princess who had been reborn in Bronia, the vital, palpable, down-to-earth Asian beauty, a queen, always serene and self-possessed. Sometimes he had the feeling that, like an ogress, Bronia had swallowed Rivkele, who continued living inside her, invisible to the outside world, invisible even to Bronia herself—but not to Hersh.

Hersh loved Bronia just as powerfully as he had loved Rivkele, and he loved his new set of children just as much as he loved the two he had lost. He usually remembered that their names were not the same, but he confused their nicknames and sometimes called the living boy and girl by the pet names of their perished predecessors. Since Bronia never corrected him, Hersh had the feeling that whatever had once been still was, that whatever belonged to his past was also part of his present.

The day just passed had been April 19th, the date of the Warsaw ghetto commemoration. It had been a beautiful, early spring day. Hersh and Bronia lived on Esplanade Avenue near Mount Royal, a district of Montreal that was home to many newly arrived Jewish immigrants. Since it was Passover, the people on the street were festively dressed. All day long groups of Jews strolled along the foot of Mount Royal—which they called *de montn*—while children cavorted on Fletcher's Field, the large expanse of land that separated Esplanade Avenue from Park Avenue and from the mountain beyond. The lilacs and jasmine were just coming into bloom.

On just such Passover days the Nazis would descend on the ghettos of Europe, intending to kill the Jews where they found them or deport them to the extermination camps. In Poland in the spring of 1943 the Nazis had descended on the Warsaw ghetto with the intention of liquidating it. The Jews of the ghetto decided to die fighting, and so the Warsaw ghetto uprising erupted on the 19th of April—Passover. It was an event commemorated every year by the Jewish community, both secular and religious, and it had come to represent for the survivors all the horrors of the not-so-distant past. It memorialized not just those who had fallen in the uprising itself but all of the innocents who had been killed in extermination camps, in labor camps, in ghettos, in forests, in fields, in pits, on highways, on streets . . .

Hersh and Bronia never missed the commemoration of the Warsaw ghetto uprising. That evening they had gone to the Jewish Community Centre for the ceremony. The hall of the Community Centre was packed with mourners. Every seat was taken, and those who could not find a place to sit stood at the back and along the sides by the auditorium walls. The ceremony began, and everyone present seemed to be bracing for the emotionally draining experience of reliving the past, of forgetting for a few hours the length of time that had passed since the nightmarish days of their youth.

This was the hour when spirits descended upon the hall of the Community Centre, when the ghosts of the past walked among the living. The choir began to sing, and one of the songs echoed in Hersh's ears. The words were by Shmerke Kaczerginski, the poet of the Vilna ghetto, who was mourning the loss of his deported bride. The song was called "Friling"—"Spring." Like a distant murmur, Hersh heard the voices of the choir intoning the refrain: "*Springtime, on your blue wings, bring back my beloved, my dearest, to me . . .*"

Hersh saw himself rise to his feet along with the rest of the assembly, all eyes riveted on the large menorah with six huge unlit candles waiting on the distant stage. The unforgotten past encroached now on the hall with such intensity that it became difficult to breathe. A male voice called out the names of the six candle lighters as each in turn climbed the steps to the menorah and lit a candle, one candle for each million of the six million. The six who had been given the honor of lighting this year's candles had each survived a different ghetto or concentration camp. The crowd stood in silence.

As usual during a ghetto commemoration Hersh felt that the pounding of his heart was heard not only by Bronia but by all the people around him. He squeezed Bronia's hand tightly and she squeezed his. He had the impression that he heard her heart pounding in rhythm with his own, that he could feel the pounding of both their hearts in the clasped palms of their hands.

They continued standing with their hands locked tightly together, one knotted inside the other. They did not say a word nor did they look at one another. They stood glued to the floor for the duration of the lighting of the first four candles, both communing with separate memories.

Then Hersh heard a name called out. It was his family name. He heard the name *Auschwitz* called out. He opened his eyes as wide as they would go. His palm grew so wet that Bronia's hand slipped from his grasp. Looking up at the menorah, he saw a tall, willowy blonde woman ascend the steps leading to the altar. The stairs seemed to be rising higher and higher into the air, and the woman rose along with them. He did not recognize the woman, yet something about her was familiar. Perhaps it was the dress. It was just the right dress for the occasion—a many-pleated gray dress of very light fabric. Hersh thought he could see the outlines of the woman's body through the folds of the fabric. He could see the texture of her skin. He was sure that he had once known that body in minute detail. He inhaled its scent, felt its delicate touch, its enticing softness. There was something intimate, something deeply his own, in the air about that woman. He seemed to foresee the manner in which she would take the auxiliary candle from the person before her and, raising her arm high, light the fifth candle.

Rivkele. It was his first wife, Rivkele. She lit the candle then handed the auxiliary candle to the person behind her and descended the stairs. There were suddenly so many stairs! She disappeared into the crowd of standing mourners. The sixth candle was lit. The choir sang Kaczerginski's "Friling" over again. Again he heard the words*"Bring back my beloved, my dearest, to me."*

Tears gathered in Hersh's eyes. Had he just seen Rivkele in the flesh? How was this possible? Where had she been all this time? And what about the children? He had searched for all of them after the liberation, searched for a long time, but never found them. It was while searching for Rivkele that he had met Bronia, who had been looking for her husband.

Bronia again reached out for Hersh's hand and clasped it tightly in her own. Hersh looked at her and noticed that tears were running down her face. Strange, he thought. He had never seen her cry before. "I have a strange premonition," she whispered. "Something is going to happen."

"I need some fresh air," Hersh whispered back, extracting his hand from hers. The candle lighting ceremony over, the crowd had sat down again, so Hersh had to squeeze past an endless row of hard, protruding knees to make his way out to the aisle. The choir was still singing

"Breng mayn gelibte, mayn libste tsurik / Bring back my beloved, my dearest, to me." Once in the aisle, Hersh scanned the faces of one crowded row of mourners after another, looking for the woman who had lighted the candle. Under his breath he called her name: "Rivkele! Rivkele!"

From a seat at the far side of the auditorium a woman turned her head in his direction. The next moment he saw her soaring toward him. She seemed to be flying, the folds of her pleated dress stretched out like wings. He never remembered Rivkele to have been so beautiful. In the past her looks had hardly mattered to him. Perhaps she was even plain looking. He could not remember. Their love, Rivkele's and his, although ecstatically erotic, had reached beyond physical appearances. Theirs had been the truest love imaginable. It was as true as his present grief.

Rivkele fell into his arms. But his arms remained empty. And suddenly he found himself outside the hall, near the doors to the Community Centre. He was alone and trying to understand what had happened when suddenly he saw the willowy blonde woman walking toward him. "It's stifling in there," she remarked as she passed him. "I need a breath of fresh air. I can't listen to speeches any more. Too many sad memories; nothing can change the past."

He followed her outside. They looked at each other, and it seemed to Hersh that they had both become transparent. Suddenly she said: "You know about the children, don't you?"

He nodded gravely. "I do. They're at home asleep."

They strolled along the street, breathing in the sweet aroma of the blossoming jasmine. The spring air seemed to absorb Hersh's breath. They came to a park. The flowering branches of the jasmine bushes looked like the arms of white angels bestowing a welcome oblivion on the world with their intoxicating white petals. Hersh sank onto a wooden bench, and the woman sat down next to him.

Nearby, children were playing in the sandbox. Hersh felt a powerful desire to see Rivkele's face again. He had not seen it for so long. He fixed his eyes on her. Yes, it was the face of his first wife—and yet it was not the face he had expected to see. The face before him was not middle-aged; it was not disfigured by pain and tears. It was not the face of a concentration camp survivor who had seen the worst that human beings are capable of, who had lost her most precious treasures, her children. No, the face before him was that of a beautiful young woman, newly arrived at adulthood.

He sat absorbed by the smooth, pale glow of Rivkele's alabaster complexion, marveling at the light in those dreamy, swimming eyes. He saw there his youth, their shared love, their home, the faces of their children as they played in the sandbox. And he felt deeply embarrassed, deeply ashamed of himself. He felt like a traitor.

"Thank God you survived," Rivkele whispered and fell silent, as if awaiting his reply. But he was so full of shame that he failed to answer. To fill the silence she asked, "Do you remember the last words that you said to me, Hershele, before the Germans separated us during the selection on the ramp at Auschwitz? Do you remember? 'Forever,' you said to me, 'forever and ever . . .'" She spoke with difficulty.

Hersh began to sob. He buried his head on the part of her shoulder where her soft hair became one with her dress. Someone was calling, "Hershie! Hershie! Where are you?"

"Someone is calling you," Rivkele whispered.

Hersh mastered himself, wiped his face with both hands, and said in a dry voice: "It's Bronia, my wife."

"I am your wife," Rivkele said in an equally dry voice.

"You are. But, forgive me, so is she. We have two children."

"We had two."

"We *have* two. Come, you must meet her."

"Gladly," Rivkele said, although Hersh felt that she was not sincere. "I have regards from her former husband."

He began pulling Rivkele toward Bronia, who was waiting in a flutter at the entrance to the Community Centre. At first Hersh did not recognize Bronia, so much did her tear-stained face resemble Rivkele's.

He heard Rivkele say, "How painful it is, Hershele, to have found you and to lose you again so soon. Thank God I am not alive."

"Don't thank God for that!" Hersh pleaded. "Never thank God for that!" He turned to Bronia. "Bronia, dearest, just think who this is."

He pointed at Rivkele.

"Oh, you scared me so terribly!" Bronia sighed with relief. "I didn't know where you had gone."

"I love you," Hersh replied. It was unclear to whom.

"So why do you want to desert me for her?" Which wife said this?

"Are you jealous?" he asked, with great tenderness in his voice.

"Why, of course. Jealousy is like love. It reaches beyond the grave."

"Rivkele has no grave. Her ashes are everywhere."

"And that makes her even more threatening," Bronia said.

An unexpected wave of resentment swept over Hersh. He remembered that he and Bronia frequently argued, that they often felt estranged from each other. Although she had never said so, he sensed that Bronia reproached him for being unlike her first husband. Hersh did not have her first husband's business sense. And she did not appreciate his sense of humor. Granted, it was a particularly morbid sense of humor that he had acquired after the liberation, yet it seemed to fit the circumstances. More than once he had read in Bronia's eyes that his wisecracks displeased her, that she thought them stupid, even though she never said a word. And then he remembered other ways in which they did not get along.

"Let's not change things, Hershie," Bronia insisted. "Let Rivkele go back where she came from."

Hersh patted Bronia's shoulder appeasingly. "She came from Auschwitz. Please understand. Let her stay. At least until tomorrow."

"How can I understand? This is beyond understanding."

"Let's leave it for tomorrow."

"How can we leave it for tomorrow when you cling so stubbornly to yesterday?" Bronia turned and walked off until she was lost in the misty depths of the street.

"Bronia! Bronia, darling, don't leave me!" Hersh began running after her.

"Hershele!" Rivkele called after him. "Don't leave me! Wait for me!"

Hersh turned to her: "Bronia refuses to meet you. You saw that for yourself. She refuses to let you stay until tomorrow."

"Why? What harm have I done her?"

"She is afraid of you."

"Why should she be afraid of me? I am just dust and ashes."

"She is terrified of you. You are a sacred memory. She knows that. She knows that I worship you, that I love you and will always love you. So she is jealous."

The sound of many voices singing the "Partisan Hymn" followed the three figures as they ran through the dark street—three escapees from a nightmare. Hersh wanted to catch up with Bronia as she disappeared down the street, but he forced himself to stop. Planting his feet firmly on the ground, he allowed Rivkele to catch up with him. There she stood in front of him. He saw his youthful past reflected in her delicate, dreamy face, and he saw there too the faces of his perished children. The white jasmine bushes in full bloom dazzled his eyes; their perfume suffocated him. He took Rivkele's beautiful hands in his. Her hands had not changed; they were still delicate and soft, as if they had never known concentration camp labor. Hands cannot conceal the truth, he said to himself—and then he remembered: Rivkele had never reached the interior of the concentration camp; she had never entered it, she had never abandoned the children. She had gone with them to the ovens.

In the dimness of the streetlights her hands shone with an otherworldly transparency. He kissed them and pressed them to his cheek. He remembered the touch of her soft fingers, the fingers of his first lover, the fingers of his children's mother. Once again the words of Kaczerginski's song echoed in Hersh's ears: "*Springtime, bring back my beloved . . .*"

"Where do you live, Rivkele?" Hersh asked.

"I live with Bronia's husband—and with all the others. We live on the outskirts of your consciousness."

Hersh felt his ordered existence slipping away. He knew that he must reclaim it. There was nothing more important for him to do than cling to the protective shell that he had built around his life. "You belong to my past," he told her.

"Yes, but your love for me did not die at Auschwitz."

"I love Bronia."

"So you do. But you love me too. Not even the Germans could undo our love."

"Go back to where you came from!"

"Would that be far enough? Do you think you will ever be able to evict me from the outskirts of your heart?" Rivkele threw her arms around Hersh and held him close.

"I have two living children," he pleaded. "They come before you or me or Bronia. That is how it must be. It is the only way we can celebrate our victory. In all other respects we are defeated and destroyed."

"That's not true!" Rivkele shook her head so violently that he could see the silken hair fall from her head in piles of ashes. "Not true at all! Only I am defeated and destroyed. But even so . . . Since you love me forever and ever, something is left that will keep us alive."

The Holocaust commemoration was over. The crowd of mourners poured out of the Community Centre. The ghosts and spirits left the building in one long endless procession, passing overhead in a dense white cloud. Without a word of goodbye, Rivkele disengaged herself from Hersh's embrace and drifted up to join the white cloud, blending into the pale vapor as it gradually disappeared behind the blazing beams of the huge projectors that sliced across Fletcher's Field at the foot of Mount Royal.

Those huge projectors illuminated a football match. The onlookers stood around the edges of the field clapping, whistling, and yelling loud encouragement to their teams. The jasmine bushes around Fletcher's Field perfumed the night with their sweet smell. Bronia emerged from the Community Centre and smiled a sad, affectionate smile at Hersh as she wiped the tears from her face.

* * *

The next day Hersh opened his eyes to find a brilliant morning. The children, still wearing their pajamas, were playing at the foot of the bed. Bronia, her head on the pillow beside him, dark hair spread out in chaotic disarray, tenderly stroked his arm.

"Do you love me?" she asked coquettishly as she snuggled up next to him.

"Forever and ever," he replied, rubbing his eyes.

"If so, then be a good boy, Hershie dear, and on this gorgeous holiday morning, you be the first to get out of bed and make us some delicious Passover pancakes for breakfast. We are starved to death."

Originally published in Jewishfiction.net. Ed. Nora Gold, 2018: https://www. jewishfiction.net/index.php/publisher/articleview/frmArticleID/17.

Bibliography

Below is a listing in chronological order of the Yiddish-language publication of the stories:

"*Der griner*" ("The Greenhorn") from *Kanadish antologie* (*Canadian Anthology*). Ed. Shmuel Rozshanski. Buenos Aires: *Yosef Lifshits-fond fun der literatur-gezelshaft baym Yivo*, 1974, 159–174.

"*Di letste leibe*" ("Last Love"). In Yiddish. *Di goldene keyt* 110–111 (1983), 117–140.

"*Dos maynsterverk*" ("The Masterpiece"). *Di goldene keyt* 112 (1984), 81–109.

"*Edgeh's nekome*" ("Edgia's Revenge"). In Yiddish. *Di goldene keyt* 126 (1989), 38–87.

"In serengeti" ("In Serengeti"). In Yiddish. *Di goldene keyt* 128 (1990), 115–156.

"François." In Yiddish. *Di goldene keyt* 135 (1993), 16–47.

"*Royt feigele*" ("Little Red Bird"). In Yiddish. *Di goldene keyt* 139 (1994), 86–98.

"*Briv tsu got*" ("Letters to God"). In Yiddish. *Di goldene keyt* 140 (1995), 51–72.

"A Friday in the Life of Sarah Zonabend" and "April 19th" were translated from unpublished manuscripts.